Then Comes Marriage

Emily B. Riddle

Cover Design by Karla Colahan of The Inspired Foundry

Library of Congress Control Number: 9798862917406

Printed in the United States of America.

This book is dedicated to my beloved grandmothers.
To Dorothy Gavin Storm, a spirited lady with a big heart,
and
to Myrtle Creekmore Broyles, who I understand was one tender and
tough cookie.
I'm so thankful for the legacy of tenacious women in my life.

1.

As Mrs. Wilkins waits patiently at the front door, I wonder how long I can hold this position. Crouched down, at the base of my living room window, my legs, thighs specifically, have started to shake, and I'm sweating. This is embarrassing. How am I not in better shape? I'm not much of a yoga person, and at closer to forty than twenty, my body no longer naturally takes the shape I put it into.

Ahh, cramp! My calf cramps on me, and I'm in agony. How do people do this for minutes on end?

"Mommy, why are you hiding from Mrs. Wilkins?"

Of course, it's Atticus who asks. At seven years old, he's my serious guy, my investigator, my inquisitive one. Ernie, barely eighteen months younger, sprawled out on the floor, playing with LEGO blocks, shows no awareness of what's happening around him.

"I'm not hiding. I'm...introverted." This is a lie. I am absolutely hiding.

Like so many of the century-old homes in our neighborhood, our house has a porch. Drive down our street and it's one after the other porch, porch, porch.

I love a porch. When we moved in over a year ago, the porch was the selling point of this very tiny, but adorable, rental. The price (low), the house (tiny, but adorable), and the porch (there was one). However, when I'm sitting on the floor of the living room, playing with the boys, as I was three minutes ago, and our landlady turns up unexpectedly, the porch makes discretion almost impossible. Between it and the long, low windows, I might as well be sitting on Mrs. Wilkins' lap.

I should feel guilty, and I do. Mrs. Wilkins, a tiny Black woman with perfectly bobbed silver hair, is in her mid-sixties, five feet, and maybe a hundred pounds, and bundled up in a puffy North Face parka. And I'm the jerk leaving her waiting on my front porch. In January.

It's been almost three minutes now, and she shows no signs of stopping. Curse you, porch and street parking!

She calls out, "Iris? Are you in there? It'd be so good to talk." She sounds frustrated. Dang it. Mrs. Wilkins is not easily frustrated.

How long can I keep avoiding her? We've got one month left, whether I like it or not. The lease is up, and we're out.

Maybe she wants to extend the lease. Hope ripples through my whole body. Is this the Holy Spirit talking? Maybe the Wilkins changed their minds. Maybe instead of selling their home, and this rental, to move to Lexington and be closer to both their daughters and grandkids, maybe they're keeping the house.

It would be surprising. Between Mr. Wilkins' recent cancer-free diagnosis, combined with the amazing offer they received for this house, the Wilkins have plenty of motivation to leave Harrisville and get closer to their grown kids.

When she gave me the news a few weeks ago and asked if we could manage to move by the end of January, what could I say? It was fantastic news for Mrs. Wilkins, especially after such an impossibly hard year.

Yes, of course, we'll find a new place. That's what I said, and I even managed a smile.

And then I added frantic nighttime Googling for "adorable two-bedroom rentals in Harrisville" to my evening activities.

Now here we are, the third of January, and I'm crouched at my window, avoiding reality.

Mrs. Wilkins knocks again. "It's really not a big deal. I just need a quick word," she says.

Maybe they are keeping the house. They'll let us keep renting. They feel sorry for me, and they've had pity.

I'll take it. Single mom, with a minimal income, I'll take whatever they want to give me.

Like a house.

Uh-oh. I feel it a moment before it happens. My legs give out, and I crash onto my butt. Well, now that I'm sprawled out flat on my back, Mrs. Wilkins definitely can't see me.

However, my thud breaks Ernie's focus. He hears Mrs. Wilkins' knock, hurtles himself at the window, and hollers, "Mrs. Wilkins!"

Our position's been given away.

"Now we know who to keep an eye on if we're ever penned down in a war zone," I grumble, as I pick myself up, adding, "Go ahead."

The two boys race to the door, me dragging stiffly and sorely behind them.

The way Mrs. Wilkins beams at each of us, you'd never know I kept her waiting. "Hello, neighbors! I hoped I'd see you and the boys again before the big move."

"What big move?"

Agh, Atticus. He's too quick.

Ernie waves and streaks off to the kitchen, shouting, "I need a snack," oblivious.

Atticus watches with large, dark eyes, concern spread across his fair, freckled face. He has my coloring—chestnut brown hair and deep brown eyes against pale white skin. It gives the impression of eyes too big for his face.

I haven't told the boys about the move yet. My instinct is to wail, "They're selling. We're in trouble. Everything's awful!"

However, this kind of parenting is discouraged. Even when you want to be truthful, it's definitely frowned upon to tear one's garments, gnash one's teeth, or otherwise give your kids the impression that you're about to be destitute like a Dickens' character.

I force a smile in Atticus' direction. "Mr. and Mrs. Wilkins are moving to be closer to their grandkids, like we are with Granny and Grandpa. So you won't see them so much anymore. Why don't you get a snack, too?"

And addressing Mrs. Wilkins, at last, I ask. "What's up?" I lean against the door, heart hammering. What if they let us stay? *Maybe maybe maybe.*

"I wanted to see how y'all were getting along. Ready for the move?"

She peers around me, taking in the room. And this is exactly what I didn't want.

While the Wilkins might be the ones putting on the pressure to be up and out in a month, it's still my responsibility to see that it happens.

And I'm failing at it.

Our whole house is about eight hundred square feet. The living room lies to my right. My bedroom is to the left. The boys' bedroom is off the living room, and the dining room and the kitchen are down the opposite hall. If you stand at the center of the hallway, you can basically see every room in the house.

Toys spill across the living room floor, and a laundry basket of clean clothes perches on an armchair. Every picture and painting on the wall is in place. Our paisley drapes adorn the living room walls. The huge living room rug, multiple throw blankets, my stack of fifty-year-old handmade quilts my grandma gave me–everything is exactly where it was when Mrs. Wilkins dropped her news on me.

Besides scouring the internet for a new home, I've done absolutely nothing to prepare for our move in twenty-eight days. Twenty-seven, actually.

But until there's a place to go, I can't find the courage to box our things. Because where are we going to put them?

Mrs. Wilkins's eyes take in the state of the place, and my heart rate rises.

"Don't worry, we'll be ready," I say. "We don't have much."

Mrs. Wilkins wouldn't be poking her head around my bedroom door. Hallelujah for small blessings.

She doesn't look reassured. "If you need time to pack, I can take the boys for an afternoon."

I nod manically, desperate to please and alleviate this discomfort. "That's so kind. That would be helpful."

She has no idea how helpful it is considering there's no way to pack the house with them anywhere in it. At night, I lie in bed and debate where to hide the boxes after I pack them.

Mrs. Wilkins' expression clears. "Great. Text me this week and I'll have them over."

She backs up a few steps. We're so close, nearly there.

Except, I remember her surprise. "Wait!" I fling up a hand, catching her attention but preventing her from coming further into the house.

My gosh, if I don't calm down she's going to think I'm running a drug ring and trying to hide the stacks of cash I have stashed around. "I have something for you. Just wait there."

Thank goodness I finished this last night. As I come back and hand Mrs. Wilkins the package, her brows knit together. "What's this?"

"Sweater. For the new baby. And...matching sweaters. For her sisters." When I decided to send Mrs. Wilkins' newest grandchild a gift, I got carried away. A present for the baby became a present for all the kids.

Mrs. Wilkins' mouth forms an "o" as she unwraps the white tissue paper to reveal three ice blue sweaters, one on top of the other, littlest to biggest. "Iris, I don't know what to say. You made these for the girls?"

I lean against the door. "Mm hmm. I thought they'd be gorgeous in that color. Kind of a *Frozen* feel but not babyish or like a franchise." I shudder. "You know?"

She's bemused. "With all the things you have going on..." She murmurs. "What do I owe you?"

"Oh, nothing. It's a gift. Congratulations." I beam.

"Well, Iris, I think I can safely say, it's the nicest gift Michelle's received with this newest addition. After two kids, people don't notice so much. Except for the mom, who's in the middle of it." She chuckles and holds the bundle in her arms, beaming at me. "This is dear. Handknit sweaters, what a thing. Thank you. And again–" she stops and looks me in the eye. "Thank you for understanding all this. I know I sprang this on you. But it's such a good offer for the house, and with my husband's health..." She stops, her voice thick with emotion.

It wrenches at my heart. Cancer-free now doesn't mean cancer-free later. "It's OK, Mrs. Wilkins, it's OK! I will...figure this out."

And I will. Because we're about to be homeless and figuring it out is my only option.

That or my old bedroom, with my twin bed, at my parents' house.

She pats my arm. "Text me about the boys."

"I will. Thanks!" I close the door and sag against it in relief. On the heels of relief comes sadness. Our home. Our lovely little home will be gone at the end of the month.

I want to cry. I love this house.

I mean, it's been a year. One measly year.

But we've loved it here. Close to the boys' school and on the same street as my best friend and her family. Ten minutes from my parents' house.

How did we get so lucky? Nostalgia washes over me, as my gaze wanders over the space. The late afternoon light sifting through the big front windows. The smell of dried lavender from vases I have set around the house. Of course, the vases will come too, but still. This is so sad.

But there's no point thinking about it right now. Ray's words come back to me, the dreaded, "I think we need to talk," and I sigh gustily. Also almost a year in, well, eight months, and he throws down, "We need to talk."

Tears well in my eyes and threaten to spill.

"MOOOOOOM," Atticus bellows. I wipe my eyes on the sleeve of my soft, rosy Anthropologie cardigan, a terrific thrift store find, and haul myself to the kitchen.

2.

"Where are my grandsons?"

My mom comes right in the house, no doorbell, no knock. My dad's there, too, and I hear him reproach her. She waves a hand. "They're expecting us."

"Hey, guys, you're fine. Come in."

After Mrs. Wilkins left, the boys and I rolled up the living room rug and spread a huge sheet of paper across the floor. Coloring keeps everyone busy, including me.

Speaking of the boys, I look around. "Atty, where's Ernie?"

Atticus, engrossed in sketching a skyscraper, shrugs. "Bathroom."

There's a whoop and a screech. Ernie is not in the bathroom. Ernie is in our dining room, stark naked, laughing.

What happened? Two minutes ago, the three of us were enjoying some quiet time. I sketched ideas for new baby sweaters while my mind drifted, and I wondered about tonight and Ray. Both boys seemed busy.

So how could Ernie be dancing around in only his Spiderman underpants now?

"That's quite an entrance, Ernest." My father is bemused.

"Ernie, where are your clothes?" My mother gapes at him.

I'm mortified scrambling to my feet and hissing, "Ernie, *come-hererightnow.*"

Miraculously, he listens. In the bathroom, he wriggles in my grip, but I'm able to yank his dark blue t-shirt back over his head. He's laughing, and, even as I'm red-cheeked and puffing, I want to laugh, too. My little nudist.

Back in the living room, I hurry them both. "Socks and shoes, both of you. Granny and Grandpa are ready, so let's hustle."

Dad's laughing, too, but I notice the crease in Mom's forehead, the eyes that follow Ernie out of the room.

"What?" I demand.

"I worry about him. A little. Atticus was never this wild. You weren't either."

"They're different kids. And so was I. Everyone has their strengths and weaknesses."

The words fall out easily; I say them often enough. She nods, but the creased brow doesn't smooth out.

"Cynthia, honey, don't worry." Dad pats her arm. "Iris knows what she's doing."

I preen at these words, a sense of self-satisfaction running through me. I do know what I'm doing. Who else has known almost every second of every day with them since they took their first breaths? Only me.

The idea catches my attention, and I feel that tug at my heart. No one will ever know them exactly the way I do. What we have is special.

Unique. Of course, I know that in a way, but sometimes an idea hits you just right, and you feel it. All the way to your–

"Let's roll," Dad announces and jolts me back. He pats his front shirt pocket locating his keys. "Ready, grandsons?"

"Anything new on house hunting?" Mom, aware of the soon-to-expire lease, sounds anxious. She sends daily emails with lists of rentals. "Any luck with what I sent?"

I shake my head. "One didn't feel comfortable renting to a self-employed single lady. I think she saw the words 'starving artist' over my head the whole time we talked." I smile ruefully. "The second one glared at Ernie and Atticus the entire time. Then said he thought he already had someone locked in." I don't mention how Ernie might have gotten to the front door first and banged the ancient knocker so hard it came off in his hand. I apologized profusely. And that knocker was low! Who puts a knocker in the center of the door?

"And the third one?" my dad prompts. Doesn't miss a trick, our Zeke Shepherd.

I give him a helpless shrug. "It was so...depressing."

"Iris–"

"I know, I know. But, Dad, really, there has to be something pretty. One needs a touch of beauty." I add, thrusting my chin out. "So I'm still looking."

He shakes his head. "Don't sink into the magical thinking on this, Iris. You have to work at things. The next house isn't just going to fall in your lap."

"I know, I know." I rub the bridge of my nose, wishing desperately it would.

Mom rubs my back, and I lean into her, thankful for her support.

"To the Bat-mobile, boys," Dad calls and adds, "Love you, daughter." I blow him a kiss.

Mom lingers while Dad leads the kids to the car.

"How are you?" Her face is etched with worry.

I wonder if other adults are as close to their parents as I am to mine? You could argue, besides Angie, Mom and Dad are my closest friends.

That is not as weird as it sounds. They're great people. And, growing up, when other kids didn't get me, didn't see my vision on a class project, or understand my worry for the class guinea pigs on weekends, my parents did. My mother, in fact, volunteered to bring those guinea pigs home every Friday afternoon and return them to school on Monday morning because I had such a hard time, imagining their loneliness.

Of course, she also said she was thrilled when second grade ended and our house stopped smelling like a petting zoo. But nonetheless, she did it.

"I'm OK. I mean, I wish all these things weren't happening at once, but I'm figuring it out." And I smile what I hope is a tired, but brave, smile. Weary, but stoic.

"Yeah?" She puts her arm around my waist. "Like you need one more thing to worry about. What's going on?"

The gesture comforts me.

"I have to figure out this thing with The Paisley Knickerbocker."

"What's up with The Paisley Knickerbocker?"

"Closing. Can you believe it? Melody has created a successful small business, a unicorn in this economy, but she says she's 'at capacity' and 'needs to self-evaluate.'" Mom's expression is hard to read, so I fill in the blank. "She's closing the store at the end of this month. She announced it right after Christmas."

"Honey, that's awful. That's...awful." I've gone too far. I've said too much, and she's panicked on my behalf. "I had no idea. She told you at

Christmas? Oh, my goodness. Iris, what does that mean for you? This is terrible."

Do I internally agree with everything she's saying? For sure. The Paisley Knickerbocker is my steady income, the place I make half my year's salary.

But as Cynthia Shepherd's one and only child for thirty-six years, I know better than to tell her everything. There's a formula, a percentage I can share, before my mom takes on my struggles as her own and loses her composure. Roughly fifty to sixty percent of truth evokes understanding without panic. More than that, I end up comforting her until she finds her equilibrium.

Which is a touch frustrating, but what can I do? She's my mom. She worries.

"It'll be OK." *Really? How?* "I'm not that worried." *Liar.* "I'm growing my booth at the farmers' market. And there's a woman from church, Andie, who's asked me to put some items in her store. That's going to make up for some of the lost business." *There it is.* Some truth, just enough to comfort her and still be honest.

She watches my face for a minute longer before nodding. "OK. If you feel good, then I feel good."

She hugs me, and when she pulls back, she smooths my hair, naturally wavy, from my face. "So pretty," she adds, holding my chin in her hand and giving it a little wiggle. It makes me laugh when she tells me that, especially as one of the compliments she and I hear the most is how much we look alike. She's blonde where I'm brunette, blue-eyed, where I'm dark-eyed, but the similarity is so strong you'd know we were mother and daughter.

And, give credit where credit's due, Mom stays put together. Her curvy form has filled out more, but she keeps her blonde hair touched up and cut in a sassy soft shoulder-length bob. She doesn't go anywhere without makeup, and she's always got some fun touch, like a soft patterned scarf or pretty broach, to brighten up an outfit. Our personal style is different, but I learned the importance of having a style at all from her.

"What are you and Ray doing tonight? I hope it's something nice."

Possibly breaking up? We're at capacity for how much bad news I can share today, so I keep the thought to myself. "I'm making dinner. Maybe we'll watch a movie. We'll see."

"That sounds nice." Mom says. "Quiet and calm. We'll be back by nine."

If you last that long. Another thought I keep to myself. My parents were amazing parents to a single girl, even a–how did the school counselor put it? Imaginative, emotional one.

But two boys, especially when one of them is Ernie, keeps them on their toes.

The passenger window rolls down. Dad calls out, " Beep, beep, Cynthia!" My father would never honk for his wife. "If we don't get going, we'll never get gone."

She kisses my cheek, then wipes away the lipstick smudge she put there. "Love you, Button. See you in a bit."

Before Mom's in the car, I whip my cell from my back pocket and hit the name at the top of my favorites list. Angie answers on the first ring, and I blurt the same thing I've said the last few times we've chatted: "What does he mean, 'we need to talk?'"

3.

"I don't know, sweetie. I don't know."

Now that I'm alone, silence permeates the space.

Silence is so hard right now. If there's silence, I'm thinking about one of three things: losing my house, losing my income, or losing my boyfriend.

"What time is he coming over?" Angie rustles through the phone.

I ask, "What are you doing?"

"Feeding Miguel. He's a food monster these days. As soon as he tasted that first avocado, he was hooked."

I smile at this. Angie's ahead and behind me when it comes to children. In the last thirteen years, she and José produced one set of twin girls and a boy three years later, then adopted a girl four years after that, and recently a precious little guy named Miguel, who just checked in at six months.

They live four houses down from us, and my boys adore their home. It is the opposite of ours. Huge, constantly being updated or repaired, and noisy and full of people, especially a dad. My kids would be there every night if they could. If I didn't spend so much of my time there sick with longing, we probably would be there every night.

"Tell him I said hi." I pause and then burst through with my top concern. "Why do we need to talk? And where did he go?"

Angie's quiet. This is her thinking voice, the silent one. "How long has it been?"

Through the phone, I hear Miguel babble, "Ba, ba, ba, baaa."

"Since what? Since he started...ghosting me?" I barely get the word out, first because it's modern and dumb and second because I think that's exactly what might be happening.

"Since you started dating," Angie clarifies.

I pretend to think about it. "About eight months, almost nine?" Even with Angie, I won't admit I've been checking off each month as it passes, watching obsessively for the break. Like every month down indicates one more month to come. So ridiculous.

While we talk, I tidy up. I'm not looking forward to tonight. But if Ray ends it, my house will not look like a pigsty when it happens. And I will make the finest Murgh Murkani he's ever had the good fortune to eat. He'll leave regretting his decision, I vow.

"Do you think it's about that?"

I pull myself back into the call with Angie. "About what?"

"You're at that point, aren't you? I mean it's not the year mark, but it's not that far off. And at our age, he's what, thirty-six?"

"Thirty-five," I grumble. Ray being six months younger than me stings every time.

"Right. Close enough. He's at the age. We're not dating for fun anymore."

"What's this 'we' stuff?" Angie and José met on a mission trip when they were twenty-one. They were married at twenty-three.

Do I envy their romance, the way they still hold hands at their kids' sports events, how they tag-team parenting, the fact that sometimes José will grab her up and goofy-dance to Beyoncé's "Crazy in Love" in the kitchen while they make dinner?

I can barely say the word yes. I envy it so badly. Except for my brief and pathetic marriage to the boys' dad, I've essentially been single my whole life.

But there's always the dream, right? The great love story, the soul mate, the One...and I just haven't met him yet.

"Iris! Snap to! I don't have forever."

"Sorry! I'm here. Anyway, what do you know about dating for fun?"

"I dated," Angie protests.

"As a teenager. Not an adult. And let me tell you, it's not for the faint of heart."

"Exactly. And that's what I'm trying to say about Ray. He's old enough to want to figure this out. I doubt he wants to date you for years and years."

"His divorce was only a few years ago. He might be leery."

"Maybe." Angie's thinking again. I fling the boys' blocks into the toy box, and we're both quiet, listening to Miguel chatting away. At last, she says, "I can't say for sure, but I wouldn't be surprised if he's wanting to have that 'talk'. The where-are-we-going talk."

Moving onto the kitchen, I sigh. "It just, it all got so weird so fast. We went from this dreamy dating spell, getting together a couple times a week, texting every day, phone calls every night. He spent time with the boys. And he seemed to enjoy it. And then Christmas happened, and now here we are!"

I can still see Ray's face. He came to our house Christmas morning after the initial melee to have lunch. My parents were there, and the boys were calmer, having worn themselves into a quiet stupor. We'd put on the original *The Grinch Who Stole Christmas*, and the four of us lounged around the living room while my father sat at the dining table reading his new book and my mother tidied my kitchen for me.

And out of the blue, Ernie said, "This day is great. I got a bike. Ray's our new dad. Everything's perfect." And then he collapsed back into my lap.

I could feel, physically feel, the change in the room. Suddenly, the heat, normally non-existent in our poorly ventilated house, felt elevated about ten degrees. The strong, familiar smell of cinnamon from the snickerdoodles left a dark, burnt scent in the air. The sounds of kitchen cabinets opening and shutting ceased as my mother froze. The chair at the dining table creaked, my dad turning to look at me.

And feeling like I was moving in slow motion, I only had eyes for Ray.

He wasn't looking at me at all, his eyes on Ernie instead. He sat next to Atticus on the sofa, his arm slung casually across the back of the couch. Looking between my boys, it felt like an eternity before he met my gaze with that unreadable expression, dark eyes, lips closed. All I could offer was a weak smile and a shrug.

Recounting this, for possibly the tenth time to Angie, the familiar sense of helpless foreboding creeps over me.

"And then he was texting less. He was more clipped on the phone, shorter. Distant."

"It's been a week," she reminds me, her tone gentle.

"Ten days!" I counter. "Something changed. The bubble popped. I mean, before that, he seemed happy. He liked seeing the boys. They liked him. It was great!"

And now Angie's tone changes, challenging me. "Is it? I mean, is that what you want for the long haul? To date a guy in a different county, a super busy farmer, who maybe sees you a couple of times a week?"

Angie doesn't have an agenda; she genuinely wants to parse it out, understand my point of view, and see where I'm coming from.

So staring out the kitchen window into our bare little backyard, I ask myself: Is this enough? Is this what I want? When I married the boys' dad, Parker, I was twenty-six. I'd been alone all of my adult life, still living with my parents. It looked a lot like my own mother's youth until she met my dad.

And the crush I had on Parker in college! The fact our dating life never came close to the life I imagined for us in my head didn't matter.

And there were so many external forces. Angie got married a few years earlier. She had twins and was pregnant again. College was several years in the rearview mirror, and while I wanted to make my art business succeed, there was no way I could afford to live independently on the income I made.

I needed a change, a fresh start, and suddenly here was the cute man-boy I idealized in my late teens wanting me, too.

By the time the charm of newlywed life wore off, I was pregnant. And he worked all the time. Again, it didn't come close to the life I fantasized about, so I kept fantasizing and I managed.

Atticus came, and suddenly I was a mom. Overwhelmed, touched out, and tired all the time. Parker received a promotion, and started traveling for more than half the year.

We grew accustomed to a routine that involved him being gone Tuesday through Friday morning. That worked better.

How he and I ever managed to summon the energy for sex that led to an unexpected pregnancy and a second baby born when Atticus was only a year and a half, I couldn't explain.

And as tough as two kids under two felt, life was better when Parker wasn't home. When he told me he had met someone else on his work trips and was leaving, I wept a few tears of betrayal. But mostly of relief.

That didn't diminish my desire to be in love, to be in a wonderful relationship. I wanted, no, I yearned for love. That big sweeping love from all the movies my mom and I watched. That romance that lasts a lifetime from every book I read as a kid because I was inside, digging into *Jane Eyre* and *Wuthering Heights* while other kids my age were traveling all weekend for soccer competitions or cheer camps. That beautiful relationship I witnessed with Angie and José.

So what did I want with Ray?

"Babe?" Angie prompts me. "Is it enough, what you two are doing now?"

On her end, there are bangs and new voices. She says, "The masses are home," and calls out to her crew, "How was the game?"

One of her twins shouts back, "We won!" and I hear her son grumble, "Lost," and her littlest girl says, "I dunno!"

Dang it. Angie needs to go, and I still have an hour before I see Ray.

"Do you need to go?" I ask, my voice more plaintive than encouraging.

She laughs. "Probably. But, hon? You don't know what he wants to talk about. So chin up, OK?"

I nod to my reflection in the kitchen window, even as I feel my old friend melancholy settle over me like a warm shawl. "Maybe it will be OK."

"That's the spirit." She laughs.

Miguel's baby-shouting, and it's not a happy sound.

Angie sighs. "I'm the one who wanted one more kid." This is something she'll only say to me because she knows I won't judge.

"And you were right to want him," I say. "Because he's gorgeous and sweet and gives the gummiest kisses."

Angie chuckles. "Keep reminding me of that."

"I will. Kiss the littles and hug the husband for me."

"Will do. Enjoy your child-free night."

"OK if I need to call…later?" My voice catches.

"Any. Time. I might be half asleep and not making any sense. But I'm right here."

I hang up with the knowledge that things are probably about to get a lot worse before they get better.

4.

Ray and I weren't supposed to last. I'm not being dramatic here, no matter what my mom or Angie might say. We weren't going to make it.

I knew his brother, Dennis, first and liked him. We were vendors at the farmers' market together, basically coworkers.

When I started at the market two summers ago, Dennis had been a vendor for several years. Bright smile, friendly, and outgoing, I was glad to be next to his booth. He was tall, dark-headed, and handsome but with such an affectionate grin and easygoing manner as to be approachable. Being friends with Dennis was easy, and that's coming from me. Friendship can take me years, if at all.

The gold band on his left ring finger offered safety. I was comfortable to talk to him without the fear it could be misconstrued.

I can't say all his female customers felt the same as me. And that wasn't my business.

"Whatcha need today?" Dennis would call over once I was set up and had a minute to chug my water.

I'd do a quick sweep of his table.

Shopping with other vendors at the farmers market is a dance. As a vendor, I have a strong sense of the effort and time it takes to produce something by hand, be it vegetables, meat, clothes, or soap. Respecting the work we all do is critical.

However, as someone earning her living as a craft vendor, Mama's on a budget. It's a constant battle. I want to invest in local, especially local food. And yet there's only so much to spend, and farmers' market goods can cost more.

And here's a rule about farmers' markets: They're not for haggling. It's not a yard sale. The price is the price. The end.

If there were any hot commodities on the table—blueberries, early tomatoes, sugar snap peas—I'd shop early and insist on full price.

"Just take–" Dennis would start, and I'd make a show of walking back to my booth, cash still in hand.

He'd give in and I'd pay him

At the end of the market, with only the leftovers, that's when I'd do my best shopping. Dennis would wave a hand and ask, "What do the boys need this week?"

Several bags of kale, mustard greens, collard greens, the leftovers I could chop and freeze, boxes of overripe tomatoes I could can or make into salsa, so much eggplant for baba ganoush, armfuls of bell peppers that froze beautifully–I'd get my fill. And pay him a measly amount.

"I can't do anything else with it," Dennis insisted, holding his hands up.

"Won't your family eat it? Or save it?"

I knew Dennis' wife wasn't much for cooking, but I was aware of the Fox family, as a whole, somewhere on the farm. Didn't those people need feeding?

Dennis shook his head again. "My mama cooks for just about everybody, so if she doesn't take it, nobody eats it. And, honestly, Iris, nobody eats all these vegetables like you." And he'd cackled, baffled by my choices.

We built a rapport. The market setup was simple. Positioned in the center of our downtown, on the square, the rules were: drive in slowly, remove your vehicle as soon as you've unpacked, and be set up by eight-fifty am. Simple.

***

Simple unless you're bringing two kids and need to be awake before six am on a Saturday. Dennis was entirely set up long before I made it. And I could count on him to help unload my car.

The morning Ray attended the market, I was late. By a lot. And there was no chance of being set up in time if I had to do it alone.

"Stay right there. Do not move!" I barked at the boys. We were extra late due to the dispute that erupted over who broke the head off the secondhand Avengers action figure that morning. By the time I finished shouting, they were in the car, riding quietly to the market while I seethed in the front seat.

Dennis' booth was set up, and I remember roaring, "Help!" in his direction, racing to the back of the car. I sensed his hesitation from the corner of my eye. "Please!" I begged, and I saw his legs move into action.

"Just get everything out of the car." Running from corner to corner, I popped my tent into place. "Hurry, please," I panted. Tents need to be weighted down, and I positioned my twenty-five-pound weights around the tent legs as fast as he could haul them out. By the time I finished securing the tent and snapping the tables into place, all the tubs were stacked neatly next to me.

"What do you want me to do with these guys?"

It wasn't Dennis' voice. And if I looked more closely, those weren't his denim-clad legs.

I snapped around to see a man standing at the back of the car, hand resting on the popped hatchback. Both boys peered out while I gaped at him.

He was tan and had dark hair sticking up all over his head. It was the first thing I noticed about him. He had dark eyes, watching me far too intently, and he was slim and wiry, like one long, lean muscle, in beaten-up Levi's and a faded black t-shirt. It was like expecting a sweet iced tea and getting a cup of strong black coffee instead. Rich coffee, but intense no matter how slowly you sip it.

"Who the hell are you?" First words out of my mouth. Not on purpose, but there you go.

"Mom!" Atticus exclaimed while Ernie cackled, "You said a swear! Mom said a swear!"

"Yes, she did." The stranger agreed, bemused.

"I, who, where did you...?" I whipped around to Dennis' booth. It was definitely the Fox Family Farm booth. But no Dennis.

"It's eight forty." The stranger said.

"Damn it!" It happened again.

"Mom!" Atticus yelled again while Ernie's laugh reached supersonic levels of delight.

"We're going, we're going." I huffed back to the driver's seat.

"Do you want me to keep an eye on them?" he asked.

I swiveled on him. "Are you crazy?"

He chuckled. "Fair enough. Can I do anything here?"

I was torn. Leaving my kids wasn't going to happen, but asking some stranger to set up my booth?

Reasonable, given the circumstances.

"There are tablecloths in the top tub." I puttered off the square, barking orders out of the open window. He kept a leisurely pace next to the car. "If you'll get those on, and the chairs set up, that would be great."

And that was how I met Ray. Demanding his help and cussing.

5.

Of course, that wasn't the official meeting. By the time the boys and I made it back to the table, me shouting at them to run, there were customers at Ray's booth. He had a wide-legged stance behind the table, hands in his pockets, chatting. As we passed, he gave me a quick chin tilt and smile.

Thank goodness Atticus couldn't hear the words inside my head. He would not have been pleased.

I can't say what it was about Ray, but I was aware of his presence all morning.

Normally I would seize the first quiet moment to inspect Dennis' booth. Today, I stayed put. I worked my booth. I sold my baby sweaters, tiny knitted toys, and toddler hats, and I kept my head down.

The market was busy, and I didn't slow down until noon—hot, thirsty, and hungry. I had just pinned my hair up off my neck and was chugging water from my thermos when I heard a voice say, "So you must be Iris."

I choked. Nothing like sputtering and spitting to set the right tone.

"Sorry. Did I startle you?" He thumped me on the back as I tried to catch my breath. His hand on my shoulder blades, the fact my t-shirt was sweaty, his nearness, it was a lot, and it wasn't just the water making me sputter.

Glancing up, I saw strong white teeth against that sun-browned skin and eyes so dark and deep they seemed bottomless.

I couldn't get my bearings.

"How'd you know my name?" Prickly immediately. *Nice, Iris, always so good with people.*

He stepped back. "Dennis mentioned you. Or mentioned having a nice neighbor. I'm putting two and two together." He held out his hand. "I'm Ray, by the way. Ray Fox."

We shook. His skin was warm, dry, and rough, and the brief touch gave me the most surprising flutter in my belly.

"Where's Dennis?" That's me, as friendly as your local district attorney dealing with a hostile witness.

"Taking a break from markets."

"Is he OK?"

Ray's eyes searched my face. I stared back, unsure of what he was looking for.

"He's fine. Giving up every Saturday for more than half the year is hard. He's got a wife who'd like to see him."

"And you don't?" Why is small talk so hard?

"I do not. I'm a footloose and fancy-free man." He held his palms out when he said it, and I think I startled us both when I laughed. He grinned. "I volunteered to come instead, give him a break."

The idea of a break shone a spotlight on my exhaustion from working every weekend for seven months of the year. "I hear that."

Ray whistled. "Must be a lot with those boys in tow."

"If there's another option, I don't have it. So here we are." I followed his gaze. By noon, the heat started to peak, and my kids petered out. They had crashed in camping chairs, reading graphic novels.

"They're good boys." He wasn't asking but making an observation.

Watching them now, you'd never know I'd threatened to put them both out on the street if they didn't *sit down* and *be quiet* only an hour ago.

"Hallelujah for the graphic novel. And they get a treat when we pack up."

"Must be a good treat?"

I rolled my eyes from side to side. "Pack of Starburst."

Ray crooked an eyebrow. "The little fruit chews?" I nodded. "One pack to split?"

"We don't see a lot of candy in our house."

He whistled again. It was endearing. "Strict mama. I'm impressed."

It was something about that "mama." It took the breath out of me, his voice deep and low, his smile mischievous, and those eyes...

I blurted, "I need to get back to my booth."

We both looked. I was already in my booth. One step and that was it. But I needed some space.

Was Ray offended? Did he laugh at such a stupid statement?

Nope. He gave a little head nod and stepped back to his booth. Over his shoulder, he called, "Come pick what you like before the market's done gone."

I didn't. I stayed put, arranging my merchandise, checking the sales on my iPad, and talking to the occasional customer. By the time the market ended, I managed to put almost an hour between us.

Instead of my usual care, I packed up haphazardly. My other market neighbor, Gretchen, watched the boys while I retrieved the car. And by the time I was back, I'd almost forgotten Ray's presence.

"It's been a pleasure, Iris."

"Agh!" My metal cashbox slipped from my hands as I swung around.

"Agh!" Ray yelped as the heavy box landed on his foot.

"Are you OK?" The box hit the ground, scattering quarters, as I moved towards him, hands out.

To do what, Iris? Kiss his boo-boo?

He was a grown man, now holding the toe of his left shoe in his hand, hopping up and down. Only when he put a hand on my shoulder did I realize how much of his personal space I had invaded.

"It's alright, Iris. I'm alright." He touched his foot to the ground gingerly, wincing. "I wear work boots for a reason. You never know where danger might be lurking."

He smiled again, his otherwise serious face wreathed in light when he did. My heart sped up, my breathing slowed down. The urge to flee overwhelmed me.

Next to the cashbox sat a carton bursting with produce.

"I wanted to bring you this." He nudged the box with his uninjured foot.

I hesitated. "Dennis told you to be nice to me?"

Ray's mouth pulled to the side, displeased. "Not a bit. I want you to have it."

Did he have some kind of magic? I didn't want to hold his gaze, but I couldn't look away.

"Mom! Ernie's peeing on the flowers!"

That'll break a spell every time. I whipped around to see my youngest's bare bottom on display and to hear him urinating on the marigolds planted around the tree.

"Ernie, for the love," I said faintly.

"All done." He zipped up, satisfied.

Atticus was disgusted. "You gotta wash your hands."

I rubbed the bridge of my nose, working to relax, and called, "Use the hand sanitizer."

When I turned around, Ray was gone.

"C'mon, boys, give a hand now."

He was at the back of my car, loading tables.

Both boys jumped into action, reveling in Ray's comments like "good man" and "toss me that, yup, there we go."

Ray was quick and athletic, lifting each table one-handed, his muscles straining against his shirt sleeves. He was tanner than Dennis, shorter, thinner, and not traditionally handsome, with his black hair stuck up all over his head, having run a hand through it too many times.

And I couldn't look away.

"Mom, why do you look like that?" Atticus frowned. Both he and Ray stared at me.

I matched his frown, hoping it hid the flush shooting up my cheeks. "I don't," I grumbled. "I don't look like anything."

"Yeah, you do. You look like this." Ernie dropped his mouth open, his eyes crossing before he burst out laughing.

Please, Lord, don't let me look like that.

Shaking my head and ruffling his hair, I said, "Who asked you anyway?" And added, "C'mon, let's get home."

To Ray, I smiled a friendly, but not too friendly, smile. We needed to be done with this and on our way. No more attentive, and, so help me, sexy farmers today. "Thank you so much for your help. And I hope your foot's OK."

His lips compressed like he was hiding a smile. "You're most welcome," he said. "And I'm sure it will be. Once I ice it. Elevate it. Maybe put it in a cast? We'll see."

"It wasn't that bad," I started and caught sight of his lips pulling apart, those teeth showing. "You're teasing me, aren't you? That's teasing."

"Why yes, I am, Iris. I'm teasing you." He beamed. Ray reminded me, here and there, of his brother, but he was different. There was a cadence to the way he spoke, a slower drawl, a use of language that harkened several decades back. Coming from him, it felt natural, like he'd been laboring on his own too long and missed the passage of time.

Yet he wasn't uncomfortable in the midst of our somewhat modern downtown area. From the corner of my eye, I'd watched him throughout the day. He spoke to pleasant single ladies and flirty sorority girls, couples, straight and gay, and grumpy old folks, with the same friendliness, always polite, thoughtful, and earnest.

He was kind. It was the only word for it.

And I could hardly bear it, the way he fixed that gaze on me. Every bit as kind as I'd seen him before but with a flavor of something else, too. A sparkle.

I had one leg already in the car, desperate to escape. "Well, it was nice to meet you. Even with the teasing."

He ducked his head to the passenger window. "Nice to meet you, too. And I hope to tease you again real soon."

With that, he thumped the top of the car once and stepped back. Tapping the gas, our car inched out of the market. I kept my eyes focused straight ahead.

What did he mean? And why, oh why, did my heart make that weird fluttering feeling at the idea of more teasing real soon?

6.

It took two more markets and my arriving without the boys to prompt the conversation of a date. Ray was already set up, and he approached my car as I crept to a stop and put it in park.

His clothes didn't change much, usually a uniform of some old, busted Levi's, a fitted t-shirt, and a pair of work boots. How did he stand it? We were in the thick of July, and I wore a t-shirt, shorts, and hiking sandals to every market. I pinned my long hair on the top of my head and still ended up pouring water down my throat, hot and dehydrated from the heat.

"Where are the young men?" Already he was pulling the tables from the back of the car. Ray chose the heaviest items first and made a point to set the tables up, too. Even as I tried to help, he brushed my efforts aside.

Being this close to him was distracting, and it was hard not to watch his strong, tanned arms at work. We were the same height, and I liked that, too. We looked right into each other's eyes, and it created an unexpected intimacy.

"Iris?"

"Hmm?"

He laughed. "I asked, where are the boys today? Or did you make them ride on the top?" He peered over the car.

It was my turn to laugh. "With my friend, Angie. One of her kids has a birthday today, and she offered to keep the boys so they can attend the party."

"How many kids?"

"What?"

"How many kids does Angie have?"

"Oh. Five."

Ray stopped and whistled. "Really?"

"Yep. I know." I shrugged, rueful. "She wanted a house full of kids."

"I'd say she got it."

Ray popped the last table into place. "I can understand it. I'm one of four."

I gaped at him. "There's four of you?"

"What, Dennis never told you that in your long talks?"

That gave me pause. Our long talks? What did that mean?

However, Ray kept going, and I worked to keep up. "Yep, Dennis at the top, then me, our sis Stephanie, and then little ol' Brandon, he's the unexpected one." He chortled at this.

"Wow." I shook my head. "I'm an only child, so that's literally the opposite of my childhood."

We continued to unload as we talked, him doing the heavy lifting while I set up my tables. He asked, "What about you? Did you want a house full of kids?"

It was a complicated question. "I didn't have plans. I was so happy when I got pregnant with Atticus. And Ernie wasn't expected, but

I was tickled about him, too. Then their dad and I divorced, and I haven't thought about more kids after that."

The back of my car was empty, and I had the keys in my hand.

"Would you go out with me?"

I paused. "What?"

Ray dropped his head and shook it, like he surprised himself. But then he looked up and met my gaze. Direct. Clear.

"I'd like to take you out on a date. Would you want to?"

He waited. I shifted from foot to foot, heart galloping, my chest hurting from nerves. "I, I have to park." That's what I blurted at him before I darted to my car.

What was wrong with me? A friendly, attractive, and seemingly sincere man asked me on a date. Asked me sweetly and while looking me in the eyes. When was the last time that happened?

Never, if I thought about it. That had never happened. I hardly dated in high school, and my few dates in college consisted of groups together, the boy of interest and I making unsure eyes at each other, both too scared to approach, until it eventually fizzled out.

It was no wonder I jumped at the chance to date Parker. Not only had he been my college crush, but he was the first guy to approach me with anything close to intelligible. He came across my booth at a spring craft fair. After I reminded him how we knew each other, his proposition went like: "Could you help me pick out something for my sister's new baby? Maybe we'll get coffee, too?" It was a sideways request and accepted with a sidelong look from me. Nothing about the two of us was clean or direct.

And since the divorce, the few dates I've accepted happened through setups from friends. Texts, direct messages, and a handful of encounters before an unsatisfactory, but unsurprising, ending.

Yet here was Ray with that genuine offer. "I'd like to take you out on a date." Could he be any more forthright?

And my response was to run away.

Great, Iris. Well done.

Ray had customers gathered around his table all day. We'd hit tomato season, and Ray offered a table full of heirlooms, German Johnson, Brandywine, and German Stripe in a rich variety of reds, orange-golds, and purples against his green and white checked table-cloth. People in East Tennessee are crazy for tomatoes. Maybe people across America are crazy for tomatoes? I couldn't say, I've only lived here. But I know the summer season is when people lose their minds for them, and today appeared to be Ray's big day.

I kept an eye on the situation. I'd made up my mind, I was going to say yes. As soon as I could catch a break between all his folks.

This never happened. It was one o'clock yet again, and he still had a customer, a young woman with long, shiny dark hair laced with purple highlights, a crop top showing flat abs with a pair of wide-legged cargo pants (impossible to imagine in this heat), and one arm of shoulder-to-fingertips tattoos, showing the world she was both pretty and rebellious, sexy and sturdy, exactly the kind of woman you could imagine a farmer taking an interest in.

Compared to this young one, in my t-shirt from the latest school fundraiser and jean shorts, my once cute topknot of hair now droop-ing down my neck, I felt frumpy and old. *I used to be artistic and fashionable,* I wanted to shout at her.

Now, I was a self-employed tired mother of two, and my jangly bracelets and big, dangly earrings were the most excitement I could pull off.

I'd noticed the way both ladies ten years younger and ten years older than him lingered at his table. And here I'd had a chance, a moment where something sparked between the two of us, and I blew it. *Classic Iris.*

I felt like molasses moving through the hot, humid air straining to hurry and too tired and sweaty to work harder.

Wrestling a table into the back of my car, I overheard Ray say, "I'm gonna need to excuse myself." A moment later, right behind me, he said, "Girl, what are you doing? You know I'm coming to help."

And there he was, next to me, with a folded table in his hand, dark eyes bright, and smiling at me fondly.

I liked all of it. I liked the way he looked at me, like he was so pleased to see me. I liked his old-fashioned way of speaking. I liked his worn, but well-fitting, jeans and t-shirts. And I really liked the way I felt around him.

Heart racing, palms sweating, I said, "Yes. That would be great."

A smile spread across his face. "Would it be now?"

"To the date," I added. "I mean, yes, to the date."

He nodded. "I knew what you meant, Iris."

And right then, when he said that? That's when I knew something was about to happen, something I hadn't expected. Something I didn't want to miss.

7.

Now months into this romance, and it's crumbling in front of me. In the middle of winter, it's dark when he arrives at five-thirty.

By the time Ray knocks on the door and quietly lets himself in, the smell of Indian butter chicken permeates the house, and I'm struggling to hold myself together.

He calls out, "Hello?"

"In the kitchen." I refuse to run to him, refuse to act as though I've spent the last two hours, two days, actually, with my stomach in knots around those words: We need to talk.

For our meal, I use Ray's tomatoes that I canned this summer and serve it with a side of his green cabbage, sauteed, spiced, and crisp. It's warm, rich, and savory, flavoring the house with its inviting fragrance.

I managed a quick shower, and, however I feel on the inside, I look fresh and smell of the local coconut soap and lavender lotion I used.

With the end in mind, I dressed my best. Wide-legged, dark blue jeans, with a mint-green, long-sleeved sweater tucked into the high waistband, and a flower-patterned scarf tied around my head. The top is so soft, mostly cashmere, an excellent find from a yard sale.

I feel pretty, my meal tastes delicious, and my house looks lovely. Will this be enough? Will Ray see this and think, "How could I ever break up with this girl? She's the embodiment of calm, collected womanhood."

No, stoppit. Whatever Ray thinks or has decided, I'm myself, and that's all I can be.

And still, I send up a fervent *Dear Lord, please let this man see what a good thing we have going. Please keep this together. Please, please, please.*

My phone pings.

Angie: **It's going to be fine. You're so loved.**

Tears prick my eyes, and I'm brushing them away when Ray gets to the kitchen. He's brought a bottle of wine, and the brown paper sack makes crinkly sounds when he removes it. With his free hand, he touches my arm.

"Is something wrong?"

I shrug and take the bottle. Fiddling with the corkscrew, I ask, "How was your day?"

"Alright, I reckon. We spent a lot of it working the cows. Dennis had some new ideas to winterize the barn, and we..."

As he talks, Ray leans against the kitchen counter, hands in his pockets. He's wearing blue Levi's tucked into his good work boots, with a dark t-shirt under a faded navy blazer. I don't know if it's him or my feelings, but watching him speak, move his head, cross and uncross his arms, it's hypnotic.

Maybe it's just me. On our first date, I felt keenly aware of him. When he opened my car door, the way he placed one hand to the top of my back as the hostess led us to our table, and how he leaned towards me when I spoke. His focus was a brand new experience for me. It pulled me in and held me captive.

And so, once we were seated, I said immediately, "I don't date."

Ray let that declaration fall between us and settle. He looked down and seemed to be thinking.

"OK then," he said at last. "Would you tell me more?"

Finding the right words was hard, like opening a door to my world before I was certain I wanted to invite him in. "I just don't. I have two little boys, and I'm solely responsible for them, outside of the money their dad sends that pays for their school. They take up most of my time, and when they're at school, I'm working so I can support us. My parents help occasionally, and they're generous at Christmas and birthdays. But I'm the one taking care of my family, paying for our house, and keeping our car running, and it takes a lot. Beyond that, I'm a fairly private person. And I need a lot of quiet time to sort of, I don't know, recharge. It doesn't leave a lot of time for dating."

He studied the table as he listened while I took in every nuance of his face. There wasn't much to read, he kept it composed.

"And you're telling me this because...?" he prompted after I fell silent.

Why was I telling him this? Did I want to scare him off? No, that didn't feel right. Was I putting my hands up and keeping him at a distance? Not exactly that either.

"I'm telling you this so you know, I'm not sure what I'm doing. Or even if I want to keep doing it. But I'm here tonight, and I hope we can have a nice time."

As soon as I said it, I heard how discouraging I sounded. "I'm here tonight"? And "I hope we can have a nice time"? Out in the world they sounded ridiculous. Pompous. Prudish.

Ray nodded again. "OK," he said. "OK, well, I hope we can have a nice time, too. When I asked you out, I imagined it would be good. Though," he went on, "I don't date much either, so who am I to say?" At that, I put my hand on his arm, and he trailed off. "Iris?"

"The last thing I said was so weird. I'm sorry. I can't believe I'm starting tonight with an apology. The best thing I could have said was, 'My life is busy, and I don't date much.' I don't know why I had to make things so awkward."

And then he smiled a real, deep smile. He gave a dip of his chin, too, and laid his hand on mine, still on his arm. "That makes me feel better. A little less like a pariah." I winced, but he laughed and rubbed his fingers over mine reassuringly. "Let me tell you about my last date. This will get you laughing. So imagine me, Dennis, his wife, and her cousin, who's about a foot taller than me, looks like a fashion model, and snaps her fingers at waiters, and we're all having dinner at the Texas Roadhouse..."

***

Ray drove me home and walked me all the way to the porch. He stopped a few feet from the door. His message was clear: I'm coming this far, but I'm not expecting to go any farther.

I opened my mouth ready to blurt something—what, I don't know. Ray put a finger, so lightly, to my lips.

"I want to say something, Iris, and I'm asking you to think about it."

I watched his face, barely breathing, wondering if I'd managed to ruin the nicest thing to happen to me in a long time before it even got going.

"I don't date much either, and I don't think I do it all that well when I do. The farm is almost always on my mind. I don't like crowds, small talk, or events, which is not appealing to most women. And I definitely don't date where I work so asking you out was a real gamble." He paused and put his hands on my forearms. I'd worn short sleeves, and his touch on my skin sent prickles down my spine. "I want to date you. Just you. And see where this goes. I don't have any expectations, and I'm not in any hurry. But I haven't enjoyed talking to a woman in years the way I like talking to you. I haven't enjoyed listening to anyone as much as I enjoy listening to you. And—there's just something about you, I can't seem to get enough of looking at you." He touched my face at this, his fingers brushing a strand of hair off my forehead. "So if that sounds like something you'd like to do, then you just nod. I'll call you tomorrow, and we'll make a plan to see each other again. And if it doesn't or if you're unsure, I'd ask you to wait and think about it before you call. I don't take these feelings lightly, and I've got no interest in fooling around. Especially when we are, for all intents and purposes, colleagues." He smiled at this, but I couldn't return the look.

And barely waiting for him to finish, I leaned in, eye to eye as we were, and kissed him.

He slipped one arm around my waist, the other hand coming up to cup my face. Our lips met, fervently brushing against one another, tender yet firm, soft but decided. Ray's kiss was powerful. It was a promise and a claim. His fingers cupping my cheek, his arm around me, his chest against me–I wanted to sink into that kiss, to fully exhale, and release into him. To be swept away.

When I stepped back, I was shaky but happy. So happy.

I managed the words, "Call me tomorrow," before hurrying inside without a backward glance.

He called me at lunchtime the next day. And we'd seen each other every week since then until Christmas when he pulled away. And it was nearly two weeks later, and he hadn't come back.

We are at the "we need to talk" conversation.

My hand slips, and the corkscrew shoots off the top of the bottle.

"May I help you with that?" Ray's next to me, taking charge of the wine.

It's too late, though. I've broken the cork, and now one chunk is out, speared on the edge of the wine opener, the other lodged inside the bottle's neck. I stare at him helplessly, feeling so lost and lonely.

Ray appears unperturbed and works at the wine in silence.

Could I keep him busy? So busy he forgets his original intention. Better yet, so busy he might remember why we're together in the first place, and not end this.

"Iris?"

Ray's peering at me, that half smile on his lips, bottle in hand, now uncorked.

"You got it out!"

"Not quite." We both look into the bottle where a chunk of cork floats in the wine. "But a little cork never hurt anyone."

"I'm sturdy," I say, and he laughs.

"It's one of the things I like most about you."

My heart lifts, then plummets. Is sturdiness a good quality? Or does it make me more disposable? *Ah, Iris, she's sturdy. You can break up with her. She'll be fine.*

He finds two glass jam jars and pours.

I sigh and take a swig of mine, only to notice Ray's extended glass. Blushing, sheepish, I touch my glass to his.

"*Slainte*" he says and sips it.

Ray's family, a few hundred years ago, hailed from Scotland and Ireland. He spent some time on their ancestry in his twenties. Of course, he did. It's so Ray.

"Ready to eat?" I don't wait for an answer. We're eating, regardless.

"What's this one called again?"

"Murgh Makhani."

His brows knit together. "Butter chicken. Indian butter chicken." He remembers. Of course, he does. That's also so Ray.

I made it on our fourth date. By that time, Ray took me out for three different meals, and I knew two things: I liked this man, and I wanted to cook for him.

Indian butter chicken is my comfort food, one of my favorite things. Do I have any tie to it? Nope. But I've spent the last fifteen years perfecting it, at least to my East Tennessee tastes. It's rich and savory, with a hint of sweetness. The boys love it, and I make it for special occasions, or when I need comfort.

When I made it for Ray, it was early August. The heat was constant and present, but I set a table on our creaky back porch, and we ate at eight, with citronella candles all around us and little twinkle lights over our heads. It was a heavy dish for summer, but I served it with a side of wilted kale and jasmine rice, and at the end of it, Ray sat back and said, "Woman, I think you've put a spell on me. That might be the best thing I've ever eaten in my life."

From the look in his eyes, I knew. That meal changed something. It hooked him.

Maybe it will work again tonight.

8.

I spend the evening on the hop, up and down. It's tricky avoiding the conversation coming.

Now that his work season has slowed down, Ray comes here. It's helpful with the boys. The farm is almost forty minutes outside of town, and, while Atticus and Ernie love it, getting there and home again is tiring. The holidays were the last time we all went. The farmers' market in Lincoln County had a Christmas fair, and Ray invited us.

It was the last day before the school break. I took the boys to lunch at our favorite tiny local place, Grandma T's, and then we drove out to the farm.

Ray took us all around the property, showing us how he was winterizing the greenhouses, the barns, and the tractors. I don't know that the boys cared, but they loved being at the farm and they loved being with Ray.

"This place is so awesome!" Ernie said this like it was a brand-new experience each time we came. At six years old, it probably felt like it was. They were all three on the new orange tractor, Ernie at the wheel, standing in front of Ray, Ray in the driver's seat pushing pedals and shifting gears, and Atticus holding onto the side.

I watched from the field, snapping pictures, and, despite the cold, feeling warm and fuzzy, fueled with holiday spirit and the magic of the evening. During moments like this, I knew we had something special, something unique.

Ray was patient with them. It was clear, he wasn't quite sure what to do with two small boys who still didn't understand the concept of personal space. At one point, Ernie swung back and bellowed in his face, "I want to be a farmer!" I watched Ray wince at the high volume coming his way but also nod and smile.

"It's honest work," he said back to Ernie. "I'd highly recommend it." And Ernie beamed like a madman because he is a madman and because he reveled in so much positive male attention.

They trundled up and down over the bare rows. Atticus whooped, overwhelmed by joy, and shouted "Faster!" Ray laughed and shook his head.

"Don't listen to what people tell you. This here's the wild one," he said and nodded at Atticus whose serious face was lit with a smile.

When it got dark, we headed to the Christmas festival, Ray leading the way in his truck as I'd take the boys home from here. It was like any small-town Christmas festival you might imagine. Located in a good-sized parking lot next to the fire station, with tents, booths, and twinkly lights overhead, it felt three times its actual size.

The boys were enraptured, heads swiveling to take it all in. There was the Second Baptist Choir on risers belting "Away in a Manger" and "Hark! The Herald Angels Sing." The fire department gave tours of the fire station and helped the kids explore the fire trucks. And there were games in the field behind the parking lot, like Buddy the Elf's Three-Legged Race and Rudolph's Egg Toss.

"What are we going to do?" Atticus' brow wrinkled, anxious from so many choices.

Ray regarded him for a moment before he said, "All of 'em, Atticus. We're going to do all of them."

And my oldest son's face smoothed, and he said, "Cool!"

Holding hands, Ray and I meandered while the boys darted ahead of us, stopping when they heard the deep tenor of Ray's voice calling, "Whoa there, fellas!"

For one special night, I'd been plucked from my normal life into this new, delightful little world of four, with the boys and me plus one. For that night, there was a second set of eyes to play lookout, another voice to chastise and praise, and these warm, strong fingers wrapped around mine.

I'd mark it a perfect evening except for one small hitch. We'd finished every single game available, taken the fire station tour, and thoroughly examined each booth. All that was left was the fire pit, tended by the fire chief, where we could toast marshmallows and purchase cups of cocoa and hot apple cider. I stood in line for drinks, noting the banner hung behind this booth read, "Lincoln County Farmers' Market."

"I didn't realize you had a farmers' market," I said as I paid.

The woman taking payments was slim and brown-skinned, with a black braid shot through with silver over one shoulder, one of the few people of color I'd seen that night. Her eyebrows rose. "I'm surprised to hear that," she said.

Immediately I felt wrong-footed. Was I supposed to know about the farmers' market?

"I'm not from here," I said, accepting my change. "We live in Harrisville. But I do attend our farmers' market there. As a craft vendor."

Overexplaining to make up for a perceived social gaffe was a talent of mine that I'd never be able to use on a resume.

She elaborated. "I assumed with Myrtle being the queen of the market you'd know all about us."

Bemused, I replied, "Who's Myrtle?"

"Sunita means me. I'm Ray's mama."

I froze in place. A woman behind the table, only moments ago camped out in a folding chair, had joined us. I looked between them, Sunita, apparently, and now this woman. Ray's mama, as she said.

Heat flooded my face. It was mortifying.

Myrtle was shorter than me by a couple of inches and full-figured, with brown hair worn in soft round layers around her full face and fair skin. She bore no resemblance to her son except for one feature: her eyes. Wide, dark, and direct. Bundled up in a heavy red quilted jacket with a pair of heavy blue jeans, probably the original mom jeans, and short lace-up Wellington boots, she rocked back and forth, watching me, expressionless.

I tried to regain my bearings. "Hi there. It's good to meet you." I extended my hand, and we shook through our gloves, hers puffy and made from some industrial water-wicking material, mine a pair of thick alpaca wool I knit myself.

"I can see we're going to have to get you some real gear," she said. "They're pretty, but not practical." She dropped my hand quickly.

These gloves were warm, wonderfully warm, in fact.

"So you're Iris?" Her eyes raked up and down me.

It was a cold night in mid-December, and there wasn't much to see. Besides my gloves that failed to measure up and my olive green parka over a pair of jeans and short boots, the only personality in my outfit was a hand-loomed scarf in a gorgeous blend of deep greens, soft gold, and flecks of gray. It bunched and doubled around my neck, and I loved it for giving a little flair to an otherwise dull look.

Don't read into this. Don't make up stories. I squared my shoulders and smiled. "I am. And you're Ray's mom."

"I am."

So big and wide was the silence that followed this, you could have driven Ray's orange tractor through it. My smile muscles kept slipping, and I kept pulling them back into place. Myrtle didn't speak, and neither did I.

"There you are." Ray slipped his arm around my waist, his tone wary. "I see the farmers' market posse is out in full effect. Ms. Sunita." He inclined his head.

"Ray." Sunita smiled back, amused.

"Mama." He turned his gaze to his mother.

"Son," she replied, her expression droll.

"You've met Iris?" Ray pulled me closer to him, but I was rigid, so out of my depth with what was happening here.

"I have." Myrtle's eyes flicked to me and back to her son. It stung.

"And you've met my mother? The great Myrtle Fox." Ray looked at me. I met his gaze but only for a moment. I wasn't gifted with a poker face, and I didn't want to show Ray my thoughts at that moment.

Myrtle sighed half-exasperated, half-amused. "You quit with that. I didn't expect to see you here tonight." The topic change was abrupt, but no one appeared startled by it. "I don't think I've seen you at the Christmas Festival since you were a kid, and I made you hand out tickets at the gate."

"It's not my normal idea of fun, but I thought Iris and the boys here might enjoy it. Hey, fellas," Ray whistled, and Atticus and Ernie's heads popped up from where they watched the fire marshal toasting marshmallows. "Come here."

And the boys raced to us as though Ray summoning them was the most normal activity. I looked to them, looked to Ray, and back to my boys, heart racing. Why would he bring them into this? This woman would eat them up. I'd spent less than five minutes in her company, and it was clear there was no affection from Myrtle to her son's new girlfriend. Why would he subject my children to her as well?

"I want to introduce you. Atticus, Ernie, this is my mother. Myrtle Fox."

Myrtle regarded them. "Atticus, Ernie, it's good to meet you."

"Hello," Atticus said. Ernie waved.

"How old are you boys?" Myrtle cocked an eyebrow, studying them. I watched her watching them. My protective instincts kicked in, ready to insert myself at any moment. Throw myself in front of them if need be.

"Seven." Atticus offered. "Going on eight."

"Five–no–six," Ernie said, and he slapped a hand to his forehead, the comedian, and giggled.

"Seven-going-on-eight and five-no-six. Hmm." Myrtle pursed her lips, continuing to watch them closely. "How much can you lift?"

The boys looked at each other and then back to her. Ernie's mouth wiggled side to side, eyes big, still holding back the chuckles. Atticus shrugged. "We don't know, Miss Myrtle."

My heart swelled. Miss Myrtle. God love my boys and their sweet hearts. They might be wild at home, but I could take them out in public and trust them to shine.

Most of the time.

Seventy-five percent of the time?

"How can you not know?" Myrtle demanded, and I felt my hackles rise. What kind of stupid question was that to ask a child? Myrtle kept on. "A hundred pounds? Fifty pounds? Twenty-five? Good grief, boys, what kind of farmhands are you going to be if you can't even lift twenty-five pounds?" Her lips twitched at the corners.

Atticus and Ernie were on to her. They squirmed and giggled at her mock-serious expression. I shifted under Ray's arm, and he responded with a small squeeze.

To the boys, he said, "Alright, guys, you get back to the marshmallows. But, hey, keep an ear on what Chief Douglas says, alright? No shenanigans near a fire."

Ernie chortled. "Shenanigans!"

"What?" Ray asked.

Atticus shook his head at Ray. "Only our mom uses that word." With an exaggerated maturity put on for his audience of Myrtle and Sunita, he added over his shoulder, "You two were made for each other."

Sunita burst out laughing at this. Ray called after him, "You keep telling her that, Atticus."

The only one not smiling at this back and forth was Myrtle.

"Don't let us keep you," she said. "It's getting late, and you've got a long drive home."

Was I the only one who heard the implied "and good riddance" at the end of this statement?

By the time the boys stuffed themselves on "a variety of high fructose corn syrup" as Ray called it, we left soon after.

At the car, he ducked his head into the back seat to see Atticus and Ernie. "I'll need you bright and early to finish pulling up that plastic."

"We've got school!" Ernie protested.

"Gah, just hired and you're already ducking work." Ray shook his head, then his mouth split in a grin. "See you soon, boys. Take care of your mama."

When he stood up, he turned and took me in his arms. Aware of the people around us and the smallness of the town, I couldn't relax.

"You know everyone here, don't you?" I said.

"Hmm?" He had one arm around my back, the other hand cupping my face.

I shifted from foot to foot, wondering who noticed us and what they might be thinking. As Ray leaned in and placed a kiss on my neck, I muttered, "Ray! We're in public."

"The boys are in the car. And you're saying it's inappropriate to kiss my woman's neck?"

Normally I'd wiggle from delight, but instead I squirmed away from the fear of observing eyes. "It's not the boys I'm thinking of."

Ray straightened. "Hey. Hey," he said again, and I met his gaze. "I'm not worried about what anyone here thinks except you and those kiddos in the back of your car. Hear me? So don't you worry about it either."

"But–"

"No buts," Ray interrupted, watching me intently. I took a deep breath, and let it out, some of my nerves slipping away. "You listen to me now, OK? I'm not thinking about what one person here thinks other than you. Not one." He pulled me in close, his face pressed next to mine. And with his lips against my ear, he murmured, "Girl, you're what I'm thinking about. All the time. I love you, Iris. Do you know that?"

That. Right there. Time slowed down, the fair and the folks, even the boys waiting in the car, all of it disappeared. Ray pulled back and touched my chin. "You got that?"

All I could do was nod. His eyes crinkled at the side, something like joy spreading across his face. "I've been wanting to say that for weeks now. Only took a crowd of strangers and a freezing cold night to muster the courage, huh?"

Somehow I managed to nod again. I couldn't find the words. They were there, but how did I say them?

If my silence troubled Ray, it wasn't obvious. He leaned down and kissed me, hard, quick kisses, one, two, three, four, enough to take my breath away.

"You get home now. Let me know when you get there." Ray pulled back, releasing me into the cold night air, the lonely drive home.

"I'll call after I get the boys to bed."

"I'll be waiting." His face was all smiles. "My girl," he added and the tenderness in his eyes made me catch my breath.

Ray Fox loved me. I was his girl.

9.

How was that six weeks ago?

As the meal winds down, Ray says less and less. I get quieter, too.

When it's the two of us mulling over empty glasses and plates, I force myself to stand up and break the spell of dinner.

"Did you want more wine?"

Ray reaches out, and his hand closes over mine.

"Just...wait," he says.

His thumb brushes back and forth across the back of my hand, and I'm hypnotized, watching it.

"I need a glass of water," I blurt as he says, "Can we talk?"

Damn.

Nowhere to run, no place to hide.

The boys are due home at nine, and it's eight now. This needs to be fast. There needs to be time to feel my feelings after this is all done.

"This...back and forth. The driving. Having to make arrangements for the boys for dates. It's a lot." Ray watches our hands as he talks.

How is this possible? Can you explain it to me, Lord? How am I about to lose my home, almost half my income, and my boyfriend in the same month?

Do you think you might have given me a little breather in between? Just throw two of these at me, possibly?

Ray is still talking. "I don't think it's been easy for you, and, while I'm not juggling the kids like you are, it's not been easy on me either."

These reminders of the hindrances children are to dating are little stabs on my heart. So much easier to grab some mid-twenty-something girl, without baggage, without strings attached. I resist the urge to scream, wanting to throw his hand off mine and tell him to get out.

"I knew this would be complicated." He finds my eyes now, his deep gaze holding steady with mine. "But I'd never met anyone like you, Iris. And it was worth it, completely worth it, to get to know you, spend time with you, be with you. You are an amazing woman."

It hurts so much. Of course, I want him to say these things, to hear these words, but it makes the ending that much worse.

"Just do it already." My voice is too loud and cold, particularly for someone who's just been told she's an amazing woman.

Ray's thumb stops. "Do what, exactly?"

Does he think I'm an idiot?

"The boys will be home soon. So can you, please, finish up?"

Ray knits his brow together. "Well, that's an unexpected tone."

"Is it? Do you normally drag these things out? Does that work out better for you?"

"Iris, drag what out? What are you talking about?"

Welp, it's official. My boyfriend thinks I'm a moron.

He's still holding my hand. I yank it back and gesture between us. "This. What you're doing right now. The breakup. Let's just do it and get it over with, OK?"

Ray's voice is quiet. "Is that what you want? To break up?" He's got his elbows resting on his knees, hands clasped, and head bowed.

"Does it matter what I want? It only takes one person to end a relationship. It's been a while since I dated, but that's my understanding of it." My heart is racing, and sobs rise in my chest. Struggling to find composure, I exclaim, "I didn't date. I told you that right at the start. And you–you said you were serious. You told me to think about it. You told me you loved me. And now here we are."

Ray's on his feet, hovering on the edges of my pacing. His hands are out, palms up as if he's trying to catch something.

"What are you saying? You want to end this?"

"Me? I'm not the one saying, 'We need to talk.'" The laugh that comes out of my mouth is maniacal and out of control. Some removed part of me knows if he hadn't made up his mind before watching me lose my mind, this will seal the deal.

It doesn't matter. I feel like a caged animal, the sadness and hurt so strong, crashing over me. I wanted this. I wanted it to work, I wanted–

Thinking back to Angie's question of what I want from this, it solidifies for me: I wanted this relationship to last. Marriage, the farm, and us becoming a family. The fantasies I sometimes indulged in, the daydreams of the future, were of Ray and me and the life we could make, the quirky, handmade, meaningful life.

And the fact its ending breaks my heart.

"Now, I did say that, but I don't know why you're," Ray stops suddenly staring past me, lost in thought. "Hold the phone. Honey, do you think I want to break up with you?"

It's the surprise on his face that slows me down. I look side to side, feeling caught out. "Isn't that, isn't that what you're doing?"

Ray takes two strides and puts both hands on my arms. "No, not at all. That's not what I want."

The feeling in the room has changed, but I don't understand it. "What?"

"I don't want to break up with you. This isn't a breakup. It's, well, it's the opposite actually." Ray's hands slide down to mine as he kneels in front of me. The room is still, nothing moving or making a sound. I can't look away from him, as he holds my fingers gently in his.

Ray's eyes are on my face. "Iris Shepherd," he says, and his voice catches in his throat, "Would you marry me?"

10.

Ray left before my parents arrived with the boys. I may have hustled him on his way.

He suggested telling my parents together. Nope, nope, nope. That would be the worst way to bring him into the family. There could be a myriad of responses to this. But my gut told me, they'd only react one way.

And with that, my father is on point at the news. "Married? In a month? Iris, that's ridiculous. You can't be considering it."

My fingers twitch, and I link them, popping my knuckles and taking a deep breath. If I'm being honest, I'm hesitant, too.

When Ray proposed, the idea took my breath away. To wake up every day to that smile, just the slightest rise at the corners of his lips? To hear that soft, easy draw at bedtime? To lean into that strong, warm chest and feel his arms around me whenever I pleased? Yes, over and over yes.

I loved this man. I couldn't put it into words at the Christmas festival, but I felt it in my bones.

And the life we could make? Memories of the farm, the taste of sun-warmed tart raspberries on my tongue, the sight of black cows chewing and watchful, the sounds of chickens muttering, the smell of freshly cut grass overwhelmed my senses. Even in my house, on that winter night, I could imagine the sun on my face, tilt my head to look at the endless blue sky overhead.

And deeper than that, the yearning in my belly. For a partner in life. A father to my children. Someone to kiss me when he walked in the door each evening. Someone to press my cold feet against in bed at night. Someone to know, or even to know and forget, my daily activities and to listen to me rattle them off throughout the day so I wouldn't forget.

The sense of that belonging, of that being known? I ached for it.

And looking at Ray's face, even as my mind reeled at the hasty proposal, my heart yelped, "Yes, yes to his face, and his hands, and his character, and his heart. Yes!"

I managed it out loud, too. Ray sprang to his feet and with both arms pulled me into his chest. His thumb traced the line of my jaw, across my cheek to my lips, and he met my gaze, his eyes dark and tender, and whispered, "I'm going to take good care of you, Iris. Know that."

We hadn't dated for long. And our lives were so separate. Ray lived almost forty minutes away. His job and his life were at the farm. Mine was here, in my little house, with my little guys and my little business.

And still. I wanted this.

Remembering all of that now is critical. "Dad, there's so much good here. What Ray and I could build, what we can do for the boys, giving them two parents, and a great guy for a dad–it's amazing." Before I yammer on about raspberries and cows, I remember, I'm talking to Zeke, not to me. Logic and reason required. "And we're at a different place than kids right out of college. We don't need to date for years and see how it goes."

"I'm hardly talking about years," Dad says.

Deep, calming breaths are required, too. He loves me, he's concerned. If I want my parents to see this as I see it, staying calm and not overreacting matters.

The difficult part of being an adult with heavily involved parents? Your parents were heavily involved.

My tone is measured. "He's certain. I'm certain. Why wait?"

He counters my question with one of his own. "Why this rush? He seems like a good man, and I believe you do care for each other. But you don't really know each other. Why can't you wait a year, eighteen months even?"

"My lease expires in a month, Dad, not a year."

Oh, no. Worst thing I could say to my father. Apparently, it's amateur hour.

I blame the pressure of my father giving me his full-fledged disapproving principal voice. As a high school principal for almost forty years, he has plenty of practice.

And I don't mean it. I want to marry Ray, lease expiration or not.

But I would make the point. Is it a coincidence that he, who has no idea of my expiring living situation, suggested marriage? Doesn't that seem a little fortuitous? A little magical, a little of God's timing, perhaps?

I feel Dad watching me. "Do not tell me you think this is God's timing, Iris. Don't you dare tell me that."

My lips flatten into a tight line, my arms across my chest.

"Why couldn't it be?"

We both look up. Cynthia Shepherd has entered the fray, unafraid of my dad's bushy eyebrows or pursed mouth.

"Zeke, they're not eloping after a month or a one-night stand."

My mother comes to the rescue. Ready to battle anyone who might suggest I was making less than ideal choices, be it the Sunday school teacher who found my decision to wear black every day for a year depressing and suggested I stay upstairs for the service if I couldn't find something cheery to wear.

Or my father suggesting my sudden engagement might be rushed.

(And as for the wearing black thing, I was thirteen, and I wanted to make a statement, though of what I couldn't say. Regardless, calm down, Miss Lori.)

My parents square off. Dad shakes his head, as he says, "I am aware of that. But the last thing our daughter and grandkids need is to rebuild from another divorce. They're still a wreck from the last one!"

I gape at him. Is that what he sees? Me, a wreck? It hurts to hear him say that.

Dad meets my gaze and shakes his head. "That isn't what I meant, Iris."

I keep my voice level. "I think it's exactly what you meant."

He steps closer, placing a hand on my shoulder. "Here's what I want you to think about." His voice is gentle. "Don't get swept away in romantic infatuation. Like with Parker."

My breathing is ragged, eyes to the ground. He has to bring up my ex-husband, too. Of course.

Had I been swept away by Parker? Yes, probably. Was I also a twenty-six-year-old woman who'd hardly dated in her entire life and was weary of living in her childhood bedroom? Yes, absolutely.

This was different. Ray was an entirely different person from Parker. I was an entirely different person from twenty-six-year-old Iris. I knew what I wanted now. A happy home for my boys and me. A job that inspired me and left plenty of time for my family. And a connection with someone I loved and admired.

Our lives were different and yet the desires Ray and I held? For a slower life, a close family, a deep intimacy? Those desires harmonized. Beautifully.

"This is different, Dad. It is." I long for him to understand. "Please be happy for me—for us—all four of us. Please."

He looks pensive, lost in thought, and I wait. At last, after one last look at me and then my mother, he sighs and nods, and hope blooms in my chest. There. If ever there was a sign this marriage was on the right track, Zeke Shepherd's agreement, even begrudgingly given, is it.

Mom hugs me and murmurs into my hair, "I hope you're very happy together."

There aren't, I soon discover, many people in immediate agreement.

When I tell Angie, her lengthy silence isn't encouraging. After a long deep inhale and slow exhale, she says, "Well, hon, if this is what you want, you have my support. Always have, always will."

And my joy is too fragile for me to ask her for more.

Nor does Ray's family say much.

He tells me about it, as we pack up my little house, a few weeks later. We wrap dishes in free months-old newspapers.

Ray told them his whole family the day after he proposed, he says, adding, "They're happy for us."

"They are?" It's a relief to do this together, mostly in companionable silence. Mrs. Wilkins, true to her word, has the boys at her house for the afternoon.

I pause my packing and glance at him. Is there more? Descriptions he could give? Exact quotes, perhaps, that he could conjure from his memory and repeat?

"Yep." Sensing my gaze, he pauses, too, and looks at me. "What is it?"

"Is that all? Didn't they say anything else?"

We study one another. Ray and I do that often, quietly collecting personal thoughts while watching each other. I don't mind the scrutiny, and neither does he.

"It's my second marriage. I'm thirty-five years old. We've not known each other that long. What did you expect them to say?" His tone is wry, his eyes looking right in mine.

I give in and look away first. "I don't know what I expected. Something more than being happy for us." Yanking the papers, I might be rougher than required.

Ray shrugs. "Who cares? They're my family, and I love them, but we're not that close."

I gape. "You work together every day–"

"Only some of us, and we're doing different jobs, away from each other, most of the time."

"You live on the same property–"

"Yep, with about a quarter of a mile between each of us, if not more."

Luckily I've set my last glass down because now I fling my hands in the air. "They're your family, Ray. If you're not close to them, who are you close to?"

He sighs. "Lordy, I don't know. Brandon and I get along pretty well. He's a goofball, and I love him. Dennis and I do alright." He stops, too, and stares at me. "Iris, what do you want from me right now?"

Nuts, it's a good question. And one I can't answer, not with words. "I don't know exactly. Couldn't they be excited for us? Happy?"

Ray gives me a sidelong look and returns to his stack of dishes. "Like your parents?"

Double nuts. He's not wrong there either. "That's, I don't know, that's different."

His lips pulled to one side. "How is that different?"

It isn't. We both know it. He's almost smiling, and that irritates me. But I give in, too, and go back to crumpling paper aggressively. "Fine, you're right. It's not different. I hoped they'd be more than happy for us, but if that's what they are, that's what they are."

I'm breathing heavily, sweating, cramming more wrapped glasses into the box and, though I hate it, on the verge of tears.

"Honey." Ray crosses the small kitchen in two quick steps. He puts his hands over mine and removes the bundled newspaper glass. "How do you feel about getting married?"

If asked to dig in on my feelings, I could write a book, a treatise on the complicated and intricate emotions coursing through me at all times these last few weeks. Excited to be getting married to Ray who I love. Terrified at moving my boys and me half an hour away from our life and into Ray's home. Joy in thinking of my kids with Ray, looking to him for help with homework, for roughhousing, for learning their way around the farm. Uncertainty at not knowing what our future will hold, but so much hope it could be something good.

Why don't I say all that and see if he runs? Ha.

I choose lightness. "How long do you have?"

"As long as you need, darlin'. That's how long I have." Ray brushes my hair back off my forehead, his fingers gentle, his gaze on mine.

My shoulders, responding to his touch, melt back into place. My breath slows. And I smile at him. "I'm happy."

He grins in return. "Alright then. Me too. And that's about all that matters, as far as I can see."

11.

There are two people whose opinions matter most, and they're the ones worrying me. While I told my parents the night of the engagement, I held off on telling the boys. Regarding those two, Ray and I were in complete agreement we needed to do this together.

And not at our familiar little house. On the drive to the farm, my stomach knots, and I grip the steering wheel. "Are you guys good? Everyone good?" I call back. I catch Atticus' eye in the rearview mirror.

His forehead furrows, and he replies, "Why do you keep asking us that?"

"Do I?" My voice is unnaturally high. I clear my throat and work on a mental pep talk. *Calm down, Iris. You're freaking them out.*

Honestly, I'm freaking myself out, too.

"Aw, I thought we were seeing tractors." Ernie has his face against the window as we pull into the gravel drive in front of Ray's house.

"We will." My heartbeat quickens at the sight of Ray. It's cold, and he's wearing his flannel coat buttoned almost to his neck, his hands tucked into his jeans while he waits for us. His grins when he sees us. "Ray wanted to show us around this part of the farm first."

"Who lives here?" Atticus' dark eyes sweep over the drive, the field across from the house, and then to the house itself. We haven't visited here, instead meeting Ray at the barns or by the fields, wherever there's work to do and room for the boys to run.

Ray's voice is easygoing. "This is my place. Have you boys been over here yet?" He follows Atticus' gaze, and for a minute it's the two of them, investigating the house. Watching the back of them, the way they both stand square to the house, it makes me want to laugh. Atticus, my mini-man.

Of course, that thought makes me want to cry.

"Iris? Honey? Are you listening?" I snap to and catch Ray and Atticus exchanging that "there she goes" look.

"I'm right here!" I scramble after them, Ernie leading the charge.

The house is fine. That's it. It's a 1950s brick rancher, one long straight shot, two big windows across the first two-thirds, one small window for the kitchen. Ray does little besides keep the patch of grass at the front mowed. No landscaping for sure, but not even a hanging basket or a potted plant.

Sadly, the interior is the same. Inoffensive, if you ignore the awful peach sofas. I've been here only a few times, and I refrained from asking about the sofas, but I'm betting they belonged to Ray's ex-wife. I haven't wanted to dig into that story anymore than Ray has told me.

Possibly I need to get over that tendency since we're getting married.

But not right now.

Walking in the front door puts you immediately in the house. Here's the living room to our left, the dining room table to your right, and the kitchen straight back.

"Can we watch a show?" Ernie heads to the sofa and flops down. "These are so squishy. Way better than home."

How. Dare. He.

"You could, but I don't know what you'd watch it on." Ray sits down, too, across from him. "You see anything that looks promising?"

Ernie glances around the room, and then his sweet face breaks into a laugh. "You don't have a TV. How do you watch shows?"

"Honestly, I don't. Not too much at least," Ray admits.

"You and Mom really are made for each other." Atticus mutters, and I can't tell if that's a compliment or complaint.

"Well, it's a good point you make." Ray catches my eye, and a shot of electricity runs between us. I know what he's thinking, and I give a little nod. He takes the tiniest breath, and then goes on. "I wouldn't mind a TV in here. Maybe right over there." He gestures across the room. There is a fireplace and some knotty pine built-in bookshelves at the other side of the room. Those are strong features–*don't get distracted, Iris!*

"What do you think? How about right there?"

Atticus perches on the edge of the sofa, his hands still in his pockets. Little boys are such funny creatures, tough and stoic, but also tender and thoughtful in a way they don't get enough credit for. Watching him, dread runs down my spine. He knows something is up.

Ernie has noticed nothing. "Yeah, that's good." He enthuses. "And then we could watch shows here."

Ray nods, glancing at me. "Yeah, that's one thought. But, there's another way we could do this, too."

"What's that?" Ernie stares at the spot where the currently imaginary television could go, almost like he might conjure it from thin air if he looks long enough.

I'm only taking a breath, wondering how we might step into this conversation. And Ray says, "I could marry your mother, and you guys could move here."

Ah, so plunging in. That's what we're doing.

But Ray's eyes are bright, his face eager. He's excited, I realize. He's hopeful they'll be excited, too.

And Ernie doesn't disappoint. "Really?" He exclaims and hops to his feet. "Are you really getting married?" He whips around to me, his whole body trembling possibly with enthusiasm.

Relief washes over me. "Yeah, we are. And we could move out here—"

"To Ray's house? And live on the farm? Yes!" He punches the air with his fist, something he's probably seen on one of the shows he covets. "This rocks! This super rocks!" Also probably from a show.

Ray meets my gaze, his smile growing wider. "I feel the same, Ernie. Since your mom said yes, I've been—"

"I'm not doing it." We all look to Atticus, who's on his feet, too. Only his hands are clenched into fists, his pale face blotchy and red. "I'm not moving. This isn't our home. And you're not our dad. I'm not going."

And that's when Atticus shoves past me and storms out the front door, banging it shut behind himself.

"What's his problem? And can we have our own rooms?" Ernie is undeterred by his brother's abrupt departure.

"Ernie, hang on, I need to…" I trail off. It's hard to find words. Ray is in front of me, already off the sofa and at the door. "I need to—"

"It's OK. He got in the car. Phew. For a minute there, I thought he might take off." He leaves the door open but comes back over to me. He's shaken, and he puts a hand on my arm. "That was unexpected. Are you OK?"

I open my mouth to say yes, but tears well up in my eyes, and I can only shake my head.

"Hey, hey, hey," Ray tugs me in for a hug. "It's OK. He's young. And this is big. He's scared, that's all."

"I've got to go talk to him. He's so upset." I choke.

Ray regards me. "Yeah, maybe you let me take this one."

I'm actually crying pretty hard, which I didn't expect. It must be the overall surprise. Sure, I was nervous, but secretly I imagined pure joy. Delight. A new house! A new dad! A new family!

"No, he needs me." I sob.

"Of course. He does. But maybe when you're calmer." Ray's still sounds gentle, but amused, too. "Let me take a crack at it, OK? Just give us a minute."

"You look like a raccoon, Mom," Ernie says conversationally. There's probably mascara streaking my face, and that's not going to help Atticus feel better. Ray heads out to the car, and I try to compose myself.

"Hey, Mom?"

I wipe my eyes, sniffing. "Yes, sweetie?"

"If Atticus doesn't come, do I get a room for myself?" His chin rests on the back of the couch, his expression is hopeful. And I can't help but laugh.

"No, you pirate," I hiccup. "Everyone is coming. So don't get any big ideas, OK? Good grief."

While Ernie gets busy building a pillow fort from the enormous couch cushions, I watch through the window. At first, Ray has the back seat door open, but he leans against the car, arms crossed, and chatting. It looks like he's talking to thin air.

However, after a few minutes, Atticus slides out of the back seat and takes a spot against the hatchback, eyes focused on the ground.

My heart aches, watching his tight posture, his downcast expression. They're talking, Ray's hands in his pockets, shoulders loose, squinting at the bright blue winter sky.

He catches me looking and beckons me out. I don't need to be asked twice, but as I head towards them, Ray mouths, "Be easy."

It's odd, being instructed on how to approach my own child. Not unpleasant, but new, and strange.

"Hot enough for you?" I joke, rubbing my arms. We left our coats inside, and the temperature, even in the sun, is near freezing.

Atticus rolls his eyes. Ray shakes his head at me, pressing his lips together to keep from laughing.

"Give me a break," I protest. "This is tense."

Ray extends an arm, encouraging me to take a place next to him. Honestly, in my high heel boots, it's uncomfortable to stay upright in the shifting gravel. But it's my moment to prove I can hang with the boys, so I stay quiet.

"You want to tell her what you told me?" Ray's so calm and easy, you'd think we were discussing the weather.

"I don't want to move," Atticus says at once.

I open my mouth to respond, and Ray taps my ankle with the side of his foot and shakes his head, mouthing, "Shhh."

I'm indignant. But I also take his point.

"I don't want to leave my school. It's the middle of the year, and I won't have any friends at a new school."

The catch in his Atticus' voice causes a catch in my heart that makes my chest throb.

"Pretty reasonable, if you ask me," Ray says and gives me a sidelong glance. "From what Atticus told me, he's not too worried about the move. But moving schools in the middle of the year is a bad deal."

My sweet, quiet, thoughtful boy. Of course, that's his worry. Like me, we both want real friends, close friends, and that doesn't come easily for either of us.

Ray's tone is conversational. "I've told Atticus, we'd need to discuss it with you, but I thought we could reach some kind of arrangement to keep them in school there for the rest of the year."

There's no way I'm pulling the boys out of their school this year; Ray and I have already worked this out. But at this moment, it feels important to weigh it. Atticus' needs some voice in the decision, and he needs to feel he's been heard.

"It's a drive to your school every day from here. And there's about four months to go. I think making the drive is worth it to keep you there the rest of the year. But it won't be easy. And you and Ernie have to be willing to get to bed earlier and wake up earlier in order to make this work. What do you think?" I glance at him.

The color in Atticus' cheeks has changed from red and angry to pink and hopeful. "I can do a drive. And I'll talk to Ernie. He can do it, too." No worries for Atticus that his brother needs a vote.

We regard each other for a long time. This boy wrecks me, the way he holds his heart stitched ever so carefully into his sleeve. At last I nod. "Alright. If you're up for this, let's do it. We move here, but we stay with your school for the year."

The joy that spreads across his face amazes me. Is that what I looked like when Ray proposed? So close to losing something precious but then ecstatic when the thing actually comes closer, draws nearer?

I'm hit with two small arms wrapped around my legs, and I squeeze back. And, to my surprise, he pauses to hug Ray, too, before racing back to the house, shouting, "Ernie, we're moving to the farm!"

I exhale only to hear the sigh mirrored next to me. Ray shakes his head at me, rueful. "I really didn't know how that would go." His eyes are bright.

"Really? You seemed so sure."

"Well, if we're doing this, then I need to be in this with you, don't I? But kids, damn. They're scary. I kept thinking, 'Don't mess it up.'" Ray laughs, a sound thick with relief. "They're such good boys, you know? The last thing I want to do is let 'em down."

And now it's my turn to fling myself at Ray, kissing him repeatedly and whooping with joy on the inside.

12.

One thing is absolutely certain: This dress was the perfect choice. I step back from the courthouse mirror, admiring my reflection. It's cream colored with a square neckline, dainty cap sleeves, a snug, flattering bodice, and a knee-length, flared skirt. I look exactly like a bride from the nineteen-fifties. My hair's pulled into a low chignon at the nape of my neck, and I'm wearing bold red lipstick. Like Grace Kelly.

Of course, Grace Kelly didn't touch up her makeup in the Lincoln County courthouse bathroom while her groom-to-be and two sons from her previous marriage wait outside.

But you can't argue that my relationship and marriage aren't romantic. I mean, I'm marrying a farmer, for goodness' sake. I'm about to be a farmer's wife. Ray's dark eyes come to mind, and I steady myself against the bathroom sink.

Visions dance in front of my eyes. The cozy home we'll make. Waking up to collect eggs, feed the animals, and drink a cup of hot, strong coffee with my husband.

My husband! I squeal. I don't mean to. It just bursts out of my lips, and I clap my hands to my mouth trying to calm down.

"Iris, honey?"

I jump and swivel. "Ray? Is that you?"

"I certainly hope so. Or else who's calling you honey at the courthouse?"

He's chuckling. Good point.

"Get out!" I practically climb on top of the sink trying to stay out of his sightline from the bathroom door. I will say, I love the old-fashioned pedestal sinks, with brass fixtures. Built at the turn of the twentieth century, this courthouse is small and, I expect, inefficient, but absolutely lovely. In the entryway, the floors are marble, and there's an actual chandelier hanging over the wide, wood staircase that cuts through the center of the room and leads folks up to the courtroom on the second floor. It might not be a fancy wedding, but, as far as courthouse weddings go, it offers a certain amount of worn grandeur.

I shout, "Please don't come in. You can't see me."

"I take your point, but I'd also remind you, I saw you when I met you and the boys at the car. And when we came inside. And right before you went into the bathroom. Where you have been for..." There's a pause, and I'm sure he's checking his wristwatch. Ray is the only person I know who wears an actual wristwatch on a leather strap. "Almost twenty minutes. I don't mean to diminish the romance here, but are you feeling OK? The boys and I are getting antsy."

I'm mortified. Has it been that long? I came in here to take off my coat, touch up my face, and collect myself. Admiring my dress and thinking about Ray, the boys, and the farm, and suddenly twenty minutes passed. "I'm fine," I speak through gritted teeth.

"Are you sure? You don't sound fine. Hang on." He's gone, and then back, and now he's in the bathroom, too.

"Ray, get out!"

He's put a hand over his eyes. With his wiry, muscular frame in his dark Levi's, white button-up cotton dress shirt, and black sport coat, he looks like a barely pulled-together Clinton Eastwood character from a seventies western my father would have watched. He's made an effort to brush his hair, but he's been running his hands through it so it sticks up all over his head. Even as I'm angry, I want to wrap my arms around his neck and bury my face in his chest.

This is him, my husband-to-be. One month ago, Ray asked me to marry him.

When Ray proposed, it took my breath away, the way he shifted the conversation from an ending to a long-term beginning, the way he went from staring at my dining room table, to down on one knee, my hand in his.

I agreed then, and I agree now. But I want him to get out of the bathroom. There's nothing romantic about this.

"I'm not looking." He's talking while still covering his face. "But I wanted to check on you. Sweetheart, are you having second thoughts?"

The idea catches me off guard. It's the opposite of what I'm feeling right now. I'm moony, starry-eyed, swept away in this whirlwind wedding....

Has it been quick? Yes. For sure. I knew that.

But this? What is happening right now? This is hardly the stuff of fairy tales.

I've stayed quiet too long, chewing my bottom lip and thinking too much.

"Iris?" Ray lowers his hand.

Instincts kick in. "Don't look! And no, no second thoughts!"

Ray doesn't make a move. He stands back and stares at me.

"You shouldn't be–you are ruining–why are you staring like that?"

"Oh, honey," is all he says.

My throat tightens, and I glance down at my dress again, suddenly unsure. "Do you like it? I found it at a vintage store. I thought it was beautiful."

He brings his hand to his face and rubs his chin, eyes cutting to the side. It's a look I've seen so many times now, but still can't read.

When he looks back, still serious, he says, "Iris Shephard, you are the most beautiful woman I have ever had the good fortune to lay eyes on."

It's like a bolt of lightning to my chest, a swipe at my knees. I want to crumble. Instead I step closer and wrap my arms around him, tension and anger melting away. He and I are almost eye to eye, and when I pull back, we're grinning stupidly right into each other's faces.

"What do you think? You ready to become Iris Fox?"

"I do. Or I am. Either one."

We laugh, almost hysterical, and Ray slips an arm around my waist. "Well, c'mon then, let's not keep those boys and that grumpy judge waiting any longer."

My mother's warnings, Angie's questions, my own bouts of uncertainty, they're all erased, swept under the antique rug we step out onto.

Ernie and Atticus, waiting on a hard wooden bench, spring to their feet. They're dressed up, but, like Ray, casual in khaki pants and sweaters I knit, a gray cable-knit for Atticus and a blue Fair Isle for Ernie. Nothing about Ray and me is typical, so why should we dress like a typical wedding party?

"Fellas, are we ready?" Ray asks. Ernie flings his arms around me, and I squeeze him close. Atticus has his hands in his pockets shifting from one foot to the other.

I catch his eye. "You OK?"

He smiles, but still looks unsure. Ray puts a hand on the back of his neck and says, "Should we lead the way, Atticus?"

Atticus nods, his little face serious, and straightens his sweater. Ernie and I hold hands and together the four of us walk into the courtroom.

13.

"Here it is." Ray and I stand outside the door of his house, his hand on the doorknob.

I touch his wrist. "Wait. Just a second." He cocks an eyebrow, and I shake my head. "I'm not ready for this to be over."

We study each other, and I flush. Our honeymoon lasted forty-seven and a half hours. Much much too short. But also as close to perfection as a time can be.

And it almost didn't happen.

Had it been left to Ray and me, we wouldn't have had a honeymoon at all. Angie and my mother, as hesitant as they were about the marriage, were adamant about the honeymoon question.

"You have to take a honeymoon. You have to," Angie said it while gripping my arm and looking about as serious as I'd ever seen her look.

I waved my free hand. "Are you kidding? We're two fully formed adults getting married for the second time. And I have kids. How in the world do we make a honeymoon work?"

Angie let go of me long enough to rub the bridge of her nose. "So you're telling me you're going to get married at the courthouse and then what? Drive over to his house, stop for fried chicken and biscuits on the way, play a game of Mousetrap, and then put the boys to bed in the room next door? On the first night of your marriage?"

I blushed. And I understood her point. The practical side of this marriage, packing my house, making room at his house for us, and talking it through with the boys, to name a few, demanded so much attention. It could be hard to remember there were other elements—love, romance, and intimacy—involved.

Angie knew she was making headway. "Trust me. Please. Take a honeymoon. Go somewhere."

"With the boys?" I snorted. "Sounds romantic."

"Of course not! I'll help. I bet your mom would help, too."

I shook my head. "She and Dad can only do so much before there's a chance Ernie sets the house on fire."

"A day. They can come here first. Do a sleepover here the first night. We'll keep them all day long. Wear them out. It'll be fine."

It was so tempting. "Two days, max. The boys couldn't cope without me for longer than that."

Angie rolled her eyes. "I think you'd be surprised. But fine. Two days."

We worked out the details, and after our wedding, Ray and I would drop the boys at Angie's house before heading off to...wherever we decided to go.

And my parents would pick them up late Saturday evening and bring them to us the following Sunday night.

Bringing the conversation up with Ray was tricky. He was already moving into the new farming season, at least mentally, thinking about improvements and prepping for spring. But we were a week until the wedding, and not approaching it was impossible if a honeymoon was going to happen.

So as we unpacked some of my boxes at his house, I made my move. "What do you think about a honeymoon?"

If anything could pull Ray out of the moment, I expect it was that. He looked up. "What do you mean, what do I think about it?"

This was something I was learning about Ray. If I made an attempt at spontaneity and said, "Let's go out for coffee," he would tilt his head to the side and say, "Well, now, why would we go out for coffee?" Then he'd need a good long think about it. Often, by the time he'd come to a decision on the subject, I was annoyed and changed my mind.

I pressed my lips into a tight line. "Would you want to take a honeymoon?"

Ray sat back, took a deep breath, and looked to the side. There he went, lost in his own thoughts.

I kept unpacking, transferring his few plates, cups, and bowls to a box bound for donation.

"What were you thinking?" he said, at last.

That much thinking to get to that question? "I don't know. Something for the weekend."

I packed. He thought. I seethed.

He asked, "What about the boys?"

"My mom and Angie are willing to help."

Ray exhaled. "Where would we go?"

"Good grief, I don't know. Nashville? Asheville? Knoxville? Pick a nearby 'ville, and we'll go there." I shoved the empty newspaper back into the box and stomped outside.

The winter had been kind. Cold, but sunny. As soon as I crossed the door's threshold, I was brought up short by the sight in front of me. Ray's small, plain yard, the private gravel road that cut through the farm property and beyond that a field with cows. There they were, chewing through what remained of the grass here and watching me with disinterested eyes.

Ray had followed me outside. "Iris, what's this about?"

Still unsettled, the cows and their gaze make me nervous. There's an electric fence keeping them in, but their presence settled me down. Instead of shouting, I said, through clenched teeth, "We're getting married, and you'd never even know it. It'd be nice to celebrate it a little. I'm fine with the courthouse–"

"Which we're only using because there isn't time to do the premarital counseling your pastors needed. And my pastor only works about half the year."

"And we're not even having a reception–"

"I thought we agreed it might be awkward to introduce all our people at a reception?"

I sighed. "I know that. I'm not saying it's wrong. I'm saying it's–it's–it's not celebratory. Or just–anything. It's nothing."

He watched me. "And you need something?" he said.

Tears pricked my eyes. Angry tears, not sad, to be clear. Sometimes Ray's calm, steady nature felt like a balm on my tumultuous soul. And sometimes it felt like bleeding out in front of an impenetrable hospital. Me dying from the intensity of my feelings and him all hard, high walls with no windows and doors.

"Yes, I want something," I said. The cows lulled me into a calm fury, a settled frustration.

And Ray slid his hand into mine and squeezed. "Alright then. Let's make something."

***

We chose the Smoky Mountains. It was beautiful, a short drive, and affordable.

Once we chose a location, he handled everything. "Here's your list." He'd made me a packing list.

Pair of jeans

Sweater

Change of underwear

Toiletries

Pajamas (optional)

That made me laugh. And shiver.

We were a stone's throw from Dollywood, a slew of restaurants, an abundance of shopping, and a lot of down home entertainment. We never left the cabin.

Ray brought in the food, carting in a tomato box packed with meat, eggs, greens, and herbs all from the farm and a brown paper bag from a local gourmet grocery store with a selection of snacks, a crusty sourdough loaf, olive oil, and two bottles of wine.

Forty-eight hours in the life of two recently wed people, two people with grown-up lives, very little downtime, and no demands was far too little time.

Standing here at the door to Ray's house, knowing my parents will arrive with my children in about forty-five minutes, I can't catch my breath.

"Are you OK?" Ray reaches for me.

"I am." But I don't move. "This weekend was almost too good, you know? How are we supposed to go back to regular life when we had all that?" The sadness surprises even me, someone accustomed to bouts of melancholy.

There's no way around it. There's no newlywed phase for us. There are kids and a home and a demanding job and no time to enjoy that fresh, shiny period of a new marriage. We don't get to play adults. We are adults.

"Hey."

I meet his eyes. "Honey, this is only the start." I open my mouth, but he holds up a hand. "This weekend? You're not wrong. That was heaven." From his expression, I know we're both back in that cabin's bedroom, gazing into each other's eyes with the same intimacy, the same intensity, his hands stroking my bare back. My stomach aches with longing at the memory. "But we have a long, long life ahead of us."

"But none like that." I hate my childish tone even as I can't stop it.

"Woman, you think that's the last time I'm taking you away for a weekend alone? If that's the case, you are crazy. Hey, y'all," he shouts to no one. "Did you hear that? I married a crazy lady. I didn't even know."

Laughter bubbles out of me. I can't hold it in.

"Instead of standing here in the cold, I say we get inside and make the most of the time alone we have before those boys get here. See how your new bedroom suits you." He wiggles his eyebrows at me, and I'm giggling. My funny, quirky, sexy husband unlocks the door, and we're inside, my blues vanishing once Ray's arms are around me.

14.

The minute my alarm sounds at five-thirty I regret the marriage.

I smack my phone so hard it tumbles off the nightstand.

When it goes off nine minutes later, I flop over the bed, see the time, and jolt up. Five thirty-nine am. This is my new wake-up time to get the boys to school.

This marriage was a terrible idea. Why did I ever agree to this? A five-thirty start is absurd. Sadistic.

Next to me, Ray shifts and drapes an arm across my chest. I fume. How dare he? I'm waking up at the crack of dawn so I can get my boys in the car in time to make the forty-minute haul from the farm to school.

"You ready to do this?" His voice is raspy, eyes still closed.

"Do what?" It's more of a hiss than a voice.

He lifts an eyelid. "Get going. Get those boys out of bed. All of it." With that, he opens both eyes, gives them a good rub, and yawns the most massive yawn. Even as I'm upset, it's fascinating to watch him wake up, his little movements and sounds, and to think, *that's my husband.*

I eye him. "You're helping?"

Ray throws back the covers and slings his legs over the side. "Well, I don't see you doing much of anything," he says and grins over his shoulder.

Right then he diffuses it. My fear, my regret. This is OK. I made the right decision.

It's not easy, waking the boys so early, but Atticus exclaims, "First day of school from the farm!" and sits bolt upright.

They're magic words. Ernie's up, too, hair on the right side of his head sticking straight up, grinning.

With Ray working away in the kitchen on lunch, I'm free to take a few minutes to get ready.

"Hey, babe?" I raise my voice as I move around the bedroom, projecting so Ray can hear me.

"Yep?"

"What does one wear for tractor driving?"

We had a brief conversation on the matter last night. Not outfits, but my working on the farm. Ray keeps saying he needs a good tractor driver, and when I suggested that might be a big jump for someone who's spent zero time on a farm, he shook his head.

"I don't need you to do much besides hold onto the steering wheel. You'll be fine."

And I believed him. When I said yes to Ray, I made the decision: no hand fluttering about the farm. Period. If Ray suggested I could do it or asked for my help, I would be in. No matter how hard, weird, or frightening. If he trusted me to handle it, I trusted him to know what he was doing.

"Are you really asking me that?" Ray asks.

I stick my head around the bedroom door. From here, I can see straight into the kitchen, into all the house, in fact.

His lips quiver. The boys are at the table, heads bobbing between us like at a tennis match.

"Are you truly asking me what kind of outfit you wear to drive a tractor?"

He's set them up perfectly. They burst out with shouts of, "Mo-om!" from Atticus and "That's so silly!" from Ernie.

I bristle. "It's not silly. I'm trying to be safe. If you say..." I struggle for a moment. "No loose scarves. Or no heels. I mean, those are things you ought to tell me before I tractor off. Don't you think? I think it's totally reasonable."

"Honey?"

"Yes?"

"No loose scarves. And, most definitely, no heels."

Atticus and Ernie whoop as I retreat back into the bedroom. They're still giggling, and complaining about me.

"What is she even thinking?" Atticus groans.

Ray replies, "We're gonna have to educate her a little better on farm living, boys," and their muttered agreement warms my heart.

They turn to Ray like sunflowers following the movements of the sun, soaking up every word he says, every morsel of attention. If thirsty can apply to two boys under the age of eight in need of a father figure, then my boys are parched.

They've spent the last six and seven years watching most of the boys around them interact with dads. They haven't complained. Atticus asked when he was a toddler. By kindergarten and the thousandth time of me saying, "No, love, your dad won't be at the Christmas concert," he gave up. Ernie took even less time. He'd point at my dad and ask,

"Da-Da?" It took a year of me shaking my head and saying, "Nope, it's just Mommy, Attie, and Ernie," for him to let it go.

They needed someone else to look to besides me. A man with a good heart and the time to care about me and these kids. Though if I did have that, I'd probably have been desperately in love with him. Straight or gay, it wouldn't have mattered. That combination is catnip to a single mom.

But my little guys had to make peace with no dad un- til–whoosh–along comes Ray. With his bright eyes, his wild hair, easy Appalachian accent, and his straightforward, amiable manner, he treated them well from the word go. He liked horseplay, roughhouse, and pranks, and that suited them fine.

Not that I introduced them early. Oh, no. From early on, we sat at my dining room table, and he said, "I'm not so sure about the fact you've got kids."

My response? "Don't worry, you won't be seeing them."

Who hasn't heard the horror stories of single moms attempting to make any friendly date into the new dad or, worse and creepy, Uncle Somebody? No, thank you. No sleepovers, no meeting the boys, and no monkey business, not on my watch. I was as serious as a heart attack.

Ray agreed, and yet still, within a few months of our first date, the boys picked up that something had changed. They watched Ray and I interact at the market, subtle though we tried to be, and suspected. It was Ray who said, "We've got to tell them something. The way Atticus looks at me, I'm starting to feel like a real liar."

That started the dominoes tumbling, time at the market turning into Ray coming to the house after the market, staying for dinner, heading home at dark, and the boys and I all going to bed Saturday night contented and happy from this new man's presence in our lives.

Now, as Ray follows us to the car, Ernie's book bag in hand, I still don't know how this actually fell into place. Just like that. Poof!

A miracle answered? A dream come true?

Whatever it is, I'm not looking too closely. I'm only thankful.

Ray kisses me good-bye, and the boys chorus, "Ewww, gross!" from the back of the car.

In my ear, he murmurs, "If you tractor back quick enough, we might be able to get up to a little something before we get to farming."

"Mom, we're going to be late!" Atticus shouts, and I slip into the driver seat and smile the entire forty minutes to school and the entire forty minutes back. All regrets at that five-thirty alarm are forgotten, replaced by my boys' faces watching their mom and new stepdad behave like a set of parents, by knowing I have, so unexpectedly, brought a loving husband and father into our lives.

15.

Ray, a thermos of coffee in one hand, is pulling the door shut behind him when I get home. Apparently, his flirtatious mood slipped away in my absence. I don't mind. Today, I want to get to work.

Ray calls, "Ready to go?"

"Yes!"

Excitement streaks up my spine. Farming! Finally! I have a job, and it's not just mine, but mine and my husband's. This is my husband's farm, and I'm poised to become an integral part of it. A critical cog. Well, not a cog. A critical component.

"I changed the game plan." We take his truck, and he drives, one hand on the steering wheel, the other holding his Thermos.

While he talks, I take a gander in the mirror. My hair's pinned up and tucked under a bandana. My navy coveralls, bought at a farm co-op store on a clearance sale, are both slimming and heavy, perfect for a brisk February day. Not bad at all.

"We're going to work in the greenhouse today where it's warmer." The truck crunches across the gravel drive, and we chug up to a row of plastic tunnels.

"They're all greenhouses?"

Ray shakes his head. "Only the first two. The rest are high tunnels."

He's moving fast, and I'm hustling to keep up. "And what's the difference?"

"Greenhouses are heated, high tunnels aren't." His strong, wiry body is quick and nimble, vibrating with energy.

I've never seen him like this. Ray tends to be fairly low-key, someone who will as happily read a book or relax on the porch as be out in the world. But now that it's his world and his love, the focused look on his face shows, he puts everything he's got into this.

It's both inspiring and unsettling.

I hear voices before I see them. Stopped at the greenhouse door, Ray's talking to the most beautiful woman in the world. I actually stutter-step at the sight of her.

She's tall, taller than me, taller than Ray. Her hair is light, light blonde, long and silky, the kind of hair found on women in Swedish clothing catalogs. Her skin is clear, tanned, and unblemished. What is she, a child? No one has skin that good after the age of twelve.

As I get closer, I see it gets worse. She looks serious, nodding at whatever Ray's saying, but there are no lines on her forehead, no creases around her large, round, blue eyes. She's some kind of old-school Hollywood movie star package, and she's standing about four inches away from my husband.

Whatever the topic, Ray's solemn, and it's clearly about work. I see that.

That doesn't stop the primal monster that rises up inside me and wants to banshee shriek, "Get away from my man!"

She's wearing straight-cut Levi's, heavy, dark brown work boots, a flannel shirt, and a waist-length Carhartt coat. She is a professional farmer.

Of course, she is. Because I've put it together even before Ray remembers my presence, and calls out, "Honey, come meet Naomi."

This is Naomi.

This gorgeous girl is his go-to guy.

They look weirdly good together. He pushes the greenhouse door, and she pulls, the two of them working quietly. He looks like the dark compliment to her blonde allure. The fact he's shorter than her makes them more compelling.

Hey, look at these two, so comfortable in their beauty that they don't even care they break the traditional male-female dynamic of who's taller. You should see them kiss!

I'm such an impostor. The overalls and bright red paisley bandanna scream amateur, and I only feel stupider when Naomi smiles, a wide, warm smile, and says, "Oh, my gosh, look at those coveralls! They're so cute."

I shove my hands into the pockets.

Ray notices my attire for the first time. He smiles. "Sweetheart, I should have said. You look right professional in those."

"Stop. They're silly," I mumble.

"No, they're great!" Naomi enthuses. "Don't listen to this guy. He'd tease a turnip if it stood still long enough." She punches his arm, and he takes the hit, feigns pain, and rubs the spot. I want to disappear into the ground. "You'll be glad you've got 'em out in the field. The wind's bitter."

I nod, unable to form words. She can't mean it, but her friendliness is almost believable.

"I like your clothes, too," I mumble, panic and insecurity pushing me into people-pleasing mode. "They're so farm-y."

She looks surprised to discover what she's wearing. "I guess they are. My mama'd burn all my clothes if I'd let her. She's so frustrated she can't get me in a dress and heels she'd like to spit nails."

Oh, dear. It's like a female Ray with the "like to" and the Southern sayings. My stomach lurches. How have I not met Naomi before this? How could she and Ray be such a tight duo, and I've never laid eyes on her until now?

Was it oversight or deliberate?

"You're sure you don't need me? Ms. Myrtle was pretty forceful this morning." Naomi looks at Ray.

He nods, lower jaw thrust out, mouth pulled to the side. "Mm-hmm. We got this. Don't we, Iris?" He slings an arm around my shoulders.

Naomi seems entirely unbothered by the gesture.

I struggle for words. "Yep. We got this."

She's satisfied. "I'll catch up with Dennis then. He's working cows today."

Ray snorts. "Dennis is always working cows. He'd live with 'em if he could."

"Well, they're a lot easier than who he lives with," Naomi murmurs, and Ray snorts and nods, a knowing look passing between them.

I'm at a loss to read it. Not that it matters. I'm feeling so stupid, so aware of what a try-hard I look like, I want to fade into the winter scenery, never to be seen again.

Naomi heads to another old pick-up truck, parked a few feet from Ray's. She gives a wave, and she's gone.

Heart hammering in my chest, cheeks flushed, I slip out from under Ray's arm, and he doesn't comment. He's preoccupied, tidying up with black, rubber hoses spread across the ground.

"Ready to get started?" he asks.

I want to shout, "No! I'm ready for you to explain how the hell you never mentioned that The Lovely Naomi is your right-hand man?"

Do I say this? I do not.

The words die in my mouth as soon as they surface. I peer into the greenhouse.

"What are we doing here?" My voice is raspy.

"You and I are going to get seeding." He claps his hands together. "It's going to be a good day."

Ray gives quick clear instructions. It's early February, and we're starting seeds for greens today—kale, collards, mustard, lettuces, and bok choy.

My lips are pinched, my shoulders tight, my whole body screams unhappy. Does Ray notice? He doesn't.

He's talking, pointing out parts of the greenhouse that he's engineered and built with his own two hands. He's bragging, and all I can give him are nods.

It's a long tunnel, encased in thick, clear plastic. There's gravel underfoot, and three rows of tables run the length of the tunnel with enough room to walk between each row without turning sideways. Ray used pallets and scrap metal for the table legs, and he's proud of them. "They'll rot at some point," he says. "But we'll get years out of them first, and they cost me nothing but the labor and the screws." His smile is boyish.

It's noticeably warmer in here, and Ray assures me when the fire gets going we'll be stripping down from the heat. He winks at this, and again I want to smile, but my mouth muscles won't work.

You are a grown woman. I speak firmly to myself. *A grown married woman. If Ray wanted Naomi, he wouldn't have married you. Think about it.*

But seeing Naomi the person and watching the ease between them shook me. I don't know that anything is going to pull me out of this. What I need is time to regroup–

"Here you go, love."

I jump.

Ray's standing next to me, gesturing to the table. "I need you to get us started while I get organized. Can you do that? Iris?" He's peering at me.

Keep it together. Breathe. You can talk about this later.

"She's so pretty," I blurt it out. There was zero chance I wasn't bringing this up.

Ray looks from side to side. "Who's so pretty?"

Now that's frustrating. I wave a hand towards the greenhouse door. "Naomi. Of course. She's so pretty."

His mouth forms an "o." "You're upset because Naomi's pretty?"

I don't appreciate this. "It's not a stupid thing to be upset about."

"No, no, I didn't say it was. I didn't expect it, that's all. I know she's pretty."

"And she's your right-hand man, right? That's what I hear."

Ray tilts his head to the side, looking away. "I don't think you heard that from me."

"You talk about her."

"When?"

This is slipping away, and I can't get it back. "You, you say, you know," and here I slip into an imitation of Ray's drawl, "'Naomi and I got all the sweet potatoes harvested today. Man, I'll be glad to not see another of those 'til next year.'" That's it, it's all I've got.

Ray's lips twitch. "Do I talk like that?"

"Ray!" I shout.

"OK, OK. You're right. I remember telling you about that." He scratches his chin, like he's waiting for the jump-scare, waiting for me to provide my evidence.

I feel all the words but can't find one to say out loud. None of them are right.

"Has it always bothered you that I work so closely with a woman?" His eyes are on me.

"She's not a woman! She's, she's, that!" I hear how silly I sound. I can't stop though. "I'm just me, just boring Iris, Iris the mom, Iris the struggling artist, with my scarves and my wrinkles. She's gorgeous. Like, stunning." And yep, tears are right there at the back of my throat.

"I don't know. You're alright," Ray says with a half-smile. I brush my cheeks, and he drops the smile, reaching for me. "Bad joke. I was trying to lighten the mood." He runs his thumb across my jaw, his touch strong and gentle. "I am not now, nor have I ever been, interested in Naomi."

"How? How is that possible?"

Ray shrugs. "Is she attractive? Sure, I can see that. But she's not someone I've ever wanted to have a relationship with."

It's Ray's deep brown eyes. They're intense, but they're always honest. I'm stumped as to how this is true, but I believe him.

Still, I keep poking at it, baffled. "Why not?"

He peers at me. "You're stuck on this, huh? Are you sure you don't have feelings for her?"

Against my will, he makes me laugh. Wiping my damp face, I say, "Maybe I do. She's that pretty."

Ray leans in again, and this time I let him pull me close. We're both laughing. Tears leak from the corners of my eyes, but I let them, resting my head on Ray's chest. There's something about the circle of his arms around me, strong and secure. Like nothing could break that grip, we're in this tiny protected space together.

"Am I interrupting?"

16.

The voice is loud, the tone wry, and, without looking, only having heard it once before in my life, I know its Myrtle.

I spring away from Ray like we've been caught necking in her minivan. She's at the doorway of the greenhouse, layered up in a heavy flannel coat like Naomi's, insulated jeans, and short, thick work boots. She's wearing heavy-duty gardening gloves.

Ray's untroubled, holding onto me as he calls out, "Hey there, Mama. Come on in. I think Iris and I have worked things out." Here he gives me a conspiratorial wink.

I don't return it. His admitting there's been a disturbance in our marriage feels worse than if she had caught us making out.

Myrtle pushes her little wheelbarrow over to a big one filled with rich, black dirt. "Glad to hear it."

"Mother dear, you're not taking my expensive organic potting soil for your marigolds are you?" Back to work, Ray carries several long black plastic wire trays over to me.

"Son, what I do is my own business." She doesn't turn around.

"Lord, forbid I ever suggest anything else, Mother. But please remember the farm pays for this costly substance so that people can eat clean food. Whereas your flowers are strictly for looks and can be grown in good old Tennessee clay if need be." He's teasing her, and for once I spot it.

"A fact I know because you remind me of it constantly, darling second born." Myrtle counters.

Ray performs a dramatic eye roll then grins at me.

"I want to set you up right here." He's back to business and talking to me. "Lay out these big trays and then fill each one with these seed germination trays." He points to a stack of small black plastic trays. "I'll get the potting mix ready."

"Not if your mom takes it all first." It's an attempt, an effort, at connection. *Look at me! Teasing people! Just like a Fox!*

The shift is immediate. I can feel it. Myrtle stops, sets her shovel down, and turns full-on to face me. She looks at me with those same dark eyes as her son. Only not warm, friendly, or inviting. "This farm and everything on it belongs to me. Every plant, every blade of grass, and every bag of potting soil. And I won't tolerate any argument from any members of this family, no matter how old or how new."

We're locked in some crazy, terrifying staredown. I'm wilting under her gaze. "OK," I croak. It's better than the "yes, ma'am" I want to murmur.

She studies me one moment longer before turning back to her business. Ray's at work, and I'm perfectly still wishing I could disappear.

When Myrtle heads out, wheelbarrow crunching over gravel, the front wheel hangs in the small rocks. I don't dare offer help. She grunts and shoves, and the wheelbarrow bows to her wishes, skittering on across the rocky ground.

Over her shoulder, Myrtle calls, "I'll see you both at dinner. And your boys."

My gaze swivels to Ray. "What's that?"

He smiles sheepishly. "I meant to tell you about it."

17.

Dinner with Ray's family, his whole family, tonight. It's unbelievable.

"Normally it's Sunday night," Ray said. "But since we were settling in last night, Mama postponed it to tonight."

"Do you eat dinner together every Sunday night?" I'm fascinated to discover this. In my mind, after hearing Ray's thoughts on his family, I assumed they rarely saw each other in social gatherings.

Ray nodded. "No, 'bout once a month."

Somewhere, early in our dating days, he had said something in passing. He sometimes had a family thing. I didn't think about it. I wasn't available for Sunday night dates because I was in the throes of getting our family ready for the week.

Tonight, we are expected for dinner at five-thirty. It is five twenty-seven, Ray is late, and my youngest is in a tree, his legs two feet above my head.

I rub my forehead, a headache waiting in the wings, and call, "Ernie, c'mon! We have to go."

"Five more minutes," he calls back.

He said that five minutes ago. And five minutes before that.

This is ridiculous. "Get out of the tree, son. We have to go." I deepen my voice; it's what they say to do with dogs. Apparently, dogs respond better to men because they find a man's deep voice commanding, whereas a woman's higher pitched tone only excites them.

I can only hope it works the same with wayward children.

Ernie laughs.

So that's a parenting fail.

My phone chimes.

"Hey, honey."

We've been married four whole days, and I already sense what's coming.

"We're stuck behind a good ol' boy and his tractor on 75. Looks like it might be a few minutes."

I start pacing. "How many minutes is a few?"

"I can't say exactly. Fifteen, maybe twenty?"

"Ray."

"I know. I'm sorry. Y'all go on up to the house. We'll come straight there. I'm not too smelly." I hear Dennis speak up, and Ray laughs. "Dennis disagrees with me, but he's not exactly pine-scented himself."

I hear him, but I'm not paying attention. Ernie's feet still dangle over my head, Atticus stands a few feet away, chewing his bottom lip and watching us. We're officially late for their family's dinner, and now Ray won't be there with us.

"Iris, are you OK?"

"No, I'm not. I'm not sure about meeting your family on our own. And Ernie won't get out of the tree, and we're late. I don't want to go." I walk away from the boys while I talk. Maybe we could turn the lights off and hide inside. No one will even know we're here.

Ray's quiet, and I wait. He sounds serious when he responds. "I didn't think about how it would feel going by yourself. Hang on a second, OK?" Again he and Dennis confer and then to me, he says, "We're going to drive like hell to get home. You sit tight. Dennis can drop me off there, and the four of us will go together. Sounds good?"

Hallelujah, yes, praise the Lord.

I consider the time it'll take. I can hear Dennis in the background, grumbling he's hungry, and that he might push Ray out while still moving.

"It's OK," I say. "We'll meet you there."

"You sure?"

No. Not at all.

"Yep." My voice has fake confidence, a veneer of cheer. "It's fine."

"OK." He sounds grateful. "If you're sure. We'll be there soon."

"Better hustle. Or else." I'm not sure I'm joking.

Ray laughs and ends the call.

If it were up to me, I'd leave this meeting for another few days, at least. I mean, what had I seen of Ray's family? Next to nothing.

His mother and father divorced when he was eleven. Myrtle, the delight that she is, never remarried.

There's Dennis, then eighteen months later came Ray and then his sister. Four years younger than Ray, Stephanie recently came back to live at home for vaguely explained reasons.

And at a refreshing twenty-one years old, there's Brandon, the oops-baby in the family, in his fourth year at Harrisville College. While almost fifteen years older, Ray gets a real kick out of his littlest sibling and told me a few stories of Brandon's hijinks that gave me pause, while I mentally subbed the word Ernie for Brandon in a mere twelve years' time.

I knew the names of the players and a general sense of geography. Dennis and Ray were on the premises but in their own homes, and Stephanie and Brandon still holed up in the family residence with Mama Myrtle.

It wasn't a biography of the Fox family. It was barely an Instagram caption.

"Do I need to come down?" Ernie asks.

No. Stay put, and I'll use you as my excuse.

"Yeah, buddy," I say instead. "We need to meet Ray."

"So we're going without him?" Atticus doesn't miss a trick.

"Just to start. By the time we're situated, I'll bet he's there."

I want to laugh at how casually I say this like I know what I'm talking about. It amazes me how you can make something up, right out of the sky, tell it to your kid, and they will believe you. Maybe not forever, but the biological hardwiring of kids to simply trust parents astonishes me.

Ernie hops down from the tree and trots inside. Atticus hesitates. Because it's Atticus and because he's my little man, I say, "We'll figure it out."

"It's a little weird. Meeting these people."

"Yeah, definitely. But we've got really good food."

"Cauliflower and spinach casserole?"

"You better believe it."

"Alright. Let's go." Atticus wriggles out of my grasp and hustles to the house.

Hearing his tone of adoration when he says cauliflower and spinach casserole reassures me.

I chose this dish with care.

When I asked Ray what might be a tasty offering at the Fox potluck, he squinted for a minute, thinking hard before he said, "Ah, hell, hon, everything you make is good. Anything you want to do."

It was so sweet. I immediately shot it down. "No. Absolutely not. What will your family like?"

He was genuinely perplexed, but I pressed. "What do people normally bring?"

"I don't know. Uh, Mama makes the meat—"

"Which is?"

"Beef or chicken, usually. The rest is some sides and usually a dessert." Ray gave me the helpless look of someone who's participated in this family tradition for the last fifteen years of his life and paid no attention to what was happening there.

I got into my recipes.

Cauliflower and spinach casserole uses two kinds of good cheese, fontina and pecorino, spinach from Ray's high tunnel, and cauliflower he grew last fall that I shredded and froze for later.

I used my Le Creuset oval casserole dish, an absolute find at our church yard sale five years ago. The lid's on, but I know underneath that lid how creamy and delicious this is, fragrant with Ray's garlic, and filled with jasmine rice.

Setting the dish in the car's front seat, I'm reassured. Who knows what they'll think of me—my thick fleece leggings under an ivory-colored cashmere tunic, another yard sale find, or the bright blue paisley scarf wrapped around my head and holding my hair out of my face—or of the boys.

But they're human beings with hearts, bellies, and noses. They will love this dish. There's no way they can't.

18.

As soon as we arrive at Myrtle's house, Ernie bolts from the car and almost kills a man.

I don't see the crash, but I hear it. By the time I'm around the corner of the car, Atticus is one step ahead of me, and there's a tangle of an old man and Ernie on the black tar driveway.

It looks like the man cushioned Ernie's fall. He's completely on his back, legs sticking out, head on the ground, Ernie sprawled across him.

"Is he dead?" Atticus demands, freckles standing out sharply on his fair skin.

"No!" *He's dead, he's dead, he's dead*, my mind beats, while I say again, "Of course not. Ernie, get off him!" I yank Ernie up.

"Are you OK?"

The man looks up, dazed. He's probably in his mid-sixties, with thick salt and pepper black hair, dark eyes, and brown skin. He's Latino, I think, and he's dressed like everyone else around here, in heavy-looking jeans and a thick coat. Voices kick up behind us.

"What in the world? What happened?"

"Ricky, what'd you do? You been drinking?"

"Brandon, that's not funny. Ricky, what happened?"

Myrtle reaches us first, a young man at her elbow.

I drop back, feeling guilty and embarrassed, like I'm the six-year-old who sent this fellow sprawling onto the ground.

"It was my son's fault." I chuck Ernie right under the metaphorical bus. "Ernie knocked him down." Awkward when I have no idea who "him" is.

Myrtle eyes me and doesn't respond.

"There's no harm done." This is from the man still lying flat on the ground. "Give an old guy a hand, Brandon."

The young guy next to Myrtle lopes over to help.

"Slow and steady now," he cautions, and Brandon (so this is Brandon!) brings him up to his feet.

We all wait, eyes on him, as he pats himself down his chest, hips, and legs. At last, he smiles at Ernie, who's still pinched in my grasp.

"I think I've still got all my parts," he jokes, and I exhale. "I'm guessing, based on what I've heard, you must be Ernie. And you must be Atticus." He looks at each of them in turn.

Suddenly they become the shyest children on earth, Ernie studying his toes and Atticus staring into the collar of his t-shirt.

I want to say I do better. But I have no idea who this man is, and there's Myrtle and Brandon, too, and I am absolutely tongue-tied. Instead of saying hello or reaching for a handshake, I hang back and hold Ernie in front of me like a shield.

Well done, Iris. So mature.

Luckily, the man my son injured has far better manners than anyone in my family. "And you're Iris." He hobbles towards me, wincing a little when he steps.

"Ricky, you're hurt." Myrtle reaches towards him, but he waves her off.

"I'm sixty-eight years old, and I just landed on my butt. Give an old guy a chance to shake it off before you start coddling him."

The boys snicker at the word butt, and he grins in their direction.

"Hi, Iris, fellas. Enrique Burgos. But you can call me Ricky. Everyone else here does."

The name's familiar.

He puts out a hand, and we shake. I keep my other hand on Ernie's shoulder. Now that he knows no one's dead, he's starting to wiggle.

"It's good to meet you." So he's Ricky, but who is Ricky in relation to everyone else here?

Ricky's eyes, darker than even Ray's, twinkle. "I'm the operations manager."

That's it! "Of course, you are!" I exclaim. "Ray's talked about you."

Myrtle rolls her eyes.

Ricky says, "I'm not surprised," but something about the quirk of his lips tells me, he's onto me. I've shown my hand.

Sometimes, just sometimes, Ray likes to talk about details and minutia about the farm's operations. And sometimes it's the end of the day, and I'm sleepy. Or it's a busy Saturday afternoon, and the boys are making a lot of noise–sometimes details about the farm get by me.

"Well, hopefully, he's mentioned me, too. I'm Brandon." The young man lopes forward with a grin.

He reminds me of Ray with his bright eyes and his smile, but he's taller and thicker like Dennis and significantly younger.

"Hi, Brandon." We shake while I hang onto Ernie. "This is Ernie, and that's Atticus."

"So, since you and Ray got hitched and these are your kids, does that make me their uncle?" Brandon peers at them with interest.

The thought hadn't occurred to me. "I think so. If you're comfortable with them thinking of you that way."

He claps his hands together. "Shoot, yeah, I am! I need someone to get into a little trouble with. Ray and Dennis got old, so they ain't no fun anymore. You guys wanna get some food?"

And just like that both boys dash after Brandon, and I'm left alone and exposed with Myrtle and Ricky.

"Coming?" Myrtle jerks her chin towards the eating.

"Oh, wait! I brought food." By the time I've got my casserole dish, Myrtle and Ricky have walked away. I plod behind them, stalling for time.

There's some cleared space for a yard with a big gazebo. Next to it, a fire pit blazes, and there are old-fashioned plastic chairs pulled around it. A picnic table sits catty-corner between the gazebo and the fire, food spread across it.

Brandon entertaining the boys is a relief, sure. But who do I talk to? What should I say? These aren't my people.

The picnic table is covered with food, and it's not what I expected. There are two roast chickens, and they look delicious. Other than that, there's a pot of macaroni, the blue box kind, a bowl of tater tots, a second pot with baked beans, and a basket of Hawaiian rolls. It's like someone flung open the pantry door thirty minutes before the gathering, grabbed cans and boxes, and here's what happened.

There's no green anything. Even thick with cheese, cream, and breadcrumbs, my spinach and cauliflower casserole is the healthiest food on this table. It's also the only from-scratch item here.

I mean, it's nothing special, right? Besides the chickens, I'm the only one who made real actual food from real actual ingredients. It's not a big deal. It's just what it is. Who I am. We can't help who we are. Some of us throw something together on the fly with lesser materials.

Some of us painstakingly craft and create something memorable and amazing.

It's whatever.

"Alright, let's eat," Myrtle calls out.

Brandon looks up from his conversation with Ernie and Atticus. "What about Ray and Dennis?"

Myrtle's expression hardens. "They're late. They'll manage."

The way she says it, flat and forceful, I feel guilty yet again for something I didn't do.

"What is that?" There's a woman next to me, eyeing my dish. Based on her dark hair, cut in a cute, sharp bob and dark eyes, plus her small, slim frame, I'd bet this is Stephanie, Ray's sister.

"It's a spinach and cauliflower casserole." I work to sound modest. As Stephanie stares at it, nerves and a touch of pride lead to me babbling. "I used Ray's spinach, and I froze some of his cauliflower from last fall. I'm Iris, by the way. Ray's wife. You probably guessed–"

"Pass." And she turns to the baked beans.

Pass?

Pass on what? My delicious homemade dish or meeting me?

Of all of Ray's family, Stephanie is the biggest mystery. I knew Ray loved his sister, mostly because he'd say, "I love my sister, but..." and follow through on what a dark horse or mystery she was. As the one family member who didn't live in town, he saw her the least. Her recent move back, he suggested, overshadowed the news of our wedding.

And she just took a pass on my beloved dish.

I step away from the table only to run into Myrtle with Dennis' wife, Shawna. I know Shawna from pictures, one Dennis showed me and one photo Ray has at the house from Dennis and Shawna's wedding. Ray had just turned thirty, he had said. Dennis is in the middle, Ray on one side, his hand on his brother's shoulder, and on his other side is Shawna clutching a bouquet big enough to bludgeon someone.

She looks the same now as the photo with a bit less makeup. She's shorter than me and smaller everywhere else, too, with straightened blonde hair, a mouth set in a tight line, and a much better handle on a strong smokey eye than I expected from someone living on a farm.

While she and Myrtle don't look friendly with each other, the way they look at me makes my palms itch.

"You're not eating?" Shawna asks.

"I'm checking on my boys," I say. Shawna's lips purse, but Myrtle nods. "I'm Iris," I say to Shawna.

"I know."

And the welcomes just keep coming.

Myrtle's still watching me. "Don't leave it too long to get a plate. Once the boys get here, they'll wolf it down."

Boys? As far as I can tell, the only boys are mine. And possibly Brandon, who just laughed at something Atticus said and slapped his knee with appreciation.

I make a beeline for them.

Hooking a thumb in my kids' direction, Brandon tells me, "These guys are a hoot. Hey, Atty, tell your mama the joke you just told me."

As Atticus proceeds to entertain me with the fisherman "catch ya later" joke, I drift.

When the boys' dad left, he took his family with him if you can take someone who wasn't involved in the first place. I suspect they were relieved to get a hall pass, a sort of "that was fun, we must be going" opportunity. They send birthday checks to each boy on their birthdays, signed "Best, Leonard & Lenore Racine" and a gift card for

Christmas. Warm folks clearly. We never hear from either of Parker's siblings.

So besides having a parenting team of one, my kids have also been limited to a family of five, the three of us and my parents. A small and quiet group.

Now here's this cheerful, noisy young man hooting over Atticus' juvenile joke and slapping Ernie on the back. Maybe besides picking up a stepfather, the boys might gain some uncles and aunts?

I'm choked up at the thought. *Stop it right now, Iris. You are not getting emotional about this in front of Ray's family. Nope.*

"Mom? MOM!"

Startled, I look at Atticus. "You spaced out again. She spaced out again," he explains to Brandon.

"She does that all the time," Ernie chimes in.

"All. The. Time." Atticus says, glaring at me.

I have embarrassed him in front of his new friend.

"Not all the time," I murmur, but they've moved on. Clapping my hands once in their direction, I add, "Guys, come fix a plate. There's cheesy spinach."

There's hesitation as they exchange glances.

"They've got Hawaiian rolls." My voice is flat.

They leave a Wile E. Coyote trail of dust in their wake as they beat a path to the table. Brandon catches my eye, his lips twitching at the corners, just like Ray's.

"Not many people can say no to a good roll." He hops to his feet. "But I'm looking forward to that spinach thing you mentioned."

19.

There's still no sign of Ray and Dennis.

"Is Naomi coming?" Brandon asks around a mouthful of macaroni.

The boys and I sit at the picnic table. The rest of the family have pulled up wobbly plastic chairs around the pit fire.

"She's with Ray and Dennis." Myrtle doesn't look up from her meal as she says this.

Shawna's head snaps up. "I didn't know she was going."

"I told them to take her."

"Why?" Shawna's tone is sharp.

Myrtle looks up from the piece of chicken speared on her plastic fork. "Because I thought it'd be helpful. Why else would I tell them to do it?"

Shawna looks back to her plate, picking at tiny portions of beans and a roll.

My casserole dish is all but untouched. The boys had some, and Brandon, true to his word, took a good spoonful. It's silly to let it bother me, but it does. Especially as most everything else has been gobbled up.

"Hello, the house!"

We all jump, except Myrtle. She turns, her face unmoved, as her two oldest sons appear from the dark.

Atticus and Ernie spring to their feet, shouting, "Ray!"

"Hey, fellas. You leave me any dinner?" Ray is just as enthusiastic as they are.

I'm suddenly on high alert, eyes swiveling to take it in. Myrtle watches the exchange without expression. I see Ricky's smile broaden, and he nods a couple of times. It's too shadowy to catch any other reactions.

"Mom made the spinach casserole, but no one likes it." Ernie slips his hand into Ray's and leads him to the table. I put my hand over my face, mortified.

"Is that right?" Ray grins at me, letting himself be guided to his mother's picnic table where he's no doubt eaten thousands of meals. "I guess we'll need to double down, won't we?"

"What's double down?" Ernie asks.

"You don't know what double down is?" Dennis is right next to them. He and Shawna exchange a look, but that's the extent of their greeting. "What are you doing with these kids, Ray? We gotta teach 'em blackjack." He grabs Atticus around the waist and carries him like a suitcase, tucked under his arm. Atticus howls with laughter.

The boys have uncles. And an aunt. Two aunts, if you include ol' pucker-mouth Shawna over there. My brain didn't keep up with calculations when I first agreed to Ray's proposal.

"Hey, honey, how are you?" Ray stops in front of my seat, ducking his face down to mine.

It's odd, feeling all eyes on us, even as they pretend not to be. I want to show off and hide at the same time.

Instead, I kiss him lightly, briefly, the warmth of his lips on mine grounding me back in him and us. Whatever the last forty-five minutes have been like, I'm not on my own in this. I want to be cold and reserved. He meets my gaze and mouths, "I'm sorry," and I immediately relent, touching his hand, feeling a shiver at the heat between the two of us.

"Here, Ray, here," Atticus trips towards Ray with a plate, and Ray launches into a generous thanks, admiring the work they've put into it.

It makes my heart hurt, watching them navigate this father figure. And Ray has stepped right into the shoes they presented him with. Other kids might balk at a stepdad's presence in their lives. Not mine. They're gulping it up like a dog at a water bowl after a long, hot run.

"Where's Naomi?" Myrtle finally speaks up.

Dennis, sorting out silverware and a glass of sweet tea for himself, replies, "She headed home."

Ray expounds on the situation. "We hit traffic in the last fifteen minutes. Broke down trailer on I-75, put everyone down to one lane. Took thirty minutes to go two miles."

"Ugh, that's the worst about these old country highways," Stephanie, who's barely looked up from her phone, grumbles.

"You don't have traffic down there in Atlanta, is that right?" Ray's expression is innocent.

Stephanie looks up only to scowl. I catch her eye and smile. Her eyebrows quirk, and she ducks back behind the screen.

"I hoped you'd show some manners and invite her to stay for dinner." Myrtle doesn't let up.

Ray meets her gaze. "Mama, we did. She wanted to go home."

"I bet she did."

This is from Shawna. What is up with her? I look between her and Dennis, but she's not looking at her husband. Instead, she watches Ray, her face inscrutable. When she catches my eye, her cheeks go red, and she looks away.

"Don't want to wear her out and have her quit on us," Ray adds.

"She'll be here in the morning. Make her a plate if that'll make you feel better." Dennis' tone is noticeably short.

"Forgive me for trying to treat our employees well." Myrtle has a quiet fire about her that makes me fold my arms over my chest. "Is she helping you work cows tomorrow?"

Ray looks at his mama again. "Nope. Well, yes actually, she is working cows. Just not with me. Dennis is helping her in the morning. I'm working the ground in the morning."

"And who's helping you with that then?"

Ray turns sideways and bestows his grin on me. It's presumptuous, but nonetheless it makes me laugh.

"It looks like I am," I say.

And to that, Myrtle only says, "Hmph."

20.

"Well, that was a night."

It's the first thing I say to Ray the next morning. The kitchen's dark except for a little lamp I've put next to the sink. Ray has come to understand, in only a matter of days, that I can't live with overhead lighting. Also that we wake the house up slowly, turning lights on only as we need them.

There's an art to waking up well.

When I said that, he laughed silently, his shoulders shaking, and said, "Yes, ma'am."

By the time we were home last night and put the boys to bed, it was late. And there were other entertaining activities to consider over discussing his family's complicated dynamics.

Now, however, I'm awake and curious.

That might not be true for Ray. He leans against the counter, waiting as the coffee brews, rubbing his stubbled jaw and yawning.

"You mean last night?"

I take a breath. *He's a man, not Angie,* I tell myself. *He has to learn how to debrief after an event.*

"Yep, exactly. I'm not sure it was smart to go without you."

"I'm glad you did. My mom wanted y'all there."

That surprises me. "She did?"

"Yeah. She knew we were late, but she'd told me to tell you to get on up to the house." He holds out his arms and draws me into them.

Interesting. And odd. "I wonder why?"

My head's nestled against his chest. He chuckles, and it trembles my cheek. "I expect she wants to spend some time with you. Get to know you."

"Hmm."

"C'mon, was it that bad? You got to meet Brandon. Steph. That's a good thing."

"Yeah, what's her deal?"

"Steph?" I feel him shift, hear him sigh. "You know as much as I do. She's been home since Christmas, and I don't think any of us have seen her besides a couple of those dinners."

That's interesting. "Why'd she pick Atlanta in the first place?"

He nods, his chin touching up and down on the top of my head. "She got scholarships to Emory. After graduation, she stayed."

"So she's a smarty." No need to hide my surprise.

"She is. The only one of us four with a lick of book sense. She got a job, found a roommate, got an apartment—the works. She only ever came home for the holidays and Mama's birthday. And then after Christmas, she shows up, says she lost her apartment, and couldn't afford a new one. And she stayed."

"Huh." It's a sad story, but feels off, too. "Just like that? She's been in Atlanta for the last twelve or thirteen years, and then she just comes back? Is she working?"

The coffee maker beeps, and Ray keeps one arm around me using the other to take down two coffee mugs. "You stay put, young lady. I'm not letting go until I have to."

He adds a small spoonful of sugar to my cup, pours in my coffee, and switches arms to hold me with his right arm, while reaching with his left, to grab the saucepan of milk on the stove. Do I heat milk for my coffee every morning? Indeed I do.

Ray does an awkward dance step, I'm laughing, and he's clutching me closer, saying, "Now, this is the tricky part, hold still." He brings the pan to my coffee cup and tips in the milk. "How was that? Did I do it right?"

How did I get this lucky? A few days into this married life and it's better than anything I imagined. Nothing like marriage to Parker, which somehow felt like playing grown-ups in the bodies of young adults.

Ray's constant touches, his smile, the way he talks to my children, it's all the best parts of our relationship. Only now we get to do this all day long.

Smitten. I am smitten with this smiling, cheeky, dark-headed man with hair sticking up in all directions and sweatpants hanging off his lanky frame.

Later that morning, after the boys were at school, I made it back to the farm and found Ray, the Fox family still on my mind.

As Ray pokes around the tractor, checking this and that, I pick up where we left off. "So does Stephanie work?"

Satisfied, Ray pushes himself up off the damp ground, brushing his hands on his pants. "She does. A remote job. She does alright, too."

"So why didn't she find a new place in Atlanta? Isn't that weird to you?"

Ray shrugs, this one with lots of shoulders. "Only the good Lord knows, Iris. I certainly don't. She doesn't talk to me. I'm not exaggerating when I say our family doesn't talk much. All I know is what my mother told me. Lost her apartment and moved home. Here she is."

He circles the tractor one more time, brushing his hands together. "So you'll have dull work. I need you to stand right here on top of this bar."

I let him guide me to the metal pole laying across the start of a dirt row. "Now you see how this pole is attached to the end of this fabric?" It's a heavy dark cloth on a feeder attached to the back of the tractor. "You're going to stand here on the pole and anchor this fabric in place. I'll drive and unroll it until the row's covered in fabric. Got it?"

"Maybe she needs someone to talk to."

"Who?"

"Stephanie."

Ray runs his hand over his head. "Honey, for the love, please pay attention. What we need to focus on is prepping this here field for planting."

I bristle. "I'm paying attention!" He cocks an eyebrow at me. "Anchor the pole with your weight. Not flattering but I get it."

Ray nods once, his mouth tweaked to the side in a small smile. "OK, then. Good woman."

"Sheesh," I murmur as he hustles up to the tractor and hops in. "But if you think we're done with this conversation, you're wrong!" I holler to the back of the machine. Ray only gives a wave.

21.

It's possible that I have died and gone to actual heaven, at least the heaven of my heart's desires. In my pajamas and wrapped in a thick cotton duvet, I'm sitting at my patio table, in my new husband's front yard, with my new husband across from me, watching my boys scramble and slide over the low, thick branches of a black walnut tree. It's not even seven, the sun's rising in front of us, and I have a cup of rich, creamy coffee in my hands.

It's been a week. The boys and I have been here a week. A week of long school drives, doing some of the more menial chores with Ray around the farm, and nights together as a family. And now here we are, bright and early Sunday morning, and it's me and these guys and this coffee and this sunrise.

"This might be my best morning ever."

Ray looks at me, surprised. "It doesn't take much with you, does it?"

I smile back, impervious to teasing. "This is it. This is all I've ever wanted. Sunshine and fresh air for my boys. Good coffee. And something beautiful to look at."

"Hopefully an adoring husband is on that list as well."

I grin at him. "Who said the adoring husband wasn't the something beautiful?"

He ducks his head. "Mrs. Fox, you are making me blush. But I have to admit I've lived in this house for four years now, and this is the best view I've ever had here."

My gaze meets his, and the look in his eyes makes my belly swoop and my heart pitter-patter. The morning is mostly quiet, punctuated by the shouts or laughter of the boys. It's only the four of us, hidden away in our private nirvana, and this man I love with all of my heart, mind, and belly is looking at me in a way I didn't believe possible. I want to be swallowed up in these feelings, to live here forever.

I look away first and say, "This feels like your farm."

"I should hope so. Goodness knows I bust my hump out here six to seven days a week trying to do right by it."

I shake my head. "I didn't mean it like that exactly. I mean, right now, at this moment, this feels like your farm. No signs of Dennis, of Myrtle, just your place."

Ray throws his head back, chortling. "Oh, if wishes were horses, then beggars would ride..."

There's silence, and I wait, hoping he'll say more. When he doesn't, I ask, "Do you ever think about it?"

Ray cocks his head to the side. "Think about what?"

I shrug. *Keep it light. Don't get intense.* "Your own farm. Doing your own thing."

Ray turns to look over the untended piece of land in front of us. "Think about leaving? And starting on my own?"

I shrug again. "People do it all the time."

He watches the boys, shaking his head, smiling. "They do. And then they close up shop. Because most small farms fail. Hell, honey, most small businesses fail. Why would I leave our thriving farm to go up to my neck in debt buying my own land, start over fresh with infrastructure, and see what happens? That'd be crazy. Pure lunacy." He shakes his head, "Ernie, looking good, fella! But be careful, OK? That branch won't hold you up if you go out any further."

Why push? It's not like I want to move. It's not like I want to start our own farm.

Except. The week hasn't been easy. All the driving to get the boys to school, and I make that drive four times a day most days. I considered staying in Harrisville, but why? I'm not going to cart all my knitting materials and tools to a coffee shop and work there. And, honestly, my brain hasn't felt invested in my work. So much change, so much new, makes it hard to concentrate.

One week. Hard to believe. In some ways, it already feels like we've been here forever.

Some of that might have to do with Ray's family. Their presence is noticeable. And it shouldn't be, not really. I mean, look at the position of our house. We're set to the side of the farm, an afterthought. Myrtle's great big place is the view turning into the farm's proper driveway. Following that paved drive eventually leads you to gravel offshoots. Not too far down from Myrtle's house is Dennis and Shawna's home, a new white and black construction with modern farmhouse siding.

We're three-quarters of a mile further down at the end of the gravel path. I might have clocked it on my odometer the other day.

Yet for our placement on the farm, we attract a lot of traffic. After a week of Fox family members stopping by unannounced, it became apparent we were out of sight, but not out of mind.

And after our third stop-by from a Fox family member in a day, who wouldn't wonder: What would our own farm be like?

The first happened right after I walked in the door from the school run. Driving wore me out, and my plan was to settle in on the sofa and get to knitting.

"Hey, there, Iris." Dennis poked his head around the door, grinning. "How you doing, lady?"

I screamed, which is a perfectly normal response to a person standing in your house who you didn't invite into your house.

"Agh, sorry!" Dennis flung both hands up. "Just me!"

"Dennis, what are you doing? You can't just walk into someone's house..."

He cocked his head to the side, eerily reminiscent of Ray. "I do it all the time."

"Really?" My hands are on my chest over my racing heart. "Well, don't do it here. We're neighborhood people. You knock."

"Aye, aye, Captain." He saluted and grinned, not the least bit chastised. "I was looking for Brother Ray. He take off already?"

"He left when I took the boys to school. I think he went to the co-op."

"Alrighty. I'll shoot him a text, see if I can get him up to the barn to help me with this steer. He's a wild thing." And then Dennis pulled out a chair at our table and sat down.

What was happening? Was he settling in for a long winter's chat?

"How's it going?"

Yes, apparently so.

"Fine, Dennis. We've been good."

Dennis ducked his head toward me, a mischievous grin spreading across his face. "Yeah? How's ol' Ray adjusting to having people around?"

We're not people. We're Ray's family.

"He's adjusting fine, we all are–" It's hard for us too, buddy. "And Dennis, I was about to get to work."

He nodded. "Any coffee still in the pot?"

What was happening?

I liked Dennis. Approachable, good-humored, his whole demeanor promised a good time. I liked him immediately whereas Ray took some warming-up time.

However, I wanted to get his butt out of my chair and out of my house. This. Very. Minute.

Dennis picked up on none of it.

And then someone honked outside. We looked at each other and simultaneously headed to the door.

It was not, as I hoped, my husband, but instead Naomi. She looked as surprised to see Dennis as I felt to see either of them. A strange expression crossed her face, glancing between the two of us, but it passed.

She stuck her head out of the cab and hollered, "Morning, Iris. Looking for the mister. Any sign of him?"

These unannounced visits were baffling, but more baffling was the casual way all the visitors were treating the visits.

"He's gone to the co-op. He'll be back soon. Or maybe at the greenhouse already?" Dennis answered on my behalf.

Naomi nodded and thumped the side of the truck once. "Alrighty then. I'll head there." She shot off and, I noticed, didn't wave this time.

"Ahh, seeing as there's no coffee…" Dennis glanced in my direction, and I shook my head, gripping my smile in place. "I guess I'll be on my way."

"Sounds good." And then I said the dumbest words ever. "Thanks for stopping by." No! No, it wasn't. Why would I say that? Stress came over me, and people-pleasing Iris popped out. I hurtled myself inside and locked the door behind me.

It didn't stop there. Only a few hours later, as I tidied up my work and was tucking several tiny new baby sweaters into my bin, someone else arrived. At least, this one knocked.

I flung the door open and blurted, "What?"

As soon as Ricky saw my face, he broke into a grin. "Hey there, Iris. I was looking for Ray."

"You and everybody else in this dang place," I muttered. To him, I added, "He's not here."

Ricky nodded, lips still twitching. "Busy day?" he asked.

I tried to calm down. Unlike Dennis and Naomi, Ricky didn't give me the feeling of wanting to close the blinds and hide inside. He stayed on the porch, hands in his pockets, no suggestion of coming inside and making himself at home.

With him, I wanted to be friendly. Like myself, he was an interloper, regardless of how long he'd worked at the farm. "I'm not used to so many unannounced visitors."

Good grief, I'd lived in a neighborhood filled with folks I know, folks I went to church with, folks whose kids were best friends with my kids, and I'd had more unexpected visitors today than I'd had in a year at our old home.

Ricky squinted to the side, nodding. "That probably won't be uncommon," he said, his voice measured, and when he met my gaze, his eyes were amused.

I ventured, "Ray's family is pretty used to stopping by when they want to?"

He gave a shrug, eyes rolling once. "You could say that. At least to Ray. I'm not so sure they would do the same to Shawna that they would to you. You know what I mean?"

Ricky's voice, with that distinct Latinox accent, is oddly soothing even as he's delivering unwanted news.

"Gotcha." I sighed and dragged the door open. "Do you want to come in?"

That made him laugh. "Not me. I'll check the big house, see if he's up there."

"That's Myrtle's?" I guessed.

He nodded, already on his way. "Keep your chin up, Iris," he called over his shoulder. "You're a foreigner in a foreign country. You'll settle in."

Emboldened by his gentle familiarity, I called back, "Did you?"

He reached his truck (What was it with trucks around here?) and glanced back. "Yes, I'd say I did."

"Quickly?"

His grin was impish. He might be in his sixties, but Ricky was a cutie. "No, I did not say that."

Sitting here with Ray on this idyllic peaceful morning and remembering Ricky's words, I want to tell him, "They're too much. Your family, your farm, all of it. I need more space."

But, from what Ray says, another farm isn't an option. We are here, on this physical land, and in the Foxes' physical presence whether I like it or not.

And so often, I don't just like it, I love it. Like right now, in this magical morning sitting in his weird front yard, with a pasture in front of us, good coffee, a sunrise, and two happy boys whooping it up in the trees.

"Iris? Are you OK?" Ray's studying me, as if he looks closely enough he'll be able to see what's inside my head.

"I'm fine. I was just wondering. Really. It's all...interesting."

Ray's still watching me, smiling that smile that feels like a thick blanket and a hot cup of coffee on a morning like this. "Alright, hon, if you're sure. Hey, are you hungry? 'Cause I've got some sausage and eggs in there that need attention."

"Are you cooking for me?" Delight washes over me.

"I might not be able to whip up a chicken makhani, but I know my way around some breakfast foods. You want a top-off before I get started?"

I hand him my mug and snuggle deeper into the duvet. "Yes, please." This is the life. A lovely, doting husband, happy boys, and all the time in the world to enjoy both. Who could complain about that?

22.

Meeting with Andie Werking of Werking Girl Collab to discuss her carrying my pieces is a relief after feeling so immersed in the farm.

I don't know Andie well. She leads our music team at church, and I've played when they needed someone in a pinch. I learned the violin growing up, and I can just make it through "Come Thou Fount" along with a few other hymns. But even years with this community, I'm still shy, especially with outgoing people like Andie.

Now here we are, and she's so upbeat and direct that I'm happy to hurry to keep up with her. And after an easy drive to school and picking up a coffee from Bread and Butter, I'm in great spirits. She expects my handmade goods to do well, and it's another buoy to my soul. I want to be a part of the farm, but I don't want my business to slip away from me.

"Why haven't we talked before?" she asks over her shoulder, leading me to her office.

"I had an exclusivity agreement with Melody at The Paisley Knickerbocker." I'm sheepish.

Why I ever agreed to exclusivity with Melody is now beyond me. I remember Angie popping an eyebrow at me when I mentioned it.

"Exclusive? What, she's a boutique in New York?"

I shrugged at the time. "She thinks it gives her store extra pull to offer items you can't find anywhere else." Telling this to Andie now, I feel silly.

She laughs. "That's Melody for you."

"These kids' things will go well here," Andie says, and her determined tone assured me. "And I think you should consider hats, gloves, and scarves for adults. I wouldn't suggest you knit a blanket or go into women's outerwear. That would be a tough market here. But people will pay for small things like hats and gloves." She extracts a chunky mitten from her pocket and waves it at me. "I had another knitter who made these, and I haven't been able to fill the void since she retired. Trust me, we need you."

Her office is a surprisingly homey place. There's a beautiful desk set in the center of the space, with two low-slung, floral patterned chairs in front of it. A long work table sits against the wall, with a few chairs there, too.

"This is cute," I say, and she looks around.

"I'm still getting used to it. Dee–you know Dee, right?" I nod.

And she continues, "She used to work here, too, and we had two of these." She pats her desk. "But now she's running her own place, so we moved her desk there. And I'm trying to make this more like a friendly workspace for everyone who works here instead of my office."

I murmur, "I can't imagine doing all this."

"Why not?" Andie rests her elbows on her desk, chin in her hand, watching me with interest. "You run your own business."

"I mean, kind of, yes. But it's only me, knitting my kid toys and sweaters for the farmers' market. It's a really different undertaking than all this." I gesture around the office, noticing the fancy coffee maker, the assortment of handmade ceramic mugs, and a bag of locally roasted coffee beans. "Between the boys and keeping up with orders, I can't imagine having time for my own shop, let alone the know-how. And now that we're out on the farm..." I drift off, not sure how to finish that thought.

"That's right! You got married." Andie taps her forehead. "Sorry, I'm bad about keeping up with other people. Just ask my friends. Tell me everything. How's that going?" Her smile is so friendly and self-deprecating. It invites me into her confidence, and honestly, I'm longing to share some real thoughts, not small talk.

"It's a lot," I say, and with it comes a deep exhale, one I didn't know I needed. "Ray is amazing. And the farm is beautiful. The boys are crazy about him, and except for the drive, they couldn't be happier. But..."

Andie holds up a hand. "Do you want coffee?"

I do, in fact, want coffee. In a few minutes, she's sitting next to me, and we're sipping coffee. And instead of discussing prices for my merchandise, I'm telling her bits and pieces of life with the Foxes, the distance from town, our house.

"Huh." Andie chews her lower lip, thinking hard. "Look, I'll tell you straight out, I'm not great at listening and holding space and all that. But I am good at seeing a problem and offering a solution. Is that OK?"

While I enjoy deep, feelings-oriented conversation, I'm intrigued by her offer. "Yes, please."

"How's your house? Your new house I mean."

"Oh, Ray's house." I pause.

Andie snaps her fingers. "See? Right there? 'Ray's house.' That's your problem."

I'm fascinated. "It is?"

She clasps her hands around her knees. "Yes. Well, maybe not your only problem. But it's one of them. You need to make that house your home. I bet you're like me, and you really like a space to be yours, to show who you are. Right?"

Yes, every word to this, yes. I nod eagerly, and Andie, clearly not afraid to share an opinion, beams and keeps going.

"First, it doesn't even sound like Ray's home is his home if you know what I mean. Like he lives there, but it's not his. And second, you've got to make it yours. Well, I guess both of yours, really."

"How?" I'm eager for instructions. Someone make this easier!

She shrugs. "I'm not great at that part, to be fair. The closer the wedding gets the more Joe and I are trying to figure out how we combine our homes. He doesn't like my idea that we live at his house when the kids are there and then live at my house when the kids are with their mom." She sighs, but she doesn't sound troubled. "I'll end up moving to his house I expect, but don't tell him yet. I don't want him to think he got that one too easily."

I can't stop laughing. Her light-heartedness breathes fresh air into my own situation.

"I'm right, aren't I? You're out of sorts because you haven't made that house your home."

I lift my hands, feeling helpless. "I want to. But Ray's so tired by the end of the day."

"Could he take a day off?"

I snort. "He's a farmer, haven't you heard? They don't get days off." The bitterness in my tone surprises me. Am I this angry? That's not fair to Ray. I knew what I was getting when I said yes. At least, I knew some of it.

I breathe and try again. "I can do a lot of it on my own. But I need to move these couches–these big box store, matching peach things," Andie wrinkles her nose, and I know she feels where I'm coming from, "out of the house and move mine in. I can't do it alone…" As I talk it out with her, a thought dawns on me. It wouldn't require Ray's help, and it wouldn't demand I do everything on my own.

"You've got it, don't you? I can see it all over your face." Andie claps her hands. "You've figured it out, and I've helped you. I keep telling Dee, I could have been an amazing therapist. She disagrees."

23.

When the boys and I left our home, we loaded everything into Ray's farm truck, making a few runs to get it all. Our nine-hundred-square-foot home packed up pretty neatly.

Some things went into the house and the rest into the storage building next to Ray's house. It was a rickety place and fairly empty, and we only put my things there with the understanding Ray's items would come out and mine would replace them.

As I start prepping the room for its makeover, I feel unsettled. What is it? I know Ray wants to help. He's said as much multiple times. "This is the best time of year to tackle a project like this," he explained as we packed up my house. "This is my slowest time of year."

Each morning, on his way out the door, he'd kiss me and say, "Tonight let's handle this furniture situation." And that evening he came in, thirty minutes to an hour later than I expected, sweaty, disheveled, and exhausted. If I brought up furniture, he'd apologize but ask for a break. "I'm beat, honey."

Yet something wasn't working on the farm. In the morning, he'd tell me, "Tonight. We'll get on it tonight."

He wouldn't say much about work, but the little bits I discerned left me wondering how much Ray carried by himself. Dennis, it appeared, was hard to find and often turned up late to work, with half his normal energy. And Brandon, a full-time student, seemed less and less available.

"He's got to prioritize his education," Ray said as we sat shoulder to shoulder in what was now our bed. "So I'm glad he's giving it his all. But I miss his help. He used to show up after lunch, with lots of energy, ready to go. Now I can't find hide or hair of him."

He ran a hand over his face and sighed. I snuggled deeper into the bed, resting my chin against his shoulder. "I wonder what's going on with Dennis?" I mused.

He snorted. "Oh, that one's always been a wild card. I wouldn't be surprised if he was at the bar these days. Shooting pool and flirting with the ladies."

"Really?" I tilted my face up to look at him. He slept in a white sleeveless undershirt and the warmth of his skin against mine made me shiver. "I wouldn't have guessed."

Ray met my eyes, his gaze straight forward. "Wouldn't you?"

There is something about his directness that makes it impossible for me to lie to him. "Maybe I would have guessed," I admit. "There's something in the way he talks to women. But if he ever talked to me that way, I didn't notice."

At least, if it was there, I pretended not to see it. I had no interest in someone else's man.

And now I was cuddled up next to Ray, the real prize, who said, "I really want to get the house fixed up, honey. I want it to feel exactly the way you want it to. I'm just so low on energy right now."

Turned towards him, my left knee resting over his right leg and his hand casually cupping my thigh while we talked, the intimacy between us took my breath away. Trailing my fingers lightly over his bare arm, feeling the tightness of his forearm and the definition of his bicep, I murmured, "It's OK, love. I'd rather you save your energy for other things."

At this some light came back into his face. "Well, now, Mrs. Fox, what exactly did you have in mind?"

And that put an end to any further conversation about Ray's family or our home furnishings situation.

But now it's after nine, and I'm wondering if he's going to show up. When I called, he assured me he was working by himself for the first part of the day, and he had plenty of time to help me and still handle his work.

I know Ray is gone for the morning, at a feedstore one county over, hoping to wrangle a better price on getting cow feed delivered in loads.

I pace and chew my lip, worrying. Is this wrong? Will Ray be upset? I could still text "never mind." I could wait. But looking around the house I'm desperate to make changes. Andie was right; making this house our home could go a long way to helping me settle down, calming my nerves which feel frayed, even here on this paradise of a farm.

I hear the truck pull up outside, and I've thrown open the door before Dennis is fully out of his truck. He grins up at me. His smile is lazy whereas Ray's is electric, and Dennis' is open to everyone whereas Ray's is only for me.

"Hey, there, Ms. Iris. You ready to get down to business?"

24.

"It won't take long," I blurt out. "You'll be in and out before you know it."

Oh, help. That sounds terrible. My cheeks burn. If Dennis notices, he doesn't say anything. He's surveying the living room, checking out the doorway.

"I think it's a pretty straight shot," he says, and he's doing a thing with his hands, raising them straight up and down, like an airman marshaller, guiding the plane down the runway. "Basically we bump this sofa over, then carry it straight out. As for the rest, it shouldn't be hard."

"Are you sure you have time for this?" I'm still in the doorway.

Dennis tilts his head at me. The fact that I'm pushing him out as soon as he walks in must feel as crazy to him as it does to me.

But what if he's giving me the time he should be putting toward the farm?

"It's my morning off, Iris. I'll be working all weekend."

My shoulders relax. "Oh, OK. Phew."

Dennis laughs. "So you don't mind taking up my time, but you won't take up the farm's time?"

I shrug. "Farm above everything else, right?"

"You got that right," he mutters, and for a minute there's an unspoken solidarity between us. Maybe Dennis isn't as keen to devote his life to the farm as Ray and Myrtle.

Curiosity rears its head, and I want to know more. I also want to get this going so for now I mentally pin those questions.

"Here's what I was thinking," Out loud, I sketch out a plan for the morning.

Dennis, to his credit, doesn't argue but gets right to work. Except for occasional prompts of "shift it to the left" or "flip it on its side", we work in silence.

It takes the entire morning. By the time we stand back and admire our handiwork, it's almost noon.

"I'll be damned," Dennis says and takes a long drink of the iced tea I offered him. "It looks like a different place."

That's a compliment I'll take. I sit at the dining room table, sweaty and tired. "I'm still not sure how Ray wound up with that old furniture in the first place. I assume it belonged to his ex?"

I give Dennis a sideways glance as I mention her, Heidi, hoping he might take that bait and spill.

He shakes his head. "Naw, when Heidi left she took the furniture with her. Ray did buy the house when he and Heidi got hitched. But that was as much lucky timing as anything. Old Bill Wiking was finally ready to sell it to him. Ray had been after him about the house for years." Dennis sighs. "It's not much to look at, but it's a helluva lot more affordable than building like I did." He looks into the bubble glass as he talks. "Anyway, when Heidi left, she decided since she brought it in, she ought to bring it back out."

I know only the bare minimum about Heidi. To be fair, Ray knows very little of Parker either. Early on, we had the conversation demanded of two divorced people attempting to enter into a relationship with one another: "What happened?"

I told him about my marriage to Parker, that shell of a relationship.

With no kids involved, Ray's story was briefer than mine. He met Heidi at a bar in Nashville on an overnight trip for Dennis' bachelor party. She was a flight attendant, flying out of Nashville. They carried on a long-distance relationship for two years before they finally decided to make it official. After they got married, she moved to the farm but continued working out of Nashville, spending several days there and driving home for a few days at a time.

"It lasted a couple of months," Ray said, his smile wry. "It was always an unrealistic proposition."

"The driving was too hard? The separation?" I wanted to know everything he did, understand each nuance, and hear all his moments.

He sighed. "More like it was too hard settling back in. We both did fine separately, her in her apartment in Nashville, me here. But her coming back, getting used to her being here all over again, it was too much. It wasn't working."

It was eerie, the way it reminded me of Parker and me in that way. "So was it mutual?"

He paused. "I think she might have kept trying. But it was wearing her down. She was doing so much driving. I suggested it, and initially she argued against it. But I said to her, 'you can't keep living like this.' And she finally agreed. We both hated it, two-month failures is how I saw it. But it wasn't ever going to work. She wasn't going to be happy finding work somewhere in the area. And I wasn't going to be happy living somewhere else."

The farm, I thought at the time. This farm, it's Ray's first love. In the same way, you could argue Atticus was my first love and Ernie, hot on his heels, my second. This farm was the first thing Ray loved with his whole heart. At that moment, I understood, don't mess around with this place. It was the ultimatum I would never want to offer.

"Iris? You still with me?"

I'm startled to find Dennis watching me over the rim of his glass. He looks bemused and something else. It's unnerving.

"Sorry. Spaced out for a minute there."

Hopping up, I serve myself more tea. "So Heidi left and Ray bought those ugly peach sofas in his depression?"

"Shawna," Dennis says, and I choke on my drink.

"Excuse me?"

Dennis' lips twitch. "Shawna offered him her old stuff. Those 'ugly peach sofas' were Shawna's when she was a single gal and had her own place."

My face is flaming.

Dennis looks tickled. I say, "That was...kind of her."

He snorts. "Shawna wanted new things for our new house."

"I didn't realize Shawna and Ray were that close."

A strange look crosses his face, but it's gone before I can read it. "They aren't. Not a bit. She wanted to help him out in a tough spot. And maybe clear the way to get the living room set she really wanted." He smiles at that, but there's bitterness, too.

"Will Shawna want her furniture back?"

Shawna's sofa and loveseat set are now relegated to the shed, and our sofa and chairs have taken their rightful spot.

"I don't imagine she wants it anymore now than she did then."

There's still a lot to do to pull this house together. And I'm feeling overwhelmed from hearing about Ray and his past. Dennis appears to be hunkering down, and I'd rather him be on his way.

That sounds cold, but it's not exactly the friendship that he and I have. And now that I'm over the thrill of having the peach furniture gone, the guilt of bringing Dennis in to help rises within me.

Dennis' phone rings and says, "Hey there, brother!" He has the nerve to wink at me.

I go hot, then cold, terrified he'll say something stupid. "Yep, I took a little time off this morning. But I'm about to get some lunch and get to it. Where do you wanna meet?"

Ray will know Dennis was here. He'll know I didn't do this work by myself. And I'm not trying to hide anything. There's nothing to hide.

Surveying the space is distracting. And I'm thrilled. It's not exactly like our old home, yet the improvement is massive.

Where those dumb peach sofas took up most of the floor space, we now have a living area. There's my short-backed, slipcovered cream sofa with our big, soft pillows, a wingback chair, and our camel-colored leather ottoman, all sitting on my gorgeous cream and black stripe rug.

It's the beginning of great. I still have so many pieces to add, scattering my plants around the room, considering where my artwork can hang on the walls.

"Duty calls." Dennis is off the phone. "Anything else I can give you a hand with?"

I shake my head and clear my throat. "This was huge, Dennis. Thank you so much."

He's been tremendously helpful. I can't let my guilt stop me from thanking him.

He pretends to tip a hat in my direction. "Happy to oblige," he says, and I'm feeling better until he adds over his shoulder, "And not a word to Ray. My lips are sealed."

25.

When I wake up, Ray's out of bed already. I tug on my robe, an ankle-length silky thing, with a sky-blue background, covered with pink and white cherry blossoms. It's so gorgeous. It's how-I-want-to-feel-on-the-inside kind of clothes.

Putting it on now reassures me. It might be a little 1950s rancher on a busy family farm, overrun by people who like to drop by unannounced and with several of them who don't seem to like me at all, but I'm still Iris Shepherd. Well, I'm Iris Shepherd Fox.

Ray's in the kitchen, and the boys are eating breakfast. Atticus studies the back of the organic cereal box. He's probably memorized it, but he needs a place to put his hungry brain. Ernie entertains himself by loading pieces of brown cereal puff in his spoon and launching them into his mouth. Cereal's scattered around his bowl, but at least he's sitting in one place.

Ray has both boys' lunch boxes open in front of him. Each shows a sandwich and a bag of fruit gummies. He's shaking baked potato chips into a bag. I pause.

"Good morning, sweetheart," he says, his voice low and warm. "How'd you sleep?"

"Great," I say. "Did you remember their–"

"Clementines? Got 'em right here." He drops two small oranges in each box then adds, "Coffee's on. I've got your cup ready."

What in the world? I swallow hard, making my coffee, noticing the pan of warm milk on the stove.

How did I get so lucky? And why do I feel unnerved by it?

He smiles back. "Good?"

"Perfect."

He leans in for a kiss, and I give it.

"Lunches made." He runs the zipper on the last one from one side to the other and sets them up next to each other. "These fellas are ready."

I lean back in for another kiss, this one longer and deeper. I meet his gaze, looking into his eyes that shift from brown to almost black and back again so subtly you never quite know where you stand. I love them and the off-balance feeling I get when he stares at me like this. He slips one finger into the belt of my robe and pulls me closer.

"You however look far from ready."

I swallow, feeling the tight feeling in my throat and my heart beating hard.

"You want me to take them today?"

Again, that strange feeling, like I've missed a step, hits me. "No, I've got it."

He quirks an eyebrow at me. "I'm happy to."

"Yeah, let Ray take us!" Ernie's suddenly paying attention and wants a vote in the conversation.

That's even more unsettling. I take my boys to school. I'm their mom. Their person. It's my job.

"You need to get to work. I can throw myself together fast," I reply, feigning ease. "I'm a master at it."

He smiles, the corners of his eyes crinkling. "I believe it."

I'm in the bedroom, doing a Superman-like quick change, when I hear Ray call, "Honey, how in the world did you get all these sofas moved by yourself?"

Nonono. I thought, maybe, I got by with it. To be fair, getting by with something feels almost as bad as getting caught.

Pulling up my long, patterned skirt, I call back, "Dennis helped."

I hustle out of the bedroom, tugging my fitted t-shirt down and meet his gaze. "Oh?"

There's a stillness to his expression, hard lines around his mouth that tell me, this is bad. He's upset.

"Mm-hmm. I wanted to surprise you."

"Right." He turns his back to me, occupied at the sink.

What is the problem? It's his brother, not some ex-boyfriend of mine.

"Go brush your teeth," I tell the boys, and they trip out of the room. "I just, I wanted, well, I mean, we'd been talking about it for a while."

"A week. We'd been talking about it for a week." Ray's eyes scan my face, and he's reading me, trying to understand something. What it is I don't know.

"I know, but a week is a long time here." It feels like a month, I want to add but don't. I sigh, a deep gusty sigh. "I missed my stuff. I needed this to feel like my house, like our house. And it wasn't happening. You're so tired every night, and I just, I couldn't wait any longer." I'm fiddling with my wedding ring when Ray's eyes dart to my hands. I stop immediately. Somehow it feels like an admission of guilt.

Of what? I didn't do anything. I helped him. I brought in someone else. I let him off the hook. I say as much.

"Dang it, Iris, I don't want to be let off the hook. I'm your husband, and if you ask me to do a thing, I want to do it. And if I don't, I want us to figure it out together. Not have you go ask Dennis." The way he spits Dennis' name out, it sounds like Ray's mortal enemy.

It doesn't make any sense. "He's your brother. If anyone else is going to help, isn't Dennis the best choice? It's not like we owe him something. Why are you so upset?"

We're stuck in this odd moment. Ray worked up, staring at me with such frustration. I'm clutching my coffee both remorseful and defiant.

At last, Ray makes a weird sound, a snort, and steps back from the counter. "You don't understand," he says, and it's not an invitation, but an end to the conversation.

When Ray turns back to me, his voice is even, his expression neutral. "You need to get going. You don't want the boys being late."

I nod, a lump rising in my throat. He rinses out his cup, puts it in the dishwasher, and brushes past me, without another word.

And just like that our argument doesn't end but ceases. Is that the meaning of a ceasefire? Nothing gets resolved. You just stop shooting at each other?

I'm confused. And so frustrated. I hear Ray and the boys talking, and there's clearly not going to be any further discussion. *I guess that's it.*

I'm out the door in plenty of time for the school run.

Ray whistles. "Y'all have one good system in place. I'm flashing back to my army training days."

That stops me at the driver's door, coffee in one hand, my purse dangling from the other.

"Army? What army?" I ask at the same time that Atticus blurts out, "You were in the army?"

Ray nods as he opens my door and takes me cup. "Sure was. Four years, two tours. And the U.S. Army, what other army would I be talking about?"

"Wow!" Atticus and Ernie exclaim.

"Wow," I repeat. Is it odd I don't know my husband was in the army? Should I know this? I mean, we weren't babies when we got married. We both lived a lot of life. But the fact I don't know at all, is that a problem?

"Were you in a war?" Ernie asks.

"Naw, nothing that noble. Just a regular ol' country boy, straight outta high school, with no plans, rebelling against being a farmer. I came back at twenty-two and put my globe-trotting days behind me."

"That's...wild." Ray tilts his head to the side, looking surprised by my response. I try again. "I mean, it's just, that's not nothing, being in the military."

He shrugs. "I thought I might use it to pay for college. Came back and decided the farm was the life. Never put a dime of that money to use. But I'm glad I did it. It gave me a chance to see places I'd probably never see in real life otherwise."

I feel small and less than hearing this. I've lived in the same place my whole life. Until we moved to the farm, I'd never lived more than fifteen minutes from my parents' house. My best friend is the same best friend I had in college, and again, until we moved to the farm, I'd never lived more than fifteen minutes from her either. Not much adventure or real life in that.

"You alright?" Ray puts the coffee cup in my hand, holding onto the driver's side door. Whatever that conversation in the kitchen was, he's worried about me now.

"I'm surprised you never mentioned it. That's all."

"Does it bother you?"

I don't know if it does, so I shrug. "We need to get going."

26.

On the drive home, I call Angie. It's after eight, and her twins are off to middle school by way of her husband. Her three youngest, fifth grade and down, are at home, ready for a day of home-schooling plus managing the baby. She answers halfway through the first ring.

"Hey, I–Simon, for the love of all that's holy, get her juice, please–what's up?"

Mostly it's clear when she's speaking to me and when she's shouting at her ten-year-old. "I have something to ask you, and it might be weird, but I don't know for sure." I switch to speakerphone.

"OK. What is it? Carmen, stop it, he's getting it. GIVE HIM A MINUTE."

"It's just–"

"Spit it out. No, not you, Car. Auntie Iris is on the phone. Let's go, lady, you know I can't do this all day. Spill."

"Ray was in the army. And I didn't know that. Is that weird?"

Angie laughs. "Probably not, considering you've known him for about five minutes. When? Recently?"

I frown. Sometimes teasing is fine, sometimes not. "After high school. I knew he didn't go to college. Apparently, he joined the army instead. Four years, and then he came back to the farm."

"So now you know." She waits, and when I'm silent, she asks, "What's the problem? You don't like that he was in the army?"

"No. I mean, I don't care. That's not right either. It's fine he was in the army. Great even! Maybe that's why he's so tidy. I just didn't know."

"Right. Again, remember five minutes. I mean, what did you think he did if he didn't go to college? And hurry, these kids are sixty seconds away from total meltdown. When he told you, 'I didn't go to college,' what did you think happened after that?"

I consider it.

"Iris!"

"I didn't think about it!" Gah, she's so bossy. "I didn't think about it. It was one conversation, and then we went off to talk about something else. It never occurred to me to ask him again."

"Hey, Carmen, get your folder, OK? Daddy left it in your room last night." I can hear her shift. From the sounds of laughing and talking fading away, I assume she's on her own for a moment except for baby Miguel, who's softly babbling nearby. "So what's up? Does it feel like he hid it?"

"No, not at all. He was so casual about it, it came out in passing this morning. He traveled all over the place."

"And?"

"I don't know. It makes him more experienced than I realized. He's traveled and done this different work. It's not the way I imagined him."

"Country farming bumpkin?"

"No! Not a bumpkin. But maybe a country farmer, yes."

"And instead, he's got some experience, and he's seen things. Things you haven't."

I grit my teeth at that last line. I don't like it. "A little, I suppose. Not a lot. But a little."

Angie's quiet, long enough for me to demand, "Are you still there?"

"Sorry, sorry. Just having a sip of my coffee and thinking. You know, he's going to be different than you imagine. They always are."

"Who?"

"The people we love. There's who we imagine them to be. And there's reality. Before we brought Car home and I only saw pictures from the agency, I thought, 'There she is. There's my little angel.' And then this hellion showed up, and the only English she knew was 'holy crap,' and she shouted it a thousand times a day, every day, and pinched everybody. And she was mad all the time."

"I remember."

"So my point is, don't walk into this with the picture already colored in. You've got a lot of lines right now, and the outline they make is Ray. But don't assume that getting married means you know each other completely. OK?"

Did I assume that? Did she think I got married and decided we now had every piece of information we could ever want about each other? Gah. C'mon.

I say, "You could give me a little more credit than that. I'm not that stupid."

Angie laughs gently. "Honey, we're all exactly that stupid. At least when it comes to spouses and kids, we're exactly that stupid. Don't let it throw you, OK? Now, I have to go. They're all here. Two laughing, one crying. We'll see how this plays out."

She hangs up, and I simmer the rest of the drive home.

Of course, I realized I didn't have years and years with Ray. Unlike Angie and José, we didn't meet in college and stay together forever, amen. But did that mean we couldn't know each other? No! That was bogus.

By the time I navigate my car into the gravel driveway, past his mother's house, then his brother's house, and finally land in our gravel drive, I know exactly what we need to do.

Except he hasn't responded to my texts and he isn't home. It's not surprising, but part of me hoped he'd be waiting, maybe pacing, ready to explain whatever the argument about Dennis was.

I drop my head against the steering wheel. *Think, Iris, think.* We need to get to know each other right now. Waiting is a terrible idea. I need to find him.

I fire up the car and turn around. He's not here, but I know where to find him.

And I'm about to uncover everything I'm missing.

27.

I'd learned Myrtle's house was ground zero for all farming operations. The greenhouses and high tunnels are most easily accessed from here. The concrete pad, with the two walk-in refrigerators and two walk-in freezers, sits behind her house. There's a double barn, stocked with animal feed and tools along with where to park the new tractor. If I need Ray and he's on the farm, there's a good chance he'll be around here.

And I'm right. As I park, I spot a group gathered around the picnic table. There's Myrtle, Ricky, Ray, and, ugh, The Lovely Naomi next to him. They're studying something on the table.

"Third night in a row. And I don't think there's anything we can do for her," Ray's saying, "We've got to–"

He stops when he spots me, and I wave. His brow furrows, his expression confused, as he comes towards me.

They all look. I wave, smiling, heart in my throat. Myrtle scowls and turns away from me. Well, that's how you kill a hopeful mood.

Ricky, who I expect noticed Myrtle's less-than-friendly greeting, waves back and calls out, "Morning, Iris! How're you today?"

Friendliness. Take it, seize it, embrace it. I beam at him hoping to generate waves of warmth. "I'm great, Ricky. How're you?"

"So-so," he says and shrugs. "I've had better mornings."

Naomi hasn't reacted to me. She's focused on the table.

"Hey, what's going on?" Ray catches my hands. "Everything OK? Boys OK?"

His response surprises me. "Yeah, everything's fine."

That seems to settle him down. "Good. I thought something might be wrong."

I refuse to be daunted. "I wanted to find you, and you weren't answering your phone."

Ray pats his pockets and comes up empty-handed. "Where'd my phone go? I felt it buzz." He looks down as if he might spot it in the grass. "I set it down somewhere."

Who doesn't know where their phone is?

Someone without kids.

It's the first thought that pops into my mind, but I know it's right. When you don't have kids at school, you have the luxury of putting your phone down and forgetting it. I haven't had that experience in years.

And that irritates me. Ray doesn't have his own kids, but he has my kids now. What if there had been an emergency with the boys? What good would he have been with his phone goodness-knows-where?

"Ray, a little help," Myrtle yells.

Ray looks at me, torn. "Honey, we're having a raccoon issue, and I've got to deal with it. Did you need me?"

Yes! I want to shout. *I need you to tell me every detail of your history. Pay special attention to your time in the army and your marriage to Heidi. GO.*

However, I hear the words in my head. And I feel the presence of people waiting impatiently for my husband.

Time to roll up my sleeves and help. "It can wait. What's going on over here?"

Ray calls, "Iris, wait!"

But it's too late. I've already seen it.

My father often said trying to get my mother and I off to school on time was like watching chickens running around with their heads cut off.

Never in my life have I imagined what that looks like.

To be fair, the chicken on the picnic table still has a head. But its face has been torn, and its neck slashed halfway open. It's breathing, but barely.

I want to say I stayed calm. Collected.

Instead, I shriek, "Holy friggin' moly!" My hands fly to my face.

The chicken rustles on the table.

"Get her out of here. She's in enough distress without that mess." Myrtle sounds frustrated.

Myrtle's kindness calms me down. Except when I glance at her, she jerks a hand in my direction, not looking at me.

Oh. I see.

The chicken is the one in distress.

I'm the one who needs to be removed.

Ray puts his hands on my shoulder. "C'mon, love. You should get back to your day."

It's an awful sight. But I'm a farmer's wife, aren't I?

It's been an urban dream of mine to keep chickens. Angie and her family have four hens in their backyard. They followed the proper steps, applied for a permit from the city, had the coop plan approved, José built it, and they got six baby chicks. Two of the chicks died early on, but they're in their second year of chicken care, and she loved it.

"Sometimes," she confided to me, "I'll say I'm going to check on the girls. But really, I scroll Instagram while they peck around me."

OK, maybe that isn't the best example of the peaceful and meditative experience Angie has with the chickens. But I know she loves it.

I shake Ray off. "I'm OK. What happened?"

Naomi speaks up. "Raccoon. We've had one in the coop every night for the last three nights."

I put my hand to my mouth. "Three nights? Does that mean three chickens like this?"

Myrtle snorts. "Are you kidding me?" She eyeballs me. "It means dozens of dead chickens. And Ray's right, we can't save this one."

I risk another glance at the chicken's neck. Oh, it's bad. *Yikes yikes yikes.* "What about a vet?"

There are five people around the table, including me, and four of them exchange a look confirming how incredibly stupid I sound.

"Ricky," Myrtle says, and he silently lopes off to the barn.

I appeal to Ray again. "Surely there's something we can do? I mean, she's a survivor. That has to count for something."

Ricky has put something in Myrtle's hand. A butcher knife, she's got a butcher knife.

"Nononono." Hands out to Myrtle, I look like an agonized traffic cop. "No."

The knife comes down fast and sure. When the head's off, Naomi bundles the hen in the plastic tarp it's on and moves it down to the grass.

To what? Bleed out? WHAT IS THIS WORLD?

"Ray!" I turn to my husband, who tries to wrap his arms around me.

"It's the most humane thing, honey. That hen was suffering."

Tears are in my eyes, hot, angry tears, but I will not let them fall. Myrtle's watching me, her expression is daring me, asking me, *What are you going to do about it?*

Ray's words make sense; this was the humane decision.

But I feel so confused by everything happening. I need something to anchor to, to give me some purpose in this awful situation.

"The other chickens, what about them?" The words pop out of my mouth.

Myrtle's gaze is unflinching. "The dozen we have left? We'll try to protect them tonight–"

I turn to Ray. "Put their coop next to our house. We'll keep an eye on them."

Ray hesitates. "Honey, I don't know–"

"Wouldn't a raccoon be less likely to come so close to a house?"

"Might be. Not a guarantee, but maybe." It's Ricky, and his expression is kind.

"I say we get rid of all of them," Myrtle says. "Let's be done with it, the whole thing."

"And do what with them?" I ask.

"Stew birds."

My gasp is so loud Ray reaches out to me. "Iris, this is farm life."

I can't afford emotion. It's so clear in the faces around me—Myrtle's displeasure, Ray's frustration, Naomi's pity. If I want them to listen to me, I have to behave like them. Steady and straightforward.

"I want to help. I'm asking for this, for my own project."

Nothing. Not one expression is different. Did they not hear that heartfelt request?

"The boys and I could do it. They'd love to be included."

"I bet your kids will love it." It's Ricky again, nodding. "It's a good idea, Myrtie."

Did he call Myrtle "Myrtie"? I'm temporarily distracted, watching the two of them. Is there a vibe here?

"Iris? Are you listening?" Ray looks bemused.

I want to say, "He called your mother 'Myrtie!'" The way Ray's eyes twinkle, I think he noticed.

Behind me, Myrtle grumbles, "Oh, for Pete's sake."

Ray keeps talking, determined to get my attention. "We'll bring the coop to the house. We'll have to wait to move the hens after dark though."

"Why?"

Ray's smiling at me. "You'll find out tonight when you help me move 'em."

28.

"This is so cool." Ernie dances on his tiptoes, wiggling with excitement.

"Alright now," Ray whispers, a hand on each boy's shoulder. "Stay still until I give the signal. Everyone knows your job?"

He looks up and down the line. There are six of us in total, with Naomi and Brandon rounding out our family of four. It's dark out, almost eight o'clock, and we're in a pasture, near a large and quiet henhouse.

It's spooky, being out in the dark, in the field. Chirps, hums, occasional howls, it makes me shiver. And in March, it's still cold.

Ray assured me all the chicken carnage from last night's chicken raid has been cleaned up. There are a dozen sleeping, healthy chickens inside.

That's where we come in.

By the time the boys and I were home from school, there were two one-and-a-half-story chicken coops in front of our house. Ray was pressure washing one. The other already looked clean. There were a few half-bales of hay stacked up next to it, along with some other tools and pieces.

"What's this?" Ernie hurtled up to the coop, chucking his backpack down in his wake.

"This is our new chicken coop, courtesy of your mother."

The coops were matching structures, each with a chicken run in a wooden frame with chicken wire and a little wooden ramp leading up to the second story of a wooden chicken house.

"What do you think?" Ray asked.

I nodded. "Great. I mean, they could be prettier, but...."

"But they're working chicken coops?" Ray supplied.

"I was going to say, 'But I can fix that later.'" I grinned at him, and he grinned back. Harmony had been restored.

"Where are the chickens?" Atticus peered inside one. Ernie had barreled inside it, crawling around on all fours.

"Still in their old house," Ray said. "That's part of our project. The three of us are going to finish getting this bad boy in shape." He petted the side of the coop. "And tonight we'll bring home the chickens."

And now, instead of getting the boys ready for bed, here we stand, ready to move some chickens.

"Are they going to wake up?" It was Atticus' biggest fear.

Ray sounds confident. "If anything happens and you get nervous, drop her. I'll catch her."

"Drop her?" Atticus looks horrified.

"Well, not hard," Ray replies with exaggerated emphasis on the hard, and Atticus laughs.

Behind us on the truck's flatbed are four dog crates. "The goal," Ray reminds us, and by us, I mean the boys and me, as Naomi and Brandon know exactly what they're doing, "is to get the chickens into the crates without waking them up. We need to do it calmly, or all hell's gonna break loose. You got it?"

Immediately both boys swing to look at me, and Atticus mouths, "Bad word."

I can't even laugh. *It's going to be fine. This is fine.*

I'm nervous. I've never touched a chicken in my life. Dogs are fine, and cats are fine, but something with feathers feels like raising the stakes.

"Alright, let's go."

This coop is almost tall enough to stand up in. Ray, Naomi, and I duck, the boys following me. There's a stinky smell, reminiscent of the petting zoo, and a faint aroma of hay that doesn't fully mask it. I wrinkle my nose but stay on task.

Ray reaches out and scoops one chicken up with one arm and a second with his other. Naomi does the same, no big deal. Before I can stop him, Ernie's got both arms wrapped around a hen. Atticus follows suit, and, when he turns to me, he's beaming.

"I can feel her heart beating," he whispers, and I give him my exaggerated mother face where I make my eyes big and nod animatedly and basically respond like he's figured out how to end world hunger.

The six who are left are asleep, undisturbed. This explains how a raccoon can come into a coop and tear it to the ground in a few minutes. Not very sensitive to danger, are they?

Ray's already back, ready for round two.

"You OK?" he mouths.

I nod. He scoops up two more and scoots past me.

"You don't have to."

It's Naomi. She's speaking so softly it's barely discernible. "If it makes you nervous, we can finish up."

And she nods as if encouraging me.

Internally, I bristle. No way am I not doing this. She's got a bird in each arm, ready to go.

No way will I be chicken shamed by The Lovely Naomi. It's now or never.

I reach one arm out, feeling feather and not much else. The hen's so light, she feels more like loosely put-together bones under a thick pillow of feathers.

It's weird but manageable.

I should go. Let Ray get the last one.

And then Naomi, apparently still hovering, whispers, "Good job, Iris."

I stiffen. The hen shifts but doesn't wake.

"Ray will get the other one," she adds and slips out the coop door.

That settles it. She might have some weird, psychic connection with my husband, but she doesn't have it with me. If she can get two chickens, so can I.

Having one feathered creature under one arm makes it awkward to scoop the second. And instead of settling my hand around the chicken's stomach, I catch her foot and accidentally pinch.

And that is when, as Ray might say, all hell breaks loose. The hen wakes up and tries to take flight. I hang on for dear life while she leaves claw marks down my wrist. In our scuffle, I drop the second hen who scuttles away. We all burst out of the coop. Naomi somehow gets involved, shouting orders at me that I ignore because, frankly, I don't want her telling me what to do. Still, she wrestles the bird away from me. The pain in my hand stops at once, the hen calms down, and peace is restored.

"I was just—just trying to calm her down," I puff.

Ray scoops up the last chicken, and she doesn't flinch.

"Are you alright?" he asks.

I'm bright red from exertion and humiliation.

"Your hand's bleeding," Naomi says.

It's throbbing, and I want to whimper. "It's nothing."

Ray comes closer. "Honey, let me take a look."

I shake him off, too.

I want to go. My hand hurts, my head throbs, and my mortification might be more painful than both of them. "I panicked," I mutter to Naomi. "I'm sorry."

And to her credit, she replies, "It's OK, don't worry. That must have been the high strung one." She smiles kindly, and my humiliation is complete.

The boys watch me, faces rapt.

"Mom, you almost killed dat chicken." Ernie's eyes are huge.

"It was an accident." I take a breath and remind myself, no one ever died of embarrassment. Or chicken scratches. Well, maybe. Someone might have died from chicken scratches.

Atticus silently stares at my bloody arm, horrified.

Once in the truck with the boys, I drop my head and exhale. I'm sore and tired, and the sight of Ray and Naomi in the rearview mirror, riding in companionable silence on the truck bed, makes my stomach throb.

Brandon, at the wheel, glances at my arm and whistles. "Make sure Ray gets a look at that when you get home."

"I will."

"And if anyone says anything tomorrow, you just tell 'em, 'You should see the other guy. What a chicken.'"

And that does it. The four of us ride back to our house howling with laughter, the tension broken.

29.

However, when Ray wakes me up earlier than our already unholy wakeup time, I'm not laughing.

"Those chickens aren't going to feed and water themselves."

I crack one eye open. "What?"

Ray kisses me lightly and says, "The chickens. Do you remember them?"

Approaching the coop this morning, my steps are hesitant, gingerly, while Atticus and Ernie dart forward. They're quiet and calm, exactly as Ray instructed them to do. Ray calls out, "Alright, fellas, let 'em out."

I whip around. "Let them out?"

Ray, leaning in the doorway of our house, coffee mug in hand, watches. "Yep."

And suddenly chickens swish past my ankles. I do a hop-step into the air and only avoid coming down on one.

"Careful!" Ray's laughing and shaking his head. "Honey, they won't bother you. They're trying to get the best grub."

"Grub?" Atticus echoes.

"Worms. Bugs. All the good stuff."

"I thought that was breakfast." Atticus points to the sacks of feed stacked up next to the coop.

"It is. We'll fill up their feeder and check their water while they're out here." Ray drains his coffee cup and heads into the yard, clapping his hands together. "Alrighty, who's ready for a lesson in livestock?"

***

Not me. I know that as I load the kids into the car twenty minutes later and head towards school. The boys are in great spirits, chattering about the hens, suggesting names, and choosing favorites. I've had to change my pants and shoes after overflowing the chicken waterer.

It's lovely. They're so happy. However, I am unsure right now.

As I slide into the driver's side, Ray follows me and says, "I'll get them put up."

I buckle and peer up at him. "Who?"

"The chickens." Ray looks startled. "They'll be a Happy Meal for some happy hawk if we leave them out."

Great. Step one thousand eighteen of the caring for chickens assignment.

Doubt floods me, worse than the water in my boots that morning.

Are chickens a terrible idea? On the drive home, I call Angie, and I don't dillydally when she answers. "Do you like keeping chickens?"

"They're fine. Why?"

I do my best to give a fast edition of what's transpired. I get sidetracked when describing Myrtle's merciless beheading, but Angie steers us back on track.

"So you're worried it's going to be messy?" she says when I finish.

I wrinkle my brow. "I don't know. They're sort of weird, chickens. They look good on Pinterest, but in real life, I don't know. You think soft and fluffy, but you pick one up, and they're all bony and pokey feathers. And claws." I add as my hand throbs.

There's an odd snuffling sound on Angie's end. "Angie? Are you OK?"

And then the peal of laughter that rips down the phone practically shakes my car windows. "Iris! Iris, you are, you are one-of-a-kind." She's hee-hawing.

Why, thank you, I think, but it doesn't sound like a compliment. "Why do you say that?"

"It's just 'they're all bony and pokey feathers.' Oh, hon, it's too good. You're too good."

I sulk while she laughs, but eventually she comes back to the conversation.

"It's a learning process," is her counsel. "They really are interesting. The kids love watching them. I think, if you give it some time, they'll settle in. And so will you."

This cheers me up. "OK. OK." I nod to myself. "I've got this. I can do this."

30.

By the time I'm home, I have a plan. The chickens and I need time together. In each other's element, breathing each other's air.

I admit the air around them isn't lovely. The coop is fresh and clean, but the barnyard smell remains. Not the nice hay smell, like when you imagine Jesus in the manger. More like hay is the air freshener used to cover up the fact animals stink.

But it won't derail me. I do some rearranging, and soon the four-person patio set is organized next to the coops. The end of winter in the south can be quite pleasant. Today the sky is blue, the temperature mild, and, after I make another cup of coffee, I'm ready to get started.

My work station is set up, a tub of yarn, my knitting needles, and my basket for completed projects. A podcast plays on my phone. And I'm knitting away, both listening to their chuffs and little trill sounds while working on a new round of baby clothes.

I've neglected my work. Andie and Werking Girl Collab wiped out the items I'd made in preparation for the market. My stock is woefully depleted, which is a great thing for money and a bad thing for the upcoming market.

As my hands work, my shoulders soften and relax, coming down from around my ears to their natural position and my breathing steadies. Maybe that's why this is the one art I've been able to maintain? It settles me down instead of winding me up.

Tires crunch across the gravel drive and my instinct is Ray.

It's Myrtle.

My shoulders shoot back up under my ears.

Instead of driving right up next to me and blowing dust all over my fine baby items, she pulls into the grass opposite the house. I hop up, and as soon as she's out of her car, I start talking.

"Thanks for that." I gesture to her parking spot. "I'm taking a risk having all this outside." And I gesture to my work.

She looks between my knitting and me and says, "I did it for the chickens."

Of course, she did.

She's rooting around at the back of the truck. "Frankly, I don't understand what it is you do. I mean, baby clothes? That keeps you and your boys fed?" She sticks her head around the side of the car and cocks an eyebrow at me.

"Yeah, it did. I mean, now with Ray and I being married, it takes some of the pressure off."

She snorts at this. Actually snorts. My temper flickers.

"Not that I married Ray for that reason." My voice rises a few octaves.

"Sure."

Is she for real? Is she standing across the gravel road, in front of Ray's two-bedroom 1950s rancher, implying I married her son for financial security?

"I mean, it's great, not being totally responsible for every single thing. But if I were marrying for money, I don't know that I'd pick a farmer."

I'm careful. In no way do I want to insult my loyal, hardworking, one-of-a-kind husband.

And yet, I can tell you right now, farmers are not well paid. Those folks at the farmers' market who want to squawk about the cost of an heirloom tomato or a pound of local ground beef? Those folks have no idea how much money these farmers pump into their infrastructure, supplies, livestock, certifications, and employees. It's a costly business.

Myrtle, however, looks unconvinced.

"You know how much Ray makes, you can hardly accuse me of being a gold digger!" I tug my heavy cardigan around myself, creating protection from her unforgiving scrutiny.

"It's a nice inheritance." Myrtle's tone is cool. "Now, Dennis mentioned you've been redecorating so I brought a few things over."

And just like that, she's moved on. But I haven't.

Struggling to stay calm, I say, "Myrtle, please understand, money didn't factor into any of this. I was doing just fine as a single mom."

"Just fine" could be an overstatement. No need to mention we were about to lose our rental house and one of my biggest clients when Ray and I got married. But that was the last month. We'd managed these last six or so years.

"All I'm saying is raising four kids on my own took a helluva lot of effort and willpower. And not everyone's got that." Myrtle unearths a small end table from her car, pins it against her hip, and turns to me.

I gape at her, but she ignores it, shoves the table into my arms, and walks back to her SUV. "Since, as you say, farming doesn't have any money in it, I thought you could use this." She's holding a lamp now, some awful thing with a glass base and a thick lampshade edged with tassels.

When I don't move, she waves a hand at me. "I don't have all day. Let's go."

And somehow I'm leading Myrtle into my house, staggering under the weight of something I never wanted in the first place.

31.

The house is messy from the morning rush. I say as much as Myrtle leads the way inside.

She surveys the place, that eyebrow always up. "I thought you got them to school hours ago."

Nuts. Of course, she knows that. She drove up to see me sitting at my patio table, knitting. I exhale and force a bright smile. "Right. That's right. But I had to get to work. I'm falling behind with all the things. Anyway, the house is a bit messy, that's all!" It doesn't help that this dumb end table is heavy, and I'm huffing to finish speaking.

The house isn't too bad, thanks to Ray. I've learned he prefers life on the tidy side. This isn't a strength of mine, but I'm trying. He cleared up the cereal bowls left in the sink, added them to the ancient dishwasher, and wiped off the table.

Still, blankets and books are scattered around. The boys' socks are everywhere, two on the living room rug, one on the sofa, and one, inexplicably, on the dining table. My tea mug is still on the end table. A basket of clean laundry graces the armchair. And the boys' art, which, yes, is mainly coloring sheets, covers the table.

Shoot. Why aren't I tidier? Why can't I be one of those women who finishes a coffee cup and carries it straight to the sink instead of being one of those women who sets her mug down, gets distracted, goes to check her phone, forgets her drink, and makes a second cup later?

"Lordy, it looks like something from a flea market."

She's not talking about the mess. She's talking about my home decor.

She's talking about the curated, styled, intentionally crafted home I've made.

I can't speak. There aren't any words.

Myrtle doesn't notice. She's looking around her and zeroes in on my dining room table. There's a centerpiece, a white porcelain tray, with a collection of pinecones and wisps of pine needles the boys and I collected, scattered around two round, squat beeswax candles. It's our winter tablescape, something we do each season. She shakes her head and uses her free arm to sweep the tablescape aside. Then she sets her lamp down, on top of the coloring papers, brushing the dust from her hands.

"Dennis said you'd been trying to redecorate, but I didn't realize it was this bad. I have more things up at the house. I'll bring another load this week."

Another load? She thinks I want "another load" of random items from her house. I'm gaping, gasping, partially because of this dumb table I'm holding. I let go, and it lands with a *thud* on the floor.

"Careful now," Myrtle warns.

My phone buzzes. I turn my back to her.

It's Ray, and there's no preamble on his part. "Hey, hon, I think my mother might be on her way to the house."

I form words through clenched jaws. "Yep, that's right."

"Ah, she's already there?"

"Yes again."

He exhales, a big gusty sigh. "OK. Look, whatever she says, don't take her too seriously. Alright? Mama's good about a lot of things, but keeping her thoughts to herself isn't one of them."

"The state of these blankets!" Myrtle stands next to the sofa, holding up a buttermilk yellow quilt my grandmother made some fifty years ago. Sure, it's threadbare, and there are patches where the fabric is thin enough to see through. But it's also as soft as cotton, heavy and cozy, and as beautiful as it was when she first made it. OK, I don't know exactly what it looked like when she made it because I wasn't alive fifty years ago. But to me, that blanket is perfect.

And now it's in Myrtle's chubby hand, and she's glaring at it, lips pursed.

"Myrtle, let me stop you right there," I say.

"Iris? Are you there?" Ray! He's still there. I put the phone back to my ear.

I've missed the last few things he's said. "What was that again?"

"The best way to handle my mother is to let her finish and then ask her advice for something else. Something you really need help with."

"Something I really need help with," I murmur, drawing a blank. What do I need help with? Where to find the best price on canned baked beans? JoAnn's versus Michael's for statement art pieces?

"Iris, I hate to be sharp, but could you put the phone down? Surely, your mother raised you better than that." Myrtle looks at me with exaggerated patience.

I open and close my mouth a few times before I say to Ray, "I have to go."

"It's going to be fine, love. I'll see you–"

I don't know when he'll see me because I've already ended the call.

I keep it simple. "I'm sorry."

She shakes her head. "It's OK. We won't worry about it. Now, I brought you this." She gestures to the lamp, which is not only ugly but big and dominating our four-person table. "I'll leave it with you. And I'll poke around the house, see what else I can find."

"Myrtle, please, don't."

She stops.

"I, this, well, you might not like it, but this is how I decorate. It's who I am."

Her jaws tighten, but I need her to understand. "These threadbare quilts, my grandmother made? I love them. And a lot of this is older, yes, but that's because I thrifted it. And I'm happy about that," I add as she opens her mouth to interrupt. "I, I don't need anything from your house. I'm sure it's lovely. But I don't need it."

Talk about looking stormy. She's offended. My stomach drops. Frustration and guilt fight for supremacy. I didn't ask for her help. This isn't my fault she's here. And, by the way, she's the one trampling all over me and my eclectic style.

This is impossible. Myrtle and I have nothing in common.

We're both silent. She glowers at me. Looking anywhere but her, my gaze lands on the window. Where I see–

"Chickens!"

Myrtle's eyes widen. "Excuse me?"

I take a breath, working to calm down. "The chickens," I try again. "Do you, do you have any advice?"

"Advice on your rescue project?" And she gives me a smile that's half friendly and half bemused.

I blink at her. "What?"

"Your rescue project. That's what we're calling it around the farm. Iris' Rescue Project."

There's a group, a "we," mocking my saving the chickens. It transports me straight back to high school, me waving my "save the whales" flyers at kids headed to class, who either laughed at me or ignored me completely.

This isn't high school. My hands are clenched, working so hard to remind myself, this is different. This is my grown-up life.

"Yeah," I say at last, thinking of my husband, who I adore, and reminding myself she is his mother. "My rescue project. Could you give me some pointers?"

32.

She's his mother. She's his mother. She's his mother.

It's my new mantra. After spending another thirty minutes with Myrtle, I have to remind myself of this.

To be fair, her chicken tutorial went far more smoothly than Ray's. She broke it down into clear, manageable pieces. I paid attention, kept up, and now I've got a sheet of tidy notes on chicken care.

As we shoo the chickens back into their coop, I wonder out loud, "Should I keep track of their egg production? Just note the days and number of eggs?"

Now, I don't naturally love data. But I've learned, through trial and error in my business, if I track how many sweaters I sell in May versus how many baby sweaters I sell in October, I'm better able to predict how many sweaters to have on hand the following May and October. And that is useful.

"That's a thought," Myrtle says, and her tone stops me. She pauses, touching her chin, considering it.

Buoyed, I mention my spreadsheets for my work. She appraises me for a long moment.

"That's pretty slick. Must help."

I nod. "It's amazing how similar the numbers are. Plus I can make an educated guess on growth, and I've been spot on so far."

"Look at you. I'm constantly on the boys to keep better records. But do they listen to me? They do not." She rolls her eyes and even chuckles. "We need more of your thinking around here."

The joy that one phrase brings me.

"Now, I've got to go."

"Are you sure?"

I think it surprises us both when I say that. But now that we're out of my house and Myrtle isn't critiquing every item I hold dear, I'm enjoying her company. Somewhat.

"Yes, I'm sure. I'm meeting Ricky at the house."

"Ooh, fun!"

She looks bemused. "Not fun. Business."

"It could be both? I mean, he's cute. Is he single? I didn't notice a ring."

Myrtle's gotten as far as opening her car door. She looks to the sky and shakes her head. "I couldn't say as to the cute, Iris. But yes, he's single. He's a widower as a matter of fact."

That gives me pause. "I'm sorry."

She nods. "It was a sad thing. His wife was a real kind lady. I liked her a lot."

"When did she pass?"

Myrtle exhales, a sound similar to the one I made when she was critiquing my home decor. "It's been about ten years now."

"Ten years! Myrtle, that's sad. But it's also a decade. That's plenty of time."

She turns and looks at me squarely. "Plenty of time for what exactly, Iris?"

If anyone has an eagle eye, it's Myrtle Fox. I squirm under the intensity of it. "You know. Have a coffee together."

"I expect we'll drink coffee today." She's wry.

"Not like that!" Why is she being so difficult?

"Goodbye, Iris."

"Bye, Myrtle. Tell Ricky I said hi."

"If you want to speak to him, you tell him yourself." And with that she climbs into her SUV, a petite, chubby, determined woman, and shoots off, without a backward glance.

33.

It's stuck with me, though. He knows my history, but I know so little of his. My parents have been married to each other for forty years now. No siblings. No close immediate family. My parents, my two boys, and me. That's the sum of who I am.

But here's Ray with a mother, a sister, and two brothers. And that doesn't bring in his sister-in-law, The Lovely Naomi, Ricky, none of them.

When Ray and I were dating, I used to imagine a solitary life for him. Lonely even. Farming during the day, him and the cows, him and the vegetables. Going to bed at night, in this little house, all on his own.

Now I wonder. Was that the right picture? Angie's words come back to me: *Don't walk into this with the picture already colored in.*

"When did your dad leave?"

I slip the question in, casually, while we clean the kitchen and the boys get their bath.

Ray pauses at the dishwasher, wet plate in hand. "What's that now?"

I close the refrigerator door and turn back. "Your dad, when did he leave?"

"O-K. That's a surprising question."

I wait. Ray sighs and returns to loading the dishwasher. "Let's see. I was eleven. So that would have been twenty-four years ago."

"And your mom never remarried?"

"As you can see, she did not."

I shrug. "She could have. She could have remarried and divorced again. Or remarried and he died. A lot can happen in twenty-four years."

Ray nods. "That's true. But it didn't. Daddy left, and Mama stayed here and took over. Well," he pauses, "really, she was always in charge. It was her daddy's farm, and she was running it with my granddad when my dad left."

"So he didn't work on the farm?"

"He did. Sparingly. He wasn't much of a worker if you know what I mean."

Thinking about what I've seen of Myrtle, that doesn't sound like her. When the boys and I head to school in the morning, we often leave by way of the big house, and we see her, out in her sunhat and gardening gloves, working in her glass greenhouse. And when we're almost home from school at four in the afternoon, her car is gone as often as not.

"I wonder what brought them together."

Ray closes the dishwasher and dries his hands on a dishtowel. "What do you mean?"

"I wonder what attracted them to each other. Why would your mom, who works so hard, marry a man who 'wasn't much of a wor ker.'"

Ray shakes his head. "I couldn't say, darlin'. We don't talk about Raymond Fox Sr. much around here."

That brings me up short. "Raymond? You're named after him?"

"I am."

He meets my gaze, direct and clear as always. Yet he can't hide the twitch in his jaw. Just the tiniest tick, not noticeable to almost anyone.

But I see it. I reach for him and slip into his arms. "Doesn't mean anything about you. Not a bit."

"You don't reckon?" Ray's tone is light, but his eyes search my face. "He wasn't a great guy, ol' Raymond. A real louse as a matter of fact."

"Then clearly you having his name doesn't mean anything. Because you might be the best man I know."

I love the way Ray's eyes crinkle at the corners when he smiles. Sure, some of its age and sun damage, but it's also the way his eyes and mouth work in tandem–he smiles with his entire face.

His face does that now, a slow shift from disheartened to joyful, and it's all for me. I bask in the sunshine of it. I want to do this the rest of my life, get this man to smile at me with that look of pure adoration.

He leans down, brushing his lips up my neck across my jaw bone. It gives me shivers as his mouth finds mine, the longing between us deep and thick. It almost overwhelms me, eyes closing slowly, while my heartbeat and breath speed up. My man. My person. My husband.

Little boy shrieks and a crash of water from the bathroom shuts the moment down. Ray pulls back, biting his lower lip. "To be continued," he says, and I nod, breathless. "I'll tag in, and we'll put these beasts to bed. And then, Mrs. Fox, I'll put you to bed, too." And that grin breaks out one more time just for me.

34.

Over the last month, we've fallen into a routine. Ray and I work together, getting everyone ready for the day, then he heads out to work while I drive the boys to school and come back. I spend my morning helping him on the farm and the afternoons building my stock of baby knits. And then it's back to pick up the boys, a few minutes to take care of the chickens, and then it's time to start dinner.

Which we may or may not eat as soon as it's ready. Ray's erratic schedule means dinner often waits thirty minutes or longer until he's home. He'll walk in the door, the boys will fall on the meal, ravenous, and Ray will say, "Aw, hon, you don't have to wait on me."

I give him the same answer each time. "We're waiting on you." He's finally stopped suggesting we eat without him.

What does he think, I got married and created this family of four so we could still behave like a family of three?

And, if I'm being honest, my hope, or possibly mission, is to guilt Ray into getting home earlier. If he knows the boys are hungry and we're waiting on him, surely that will get him moving faster? I don't want us to eat as a family of four. I want my husband home by six. My goodness, he started his work day at seven thirty. Can't he commit to being home almost eleven hours later?

It's working. Sort of. He's home on time more days than he's not. Sometimes he's cranky and mutters about "just needed five more minutes to finish repairing that irrigation system." Fine, be irritable. We're irritable, too. We're hungry.

The weekends feel less complicated. Ray works some Saturdays, but he's always home before lunch, and we have the rest of the weekend to ourselves. And Sunday is my sweet spot. Yes, it's another day of driving to Harrisville, but I'm in the passenger seat, relaxed, watching the green hills and pastures roll by turning into stores and neighborhoods, as Ray gets us to my church, our church, for the morning service.

"Iris, we're so glad you guys are still here with us," Deacon Beth tells me during the passing of the peace. We hug, and she adds, "Of course, we'd understand if you found a church there. But we want you here."

"Trust me, I'd rather be here."

Deacon Beth's eyes widen, but she's smiling. Perhaps that sounds more aggressive than I meant.

Moving through the people back to Ray and the boys, they're chatting with our friends and former neighbors, Dee and Derrick and Tom and Rishi. Seeing them brings up a wave of sadness. We lived right down the street from Tom and Rishi and a street over from Dee and Derrick. Plenty of Sundays we saw each other walking to church. Now we're hauling it in from thirty-plus minutes away. And they're all here, fresh and happy, life untouched by dramatic and sweeping change.

Or, I mean, so I imagine. I could be wrong.

"Iris, when are you going to play again?" Rishi has the sweetest smile. Seeing him and Tom together makes me laugh, Rishi is bright-eyed, cheerful, hands moving while he chats. Tom has his hands in his pockets, looking off to the side, clearly ready to be removed from all the small talk. Ray and Tom, I've noticed, often seem happy to stand next to each other and say absolutely nothing. Introverts unite.

Ray nudges me. "Honey, you drifted again." He catches my eye and squeezes my hand.

While I don't love the drive, I do love being at my church with my beloved congregation holding my husband's hand.

"Sorry! Sorry, Rishi. And honestly, I don't know. Probably not soon. With our drive in the morning, it's harder to get here any earlier."

"Yeah, you guys are doing great getting here by kickoff." Derrick gestures to his wife and daughters behind him. "No way these ladies could, especially now that this one discovered makeup."

Tasha, his older daughter, is wearing makeup, her already gorgeous chestnut skin enhanced by a glowing blush and soft pink lipstick.

"Do you miss it?" Rishi wants to know.

"Playing with the church band?" I consider it. "I do. But I'm pretty limited. I've got about eight songs I feel good about, and then it's beyond me."

It's not until we're driving home, the boys quiet and sleepy in the back, Ray says, "If you miss playing, we could get there earlier. You know I'm an early bird, and these boys do OK. We don't have to worry about cosmetics. Just yet," and he grins.

I laugh. "Maybe. I do love to play. Of course, it'd help if I practiced more and learned some new songs."

"No reason in the world you can't. Dedication rarely makes things worse."

My ears prick. What's this about?

"I'm dedicated enough. Volunteering for the music team at church isn't exactly something I need to excel at."

Ray shrugs, eyes never leaving the road. "If you're gonna do a thing, might as well do it well."

"Is that supposed to mean anything?"

He slides a look in my direction. What does he notice? My crossed arms? Stiff neck? Scowl? Ray sighs. "Honey, it's not a criticism. I notice how you do a lot of different things. And I wonder if maybe you narrowed it down to a few things, you might do those things well."

It's uncanny, hearing similar words to ones I heard throughout my childhood. Teachers, tutors, after school programs leaders, and especially my father loved to point to my skill and then fret over my commitment.

"She's so talented at the piano...if she would practice more..."

"Iris, if you're interested in pottery, you'll need to stick with it..."

"I believe Iris has natural skill with painting, but she's not showing the dedication she needs to really build her craft..."

Keeping my voice low, I murmur to Ray, "I think I do just fine at narrowing down. I think some of us could do better to expand our interests."

Behind us, the boys are quiet, playing some kind of trading card game I don't understand.

Ray grips the steering wheel, eyes focused straight ahead. "I assume this is some kind of critique about how much time I work. And you're right, I work a lot."

"All the time. You work all the time, Ray."

"Yes, well, until we got married, Iris, I could work all the time. The farm was my one and only demand. But I hope you know I am trying to make time for our family and to invest in that as well." He's keeping his voice low and measured, and while I understand it, it grates on my nerves, too. How can he stay so calm? Doesn't he care? His set jaw, his careful way of speaking, it's like he doesn't want to talk about this at all.

And now that I've started, it's hard to stop. "Are you? Because I'm not sure it feels like you're any more present now that we all live in the same house than you were when we lived half an hour away."

His jaw goes slack, his mouth open, shocked. How can he be shocked? He's there.

"If you knew how hard I'm working to fit my day into less hours," he starts.

"But you're gone all day. You leave the house when I take the boys to school, and you're not back until six or even seven some nights. And it's not like you get paid so much to make that more bearable."

Oh, dear. I didn't mean to say that. Not at all. I know it bothers Ray that he doesn't make a larger salary. It's his tender spot, and now I've not only touched it, but I've stomped all over it.

"I didn't mean that. I'm so sorry," I gabble, trying to walk it back. "What you make is fine. It's great. It's not that–"

"It got you out of the position you were in." There's a muscle working in his jaw.

I pause. "What position was that?"

"About to lose your house. And needing my help to get out of it." His words are quiet, and when he's done, we're both silent.

My cheeks burn with color, my emotions in a jumble of shame for that situation, anger that he's used it against me and confusion that he knew at all.

I pick the simplest one to handle. "How did you know about the house?"

Ray turns the car onto the farm road. He sighs. "Your mother said something. And I shouldn't have said it like that. I'm sorry."

We slow to a stop outside of the house. Both boys unbuckle and hop out, hurtling to the front door.

I can feel his eyes on me. "Honey, it doesn't matter to me. I wanted to marry you. I believe you wanted to marry me."

I've got nothing to give him. I'm hurt that he's held this against me this way. And humiliated that he knows about the house. How could my mother betray me like that?

"Iris? What are you thinking?"

I rub my forehead again, exhausted. "I need to make lunch."

Ray gapes. "Now? We're in the middle of a conversation."

I meet his gaze, and my face must look awful because he blanches and reaches for me. "Iris, please, let's talk about this."

"The boys need lunch. And laundry has to get done. And homework needs to get checked. This family is my work." As I climb from the car, I throw over my shoulder, "I'm clearly the only one who's going to do it. "

35.

Everything feels achy the next morning. My head, my throat, my shoulders, my eyes. Can eyes ache? Mine do.

Ray's already out of bed. I get dressed in the dark; arguing in pajamas is too vulnerable. How do married people do it? How do they have fights in their towels, their underwear, or their flowered nightgowns? Parker and I were married so briefly, and he was gone so often that we rarely had the opportunity to argue. And I was always fully clothed, even if it was in a baby spit-covered t-shirt and stained yoga pants.

By the time I've done everything from putting my hair up in a loose knot on my head to brushing my teeth, Ray's waking the boys up. And as angry as I feel still, give credit where credit's due: When Ray is home, he's actively in our lives.

If only he were home more.

I want him to know how hurt I am. Heartbroken. Betrayed. But I want to convey this to him without saying a word or making eye contact. It's not easy.

I stay by the front door, slipping my shoes on, while he makes himself an egg. When he offers to make one for me, I say, "I don't have an appetite," and it's the one time we meet each other's eyes. *There, Ray Fox, you take that. That's my broken heart for you. Do you see that?*

And he has the nerve to smile at me. To actually smile! It's a small one, and he tries to hide it behind his cup of coffee, but I see it. How dare he?

"Maybe I'll put a breakfast bar in your bag. Just in case you change your mind."

The gall of this man.

I'm desperate to talk about what's happened, but not with Ray. As soon as the boys are safely deposited at school, I will be phoning a friend about all this.

However, we've halfway to school when Atticus brings me up short. "Are you mad at Ray?"

He's looking out his window, his normally smooth forehead creased, his little mouth puckered.

I tread carefully. "What makes you say that, love?"

He shrugs. Man, I wish we could remove the ability to shrug from kids, zap it right out of them. It's their secret weapon against adults, a gesture that speaks volumes yet reveals nothing. It says: *Something's wrong, and I'm not telling what.*

"Honey?"

"You're all quiety. You get quiety when you're mad." Ernie, the great truth teller, enters the fray.

I rub my forehead. "Really?"

"Yeah. Or you say stuff to yourself. Like this," and Ernie makes soft, muttery sounds under his breath.

I catch a glimpse of myself in the rearview mirror, and it's shocking how perfectly Ernie's face reflects my expression.

I work to pull my lips apart from each other and relax my jaw. "I didn't realize that."

"It's exactly what you do." Now Atticus has things to say.

What to tell them? Was it easier when they only had to handle my struggles? Now it's my struggles and my married struggles. "Guys, it's fine. Ray and I had a little argument. People do. But we're fine." I try to smile reassuringly while also keeping my eyes on the road.

This is another impossible hard thing with parenting. I'm determined to be as honest as I can with my kids, but only within reason. I want them to trust me, to ask for the truth, and to give it as best I can.

And yet, they're little kids, and the last thing they need is some kind of blow-by-blow of a problem. Walking that tightrope is one of the trickiest parts of this job.

"A disagreement or a fight?" Atticus challenges me.

What in the world? "It's a disagreement. And where did you learn that?"

"Ms. Sonya. Ms. Sonya says everyone disagrees, right? But fights are bad."

Alright then. Thank you, Ms. Sonya, for sharing these discerning lessons with my seven-year-old, who's actually listening.

"So if you and Ray are having a disagreement, it's OK. But a fight would be bad." He meets my gaze, then looks straight back out the window.

"Atty? Is there something you're not saying?

Ernie pipes up again. "We don't want you to get divorced. We're here! Race you!"

He's already unsnapping himself from his booster seat while Ms. Sonya the Peacemaker opens the door and ducks her head in. "Morning, everyone!" she sings out. "How're we—you OK, Iris?"

No. The answer is no.

But I don't get a chance to answer. "She and my stepdad are having a disagreement," Atticus offers, pushing his way out of the back seat, hot on Ernie's heels. "But it's no big deal."

"Ah." Ms. Sonya looks amused, and gives me a wink. "Marriage, right? I've been there." Then she shuts the car door and leaves me alone with my thoughts.

36.

When my mother answers the phone, she sounds bleary. My dad is the early riser; my mom can easily sleep until eight or nine, which might as well be noon by most older folks' standards.

"Iris, honey, is everything OK?"

"How could you do that?"

"What? Do what?" She yawns.

"Tell Ray about the house."

"What? I never have!" She adds, "What house?"

I roll my eyes to no one. "You told Ray I was losing the house."

"I did no such thing..." She starts big, and then her voice fades. "Oh, wait..."

There's silence, and then, at last, she admits, "Alright, I might have done that."

"Mom!" I groan, and she exclaims, "It was an accident! You know I'd never say anything on purpose."

We're both quiet, giving her time to collect her thoughts. Outside, the scenery changes from city to country, but I barely notice anymore.

Mom sighs. "It was so crazy, helping you pack and getting you moved. I remember I went to get sandwiches. I was asking Ray for his sandwich order. And I might–just might–have said something about–"

"About what? About what, Mom?" I bellow into the phone.

"About the Wilkins selling their house. Well, selling their rental. And what perfect timing this was, what with you needing to move anyway."

That's it. There it is.

"Oh, Mom," I murmur.

"I don't see what's so bad about that. It was a good thing. Y'all getting married was great timing because you were about to be homeless. Oh. Well. OK, I can see how that doesn't sound so good."

"Oh, Mom," I can't help but repeat. And yet. What should I say? Yelling at her won't change it.

And, God bless my mom, this is classic Cynthia Shepherd. If it's in her head, it's likely to come out of her mouth. A character flaw, perhaps, but it's the deal.

It's also true. And it's not ideal that I'm hiding it from Ray. What does that say about me?

"What if Ray thinks I married him because I was desperate? And we weren't going to be homeless," I add. "I would have found us another home. I have always taken care of us."

"Of course, you have, sweetheart." She's using her soothing voice. It's working. I'm a grown woman, and my mom's calming voice still works on me.

"No one, not Ray or me, would ever accuse you of being incapable or unable to handle the situation."

Myrtle would. I keep it to myself.

"That doesn't make Ray's proposal any less timely."

"What if he doesn't see it that way?"

"Have you asked him?"

"No." And my voice is tiny.

And then she surprises me with her response. "That's fine. You don't have to go home demanding that Ray tell you all his thoughts and feelings."

Relief rushes through me. "I don't?"

"Of course not. Leave it alone. It was a silly thing, said by a silly old woman."

"Mom!" I've switched from being her accuser to her defender. My mom has that kind of charm.

"It was. You give it some room to breathe. It'll sort itself out soon enough."

There's so much relief in this advice. And yet, it does make me squirm. Would Dad agree?

She's undaunted. "You're newlyweds. The last thing you need right now are a bunch of big, tough conversations." I nod along, more than satisfied with the Cynthia Shepherd method of marriage counseling than anyone else I've spoken with recently. "It's in the rearview mirror, alright? You married each other for all the right reasons. And these are growing pains. Don't worry about it, alright?"

Tears pool in my eyes and slip down my cheeks. I manage, "OK, Mom."

Her voice is tender. "My poor girl. You're doing fine, you hear me? You are doing fine, and this is all going to work itself out."

We say our goodbyes, and I'm feeling better as I wipe at my damp face. Cynthia Shepherd might be the first one to put her foot in it, but she's also the first one to put a thing right when it feels like everything's falling apart.

How she put it right, I can't say exactly. But I know, after a talk with my mom, hearing her praise and encouragement, I always walk away feeling better.

Even if the voice that niggles at the back of my brain reminds me, nothing's been sorted out or made right, not between Ray and me. Not at all, in fact.

37.

Why don't people cry more? Gah, the relief. I cry all the time, nearly every day, over something. Sometimes happy, sometimes sad, but there's always some moment, some conversation, a memory, a word, something that deserves a tear or two.

It's quiet when I pull up to our house. For once, I don't want it to be quiet.

Instead, I text Ray. **Where are you working today?**

Its seconds, and he responds, **Greenhouse. Starting more seeds.**

We moved to a farm to experience this life. Phone tucked in my back pocket, I set off on foot to the greenhouse.

They drive so much, the Foxes. Everyone has a truck. They roar them all over the farm. Why? Why not get out on foot and enjoy the land that is your birthright? Take in the sights of your hills, your pastures, the smell of your green grass, the scent of livestock, and the feel of the breeze on your face. They're so strange, this whole family, so closed off and shut down.

It's a longer walk than I expected. That's weird. It feels like a matter of seconds in Ray's truck. There's also a moment when I get a little turned around. Is the greenhouse more to the left or to the right? Ray could probably point me with directions like "bear southeast." But I wouldn't understand it, and besides, I'm not telling him I'm coming. Isn't one of the gifts from working, essentially, from home a delightful surprise visit from your loving wife?

When the greenhouse appears, I'm flooded with relief. I'm also flooded with sweat. Between the surprisingly long walk and my heavy winter coat, it took a lot more effort to get here than I imagined. I'm definitely red-faced, and I brush sweat off my forehead a few times. Touching at the loose tendrils around my face, I smooth my hair. Windswept, it's a style. Just look at any Jane Austen heroine.

Doesn't matter. The large, sliding door on the greenhouse is open just enough I can squeeze in.

And I do.

Only to be greeted by the sight of my husband and The Lovely Naomi in an intimate tete-a-tete.

There's a roaring sound in my head, like a train thundering right through my brain. I stop, clutching the doorframe.

Yes, that's definitely them. They're each perched on an upside down barrel, turned towards each other, so close their knees almost touch. Ray's hands are clasped between his knees, and he's speaking softly, his head bowed. Naomi is—good grief, is she crying? There's a snuffling sound, and she's wrapped her arms around her middle, her face averted.

Besides Naomi's crying, the greenhouse is silent. I can't—I don't—what do I do now?

Gravel moves under my feet, and the crunching noises catch Ray's attention. He jumps up, like a scalded cat. Why? Is he guilty? And of what?

He darts towards me, hands reaching for me. "Iris, honey, is everything OK?" His face is concerned.

I look between the two of them. Over his shoulder, I see Naomi stand, touching her face, wiping away tears. She turns her back to us.

WHY? What is happening?

"Honey?" Ray repeats, and he touches my face, his eyes meeting mine, searching.

They weren't—doing anything. Yet they were so close. I don't sit that close to anyone, except my kids and Ray. That's it. Well, maybe Angie, if she's upset. I'll hug her, sit with an arm around her.

Is that what this is? Is my husband comforting his friend? Or is he, is he—I can't finish the thought. My insides turn icy at the thought of Ray being unfaithful.

"Baby, you're all red. Come sit down." He guides me further into the greenhouse, and there's a seat under me, a proper folding chair in this case, not a makeshift barrel. "Let me get you some water."

With Ray scurrying around, I work to compose myself.

I don't know what's going on. Something weird for sure. But what exactly that weird thing is, that's yet to be determined.

And what I know absolutely is I will not be asking Ray a word about this, not with The Lovely Naomi standing ten feet away. No chance.

If something is going on, if Ray's—whatever is happening, no way am I finding that out in front of Naomi. No freaking way.

So I wait quietly, drink the water Ray handed me, and wait, while Ray leans in close to me, murmuring, "I need a minute to get Naomi squared away. And then we will figure out whatever is going on. OK?"

When Ray asks that, it's not a throwaway question. He waits next to me, and when I look up, his dark eyes are fixed on my face.

I nod. He squeezes my knee and stands up.

I know for a fact he wasn't touching Naomi. For an almost fact. Actually, I have no idea. They were too far away, and I'm wearing my contacts.

What is going on here?

Ray says a few things to Naomi. He's looking at her with that same direct stare he gives his customers, his mother. It's different from the way he looks at me.

I'm almost certain it's different.

Naomi's still snuffling, the big crybaby, but she's nodding, too. When he's done talking, she gives a little smile.

And she heads for the door. She passes me, and I keep my head down. Whatever's happening, I'm not invited into it. That much is clear.

"See ya, Iris," she murmurs, and I blurt, "Yep, yeah, OK. Bye."

Lordy, I am smooth under pressure.

The greenhouse is warm, and I want to take off my jacket. I'm also not sure if I'm going to be storming out of here in two minutes, and if so, I need to be prepared.

Once we hear Naomi's truck tires outside, I breathe out. Here we go. Moment of truth. Let's hear what he has to say.

Ray settles down in the folding chair next to me. They're incredibly awkward, these light metal chairs balanced in slippery gravel and already mine has shifted a few times, throwing me off balance. Maybe the barrels are the smart seating option.

I wait. And wait. And wait. Minutes tick by. Ray says nothing. When I look up, he's watching me.

Waiting?

Is this it? Did you marry me and bring my boys and me to your farm only to two-time me with your beautiful farmhand?

"Well?" I say, and my voice is tremulous. Surely that sums it up for him.

And Ray peers back at me and says, "Well what, honey?" He's rubbing my back, soothing circular motions, and it's comforting. Dang it! My body instinctively leans towards him.

But no! He's the one with the explaining to do. What is going on?

"Are you, do you have, what do you have to say? For yourself?"

Ray looks started. "Say for myself? I don't know that I'm following you."

Now I'm starting to seethe. It happens so quickly how I move from sobbing to shouting. Angie, herself a steady person, who often struggles to get angry, has complimented me on it, my range of emotions.

I think it was a compliment.

I stand up and move around. "Ray, what was happening just now? Between you and Naomi?" It's hard to say her name.

"We were trying to get seeds started. As you could see, it wasn't going great, but we got a little bit done."

Is he serious? Am I crazy?

I'm pacing, and between the steady crunch of gravel and my racing heart, it feels like a scene from a film. Like at any moment I should scream, *Did you order the code red?* and then prepare for my Oscar nomination.

However, my co-star isn't doing his part. Instead of pushing back, instead of shouting, *You can't handle the truth!* and going red and veiny, Ray looks stumped.

"Well, no, we weren't working when you came in," he says. "Iris, what's going on? Is something wrong?"

"What were you talking about?" Not as compelling as Tom Cruise's line, but as close to a direct question as I can find right now.

And that, at last, gives him pause. Ray sits up straighter, rubbing his thighs, and sighs. "With Naomi?"

I'm about to start pulling fistfuls of hair out of my head. "Yes, Ray. With Naomi." What is wrong with this man? Who is this soulless automaton answering my questions like a robot?

"Honey, I can't say."

Swinging around, finger about to jab at him, his answer stops me. "You–what?"

He shakes his head. "I can't, I can't answer that question."

My mouth opens and closes, but there's no noise. I have no idea what to say to this. Ray stands up, hands out, palms up, and reaches for me. "Please understand me. It's not mine to share. That's why I can't tell you. But I can say, Naomi needed to talk so I listened. That's it."

He won't tell me. He's got a secret with Naomi. They're on one side, and I'm on the other.

Is that right?

Ray's friend asked him to listen to her. And she wants him to keep what she said private.

Is that right?

My mind churns trying to sort through the pieces. Is this wrong? Or right? Is he being a dishonorable husband or an honorable friend?

He's waiting patiently for a response.

"Alright then." It's all I can manage to say through tight lips.

Ray grabs my hand and squeezes. "You understand?"

I meet his gaze. His eyes are as clear as ever.

And I still remember what I saw, those two so close, speaking softly, something I can't know.

It makes my stomach clench.

The most I can give him is a jerky nod. "I can try."

He brings my hands to his lips, kisses them. "Iris, you can trust me. I'd never lie to you or deceive you. Understand me?"

I nod again, a softer, gentler compromise, and he pulls me close, holding me against his chest, his nose buried in my hair, breathing it in. "I love you, Iris Fox. You don't ever need to doubt that."

But if that's true, why don't I feel safe now, my mind pleads. If only my mouth could find a way to say it out loud.

38.

There's no more putting this off. In my rearview mirror, I see the awful tasseled lamp and the end table. I can't keep these things in my house. And it's dishonest to stick them in our shed, pretending I want them. Instead of going straight to my house, I park outside the big house, remove the items from the back of the car, and set them near the back door. And take a few deep breaths. I have no idea how Myrtle will respond.

There are voices coming from Myrtle's greenhouse.

I've been curious about the greenhouse for a while. It's a lovely, all-glass room attached to the back of the house. It's hard to see much besides greenery.

Myrtle grows and sells flowers at the Lincoln County Farmers' Market, a small, quaint market, Ray's told me, open June through September. "She wants us to sell there, and I have in the past. But then I picked up the Harrisville Market for Dennis, and he's taking Saturdays off. And my mother's not hauling coolers of vegetables and meat there. So she sells hanging baskets and potted plants, and that seems to be enough." Based on the hesitation around that phrase "seems to be enough," I didn't believe him. I don't think Ray believed himself. And I don't believe Myrtle was happy not having her wishes obeyed.

Still, there's something magical, stepping into the greenhouse, the way the sunlight hits the glass walls, the scent of damp, warm earth, the air wet on my skin. There are long wooden tables covered in black plastic trays with seeds started. Planters hang around the ceiling, the place thick with greenery and trailing vines.

Is this OK? Can I walk right in? It's not like it's her kitchen.

And nothing stops the Foxes from walking in on me, right?

I approach quietly. And I'm glad I do.

"I don't understand why you left in the first place if you hate being here so much!" Myrtle shouts. She's holding a metal spade in one hand, a small ceramic pot in the other.

"I guess I hated being in Atlanta even more than I hate being here!" a woman screams back.

Oh. No.

Stephanie's come into view, across the table from Myrtle, more animated than I've ever seen her.

"Well, isn't that just dandy?" Myrtle stabs her spade into the nearest pot, driving it into the soil. The bitterness in her tone makes me wince. "I give you everything—the best college education money can buy, a down payment on an apartment, supplement your rent—and this is the thanks I get. You hate it here." She hits the word "hate" with special emphasis, her round cheeks flushed, eyes bright. I want to reach out and put an arm around her. What an awful, hurtful thing to hear your adult child say.

Yet Stephanie looks even worse than Myrtle. In old, grubby sweats, her dark hair lank and dull, she doesn't appear to be holding it together.

"I just–I didn't think I'd be–ugh! You don't understand anything!" Stephanie waves two fists in the air, her face pinched in frustration. Now, my heart aches for her. Who knows what she was about to say, but I certainly understand feeling unheard and misunderstood.

"How can I? You don't say anything! You walk around with your face stuck in that phone. I hate that thing. I want to throw it out the window." Myrtle's face twists viciously at the word. Having witnessed Stephanie's screen time, almost compulsive in how it holds her attention, I empathize.

Stephanie, clutching her phone to her chest, gasps, "You wouldn't!"

"I pay for the dang thing. I'll do whatever I–"

Crash!

We all jump. Two heads whip around to gape at me while I gape at the floor. There's a planter on the ground, smashed to pieces. Dirt's everywhere, including all over my ballet flats.

I must have knocked it with my elbow, probably from squirming. Squirming's my natural response to conflict.

"I'll clean it up!" I exclaim.

"This is all I need," Myrtle grumbles while Stephanie stays quiet and stares at me with red-rimmed eyes.

"Where's a, I need a broom...." Turning in a circle, my forehead smacks a hanging plant, scattering more dirt on the floor. I rub my forehead. "It's OK. I'm OK."

"Iris, stop." Myrtle holds her hands held up like a policeman. "Please. I'm begging you. Stop."

I look between the two of them, helplessness rising inside me. This has gone so wrong. "I really want to help."

"I believe that, all actions to the contrary." Myrtle takes a deep breath. "Look, you want to help? What are you doing today?"

I consider it. "Grocery shopping. And picking the boys up from school."

Myrtle nods. "Great. Perfect. Take her with you." And she points to Stephanie.

"What?" Stephanie says.

"What?" I echo.

"You need to get out of the house. No! I don't want to hear it." Myrtle throws up a hand before Stephanie can protest. "I don't care if you want to. You live in my house on my dime. If I say so, you'll go." Stephanie looks madder than ever. "Say one word and see if I don't send you to Dennis' house. Is that what you want?" Myrtle deadeyes her one and only daughter, and after several, breath-holding moments, Stephanie drops her gaze, her shoulders sagging.

It's acquiescence at its most pitiful.

"What I thought," Myrtle says, but it's a hollow victory. She turns away from Stephanie, her own round shoulders drooping. "Y'all get going. And you," she turns hard eyes on Stephanie one more time, "leave that damn phone here."

We've been dismissed.

39.

Stephanie doesn't leave her phone.

It's in her hand the entire drive to the grocery store. I tolerate it until I park. And then I have to say something.

Swinging around in my seat to face her, I think of my mom. How she's unendingly sympathetic and kind to me. I work for that kind of gentleness, like I might find for my own boys. "I think your mom's hoping we might spend some time together. You know, bond."

Stephanie raises her eyes. "I think I'll stay here."

Oh, no. No no no no no. Absolutely not.

Myrtle instructions were explicit: Take Stephanie, and Stephanie, stay off your phone. She most certainly didn't tell me to take Stephanie so Stephanie could hole up in my car while I shop.

Also, Stephanie needs help. That's clear. She doesn't look like she's showered in days. Having your face stuck in a phone like that can't be healthy, can it? And she's Ray's sister. There are so many reasons I need to intercede.

"Would you come inside? Please? I think it might help."

"Have you seen me? I shouldn't be in public." Stephanie runs a scathing glance over her own body.

At least, she recognizes she's not at her best.

"It's the Lincoln County grocery," I say. "You'll be more pulled together than half the customers and everyone working the baked goods counter."

That, of all things, brings out a tiny chuckle. And then, miracle of miracles, Stephanie tucks her phone into her pocket.

"So this is the store these days?" Stephanie ambles alongside me, hands shoved into her pockets.

I'm pushing the buggy, but at those words, I stop. "Have you not been here?"

She shrugs. "Not since high school. Actually, I think I came a few years ago when Brandon was underage and asked me to buy him and his buddies beer."

My mouth falls open. "You've been home since December. It's March."

Stephanie flinches, but her chin juts out determinedly. "Yeah, well, I don't cook, do I?"

I'm still reeling. "Don't you need, I don't know, deodorant? Razors? Pads, something?"

She studies the bag of bread in front of her, avoiding my gaze. "I put it on the grocery list."

It hangs between us: *and Myrtle brings it home.*

Stephanie's been home for over three months, and her mother is already back to looking after her like she's sixteen.

What in the world is she thinking? How can Stephanie get so angry with her mother in one breath, for speaking to her like a child, and then be happy to be treated like a child in other circumstances, like having all her meals and necessities provided for her?

Said like that, it's an easy answer. Sometimes we pick and choose based on what suits us.

Tread lightly. This is what I remind myself of. Stephanie's my sister-in-law. I'd like us to be friends or, at least, friendly.

We make our way through the aisles, and I keep my eyes on the groceries and off Stephanie. "This must be pretty different from Atlanta."

She snorts. "Uh, yeah. Why do you think I left?"

It's not clear if she means left here or left Atlanta. "Do you miss it?"

"Yeah. A lot. I've lived there since I was eighteen. That's home."

I notice the present tense but let it pass. Instead, I compare flours, the one organic variety to the rest. "Did you have a roommate? I think that's what Ray told me."

Her shoulders stiffen and creep up. It's minuscule, but if anyone knows how to watch body language, it's me. There's something there.

"I did."

"What was her name?A pause, so faint you have to strain for it. "Em."

"Were you close?"

"Yep."

I choose the organic flour. There's a bit more money for groceries now that Ray and I combined households. "That's hard, leaving friends behind. Were you roommates long?"

"Ever since we graduated." There's no missing it. Stephanie's struggling.

I stop again in front of the oils and turn to her. "Are you OK?" It's a risk, but I give her arm a squeeze. It's the kind of light touch I'd give one of my sons if he was feeling tender and standoff-ish. "I'm not trying to bring up the hard stuff. We don't have to talk about it."

OK, I'm a little bit bringing up the hard stuff. How else will I get to know her? These dang Foxes and their closed-mouth approach to life. How am I supposed to get to know any of them if they won't talk?

Stephanie turns towards me, too, her eyes, large and dark, like Ray's and Myrtle's I realize, swimming with tears.

"Oh, Steph," I blurt even though I don't know her well enough for the nickname. But, man, does my heart swell at the sight of her distressed face. She suddenly seems younger and more vulnerable like one of my kids instead of my peer.

And then there's a *ping*. Instinctively I glance at her pocket.

Brushing at her cheeks, Stephanie shakes her head. "Don't look at me."

It's me. Of course. My ringer's always on.

The moment to connect is sliding away, but I have to look. And when I do, it gives me pause. "It's Dennis."

Stephanie starts. "My brother?"

"Yeah. He says, 'You around?'" I'm annoyed but send back "yes" before I put my full attention back on Stephanie. "So are you and Em still in touch?"

Maybe that's the constant texting. She's trying to hang onto a friendship, maybe even a best friend, from a distance of two hundred-plus miles away.

Studying a bottle of olive oil, she shakes her head.

"That's awful!" I probably need to lower my voice. And reconsider my comforting skills. But the words pour out before I can stop them. "First, you lose your apartment and then your best friend. No wonder this has been so hard. Stephanie, what happened?"

Maybe my wailing was OK because she turns to me again, eyes finding mine and mouth open.

My phone pings again.

"Ignore it!" I exclaim, but she's closing back up again. I can see it.

"You should check. It's weird that Dennis is texting."

It is weird. However, that doesn't lessen my annoyance especially when I see: **You come get me?**

I read it out loud, exasperated. As I finish, he adds, **You owe me.**

And the most frustrating part is, he's right. I do owe him.

When I look up, Stephanie's watching me, her gaze curious. "Why does he think you owe him?"

I do not feel like getting into this right now. "I do probably have to go get him," I admit. I've already sent back: **WHERE?**

The word pops up, and I read out loud, "Shirley's. What in the world is Shirley's?"

Stephanie looks amused. "Shirley's Bar and Tavern."

"Where is that?" I'm starting to text back, but she stops me.

"I can show you."

40.

And somehow, instead of finishing my grocery trip or our conversation, Stephanie and I leave the store. We stop only to turn our shopping cart over to a cashier so the food doesn't spoil. Stephanie rolls her eyes at me, and I ignore her. Food waste should be a crime.

Shirley's is in the opposite direction of Harrisville, on the outskirts of Lincoln County. No wonder I haven't heard of it. I never come this way, and Ray certainly doesn't go here.

It's a dinky little place, with cement walls painted white and a single glass door. There are no windows. Most telling is the faded, painted image of a lady, circa 1950-something, turned to the side. She's wearing tiny shorts on her unbelievably round bottom and a red and white plaid shirt tied at her unbelievably small waist and barely covering her unbelievably large breasts. Her whole look is finished off with a cowboy hat and a coquettish expression.

"No wonder women have body images," I grumble, and Stephanie laughs.

There are two cars in the parking lot—a small sedan and Dennis' truck. A heavyset young guy, with blonde hair in a low ponytail, stands next to Dennis' truck.

As we clamber out of my car, he calls out, "Hey there, Steph. Long time, no see."

"Hey, Trevor." She nods at him. "You working here?" It's the first time I've heard her sound remotely like either of her brothers.

"Running the place now. Dad's taken early retirement." Trevor, who is probably closer to Stephanie's age than I first thought, shrugs.

"What's she doing here?"

The voice comes from inside the truck. Two boots stick out of the driver's side, and when I poke my head around, there's Dennis, laid out across the truck's bench seat, his cowboy hat pulled over his face.

"What are you doing here is the real question?" I fire back.

He tilts his hat off his face and brightens. "So you did come." There's something disconcerting about the familiar way he says it. I'm aware of Stephanie and Trevor watching us.

"I thought it might be an emergency. What is going on?" Frustration helps cover my mortification.

Dennis drops back in his seat, hat back over his face. "Mechanical malfunction."

"More like operator error." Trevor rolls his eyes. "I left him here last night, passed out. Took his car keys. Woke him up when I got here."

I'm horrified. "Dennis! You spent the night here? Does Shawna know?"

"Shawna's at her mother's. Has been for a bit."

I exchange a look with Stephanie, but she appears as mystified as me.

My patience is running thin. So far, I've managed to get zero of my shopping done, I've made no headway with Stephanie, and now

I'm standing outside a dive bar. I'm hungry and tired and want to go home.

"Go home, Dennis." I burst out. "You shouldn't be here."

He sits up abruptly, hat sliding to the ground, and gives me the goofiest grin. "Will do, ma'am. Just tell him to give me the keys."

The waves of alcohol wafting off of him make me pinch my nose. "My gosh, Dennis, how drunk were you?"

"Are you," Trevor corrects me. "That's why I'm not giving him his keys. He was drunker than Cooter Brown last night, and he's only a tiny bit more sober this morning. He doesn't need to be driving."

"I want to go hooome!" Dennis bellows.

"Stop it," I say at once, and the mom voice that comes out is instinctual. "Trevor here—also, hi, Trevor, it's nice to meet you. I'm Iris, this dummy's sister-in-law." Trevor nods his chin in my direction, hands tucked in his pockets, looking bemused. Rounding on Dennis, I continue, "You stop it right now. You're embarrassing yourself. You're a grown man, it is eleven in the morning, and I'm outside a honky-tonk and—and," I'm running out of steam. All three of them wait, and I give up, exasperated. "The point is, you need to go. We all need to go. And Trevor needs to work."

I run my hands through my hair, thinking. "Here's what we do. Stephanie, we came in one car. You drive Dennis back—"

"I can't drive him back," Stephanie says at once.

I want to scream.

Summoning all the calm I can muster, I ask, "Why not?"

"I don't drive anymore."

She's being precious. I don't have time for this. "How'd you get around Atlanta?"

"MARTA," she says at once, and I sag against the truck, defeated.

"What about my car? It's smaller."

She eyeballs my Outback and shrugs. "I guess."

With that weak agreement, we settle that I'll drive Dennis' truck, and Stephanie will follow behind in my car.

"Get in." I poke Dennis' feet hard with his keys.

He scoots, falls into his seat, and laughs. I'm going to murder this man.

"Trevor?" I turn back to him, wishing he didn't look so curious. "Thank you for your help with this." I can't help but ask, "Do you usually let people get so drunk?"

Trevor, instead of appearing chastised, looks thoughtful. "It's not normally this bad," he says.

"Normally?"

"Yeah. Normally, he gets a little drunk. I tell him to sleep it off in his truck, and he passes out for a couple of hours, wakes up, and drives himself home. But last week, he was still here in the morning. At least then, he was sober enough to drive home. Today, I noticed that." He points, and I look to see an empty Jack Daniels bottle on the floor of the passenger seat. "And woke him up, had him call you. Apparently, he came out here and kept partying by himself last night."

"Wow." That's all I've got. I'm cold even in the winter's sunshine, trying to parse out what's happened. Does my brand new brother-in-law have a drinking problem? More than that, was my friend from the farmers' market an alcoholic and I had no idea?

"Yeah, I know. He's definitely depressed." I raise an eyebrow, and Trevor smiles sheepishly. "I'm also a psychology major at the community college up the road."

"Good for you!" I say, and he smiles. Dennis has either fallen asleep or passed out, his head tipped up on the back of his seat. "What's your diagnosis of this guy?"

"Very, very unhappy. And it's only gotten worse in the last month."
At that, Trevor gives me a long look, an expression I can't read.

It leaves me uneasy. "We better get out of here. Before Stephanie loses her nerve, I'm trying to get all the people back to the farm."

He laughs. "Good luck with that. I don't envy you."

And I don't dare to ask him to elaborate.

41.

Driving up to Dennis' house, I grip the steering wheel, shoulders and neck tight. What in the actual world is happening with Dennis?

He's slumped against the window, snoring, and drool leaks from the corner of his mouth. As someone who grew up with teetotaler parents and who gets a headache after two glasses of wine, I'm out of my depth. Is he asleep or unconscious?

When I slam the driver's door, Dennis doesn't flinch. Unconscious, I guess.

Stephanie stayed right behind me, and she's there now, climbing out of my car.

"How was it?"

It's surprising, her bright eyes. "Good! I thought I wouldn't remember all the things. But it was fine."

I peer at her, a new thought dawning. "How in the world would you get home if you don't drive?"

Stephanie's cheeks go pink. "Plane."

"You flew? You flew the two hundred miles from Knoxville to Atlanta?"

She thrusts her chin in the air. "I got work done on the flight."

I'm still so curious about her leaving Atlanta that I don't want to risk upsetting her before she might share more, so I don't press the issue.

I switch gears. "He's asleep. And he's not waking up."

"At least Shawna's not here," she says, and I nod. But I'm uneasy. How long has Shawna been at her mother's? When is she coming back? Is she coming back?

Jangling his key ring, I realize there are about a hundred keys on it. "What is he, a janitor in his time off?"

"It's all the farm stuff," Stephanie says. "Ray's got the same thing. He keeps a second set of keys for work."

I stiffen. Is it not clear to people that I'm tired of them educating me on my husband? Maybe I don't know that information; that's true. But do you know what I don't need? Everyone in his family showing me how much they know about him.

I focus on the keys. "I guess I'll start trying–"

"We're in."

Stephanie's at the front door, which is now open, holding her hands in front of it, Vanna White style.

"How'd you..."

"It wasn't locked." Her tone is even more cheerful. Who knew today would put such a bounce in her step? "Hardly anyone on the farm locks their doors."

"Ray does," I say and keep *so there!* to myself. *See, Ms. Smarty Sister, I know something about him you don't.*

She's unfazed. "He probably started because you guys are there now. All set?"

I blink. "We have to get him inside."

"Do we?"

"Yes?"

She shrugs. "I mean, he's home. Right? Whether he's in the car or the house, he's here safe and sound. Job done."

"That's not—we don't—I mean, we can't leave him there."

"He's the idiot who got himself into this mess."

"Stephanie! He's in his car. It's bad enough he spent the night like this. Please. Let's at least get him to the living room."

I march to the car, pretending I don't care if she follows but praying she does. He's a big guy. I'll hurt myself trying to move him alone.

Stephanie follows. Victory!

Dennis is dead weight. Between the two of us, we wrestle him out of the car and into the house.

"The living room," I pant as we drag him over the threshold. "Just...get...him...to the couch."

"Dennis!" Stephanie screams it, inches from his ear.

I'm so surprised I shriek, too. But it works. Dennis's eyes pop open, and his head moves slowly, looking between the two of us.

"What? Huh?"

"You're drunk, and you're home," she growls in his face. He laughs, and she recoils. "And you stink." She's glaring at him.

"You're both here. Steph. Iris. I knew you'd come," he adds, and he's looking at me when he speaks. Stephanie isn't wrong. His breath is atrocious.

"Yep, I did."

"Iris, Iris, Iris," he murmurs, setting off alarm bells in my head. "You were mine first, you know that? Mine."

I flush, but I don't say a word.

"Ray stole you. But I knew you first."

I'm aware of Stephanie watching me while I ignore Dennis.

We're almost to the couch. My calves are seizing up, my shoulders aching, I don't think I can go another step until–

"Done!" Stephanie's quick to drop him where he lands mostly on the sofa. "I'm getting a soda. Want anything?" She's off to the kitchen.

"No, thanks." All I want is to get out of this house. Wrestling out from under Dennis' arm, I stand up and give it a quick look around.

It's all tall ceilings, a wall of French doors leading outside. There's a gas log fireplace, and everything's painted in sharp white with lots of white furniture, almost no reprieve except for some gray and strong touches of black. It's very trendy.

And cold, my brain adds, but I ignore it. Not my business.

"You know it's not fair."

Dennis's voice startles me. He's looking up at me, his eyes half-closed, smiling. I'm so tempted to ignore him, but on the off-chance he remembers any of this, I don't need to make any more enemies in this family.

"What's not fair?" I keep my voice quiet and neutral.

"Ray getting you. I set up next to you for two years. And then he swings in and takes you. How'd that even happen?"

It feels like the world is slipping into slow motion around me. My palms are sweaty, and my breath speeds up.

"Dennis, I don't know what you mean. You're married." I whisper, talking fast.

He shakes his head and closes his eyes. "Me and Shawna, we're no good. She moved out, the day after that last Sunday supper."

The words hit me like a gut punch. Shawna moved out? Does anyone here know?

Dennis, however, is semi-awake and chatty. "She was the prettiest girl in our high school. I felt like I was getting a trophy the day she agreed to go out with me. But it was a mistake, all of it. She hates it here."

This is better. Far safer. "I'm sorry to hear that," I say. "That sounds hard."

Dennis shrugs. His hands are folded across his chest, and he's talking with his eyes closed. "I got what I deserved. She wanted Ray. All through high school. For whatever reason. And he wasn't interested. So when she said yes to a date with me, I thought, 'I win.' Crazy, huh? And then he goes and gets you. And I'm the all-around loser, aren't I?"

It's too much information. I lean over him, holding my breath, absorbing every word like he's on his deathbed and I'm taking his last confession. "Shawna wanted Ray? Is that true?"

He pops one eye open and gives me a crooked grin. "Girl, is that all that matters to you? How it affects your man." He slips into a draw so Appalachian it's identical to his brother. "Well, you're showing me what kind of shot I have. None."

I hear a slam and startle, springing up. It's Stephanie shutting the refrigerator door.

"Do you want anything?" She's holding a bag of tortilla chips in one hand and a can of soda in the other.

"You can't take those!"

She shrugs. "Sure I can. Payment for getting his dumb ass home." She pops a chip in her mouth with a *crunch*. "You ready?"

There's no doubt Dennis is out. "Yep, I am. Let's get out of here."

42.

Dennis liked me? Likes me? The suggestion is so absurd. He's married. He's been married as long as I've known him. Did he think I was–

My brain won't finish the thought. I know what infidelity feels like. It's painful. I didn't deeply love Parker, but if someone who's meant to love and cherish or, at the very least, respect you, steps out on you, it hurts. I can only imagine how Shawna would feel if she knew.

Does she know? Thoughts tumble one over the other. Dennis hasn't told her, has he? Of course not. Who would do that? A crazy person, that's who.

Or a drunk. Which Dennis appears to be. And look what he managed to blab to me in an eight-minute span of time. The stuff about Shawna and Ray–

And Shawna liked Ray? I can't say which feels worse—Dennis' unexpected and inappropriate declaration of something or learning that Dennis' wife once had strong feelings for Ray. Did she still? Did Ray ever?

What am I supposed to do with all this information?

"Gah, this place!" I bark into the silence.

Stephanie turns to me, popping an eyebrow. "What's wrong?"

Shoot. I almost forgot she was here. I've been a mom for so long noisy eaters are just background noise to me. "I don't know. Nothing." I shake my head.

"C'mon, you brought me here. So spill."

She's right. Instead of taking Stephanie back to Myrtle's, we're parked outside of my house.

"Damn it!" I howl, and this gets a jaw drop from Stephanie.

And a cheer. "Yes! Let's go! The Fox family effect is finally happening."

"What do you mean?"

"This! You say 'this place.' And you're cursing. It's this farm. It's this family. It does that. It ruins you." And she takes a loud chomp of her chip.

"Does what?"

"Sucks the life right out of you," and she says it while staring straight into my eyes. And chewing vigorously.

"You're not helpful," I say, and she laughs.

It's infuriating. I get out of the car, slamming the door. I need space. I need fewer people. Fewer Foxes.

Except that doesn't work. I'm married to a Fox. I am a Fox. And even thinking that means, somehow, Stephanie might be right.

I pace, running my hands through my hair. Maybe this is why Ray's hair sticks up constantly? His family and their dysfunction?

There's a spiral right in front of me, and I'm only a hair's breadth from taking it. It starts with the thought: *What have I done?* After that, hot on its heels: *I'm trapped.* And behind that, finishing the triad of hateful thoughts: *I have to escape.*

"You gonna take me home?"

I whirl around. Stephanie sits half out of the car, munching her stupid chips and watching me curiously.

"Why don't you walk?" I snap back.

She recoils. "Hey, hey, OK. Hang on." She puts one last chip in her mouth, wipes her hands on her pants, and stands up. "Let's talk."

I throw my head back and laugh. "Now you want to talk? Now? I haven't gotten four words from you since I met you two months ago. But now, you want to talk. Fantastic."

"That's not fair."

She shifts from foot to foot under my disbelieving stare then relents. "It's a little fair. But can you see why? This place will make you crazy. I've been home since December. Escaping into my phone is the only thing that's keeping me together."

"So go back to Atlanta!" I bellow, and the sneaky thought pops up: *Can I go back to Harrisville?*

"I can't!" she shouts back.

"Why? There are other apartments. Other roommates. You're being a baby."

"Em wasn't my roommate. We were in love!" she shrieks at me, and that stops me in my tracks.

Stephanie was in love with her roommate? They were a couple? This is enough to throw me off my tailspin. "So you are—that means—what does that mean?"

She gulps in air, glaring up at the sky. "We, Em and I, we weren't roommates. We were a couple."

"And she—"

"He."

Well, that's a bit more clarity. I clear my throat. "He ended it?"

And I'll be darned if tears aren't leaking from Stephanie's eyes. She nods, staring off to the side, arms crossed over her chest.

"Oh," I say. "I'm sorry." We're both quiet, and then I can't help but ask, "And you're sure he's–it's over?"

"I can't change, so yep, it's over."

I'm longing to ask what she means, but I can't find the boundaries in this conversation.

But I want to try. "So Em–"

"Emad."

"Emad," I echo, and there's an inkling of what might be happening. "You and Emad lived together?"

"Yep."

"For a while?"

"Since we graduated from Emory."

"And then something happened..."

"Nothing happened. That was the problem. I wouldn't–" There's a long pause, and Stepanie exhales– "I couldn't change."

"Which means?"

"I wouldn't bring him home. I wouldn't introduce him to my family. My mom. Any of it." She shakes her head and starts crying hard now, tears streaking down her face. "How could I? How am I supposed to bring Emad Hatim home to Lincoln County to meet Myrtle Fox?"

She glares at me. "Hmm? What do you propose, Ms. Let's Talk About Everything?"

I hold my hands up. "Yeah. OK. I won't argue that with you."

I'm desperate for quiet, but she can't go home in this state. She needs to talk; she needs a friend.

"Come inside. I'll make lunch, and you can talk about it."

"I don't want to talk about it!" she fires back.

My hands go up again, the international gesture for *please don't come at me.* "OK. We won't talk. I'll make lunch. No talking. I promise?"

43.

Stephanie can't stop talking. I make hot tea for both of us and then work on lunch.

"This tea reminds me of Em," she says. And the words pour out from there. How they met as freshmen, how they were both engineering majors. She liked him immediately and knew without a doubt she couldn't pursue it. Ever. "I know it's a new century and all that, but there were a handful of Black families in Lincoln County when I was growing up. Maybe twice as many Hispanic families. And they're all Christian."

Em, it turns out, was most definitely not.

"He's not a devout Muslim," Stephanie admits. "His family is fairly liberal in their thinking. His parents didn't love that we weren't married and living together. But they understood. They tried. Can you imagine what Myrtle would say if I brought home this Saudi man with his brown skin and introduced him as my boyfriend?"

Hmm. I could think of another man with brown skin who I was pretty sure Myrtle harbored more than a passing interest in. But that was a guess, and it wasn't mine to say.

"So you've never told your mom about him? Did she even know you were living with a man?" I slide a plate in front of her.

I've made my classic chicken salad sandwich with a smear of my homemade pesto. I prep a bunch of pesto in the summer with Ray's basil and freeze it. It's delicious. Stephanie digs in and says nothing. This family. How do they own and operate this farm when they're such philistines about food?

Stephanie snorts with her mouth full. "Tell my mother I live with a man? Are you crazy?"

"So you told her Em was a woman?" Sounds pretty crazy to me, but I refrain from commenting.

Stephanie's eaten everything but the crust of her bread. "I don't know if I ever said it exactly. I just, you know, referred to Em."

Somehow this seems familiar, and I remember a conversation with Tom from church. "It's kind of like the pronoun game."

She cocks an eyebrow. "Huh?"

"A friend of mine who's gay told me about when he first started dating but hadn't come out to his family. He'd use vague pronouns, like 'they,' or he'd use 'we' a lot to avoid gendering the guy he was seeing. This is kind of like that, and that's tough."

"You have gay people at your church?"

"Several."

Stephanie shakes her head. "You did not grow up here," is all she says.

I want to understand better than I do. "What's the bad piece? That you're in love with a Muslim man? Or that you're living with him and not married?"

"Both." Stephanie sighs. "But, honestly, it's the Muslim piece. If he were white or, at least, if he were Christian, this would be so much easier. I mean, we would have gotten married, and that would have taken care of the other thing."

This announcement quiets the room. For a few minutes, I can only stare at her.

"So you're telling me you would have married him if he weren't Muslim? It was that serious?"

"Yeah, of course. We've lived together for eight years. I love him. He makes me nuts, but he's my world."

It's too much. I have to pace. "Oh, Steph. This is so hard."

She has her head on her arms, her cheek pressed into her arms. "I know. I mean, I'm hardly a practicing Christian these days. I had a church, but the harder it got with Em, the more he felt like I was embarrassed of him, the less I went. I couldn't talk to anyone about this. You're the first person, in fact."

"Wow. Thanks, I guess?" My heart aches for her. What an impossible predicament. "What does he, Em, say about all of this?"

She waves a hand. "He was fine with it. Lovely even. Em was actually open to Christianity. He came to church with me a few times. He thought it was interesting."

I freeze. "What?"

"I know." Stephanie shakes her head. "If I'd wanted him to attend church, to be part of it, he'd have done it. Good guy, right?"

I can't. Rounding on her, I put both my hands on the back of my dining room chair and say, "Stephanie, what in the world is holding you back?"

"You don't know what it's like. You don't know Myrtle. She's, she's like a force of nature, bigger and stronger than anyone else in the family. If she doesn't like something, she'll exert pressure until you can't resist, until you cave and give in. If I brought Em home, and she didn't like it, she would have ended it somehow. I couldn't risk it."

I want to push back, but I can't. I've experienced the power of Myrtle's words, haven't I? I feel like I've been holding my hands up in front of me, working hard to stem the tide of her mighty personality. And that was over a lamp and a table. Over her showing up announced, of her implying I married her son for his money.

Imagine if it were something as life-changing as a marriage.

What can be done when a person has such authority, such presence that she can end a relationship one state away that she doesn't even know exists? How do you reckon with that kind of force?

Sighing, I run a hand over my face. "So the issue isn't really Emad and you. It's Myrtle."

Stephanie stares at the table. "I guess that's one way to say it."

I plunk down at the table and lean back in my seat. "How are you?"

When Stephanie looks at me, her eyes are red and damp. "Awful, honestly." She laughs. "I thought it was bad when we broke up, but then I got here. And it turns out the only thing worse than losing the love of your life is never talking to or hearing from him again. I'd trade those last weeks in the apartment with all the arguing and me pleading and begging," she stops there, tearful, "than live like this."

"How long has it been?"

"Since I left. He said no contact. I've tried, though, trust me. I've texted. Called."

"Any response?" I know the answer. I can see it all over her miserable face, slumped shoulders, the way she buries herself in her phone.

"No. When Em says a thing, he means it."

"That's usually a good quality."

"Yes, it is."

We're quiet. Finally, I retrieve the tea kettle and fill up our cups.

"Can you still see his socials?" I ask. She nods. I put out a hand. "C'mon, let's see."

She's so quick I wonder if that's where all the phone time goes, watching and mourning the loss of her love.

His Instagram is active. A couple of pictures a week—food and buildings, interesting architecture. However, if I scroll back far enough–

"Ouch." I wince as I reach last November right before their breakup.

His grid is riddled with pictures of them and so many shots of Stephanie. It pains me to look. There's Stephanie but not like the woman sitting across from me. In these photos, her eyes twinkle, and her face is constantly in a half-smile. There's a photo of them from last summer, a selfie, Em turned to gaze at her, and the raw, open affection in his face makes me set the phone down.

They were so in love. Stephanie watches me, eyes wide, lips trembling.

"Well?" she asks.

I lift my shoulders once. "What?"

"What do I do?" Her plaintive voice hurts my heart. It's pitiable. What an impossible situation. A hard situation to navigate, the different faiths, but manageable except for that one absent yet always present person: Myrtle.

"Come to church with us this weekend." These are the words that come out of my mouth. And if I sit quietly for a minute longer, I stand by them.

"Why?"

"It feels like the right thing to do. Come to church, get some space from your mom, and meet some people you didn't go to high school with. Just come. Sit quietly. See if you get any ideas."

And, surprising both of us, she agrees.

44.

Sunday morning I wake up first, which in itself is a first. Next to me, Ray's asleep, snoring a little. How funny. I don't see him like this often. He's usually nudging me awake with a cup of coffee and a "darlin', you gotta get up."

The house is quiet. It's dark outside. I roll to reach my side table, fumble for my phone and find the time. Almost six. We'll need to be up soon.

"Where do you think you're going?"

Ray's arms encircle me. He kisses my shoulder and holds me close. I sink into him, thankful for his warmth. Thankful for him.

"Why don't we do this every morning?" His mouth is against my ear, his voice low.

"I don't know," I murmur.

"Is it because you prioritize sleep over everything else?"

"How dare you," I whisper back, and we're both giggling.

The relief of this lighthearted interaction floods over me. Yesterday, with Stephanie's romantic entanglement confession and returning

Ray's older brother to his home and all that entailed, Fox family secrets overwhelmed me.

I have no idea what I can tell my husband and what I can't. "Your sister's in love with a first-generation Saudi. Your brother's wife left him. And your brother might have a drinking problem. Plus some unresolved emotional attachment to me…"

Nope, I can't even touch that one. If I am pushing anything to the back of my mind right now, it's that.

So it's possible I was distracted and jumpy last night, saying, "What?" repeatedly and darting away from Ray any time he came close to me. Having these secrets from him about his people makes it harder for me to connect with him.

Waking up, feeling Ray's strong, wiry arms around me, the two of us whispering in the darkness restores some of that divide that felt so present last night.

"What's on the roster for today?" Ray asks.

I roll onto my back, and he stays on his side, propped up on his elbow. His hand draws lazy circles on my stomach, but I can't focus on it.

Being married is so much work. There are times when it's soft, easy, effortless. But then weird tensions, the conversations we actively work to not have and, Lord help me, the occasional arguments pop up, and it feels like a battlefield between the two of us.

I never could have imagined it. When it was only Ray, the boys, and I, it felt so easy. Now that we're here together and with the presence of his family always around, it's a fight to stick it out. I actively work to ignore that piece of it because it feels so awful.

"Church. And that's about it."

"That sounds like a great day to me," Ray says. "Get some time away." His eyes flicker over my face, checking on me. I've realized

Ray might not want to discuss feelings, but more often than not, he's gauging mine, working out how I'm doing and trying to help when I need it. "A day with just us. No Foxes allowed. Besides you and me, that is." And he smiles at this. To a certain extent, he understands that his family and their presence are challenging.

And I have to correct him of this misapprehension.

His hand is warm on my stomach, but I'm squirming away from it now. "About that…"

***

"I don't understand why my sister is coming to church with us." Ray's hands are busy at his collar, finishing his necktie. He wears jeans and clean work boots along with a white or blue Oxford button-up shirt to church. He also wears a tie, one of the three that he owns.

As someone who takes a lot of joy from her large and varied wardrobe, it's interesting to see how Ray dresses himself. I've learned if he likes a thing, then that's it. So if a blue Oxford button-up works, he buys two of those plus a white one, and those are his fancy clothes. Black t-shirt good for work? Buy two packs of four, and your workday uniform is ready.

"You'd have done great at a school with a uniform." I adjust his tie and smile at him.

He plants a kiss on my lips but jumps back as if stung and yelps, "No! You will not distract me with smiles and kisses. Tell me, why is my sister coming to church with us?"

Dang it. I thought I'd managed a subject change.

"Your sister needs to get out of the house. She needs to see someone other than your mother."

Ray quirks an eyebrow. "So she'll hang out with her brother instead?"

"Sure!" I lift my shoulders once, feeling helpless. "Better than her mama. Look, she's been here for months, and she's barely gotten out of her sweats. She needs a change of scenery. And a friend."

"And that's gotta be you, does it?" As we talk, we're moving the boys out of the house. Ray picked up the little backpack with snacks and water for the boys. I've got my purse, keys in hand, locking the door behind us. It's effortless, unspoken, working as a team.

"I don't see anyone else signing up for the job."

The boys are already buckling up in the back seat, and Ray and I stand on opposite sides of the car, regarding each other. He gives first, looking away and shaking his head. "Don't ever let it be said that Iris Shepherd, now Fox, doesn't have one of the biggest hearts I've seen," he said. And I smile. There's defeat in his voice, but something else, too. Pride, maybe? Appreciation?

The sound of crunching gravel alerts me to Stephanie pulling up before I even look up. "Here she is!" I wave, and she rolls her eyes before climbing out of her car. "Please," I say to Ray, voice lowered. "Encourage her, OK? She needs it."

And it hurts my heart, not being able to share with him exactly what that means. But I keep my mouth closed.

45.

Stephanie isn't easy with people or a new environment. Having never seen her off the farm, I didn't know what to expect. She's hesitant, hanging back behind Ray and me, eyes darting side to side as if expecting to be accosted at any minute. Is this natural personality, the result of living in a big city for so long, or further evidence of how only seeing Myrtle Fox can cow a person?

Maybe all three.

My kids help. I've enlisted them as Stephanie's personal tour guides, and they're delighted to share the important pieces of church with her.

"Over here, we play touch football when it's over." Atticus points to a spot in the church yard on our way in. "And over there is where they set up the coffee for grown-ups." He points to a strategically placed table on the opposite side from where the football gets thrown. "And up at the front? That's where we do all our performances, like the nativity play. The water fountain is through those doors. And downstairs are the kids' rooms, but once you're seven, you have to stay upstairs. Ernie still has to go downstairs."

Of course, what's important to a seven year old is different from what's important to his mother, I guess.

I offer her a quick rundown as to where the bathrooms are located, make sure she has a bulletin to follow our liturgical service, and give a quick idea of how communion goes.

"Do you have communion every week?" I nod. "I'm only used to it for Christmas Eve and Easter."

Scooting into the pew, I mutter from the side of my mouth, "Well, buckle up then, because the communion wine isn't grape juice either."

The nonplussed look on her face makes me laugh as the priest asks us to stand.

Slipping up behind Ray, as we sip coffee on the front lawn and avoid getting pegged by a wayward Nerf football, I whisper, "I was right. Wasn't I?"

He's finished his conversation with Pastor Robin and turns towards me. "Always, my love, but what do you mean right now?"

I gesture to Stephanie. She's in conversation with Andie and Andie's fiancé, Joe. There's a lot of smiling, and Stephanie looks more at ease than I've seen her—ever. Just ever.

Ray acquiesces. "Yes. You were. She looks happy. Honestly, I'm not sure I've seen a smile like that on Steph since we were kids." He looks conflicted, pleased and sad.

There's a reason for that! I want to say.

But it's not my place. I can't share Stephanie's secret even when I know it would give her brother the same window into her sullen and standoff-ish demeanor it gave me. She doesn't hate anyone at the farm. She's afraid, afraid of their judgment, of their criticism, of their rejection. Afraid of what it would mean to all of them if they knew who she loved.

I squeeze his hand and slip off to check on Stephanie.

"Doing OK?"

She's beaming. Stephanie, normally slumped and glum, is lit up from the inside. She's also clean, with shiny dark hair, wearing red lipstick and a black and white patterned wrap dress.

"Did your mom see you this morning?" I blurt before I can stop myself.

Some of her shine dims. "No. She's in charge of coffee at church. She'd left before I came downstairs. She wasn't very happy I wasn't coming with her."

Nuts. The last thing I wanted to do was lower the mood. I take her arm and say, "Come meet more of my friends."

Tom and Rishi are only a few steps away. "Hey, guys! Let me introduce you to my sister-in-law. Stephanie Fox, this is Tom, and this is Rishi."

I don't mention their last names as I'm terrible with last names, and I can't remember if they've each kept their own or hyphenated. However, the fact they're holding hands and wearing wedding rings should make their relationship status apparent.

It makes me giggle to myself, watching Stephanie pick up clues. She thrusts out a hand, working to cover her awkwardness. I notice Tom smiles behind his paper cup of coffee.

Rishi, though, who puts the extra in extrovert, grabs her hand, gushing, "It's great to meet another Fox. We love your brother. When Iris told everyone the good news, I whooped. I actually whooped."

"Is that because you love Ray or because my perpetually single status made you sad?" I tease him, and a blush spreads across his dark skin.

"Both," he admits, and Tom and I laugh.

Stephanie, however, doesn't. She's staring at the two of them, like an exhibit at the zoo. It makes me nervous until she blurts out, "Is it hard? Being an interracial couple?"

Well, look at that. Going straight for the heart of the matter.

Tom and Rishi exchange a look. Tom is bemused. "Honestly, people tend to notice the both-boys thing before they notice the white-Indian thing," he says.

Stephanie blushes. "Sure, sure. Sorry. I didn't mean to be awkward. I just..."

We wait, but she's fallen silent.

"Stephanie's trying to work out some relationship questions," I say, and she gives me a grateful expression. I ask, "Once everyone got past the both-boys thing, did y'all have a religion component to figure out?"

Tom and Rishi exchange a look, and Rishi shakes his head. "Not really. My grandparents were Hindi, but after my parents came to the U.S., they became Christians. I was raised this way."

We all see the change in how the light fades from Stephanie's face, her mouth tugging down at the corners, lowering her gaze.

And it's Tom of all people who says, "I don't know your situation—and I'm not asking—but there being a challenge to a relationship doesn't mean it isn't worth it. In my experience, it's easier to sort through big issues, like religion or race, than to make genuine incompatibilities work. So the question might not be, can we figure out this big subject, but do we have enough in common, enough that binds us, to make figuring this out worth it?"

"Spoken like a true professor." Rishi beams at his husband.

Tom sips his coffee and shakes his head, emotions tidily packed up and put away.

Rishi takes Stephanie's elbow and asks, "Do you want to talk?"

And to my astonishment, she nods, and they separate themselves, heads close, Stephanie's mouth moving fast.

"Iris? Are you OK?" Tom's staring at me.

I swallow, forcing myself to be calm. "Yeah, fine. Gonna grab more coffee." I gesture with my cup, and coffee spills over the rim.

But Tom only nods and looks happy to stand on his own, waiting out the social time.

What are "genuine incompatibilities"? How do you know if you have them?

On the outside, Ray and I look easy. We're the same race, opposite gender, same faith, general age, and general financial status—if you ignore Myrtle's suggestion I'm a gold digger.

But what about priorities? Family versus work. Marriage versus family of origin.

Faithful versus unfaithful?

My eyes search until I find Ray in conversation with Jenna and Sangyoo. He's sipping his coffee, nodding as Jenna talks with her hands, and Sangyoo bounces their baby, Olivia, in his arms.

Seeing Ray at a distance, unaware I'm watching him, makes my heart race. His eyes, his wild hair, the way he's listening closely to what Jenna says, the way he laughs. The way his eyes, maybe sensing me, find mine. And he smiles.

I raise a hand in greeting, feeling flushed, almost sick, with affection. I'm in so deep. The feelings Ray brings up in me, I haven't felt this way before.

But, Tom's voice echoes in my head. *Do we have enough in common, enough that binds us, to make figuring this out worth it?*

46.

I can't get my bearings. It's Wednesday, the boys are at school, and I'm still in Harrisville, handling work. I've dropped off my tiny baby knits for Andie. She was a delight, she and Jenna, admiring my delicate stitchwork, the tininess of the items. And the prototypes of adult gloves and toboggans I made went over beautifully. She signed off on all of them and put in an order for these items starting this summer.

When that's all done and I'm back in my car, I call Angie to see about stopping by. "Oh, hon, I wish we could!" she says, her voice full of remorse. "I'm taking some of these beasts to the Chattanooga aquarium today. We're already halfway there. I could turn around…"

I laugh at the absurdity of it. "Stop it. It's fine. It was a last-minute thing anyway."

Hanging up, I shake my head, shaking away tears that leak from the corners of my eyes. This isn't weird, but between the stream of Foxes stopping by and the mental struggle I've had over Tom's question since Sunday, I'm feeling extra tender.

I need downtime, alone time. Yet being away from the farm, stressful as it feels, also is its own weirdness. I suddenly exist in two separate places but call neither of those places home. How can that possibly be?

There's so much time before I need to pick up the boys from school.

I drive to Bread and Butter for coffee and a place to work. It's quiet, almost lunchtime, and there's a small table open where I can spread out with my sketchpad.

Liz isn't taking orders, but she's behind the counter and welcomes me.

"Doing inventory?" I guess, and she laughs.

"Always. It consumes me."

"Only because she's a stickler," says the man at her elbow, a young Black man who's worked for Liz for years. I think his name is Michael. I speak to him almost every time I come in, and mostly I try not to stare because he might be the best-looking person I've ever seen in real life. "She'd count the coffee beans if you let her."

He's grinning at her. Liz blushes and laughs. "I don't mean to be. But the more data we have the better we can plan."

He shakes his head. "That's our Liz, planning planner extraordinaire."

Their camaraderie is a balm, shaking me out of my current funk. I laugh, too, and say, "If only I had half of your skills for planning, my life might not feel like such a mess right now."

It doesn't come off light and cheery, the way I heard it in my head. Liz pauses, and Michael silently puts my coffee in front of me, smiles, and disappears.

"You OK?" Liz is quiet.

I clear my throat; it's too loud. "Yeah. Of course. I'm fine. I'm just, you know, a new marriage, new home, new life. It's a lot." And then I laugh like a maniac, sip my coffee to cover the awkwardness, and burn the inside of my mouth.

So that's the kind of day it's going to be, eh?

Liz's eyes are kind as she asks, "Do you want to chat? I can take a break."

"Sure. If you want to." Like this is for Liz. Like she needs it.

When she joins me at the table, she has a mug in her hand. "Coffee?" I hazard. She shakes her head.

"Hot tea. My coffee cutoff is eleven. So," Liz shifts in her seat. "How's married life?"

I scrutinize her face. Her gaze is level, calm, and patient. Genuine. "Hard," I say and the words bring a river of relief. "Just really hard."

Liz nods. "I bet. You want to tell me more?"

So I do. The always present Fox family, not only around the house but sometimes in my house, and definitely coming between my husband and me. I even bring up Naomi though I tread lightly there. Why?

Because I'm afraid to hear someone else's perspective. A difficult family? Manageable. A gorgeous young woman who works closely with my husband and with whom he appears to be harboring some kind of secret?

Just forming the thought makes my belly hurt.

Liz listens and nods. She sips her tea, her eyes on my face, unphased when the bell on the door rings or a line forms at the counter. It's such a gift to have an attentive and unbiased audience. I talk and talk, and I eventually stop to breathe and take a long swig of coffee.

Truthfully, I don't know Liz that well. Probably not well enough to have shared so many intimate details with.

But if she's disconcerted by me, she doesn't show it.

"It sounds like a lot," she says. "You're not only adjusting to marriage and having a stepfather to your kids. You're adjusting to a new home. With a really present new family."

I'm hanging on each word. *Diagnose me, Dr. Liz. Help me, please.*

"It sounds hard, Iris. For sure. I," she stumbles but pushes through, "Haven't been married for years. So I'm not sure I'm the best to give advice."

"You've just listened to all that. You seem like the perfect person," I say honestly, and she laughs.

"I wonder if your husband really understands how you're feeling? Maybe it's not clear to him how hard all this is."

I nod, once, twice, three times. Do her words make sense? Yes. Definitely.

Do I want to try another hard conversation with Ray? Yet one more that could very well lead to a fight?

The answer is one long sigh.

Liz hears the sigh and immediately looks guilt stricken.

"I'm sorry." She pats my hand. "Really, I think you're doing great. This sounds like a lot. And you're trying. You're working on it. I'm sure you'll figure this out." Her smile is so encouraging I let it buoy me. I'm not ready for more straight talk with Ray. But I am ready to believe that this will get better and I might not be in the mess I thought I was.

"Think about it, Iris, you're living a dream. You married this amazing man, and now you live on a beautiful farm–it is beautiful, right?" I nod. Liz puts her hands in the air as if to say, *So there!* "Happy remarriage on an honest-to-goodness farm! How many women do I know who would love this story? Single or otherwise," she adds and gives me a wry smile.

It's true. All of it is absolutely true. Liz's words slide across my view and expand my vision. Don't zoom in, pull back. Look from a bigger lens, a larger perspective. There is so much good in this story. Who would complain about a few missteps or minor disturbances?

"You're right." I meet her gaze and nod. "You're so right. These issues, they're tiny. Why am I worried?"

Liz's brow creases. "I'm not saying that exactly. I hope you don't think I meant that–"

I wave my hand. "Oh, no, you're great. I think you're spot on. If I don't remind myself of all the good there is, I'll stay in this funk. And who wants to live like that?" I laugh.

Liz shakes her head adamantly and says, "No, wait."

At that moment, my phone lights up with an image of Ray, and I reach for it. "I really appreciate it, Liz. Thank you for this."

I'm not sure why, but she looks uncertain as she stands up. "If you're sure?"

I nod eagerly. "I am! Thank you. Now I'm going to take this." I answer as Liz walks back to the coffee counter, glancing back at me as she goes. "Hey, babe! How's it going?"

"It's, a, it's a going," Ray says, his tone also jovial, almost overly so. "Is there any chance you're still in Harrisville?"

I feel a ding of guilt. While I did tell him I'd be dropping new merchandise off at Andie's store, I didn't mention my plan to stay in town.

After being a single woman for so long, it's hard to remember to share every piece of information with your partner. And sometimes I like some privacy. Is that wrong?

"Yeah, I'm still here. I actually—" I start, but Ray cuts me off.

"That's great! That's great news, honey. Is there any way you could do a favor for me?"

"Yes, of course. What's up?"

"There's a meeting at the house today, some stuff with the farm lawyer at three-thirty. And we need Brandon here for it. Problem is, he's not answering his phone."

"O-K."

There's silence, and I wait.

"I don't suppose you could run by his school and tell him?" He says it in a rush, one long line: idon'tsupposeyoucouldrunbyhis-schoolandtellhim.

I pause. It seems like a small thing. A weird thing, but a small thing. So why does this feel so strange?

"I don't know where to find him," I hedge. "Can you tell me?"

It's quiet on Ray's end. "Honestly, I've never set foot on the campus," he says, and for the first time in this conversation, he sounds like himself. "Look, don't worry about it. OK? It's a ridiculous thing to ask."

"No, wait. I'm not saying I won't do it."

"Really, Iris, it's fine."

"No, I'm sure I can figure it out. He's in the College of Agriculture, right?"

Ray's quiet again, and I wait. At last, he sighs. "Yep, that's right."

I can't explain why he's hesitating and seems frustrated as we hang up.

It is weird, tracking down his little brother on campus. However, it's no weirder than a lot of situations I've witnessed or been part of since joining the Fox family. Why balk now?

47.

As a Harrisville College alum, I know my way around. Goodness, I love the campus. It's a small liberal arts school with lots of sharp white molding contrasting the red brick and rolling green lawns between buildings.

Attending school here was the first time I felt like I belonged, like I fit. In fact, walking the campus I'm reminded of how much I loved it. I lived at home through college, but my schedule was such that I felt the most independence I'd ever experienced. And after feeling awkward and friendless throughout my school years, I made a few friends, which to me was a tremendous accomplishment.

It's springtime, and the sun is out with dogwoods and crepe myrtles starting to bloom and buttercups and tulips shooting up green leaves from beautifully manicured beds.

I have a vague recollection of passing the Agriculture building on my way to classes at the College of Arts and Sciences, and finding my way there now is easy. Class ends, students pour out, and there's no Brandon with them.

I text Ray. **You're sure he's out of class now?**

He shoots back, almost as if he's watching his phone waiting for me, **Yep, done by this time every day.**

Nuts. Why is Brandon the one twenty-something kid who isn't living with his phone in his hand?

I head into the building, to the office, and find a student working the desk.

"Hi." Shyness creeps in, but I remind myself I'm the grown-up here. "I'm trying to find Brandon Fox. He doesn't have his phone on, and he didn't come out after class."

She eyes me. "Are you sure he's in class today?"

I nod. "Yep. And should be done now."

"Maybe he's in a study group? Or talking to a professor?"

My smile freezes. These are excellent suggestions. But how in the world am I going to find him if that's true? "Yes, that's possible. Hmm. I don't want to bother him, but he's needed at home."

She's got one elbow on the desk, chin in her hand, and she reacts to nothing I've said.

My will is fading, but I won't give up. "Is there–is there a paging system?"

"So I could do what? Call him to the office?" She shakes her head at me. "This isn't high school."

Good grief. She's not wrong either, but could I get a little customer service?

"Do you need something?" I startle, realizing she's moved on to a student who's come up behind me. I step to the side. The kid finishes, but another woman comes up, clearly one of the actual staff, an Asian woman in her forties, I'd guess, wearing a boring blue pantsuit with a stunning brightly colored handkerchief tied around her neck.

"I love that neckerchief," I say absentmindedly. "Is it silk?"

She smiles and nods. "It is."

Then she returns to her business with the receptionist, and I'm back to square one.

What am I supposed to do? *Think, Iris, think.*

Ray's made it clear, this isn't my problem. Even asking the question seemed stressful for him. If I text now and say, *He isn't here*, Ray will understand. He'll be confused, but he'll understand.

But I want it to be my problem. Don't I? Isn't this how I'm going to become a Fox? By being treated like one of them, even when it comes to being tasked with the totally ridiculous job of tracking down a kid on a campus filled with students.

I turn back to the desk. My smile is on and bigger, friendlier. The student receptionist appears unmoved to see me. That doesn't stop me.

"I'm so sorry. I know this isn't your problem," is how I start. "But I need to find Brandon. We have a situation at home. And it's important to my husband. He needs to be there."

The woman with the scarf is still at the desk. "Surely we could see where he was supposed to be?"

Oh-ho! Could we? I smile at her, and I mean it this time.

The student sighs. "Fine. Let me look him up. Maybe you've got his schedule wrong."

Relief washes over me. "Yes! Maybe I do."

I give his name and wait, resisting the urge to drum my fingers. There's a big clock on the wall, the same clock in every school and college across America I expect, and it's telling me it's almost two. If we're going to make it back to Harrisville for this meeting, we have to hustle.

The student frowns, studying her screen. "Brandon Fox?"

"Yep, that's right."

The other woman has dug in, too, leaning over the screen. She frowns, too. "And you're saying he's in Agriculture?"

"That's right. And, gosh, I am sorry to hurry you, but if we don't get going, we're going to miss something important. Really important." Working so hard not to lie, I'm walking a fine line here. Please don't let them ask me what's so important.

They exchange a look, and the staff member takes charge. "Well, since it's an emergency–" I never said that. But I also don't correct her– "Your husband isn't in the College of Agriculture. He's in Engineering."

Of anything they might have said, that wasn't it. I let the husband comment fly right over my head. "Say what?"

She draws a deep breath and nods. "Yes. I hope that's not a problem. But since it's an emergency," and she's picking up a piece of paper, scribbling something down, "this is the Engineering building, and here are directions. It's quite close."

I snap the paper from her, muttering, "Thanks," and fleeing.

What? There's no time to mull, but I follow what's written down. Before I'm even up the stairs leading to the building, there's Brandon. He leans against the steps' rail, chatting with two other kids.

"Brandon!"

His head whips around, mouth falling open. I stay put, beckoning like mad. He says something to his peers, they both glance my way, and then he hotfoots it down to me.

"Iris! Hey, fancy meeting you here!" He's all smiles and friendliness. "It's a miracle you found me. Normally I'd be a couple buildings down at Ag, but today I got pulled into–"

"Cut it out. I know you're in Engineering," I snap, and he freezes.

"What, what, how do you mean?"

I stomp my foot, furious. "Brandon! Your family thinks you're getting a degree in Agriculture. What are you doing in Engineering?"

"Look, Iris, there must be some mistake," Brandon starts.

"Oh, good, you found him!" We both turn, and the lady with the beautiful scarf is passing by with a small group of people.

To the man next to her, she adds, loud enough for us to hear, "She couldn't find her husband, and we had to send her in the right direction."

Brandon looks at me, eyebrow raised. "Husband?"

I wave a hand, flushing. "Not the issue. Seriously, what is going on?"

Brandon drops his head and takes a big breath. "Can we sit?"

I meet his gaze. He looks more like Dennis, tall and thick with the same fast smile that Dennis has. But right now, his eyes are plaintive like Ray's, worried and open.

I take a breath. "Yes, OK."

48.

As soon as Brandon starts talking, he can't stop. These Foxes and their "I don't want to talk about it."

We choose a bench across from the Engineering building, and he tells me everything.

How he loves the farm, he does, but it doesn't hold his interest. It's what he knows, and he's good at it. He gets to work with Ray and Dennis, and that always seemed good enough. He was content, at the ripe age of eighteen, to commit to farming as his lifelong career.

Then he got to college. "I didn't even want to go," he says, his voice plaintive. "Mama and Ray made me." He rests his elbows on his knees, hands clasped together, and head bowed while he talks. "I'd had enough of school. But they said I needed a degree. Something in agriculture or marketing, something that could help the business."

He shakes his head. "I loved all the math. Calculus. Statistics. It's like they spoke my language." I laugh, and he shoots me a suspicious look.

"Sorry." I put up both hands. "That's just, that's the opposite of anything I have ever said in my life. Please, continue."

Brandon shrugs. "It was the math that did it. And then some science. I was taking some of these classes for fun, as electives, and some of my buddies kept asking, 'Why agriculture?' Or 'Have you thought about engineering? Math major? L & T?'" I pop an eyebrow. "Logistics and Transportation."

"Thank goodness. It sounded dirty."

Brandon laughs and with it relaxes. He sits up and leans back, watching people pass. "I don't know how I got into this. I mean, what the hell am I gonna do?"

I lean back, too, crossing my arms over my stomach, thinking. "Does an engineering degree have anything to do with the farm?"

He shrugs. "It could be helpful. When we build and plan, I can do a lot of good."

"And otherwise?"

He shakes his head.

What a mess. "Brandon, what were you thinking? Why didn't you tell someone?"

"I don't know. I had to switch majors to take the classes I wanted so I just did it."

"When?"

He won't meet my eyes. "Last year."

"Brandon!" I yelp. It's all there is to say.

We fall silent.

He's so young. I hate platitudes, but he has his whole life in front of him. And if anyone can understand going against the grain, following a career path other people question, isn't it me?

"Would it be enough for you? Getting this degree and going back to the farm?"

He doesn't say anything.

I nudge him with my foot. "Brandon?"

He looks at me, his expression agonized. "I don't think so. Not after seeing all the things I could be doing."

There's fourteen years between us, but at that moment, he reminds me so much of my boys, that open, honest desire for something mixed with so much fear he can't have it. "I didn't want this to happen, Iris," he says, and he sounds tearful. "I love my family. I want to be there for them. But this is the rest of my life, and I, I don't think I'm meant to live it in Lincoln County on the farm."

I nod. "Welp, that's that then."

"What do you mean?"

"It's not a matter of if, is it? It's a matter of how and when. That's what we have to figure out. When to tell them and how."

The force that hits me is so strong my brain shrieks, *Attack, attack!* until I realize it's Brandon, bear hugging the ever-loving breath from my body. "Thank you, thank you, thank you," he says into my hair.

Meanwhile, I'm slapping his back, gasping, "I can't breathe. Brandon! Help!"

He backs off, grinning, and I try to catch my breath.

"Aw, looks like you worked it out." It's the lady in the scarf again, headed back to the Ag building. She's beaming at us and shoots me a thumbs up.

I wave, force a smile, and remind myself I can't come back to this campus until Brandon has graduated and many years have passed.

"Hang on. Why did she call me your husband?" Brandon raises an eyebrow at me.

"Just go with it," I hiss through my teeth. "And get your stuff together. We've got to get our butts back to Lincoln County."

49.

It turns out, it's only Brandon who has to get his butt back to Lincoln County. Once we get to our cars and he's following me out of the parking lot, I call Ray and share some of the good news.

"I got him!"

He actually whoops. "That's my woman, taking care of business!"

"Brandon's headed back now, but I've still got to get the boys. Is that going to be a problem?"

What I mean is, will that be a problem for Myrtle?

Ray, however, says, "No, don't worry about it. You take your time. This thing should be over by five, and I'll come straight home."

This isn't adding up. "But if the meeting's at three-thirty, shouldn't I come straight to your mom's house? Catch up on what I can?"

"Oh, Lord, no, honey. You've done your part. Don't worry about this. Besides, it's just for the family."

The words hit me harder than Brandon's big boy hug moments earlier. Tears prick my eyes, and my hands clench the steering wheel.

"Iris? Are you there?"

I lick my lips, suddenly dry, and echo, "Just for the family?"

He's quiet. "Well, now, I don't mean it hatefully. That's a good thing. You don't have to be mixed up in all this."

"Mixed up in the family?" I laugh, and it's a hard, hollow sound. "Alright then, Ray. Good to know."

"Hang on a second. That's not what I said."

"Never mind. I'm going to go." And I hang up even as my husband sputters excuses at me. He calls back, and I ignore it.

Just for the family? How can he say that? How can he even think that?

I'm so frustrated I bump the steering wheel with the heel of my hand. That both hurts me and honks the horn, earning me a surprised then hateful look from the car stopped in front of me in the pickup line. I wave apologetically, but he shakes his head and drives off as soon as his kid gets loaded into the back of his car.

What's the point of me hustling out to Harrisville College and tracking down Ray's brother if I'm not part of the family? Would a stranger do that? A friend? Hardly. And yet here I am, wearing myself out only to be told the meeting is "just for the family."

What would it take with him? We're married. We have been for two months now! I realize two months isn't twenty years. It's not even two. But it's something, at least to me. To Ray, it doesn't seem to mean anything.

Thinking of the last few days, of Dennis' drunken behavior, of Steph's big love admission, and now discovering Brandon's well-kept secret, I want to scream. I'm good enough to hold all these family secrets but not to be part of the family. That's what this is?

"Hey there, Ms. Iris!" It's one of the after school teachers, Ms. Jade, in all her sunny glory. I turn to say hello, and she blanches. "Oh, Iris, are you OK?"

A quick mirror check shows me I've got mascara streaks and a bright red nose. Rubbing at my cheeks, I gulp. "I'm OK. It's been a tough day."

She tilts her head, looking sympathetic, even as she nimbly loads the boys into the back seat and helps them buckle up. "I hope it gets better."

I force a smile. "I'm sure it will. Thanks, Ms. Jade."

"What's wrong with you, Mom?" Atticus demands.

"Oh, I'm fine, lovey."

"But you've got raccoon eyes!" Ernie exclaims.

I wince as much from the noise as the truth and dab my eyes. "It's fine. I'm fine."

"Were you cryinggg?" He holds the 'g' for reasons only he could fathom.

"A little. And Ernie, stop shouting. You're going to bust all our eardrums."

He opens his mouth, but I catch his eye, and he settles down in his seat.

We have a thirty-minute drive in front of us, and bawling all the way home isn't an option. No matter how appealing. I straighten up in my seat and focus. "How was your day?"

Atticus shrugs. "Fine. I've got to finish a math sheet, and I need testing on spelling words."

My gosh, this kid makes it easy. Ask him what needs to happen next, and he'll spit out all instructions, plus a timeline for when he'll have them done and probably a few suggestions on extra credit he might get or how you can best assist him. I give him a wink. "I'd love to help."

"It's OK. Ray said he'd do it." Atticus is face open and honest.

I grip the steering wheel a little tighter. "But honey, I love helping you."

"I know. But I want Ray to."

I'm baffled. And hurt. Here's Ray, telling me something is just for his family. And now here's my son, preferring Ray to me. Openly embracing this stepparent person. Where was the fairness? The humanity? I press forward. "Why Ray? This has been our thing for, I don't know, your whole life."

At this, Atticus shrugs. Alright then. Clear as mud, as my dad says.

Lips pressed tight, I only nod. "What about you, Ernie?"

Now it's Ernie's turn to shrug. Apparently, it's contagious. "Don't know."

My eye falls to his backpack. There's Atticus's dark blue, closed. There's Ernie's red one, top open wide, with a handful of Xerox sheets sticking out of the top. At least someone would still need my help.

It's a quiet drive home. Besides asking about lunch, it's usually a silent ride, and I think we all enjoy it.

It's all the time Ernie needs to recharge, and by the time we pull up in front of the house, he's spilling out of the car, shouting, "Ray's home!"

He's right, too. It's only a little after four, but Ray's truck is in the driveway, Ray still in it. He climbs out when he sees us.

Both boys bolt for him, and he rewards them each with a hug, a clap on the back, and a hearty, "Howdy-ho, boys! How goes it today?"

He glances in my direction and waves. My eyes are welling up, and I can't bring myself to get out.

I stay in the car for two reasons. First, I'd rather not start sobbing in front of my boys. And second, I do want to check my face one more time, surreptitiously, and make sure my eyes aren't covered in gunk.

Of course, it's hard to dab at my eye makeup when I keep welling up.

It's probably silly. I'm probably overreacting. Goodness knows I've heard these two accusations my whole life: Iris, you're being silly, and Iris, stop overreacting.

But it hurt when Ray said this meeting was just for family. It hurt a lot. If I'm not family, who is? If my kids want him to do spelling, if they light up at the sight of him, hurling themselves from still moving cars to go greet him, what are they to him? How can he be so cold?

Something makes a click-click sound against my window, and I jump.

Ray's leaning against the side of the car. He makes a rolling gesture with his finger, and I obediently open the window, like I'm pulled over at a traffic stop.

"You think you're gonna come in?"

I open my mouth to answer and instead start sobbing.

Ray's face falls, and he exclaims, "Oh, Lord, Iris, what is it?" At the same time, he's opening the car door and helping me out.

"Where are the boys?" I manage.

"I sent 'em inside. Told them to turn on the TV and get to undoing all the good work school did today."

I nod and cry harder.

Ray's mouth is open, eyes confused. "Honey, what is happening?"

The thoughts make sense in my head, but somehow, with Ray's arms around me, his eyes on my face, I struggle to verbalize them.

"I wanted to come to the meeting." It's the best thing I can land on.

If Ray looked confused before, he looks doubly so now. "The farm meeting?"

"The family meeting." I study the ground, feeling embarrassed, as if the exclusion is somehow my fault.

"Why?" he says.

How can he not get this? Is he deliberately misunderstanding?

My heart thunders, my chest heaving. Sadness shifts into frustration and anger. If he can't or, more likely, won't get it, I'm not spelling it out for him.

Jaw set, tears dry, I shake my head. "Nothing. It's nothing."

I step away, but he keeps his hold on me. "Iris, this ain't nothing. I saw your face. Honey, you look heartbroken. It was only a meeting."

"Just a meeting I had to track Brandon down for? So no big deal then, but I had to drive over to the college and find him for it?"

A look passes Ray's face, some kind of comprehension, and he draws back now. Hands in his pockets, he ducks his head. "Yeah, OK. I get that. I am sorry, Iris. I wouldn't have asked, but..." We stare at each other as his voice trails off. What he's saying doesn't click for me, and when he doesn't finish his thought, I remain at a loss. He looks away first. It's like he's embarrassed. But of what? Not inviting me? That doesn't feel like it.

He says, "Look, my mother asked me to ask you. She knew you were in Harrisville, and she really wanted Brandon there. I told her it was wrong to ask you to stop your day to deal with her problem, but she was adamant, and I gave in. I'm not proud of myself."

He looks me straight in the eye and says, "I won't ask you to do anything like that again,"

That's what he thinks I'm upset about? I want to pull my hair out. This is maddening. We don't even agree as to why we're upset.

"It's not being asked to find Brandon. It's being kept out of the meeting. The family meeting."

Ray's forehead wrinkles, and he opens his mouth. But then Atticus shouts, and we both turn to see him running towards us. "Ernie let the chickens out!" he howls, cheeks pink and blotchy with indignation. "I told him not to, and he did, Mom!"

From a distance, Ernie shouts, "It's OK! I can get them!"

Ray's in action, striding away and calling, "I'll get them," over his shoulder.

"Oh, good grief." I instinctively reach out to rub Atticus' back.

And I take Atticus inside. I'm finished with this conversation.

50.

"Is everything OK?" My mother, sounding unnecessarily anxious, answers the phone after one ring.

Pulling from the school parking lot, I drop my sunglasses on my face and take a long drink of coffee. This morning, it wasn't pretty. Ray left early. He'd warned me he needed an early start to the day. But, when my alarm went off this morning, I'd forgotten. I pressed snooze like I always do knowing Ray would wake me up if I slept through my second and third alarms.

So two things happened: I overslept, making us late, and I realized how dependent I've become on him in less than three months. This marriage is so new, and yet so much of he and I and how we work is sewn into the fabric of my life now. When he's not where I expect him, I miss a stitch, and a hole opens up.

We made it out of the house, me throwing an actual box of cereal into the back seat with the boys, like feeding a pack of wild animals, and then driving like I was being chased by the devil. The car line teacher locked the school's front door as we arrived, forcing me into the parent walk of shame, in my sweatpants and the t-shirt I had slept in, to escort the boys inside.

And now, the car is quiet. I'm headed home and think, *You know who could comfort me? Who could bring some perspective and help to this day? Angie.*

But she isn't home.

So now I've called my mother, who's apparently been in a quiet crisis over my lack of phone calls recently. "We've been worried." Translation: She's been worried.

"Mom, we talked a couple of days ago."

"We texted. Texting isn't talking. And it was working out schedules for the boys. That's hardly talking. What's going on?"

That tender sad feeling wells up again, and my chest starts rising and falling as I fight back the tears. "It's just been hard," I mumble. I will not cry, no matter how badly I might want to.

"What's happening? What's wrong?" There's not much subtlety to my mom. Her voice rises, her words start to fall over each other, instant panic at its most powerful. "It's Iris. She's upset," I hear her say off to the side. "Button, what is it?"

It's the ding-dang 'Button' that does it. I start blubbing.

To this, she exclaims, "Oh, no, Iris!" And then off the phone she's shouting, "Zeke! Come here, something's wrong with Iris!"

"No, no, nothing's wrong." I weep in the direction of my speaker-phone. "Look, Mom, I should go. I need to drive."

"Come over here," she says and sounds firm for once.

And to my surprise, and probably hers too, I listen to her.

My parents have lived in the same house my entire life. They bought it as older newlyweds, a two-bedroom, one-bathroom cottage in one of Harrisville's older and well-established neighborhoods. Mom always laughs, in a posh neighborhood like this, it was either this or a sturdy box. But truthfully, it never felt tiny.

And we always got along. It was only the three of us, making our way through the day-to-day, Dad a principal at a high school several neighborhoods over and Mom a happy stay-at-home mom.

They met working at that high school. Dad got the job, moving from Knoxville to Harrisville. Mom was one of the two women who worked in the office, a single lady, in her late twenties, living with her parents, going to church on Sunday mornings and nights and Wednesday nights, and working her job. Dad was almost five years older than her, and he says his family believed, a confirmed bachelor. Nonetheless, after a slow warm-up, they started dating. And continued to date for nearly two years until on her thirtieth birthday, Mom gave Dad an ultimatum: propose or she'd be accepting the new gym teacher's, Coach Holland's, invitation to dinner the next weekend. Coach Holland, Dad will say when he tells the story, was a rambunctious, impulsive man. "I knew," Dad says, "if I was up against Coach Holland, my days were numbered."

And here they are, at their new kitchen table, having recently turned the tiny dining room into Dad's office and library.

As Mom makes coffee, I ask, "Why didn't you make my bedroom your office?"

It's not that the kitchen isn't lovely. The new table is sweet, a round, cheery yellow table, with matching yellow chairs and cushions with bluebirds, my mom's favorite bird. Because my mom is exactly the kind of person to have a favorite bird. But with the table and the kitchen island, plus normal kitchen cabinets and appliances, it's packed tight now.

"Why do we need a dining room? It's only your dad and me." Mom stirs two spoonfuls of sugar and warm milk into my coffee. It's comforting that she still knows my coffee order. And at the same time, it reminds me of Ray, who's just learned it.

"Besides," Mom sets the cup in front of me, "there might be an emergency. You could need your room."

"Cynthia," Dad says at the same time I bristle and say, "Why? Why would I need my room?"

Mom lifts her shoulders, an elegant shrug. "I don't know. That's why it would be an emergency."

Dad sighs and shakes his head.

"Now what's going on? You sounded awful in the car, honey." Mom meets my eyes, direct emotional confrontation one of her skills. "And you don't look good, Button, if I'm honest."

"Mom!" I say again while Dad laughs.

"I don't mean to hurt your feelings. But it's true. What's going on?"

My mom hasn't worked in a school office in thirty-six years. She stayed home because she wanted me to have the best care possible, which, apparently, meant her. Dad would often make the point, as I reached grade school and beyond, I probably didn't need quite such excellent care anymore. And Mom would lift her shoulders, that ladylike shrug, and say, "If we thought someone else could take care of us as well as she did, well, hire that lady and she'd get straight back to work." It was enough to make Dad recede behind his newspaper and leave it alone.

Now that I'm here, I'm not sure what to say. Some of the sadness has passed. Seeing them helps. "I don't know. It's not, nothing's wrong exactly. It's just, it's hard."

"Marriage is hard. Whoever says otherwise isn't doing it right," Dad says.

I resist the urge to roll my eyes at him. King of the platitudes, my dad.

Lips pressed together, I lean my elbows on the table, working to find the words. "I know it is. And it's OK," I add as my mom's mouth pops open. "But it is hard. And I think this might be extra hard, being there with Ray's family like we are."

Mom shoots a look at Dad, eyebrows raised to her platinum-blonde hairline. "What did I tell you? I told him, I told your father, this living on the farm is going to be a mess. A real mess. Is it awful? Are they terrible?"

"No!" I exclaim, not because it's true but because I instinctively disagree with my mother's big, bold declarations. And so many of the things she says are big, bold declarations.

She sips her coffee, waiting.

"They're not awful," I say. "But they're not easy either. They're, I don't know, they're all there, all the time."

"It's a family business with all people living on the premises. So that would make sense," Dad, Mr. Logical to a Fault, says.

"I know that. I thought we'd have our own space, but they kind of show up whenever they want."

Dad frowns. "That's not OK."

"Right? Thank you!" I throw my hands up, relieved. If my dad's thrown off, I can't be on the wrong path. "It's so weird. They just stop by–his mother, his brother, the farm manager, whoever–and that's normal for them apparently. But then, they don't–" I halt, unable to actually form the words hovering at the edge of my lips.

"Iris? What is it? Just say it, sweetie." Mom's eyes are wide, hanging on every word.

It needs to be said. I don't want to do it, but I want to be honest. *Tell the truth, tell the truth, tell the truth.*

I swallow, face my parents, and say, "They don't like me."

51.

"What?" Mom's appalled, shooting to her feet and banging her mug on the table.

At the same time, my father puts up his hands and says, "Hold on."

Mom isn't having a "hold on." "How could they not like you? You're the most likable person I know!"

My father coughs at this declaration, and even I squirm. That's a strong statement. Still, I appreciate the effort.

"It's true. You're kind, you're funny, you make beautiful art, and your boys are, are, are spunky!" It makes me laugh where she lands. "Spunky" feels like the median of my kids. It's too strong for thoughtful, quiet Atticus but far too mild for wild, reckless Ernie. "What wouldn't they like about you?" Mom's tone is so plaintive, her eyes wide with wonder. I realize she's taking this personally, too. I am her daughter. If someone didn't like one, or both, of my boys, I'd probably feel the same.

I squeeze her hand. "At least, I've got you guys in my corner."

"Darn tootin' you do." Her eyes are blazing. "And your bedroom is always here if you ever–"

"Mom," I warn at the same time Dad says, "Cynthia, please."

Then he fixes me with his severe look. While my mom's all softness with her shoulder-length blonde hair and an every softening, rounding form, my dad's all dark and angles, tall and lanky, with dark brown dark hair that's gone gray and bushy eyebrows that are completely silver.

He stares at me. "What makes you think they don't like you?"

That tone, solemn, searching for the truth–I've joked my dad missed his calling as a lawyer. A prosecuting attorney to be clear. He insists his voice and his stare have done wonders on errant teenagers for the last forty years, and he doesn't regret his professional choices a whit.

Unlike kids at his school, I've grown up under that gaze. Shake me? Just try.

Shoulders squared, chin out, I meet his gaze and throw down my gauntlet. "It's a feeling I have."

"There, you see?" Mom flings her hands in the air while my dad shakes his head.

"Goodness, Iris, here we go again. You and your 'feelings.'"

"Don't put it in quotation marks." I glare at him.

"I didn't," he says back, calm and collected.

"I could feel the quotations," I shoot back, and we eyeball each other.

He gives in first. As usual. Instead of pushing back, he leans back in his chair. "A feeling is not evidence. I'm not saying it doesn't have validity, but that doesn't make it fact either."

"It's a very strong feeling," I say, and Mom gives him a triumphant look. It's a bit much, and I want to ask her to tone it down. However, as my one and only ally in this ongoing familiar dispute, I don't want to risk alienating her either. "It's the way his mother looks at me. It's how they all look at me, honestly." Recalling so many expressions, Brandon's mirth the night of the chicken debacle, Naomi's gentle condescension, Stephanie's complete exclusion.

Really, Iris? Is that absolutely fair? The problem with being raised with a dad like Zeke Shepherd is, after enough questions on truth and accuracy, it does lead to occasional self-examination that doesn't always prove me as blameless as I might hope.

At the moment, I'm aware of the fact, Stephanie blanked everyone, not just me. And since her great reveal about her love life, that's changed. She's texting me daily and plans to keep attending church with us.

And Brandon, while we haven't spoken again, sent me a simple thank you text, including an old-fashioned smiley face made up of semicolon eyes and a parenthesis mouth. He's not ungrateful.

"What are you thinking about?" It's my dad. My mom bangs around the kitchen looking for food I bet.

Yep! She returns to the table with a box of frozen Thin Mints, saved from the last Girl Scout cookie sale, and she's muttering as she tears into a sleeve and empties it onto a plate for us to share. Never mind that it's nine-thirty in the morning.

"Not like you. How dare they. What a bunch of–"

"Cynthia," Dad says again. It's quiet for a bit except for the companionable sound of Mom and me crunching on cold cookies.

I ignore Dad's question and consider the kitchen instead. It's so nice here. Exactly how I remember it, bright, cozy, smelling of Mom's favorite vanilla cinnamon candle. The sunlight falling through the kitchen window warms me up, and I'm so tempted to head up to my old room, perfectly intact, and take a nap on my white wrought iron daybed.

Why couldn't I come back here? It would be so easy. More help from Mom and Dad with the boys. No more new relationships, trying new things, meeting new people, and working so damn hard to sell baby sweaters and knitted blocks to people who really don't need them except they're soft, beautiful, and bougie. Maybe I could work on my art? Really explore what it is I want to do. Maybe I could learn that weaving machine or spend more time with acrylic paint?

Or–I'm gripped by the thought–go back to school. There could be a world of work out there I'm not aware of. Actually, what a ridiculous thing to say. Of course, there's a whole world of work out there I'm not aware of.

"Iris? Why do you look like that?" The concern in my father's eyes brings me back to here and now. A married woman. With two kids. Visiting, not living, with her parents. Stress eating cold Thin Mints with her mother because life feels overwhelming at the moment.

I meet his gaze. "Nothing." It's the best response. He's got his chin down, gaze suspicious. "Nothing, really. Just considering how I can build bridges with Ray's family."

Mom snorts. "Pah. They should be building bridges with you." She brushes cookie crumbs off her chest and glares out the window.

"Honey. I don't think you need to work so hard on it. Why not just be yourself? Give it some time and let them get to know you. You are, in fact, a fairly likable person."

"Am I?" I deadpan, and he grins.

"That's the spirit. Don't let 'em get you down and don't give up! Now, let me tell you about that hooligan Jake Marshall and the skins protest I heard he led last week."

"Skins?" I echo, concern washing over me

"Yes, skins. Apparently, Jake has taken up the cause of women being forced to cover their breasts in public. And he believes, this sixteen-year-old delinquent does, that women should be allowed to disrobe exactly the same as men. So his protest was meant to be a campus-wide walkout at lunchtime with everyone, males and most definitely females–"

"Topless," I supply.

Dad winks at me. "You guessed it."

52.

"I still don't understand why we're doing this." Ray kneels at the grill, trying to work out why the propane won't light. There's a pop, and he falls back, swearing, flicking his burned fingers, then looks at me with a straight face. "Think I fixed the grill."

"We've been married for two and a half months. We're all settled in. And there hasn't been one of these suppers since the boys and I got here. Why shouldn't we do one?"

"I can quite literally think of a hundred different reasons. But I can see by the look in your eyes, you won't care for one of them." He fires up the grill, where flames dance to life, before he turns it off and closes the top. "Has anyone ever told you you're a very stubborn woman, Iris Shepherd now Fox?"

All the time, I think, but only shoot him a sunny smile and go back to my work, which is spray painting the wrought iron table. To be clear, I'm not painting a new color, but touching up its faded peeling black.

In one week, we're holding a Sunday family supper. It was never made clear to me why the suppers stopped after we attended our first one. But they did. And I was going to bring them back to life.

So I proposed the idea to Myrtle yesterday, and she was delighted.

Well, she wasn't delighted. I don't know if Myrtle ever feels delight in her life. She looked at me with a serious face, snorted, and shook her head. I took that as a yes.

Everyone in the family knows to come here. Ricky and Naomi have both been invited as have my parents. And in one final brilliant move, I've told people not to bring food. Instead of the usual Sunday potluck, we will have one Iris Shepherd Fox feast.

Ray shakes his head. "And because we're having this party–"

"Supper," I interject. "It is a casual Sunday supper. Same as the one y'all have. Or used to have."

"Right. Except this one involves more people, it's here, we have to clean up for it, and we're making all of the food."

I nod. "Yes."

"So exactly like the normal Sunday supper. But the point is, even though this meal isn't for another week, we have to get ready for it today. Is that right?"

"Yes," I say again, this time more firmly.

With only a week to go, we're in the thick of preparation. The boys are currently hanging upside down from the trees. Ray's working on cleaning up the grill and grill area, and I'm determined to make this outdoor space in front of the house beautiful in the time we have allotted.

"And we couldn't get ready for this party, say Saturday? Or better yet, Sunday when we have it?"

I look at him. "Do you remember what happened last Saturday? As in yesterday?"

He has the grace to look abashed. Market season is bearing down on us, and Ray promised these next few weeks of free Saturdays we'd spend together as a family. Until Dennis got a call from a farmer up the road about a bull going up for auction yesterday afternoon. This meant, instead of getting in the car with us in the morning to drive to a nearby state park and take an easy hike, Ray got in his brother's smelly truck and drove forty minutes north to the auction. He returned two hours later than he told me he would, with, yes, a bill of sale in hand for the bull, but also definite black marks next to his name, at least in my book.

"That was a once-in-a-lifetime opportunity."

I resist the urge to roll my eyes. That was Angie's advice when Ray and I got married. "No eye-rolling," she said.

"But what if he says something really, really stupid? And I really, really need to roll them?"

"Don't do it. It's the death of a marriage."

"Says who?"

She shrugged. "Can't remember their names. But they're professional marriage therapists, who've been married to each other for a billion years, and they absolutely, totally, without a doubt, say, 'No eye-rolling!'"

I studied her. "So you never eye-roll José?" She paused, mouth open. "You're saying this in front of God, not just me!" I added.

"OK. I might eye-roll him sometimes. But only on the inside!" I cocked an eyebrow and pointed heavenward. Angie sighed and relented. "Or where he can't see me do it."

Well, this is me now, eye-rolling my sweet, kind, sexy husband on the inside, because while he might have the best of intentions, the amount of time he spends working during his free time is staggering.

And Ray doesn't have boundless energy. He's not one of these types who can interact, socialize, and stay busy until the proverbial cows come home, then come home himself and do seven more things.

Now give him a solitary project to work on, and he's locked in for hours. But put him in a truck with Dennis, then in a roomful of other farmers at auction, and back in that said truck? By the time he's waded through the waters of listening to Dennis ramble, spitting and chatting with other farmers, negotiating an auction, and then doing the drive with Dennis again, Ray is done. Kaput. He has no more energy left to give us. So yesterday when he arrived home from said auction, all he could offer was to put on a Pixar movie with the boys and sit on the sofa, occasionally asking questions like, "Yeah, but why does the dog talk? And I still don't get the balloons. They were pretty, but they don't seem to tie into the rest of this movie at all."

I know Atticus and Ernie were disappointed. They wanted to do something amazing like hike with Ray or at least go drive farm equipment in the fields, maybe holler at the cows and put out the hay. I saw their faces when Ray found the remote control and patted the spots on each side of him on the sofa. They were disappointed but grateful. Thankful to have anyone father-like who wanted to spend time with them. They watched *Up* again like it was the most riveting movie they'd ever seen.

The angry flare that flickers in my chest causes me to drop my eyes and focus on my painting. *Don't say words, just breathe, and get through this.* If I don't focus on how much Ray works, on how often he's missing without ever noticing he's absent, maybe I'll be able to maintain my composure and stay calm.

"Hey, Iris?"

I pause my painting, hand in mid-air, and look up to meet Ray's eyes. He waits until he has my gaze and holds it. "I'm glad we're doing this. I'm glad you suggested it."

And then he smiles a tiny smile just for me. My breath catches in my throat, the urge to cry at such tenderness, such authenticity, rising up in me. I smile, nod once, and look back at my work. It's the only way I can keep from giving my whole heart away.

Because somehow he does this. He makes me want to pull my hair out, see red angry, so crazy with frustration, and just when I think it's time to start running or yelling, he holds my gaze and, in the simplest way, lets me know his whole heart is in this. With me. Him and me. Me and him.

And it's enough to make me want to beam and weep at the same time.

53.

Pulling up to my house, coming from the back from the school drive, I'm desperate for a quiet morning. The boys are at school. Ray is on the farm. With this Sunday supper staring us down, I need a little alone time to reset my mind. Reset my spirit.

But apparently, not today. There's a big truck outside, and I recognize it. Not my husband's. Not Ricky's. Not even Naomi's.

Dennis' truck. And sitting at my freshly spray-painted patio table, long, denim-clad legs stretched out in front of him and crossed at the ankles is Dennis.

"Iris." He smiles.

I approach with caution. The best possible means of handling this is to be cool and easygoing and pretend as if nothing happened. Not a word about anything.

Pasting on a smile, I hop out of my car, trip, drop my bag, and spill the contents everywhere. Wallet, cell phone, hair ties, half-eaten breakfast bar, Kleenex, reusable bags of animal crackers, a hairbrush, a few action figures, Matchbox racing cars, and so much more.

How to be confident while on the ground, scrabbling around for random items and bric-a-brac? It doesn't help when Dennis gets down on all fours, too, handing me things and laughing.

"Iris, always cool under pressure," he says, as if he read my mind and knew my intentions. Maybe he did. Recalling his words about our time at the farmers' markets those years before Ray came, I feel a little shiver.

It's hanging over me, what Dennis said. Not intentionally and not during daylight hours. I shove those words away when I'm with the boys and Ray. But at night when the house is quiet and Ray is asleep, Dennis' words creep into my brain, and they leave me wondering.

Was I as innocent as I thought? I liked that Dennis was married. Married meant taken. Married meant off the market. It meant we could joke and chat without any question of anything beyond friendship.

I know, for sure, I never imagined anything other than friendship. But did I...had I possibly been more intimate, more honest than I should have been with a married man? It's so hard to find the lines. I absolutely believe women and men can be friends outside of a romantic relationship. But when I cast my mind around, considering my male friends, I come up with only married men. And, in both cases, I'm friendly with their spouse.

None of that was the case with Dennis.

My throat tightens up, my stomach in knots. Did I lead him on?

Kneeling next to him in the hard and unforgiving gravel driveway, these thoughts rush over me, and, before I can stop myself, words start spilling out. I have to assuage myself of this guilt.

"Dennis, I hope you know I never meant to cross lines. Or boundaries. I wasn't thinking, or at least I was thinking, but I genuinely thought it was just friendly, just two people who enjoyed each other's company hanging out and chatting. And I don't have anything to compare it to. I mean, I've been a work-from-home mom my whole life, well, my whole mom life, and I have so little interaction with men, besides customers and that's different. I saw the markets as my office. And here were you and I having a great time and passing the work day like good co-workers, colleagues, honestly. And now I keep thinking about it, and I feel so bad. I'm so sorry, Dennis. Can you see where I was coming from?"

He's gotten still, watching me. When I stop and draw in one long, shuddery breath, his expression doesn't change. It's in his eyes where I see it—hurt. He's hurt, and there's no way around it. Maybe he's more hurt hearing me say it was always a friend thing to me. I did say that, didn't I?

I've made this huge, hurtful mistake, and I have no idea how to correct it.

And then Dennis says, "You work so hard, Iris. All the time. With your boys. Trying to make your nutty business take off. Making all that crazy healthy food. Just being nice to people."

Something in his voice pulls me upright. Sitting back on my haunches, hands on my knees, I meet his gaze, and he meets mine.

When he speaks, his voice is clear and firm. "You're a good person, Iris. I don't doubt that. Not for a second. I hope you don't either. Don't let one pathetic guy's disillusionment mess with your head, OK?"

You're a good person. The words hit almost like a punch. I struggle to catch my breath. The thing I've felt so far from, the thing I've wanted these people in this family to notice, and Dennis has just said it. Simply, you're a good person.

"You hear me?" He's looking hard at me.

I nod, brushing at my face and trying to maintain my composure—or what's left of it.

Dennis nods, too. "Good," he says. His tone is clear: This is done.

Relief floods through me. That's it. It's over.

There's the crunch of gravel, and we both turn. I don't know what I expect, but it's not Ray in the cab of his truck, watching us with hard, blank eyes.

54.

Goodness, Dennis is never phased. He doesn't hurry to stand up, doesn't move an inch.

"Howdy-ho, brother," he calls.

Ray moves slowly, expressionless. He approaches the two of us gunslinger style, cool and calm, and stops a few feet away.

"What brought you here, Dennis?" he asks. I swear to goodness, if he had a revolver on his hip, he'd rest his hand on it right now.

I open my mouth, excuses springing to my lips.

"Ah, I had something to say to Iris," Dennis says without hesitating.

What? Why? Why would he say that?

"We needed to talk about–about–" I falter. Dennis isn't looking at me. Ray isn't either.

That's when understanding dawns. This isn't about me. Or if it is, it's only about me as an object, a prize.

But, really, this is about these brothers, fighting out some battle that started a long time before I was ever here and will probably go on long after I'm gone.

And why did I just think that? Where am I going?

There's a thrumming in my head, blood rushing to my face. I shove myself up off the ground, staggering a little from my legs falling asleep and catching myself on the patio table. *Graceful as always, Iris.*

Even that doesn't stop me. "This is ridiculous." I'm glaring first at Ray first and then at Dennis. "You are brothers. You've always known each other. Do you know how lucky you are? Do you? Some of us have wanted our entire lives to feel that kind of long-lived connection with someone else. And what do you two do? You throw it away in some stupid rivalry in this, this pissing contest! It's disgusting. You're both idiots."

And, with my bag clutched to my chest, on shaky legs, I storm into the house, letting the door bang shut behind me.

55.

Only Ray follows me inside.

I don't know how long I've been alone, ten minutes, maybe longer. And remembering my life before men, before marriage, before this farm, I've asked myself, *If you were home, what would you be doing now?*

The simple answer is lunch. So that's what I do now. Ray finds me finishing up, a simple tuna fish sandwich on some sourdough I made last weekend. I top it with baby spinach from Ray's spring garden and add a few slices of cheese to the mix. Absolutely perfect.

While he hovers in the doorway, I take a seat at the table with my plate, toss up a quick, silent prayer for my meal, and take a bite. It's delicious.

"We should talk," Ray says.

"No." I chew and dab at my mouth with my napkin.

Both his eyebrows move slowly up his forehead. "What's that now?"

"No," I repeat with more emphasis. "I don't want to talk. I want to eat my lunch."

I take another bite of the sandwich. In two days, this bread will be tough, but today it's soft and chewy.

The house is quiet. Sunlight streams through the three windows though the house is still never bright. In the distance, faintly, I can hear the highway that runs by the main house. Otherwise, it's only my chewing to break up the stillness.

I'm not exactly enjoying it. It's a relief to eat uninterrupted, but the tension in the room hangs over both of us. For the first time I can remember, I wish Ray wasn't home.

Ray, to his credit, doesn't rush me. He leans against the back of the sofa, arms crossed, legs stuck out in front of him, studying his boots. His posture is an uncanny imitation of Dennis, something I doubt he wants to hear.

I finish, wipe my mouth again, and lay my napkin down. And then I look up at Ray. His lips quirk up at the edges. His dark hair sticks up all over his head. He's down to a t-shirt today, the weather pushing into the mid-seventies lately, and a pair of busted-up old chinos, the knees threatening to split open they're so frayed.

"May I?" He indicates the table, and I nod, working to stay neutral, expressionless.

We're both quiet. I'm aware of the time. I have two hours before I need to leave for the boys.

"Iris," he says exactly as I say, "Ray, look."

We pause and eye each other.

Is this marriage? You'd think we'd be on the same team. Instead, we watch each other like opponents, eyeing up the competition, testing the ground. There's no sense of camaraderie. This is a battle, a quiet one, sure, but two people drawing lines in the sand. Here's my stake, here's yours. And we both want to win. Is this what a long-term relationship is? Two people vying for victory.

"Go ahead." Ray nods.

I almost push back and say, "No, no, you go." But before my more moderate self can intercede, I burst out, "Nothing is going on between your brother and me! You have to stop behaving like there is."

He's silent for so long that I know he doesn't believe me. I drop my head back, sighing with exasperation. "This is ridiculous. I am married to you. Why would I do that if I had some sort of, I don't know, feeling for Dennis?"

Ray shrugs, the lightest gesture, and it stings, him behaving so cavalierly.

"Fine." I push back so hard from the table, my chair tips over. Shaking, hurt, I ram it back into place. "Fine. Think what you will. Don't care about what I have to say."

"Iris, please. Will you sit down?"

I round on him. How can he be so calm? He's perfectly poised in his chair, both hands on the table in front of him, looking up at me with hard-to-read eyes.

"No, I won't."

"Why?"

What is wrong with him? I throw my hands out in front of me, palms up. "I'm upset, Ray."

"About what?"

"Everything! You think I'm having some kind of thing with your brother. Your mother hates me."

"My mother doesn't hate you," he starts.

I barrel on. "Yes, she does. She wishes you and I had never got married."

"What in the world makes you say that?"

Nothing springs immediately to mind so I say, "It's a feeling. I feel it, OK?"

He drops his head back, guffawing at the ceiling. "Ah. I see. More of Iris' 'feelings.'"

It's uncanny how he sounds like my father, and my back goes up so hard I can feel it in my shoulders, in my neck, in my jaws. "What?"

Ray looks at me point-blank, and, finally, he looks like himself. "Iris, you and your feelings run this damn place, have you ever noticed that? You're mad, and you show it. You're sad, and you show it. You're happy, and forgive me for sounding like a song, we all know it. You can't keep anything on the inside for two seconds."

"I, I thought you liked that about me. My, I don't know, honesty. It's real." I thrust my chin in the air, but internally I'm reeling. Does that bother him?

"I like that you're in touch with your feelings. I just wish they'd stop calling all the shots for one minute."

Whatever I wanted to say before now has flown right out of my head. My feelings are hard for Ray to manage? That's why he's upset?

Is this the first time I've heard an argument like this?

Hardly.

Yet hearing it come from Ray's mouth makes me so angry I'm trembling. "How dare you–" flies out of my mouth.

And Ray, neither abashed nor concerned, says, "Honey, please, don't be so dramatic."

And with that, I grab my bag and storm right past him to the car.

56.

It's the weekend, and I've never been more thankful to be free of the drive to Harrisville and back. My boys don't sleep any later than usual, but they can make their own bowls of cereal and settle in front of the television as soon as they wake up. And this is precisely what I've given them permission to do.

Atticus and Ernie are delighted. I hear them whispering to each other, giggling, as they pile into the kitchen and bang cabinets and drawers finding what they need.

Sleep was my goal, but I've failed. Between the argument with Ray and preparing for people to come to supper tomorrow, I'm exhausted. My body craves sleep, hours and hours of it.

Last night I went to bed silently seething, lying in bed for hours wondering what I've gotten myself into and how to get myself back out of it. Sleep didn't come until the early morning hours. And then I felt the rustle of the blankets, Ray slipping out of bed to get ready for the day, and suddenly I was wide awake.

Now I've lain here for an hour more, thoughts drifting.

There's a bang, the fridge door, and I jolt.

"Sssh, you're going to wake Mom up!" Atticus hisses.

"Will not," Ernie shoots back, but he's whispering, too.

News flash, boys: Mom's awake. Staying in bed is pointless.

However, when I walk into the living room, pulling my robe around myself, I'm greeted by, "Awww, no!" and "Mom, you're not supposed to be up!"

"Can't a mom spend time with her kids?" I climb onto the sofa, dragging a blanket over myself.

"Do we have to turn off the TV?" Atticus asks, and they eye me suspiciously. I shake my head, and they both sigh.

Neither of them asks about Ray. It's silly to think they would. As the season gets busier, he's leaving earlier and coming home later. Waking up and finding him gone doesn't unsettle them.

I don't know if I find that encouraging or worrisome. It's a reminder, I suppose, my boys and I are a threesome, The Three Musketeers, accustomed to life on our own.

That thought leaves me sad.

And wistful for our old home, our old town, our old life.

57.

"Well, this is different."

It's not surprising these are the first words out of Myrtle's mouth. Does it cause me to drop my chin to my chest, a few seconds of total defeat? Yes, it does.

Do I pick my head back up and rally?

Sort of.

Besides, she's not wrong. If the definition of "different" is simple, beautiful, and inviting then yes, this is different.

The scrappy front yard is about the same, a weird mix of patchy grass sprinkled with loose gravel. We've strung together two of our farmers' market tables and, for lack of proper tablecloths, draped them with quickly hemmed sheets that have the most delicate flower pattern. Somehow I've managed to pull together ten place settings, plus two kids' plates and cups. But it's the lighting that brings that touch of fairy dust to the evening.

Never forget, the underappreciated workhorse of decorating is good lighting.

It's spring and it's still getting dark at six. A dozen mason jars lit by tiny electric lights and covered with ribbon twists of burlap make a row up the center of the tables. Ray erected poles around the outside area, and we've strung Edison bulbs across them. It's all softly illuminated, glowing, and romantic.

The boys run around the yard hooting in a noisy game of tag. Ray's at the grill where he's spent the last hour finishing off pork ribs at the lowest of temperatures (because nothing says classy night like eating BBQ with your fingers). I've gone for a sober evening, Dennis at the back of my mind, and we have pitchers of sweet iced tea and lemon water.

To my relief, our guests arrive at the same time, averting any awkward moments of entertaining the early ones. Thank goodness. Pretending you have nothing better to do than small talk with the people who arrive fifteen minutes early while you're still putting the finishing touches on the evening is mental torture for me.

Not tonight. Myrtle arrived first with Stephanie and Brandon in tow. And pulling in right behind them were my parents, followed closely by Naomi.

My stomach drops at the sight of her, but I'm the only one to blame for her attendance. When I mentioned inviting her to Ray, he said, "Why would you do that?"

"Why wouldn't I?" I shot back, silently challenging him to tell me a good reason.

He shrugged. "I thought this was family only."

"She practically is family." I did my best to keep my tone even. "She's been around a lot longer than me."

At that he gave me a strange look and dropped it.

I force myself to greet her first. "I'm so glad you could make it!" I enthuse, lying through my teeth.

Naomi nods and tries to smile. Up close, it's apparent she's been crying. Her eyes and her nose are red. How is she still so pretty when she's all pink and puffy like this?

I force myself to draw closer to her and ask quietly, "Are you OK?"

Naomi meets my gaze, and for a moment she almost looks thankful to me. "It's been a long day," she says.

Cryptic. It's Sunday. She doesn't work Sunday. Ray and Dennis get pulled into work on Sundays, but they're the only ones.

"Can I help?" I don't know what else to offer her, but I'm nervous and my need to help kicks in. "Do you, do you want to freshen up? I can point you to the bathroom."

Naomi nods, tearing up again. "Yeah, that'd be great." She rubs her eyes with the carelessness of a woman who's never needed a dab of mascara in her life. "But you don't have to show me. I know where it is."

I don't like that at all. However, she pats my arm and murmurs, "Thank you, Iris," before pushing past me and heading into Ray's house—our house—and there's nothing more for me to say about it.

"Honey, this is gorgeous!" Mom bustles up in her flower print wrap dress, a heavy cream-colored shawl around her shoulders. She thrusts a gift bag, with yellow and green tissue paper spewing from the top of it into my hands.

I hug her and absentmindedly accept it. "Thank you. We worked hard. What's this?"

"Hostess present!" she trills, stepping past me to hug Ray. "You lovebirds never had a housewarming."

Ah, the other side of my mom. Besides being my biggest cheerleader, she's never quite learned that adult children don't get gifted with the same regularity as young children. It's common for the boys and me to get Valentine's gifts, Easter presents, 4th of July prizes, and the occasional Halloween goody basket.

Dad's patting my back, murmuring in my ear, "You know your mother, just leave it be."

"We didn't know presents were expected," says Myrtle, her tone so dry I can hear the crinkle in her voice.

Mom turns to shoot Myrtle a glance.

"I have never been one to say no to a present, and Cynthia's already figured that out about me." Ray gives Mom a hug and turns to smile at me, his arm still around her. "And on that note, I should do my hosting duties. Cynthia, Zeke, this is my mother, Myrtle Fox. Mother, these are Iris' parents."

Mom, her lips pressed tightly together, flicks Myrtle a nod. My father, however, steps closer, hand outstretched, and they shake.

"Delighted to meet you," he says. "Honestly, it's a crime we haven't met sooner."

"These two didn't give us much time, did they?" Myrtle says dryly, and I tense. Dad, however, laughs, and he sounds genuinely amused.

"No, they sure didn't," he agrees.

"In our day, in a hurry meant one thing. But with these two," she glances between Ray and me, "I think we've dodged that bullet. We've got two impetuous youths on our hands."

"Well, that's the first time I've been called a 'youth' in some time," Ray speaks up, and my shoulders loosen at his tone. He gives me a wink.

It's enough, and I'm able to speak. "We're so glad y'all came." I'm still sweaty and stressed, but Ray and I are in this together.

Mom's eyeballing Myrtle, but at those words, she turns to me and says, "Go on, open it!"

Why, Lord? Why me? I rub my lips together, stalling. "Now?"

"Well, not later, that's for sure." She laughs and looks at Ray shaking her head, as if to say, "This silly daughter of mine!"

How I loathe this side of the gift-giving. Mom loves to give gifts. She also loves to bathe in the blessing of gratitude she anticipates on the other side of giving gifts.

Ricky pulled up, parked, and climbed out. He stands next to Myrtle, watching with bright eyes. And the boys poke at the table with Ernie whining, "I'm hu-n-n-n-gry," loud enough for everyone to hear.

I look to Ray who gives me the tiniest eye roll. He and I are united against this ridiculous situation.

In the bag there's a card. *You've got to be kidding me.* I give myself a papercut down the side of my pointer finger trying to get through this quickly.

Keeping my cussing on the inside, I find a hardware store gift card in my hands. "It's a gift card!" I sing out, forcing a smile for the crowd.

"You can't ever have too many of those," Ricky says, and there's a rumble of innocuous agreement.

"Iris, slow down. You didn't read the card."

I swallow. Don't think I didn't know this was coming.

Mom removes the bundle from my hands. "My daughter, brought up with no manners apparently. The card says: 'Roses are red, violets are blue, you two are a blessing, and we love you.'" She beams at the group.

Ricky smiles and nods, and Naomi, who is apparently refreshed, says, "Aww." The Foxes are silent.

My mother is undeterred. Clearing her throat, she gets to the handwritten portion. "'Dear Iris and Ray, we couldn't be happier for you two and the love you share. Wishing you many years of blessings and welcome to our family, Ray. We're so happy to have you.'"

She doesn't announce the amount on the gift card, which is a relief. Instead, she goes through the motions of reassembling the gift and handing it back to me. "Dad and I mean it. We couldn't be happier having you in our family, Ray."

And it's not the way she looks at my husband so much as the way she doesn't look at my mother-in-law that leaves me both appreciative and mortified.

"Any chance we can eat now?"

We all turn to Myrtle who's watching this scene with both eyebrows raised. "Like Ernie said, I'm hungry."

And that is how we kick off this family Sunday supper.

58.

Somewhere between the ribs and bringing out the strawberry cake, made with strawberries the boys and I picked and froze the previous year, I start to wonder how long is too long to sit in the bathroom and wait this night out.

Ray's still smiling and chatting, but every so often, he catches my eye. And I think if I try to escape, I'll be fighting him for the rights to that room.

What's the hardest part? It's hard to say.

Is it the multiple times my mother says to Ray, "We couldn't be happier you are part of our family"?

Is it each time my father, in full principal mode, attempts to engage Myrtle in conversation, and she, in full Appalachian reticence, answers with a deadeye yes or no response?

Dad: Myrtle, was it always your dream to run the family farm?

Myrtle, meeting his gaze, expressionless: No.

Dad: Did you have something else you might have preferred?

Myrtle: Can't say there was.

Dad: Well, it might not have been your dream, but you've certainly created a thriving operation from the sound of things.

Myrtle: Maybe.

Perhaps it's the fact Atticus and Ernie have been left to their own devices and sit under the table making farting sounds with their armpits. Or possibly it's the fact that Naomi alternates between a cold fish expression and red, weepy eyes. It doesn't help that I've caught her glancing at Ray only to see him giving her a return look of helplessness.

Do we think that's what's hardest to bear?

No matter. Before I can dig in on that subject, a truck roars up the road, driving at surprising speeds for our little gravel drive, lights blaring. Hands fly up in front of faces, headlights startling our guests. Dennis steps down with his typical swagger. Am I the only one who notices that he stumbles when his boots hit the ground and he hastily catches onto the side mirror to stay upright?

"Well, hey there, Dennis." Ray is on his feet. We're on the same side of the table at the center, the boys seated between us. "We'd given you up for lost."

"Doubt that would have bothered you much," Dennis replies.

My spine tingles, and the little hairs on my arms stand on end. I work to keep my expression neutral, eyes darting between them, like a moderator at a political debate, wondering when I might need to jump in and shut down a microphone.

Ray sighs. "You wanna turn those headlights off? Our guests are seeing stars at this point."

Dennis obliges. Darkness returns, sharper than ever after the burst of light. My twinkle lights suddenly don't seem strong enough to illuminate us anymore.

The charm is gone. It's chilly. No one is eating dessert, and except for the occasional mouth fart of a little boy, nothing about this feels fun anymore if it ever did.

It's quiet, the two men staring at each other, and jangly nerves send me to my feet. I blurt out, "Come eat, we've got plenty."

Dennis looks at me, and a smile spreads across his face, incongruous with any expression a man should ever give his brother's wife or give any person with whom he's not intimately involved. It horrifies and infuriates me. How dare he look at me like that, like we have some knowledge of each other that allows for that kind of familiarity?

My gaze darts to Ray, and he's watching Dennis, his jaw working. Still, he manages the words, "Maybe food will do you some good. Sober you up a bit."

Squinting at Ray, Dennis asks, "You calling me a drunk?" His tone is more quizzical than outraged, more amused than off put.

"I'm calling it like I see it. You're drunk, and you need to go home." And with that Ray starts around the table.

The citronella candles crackle, their sharp lemony scent permeating the air.

These are things I notice during this ridiculous, awful conversation.

Why doesn't Myrtle say something? Why doesn't she do something? I look at her, at Stephanie, at Brandon, and not one of them meets my eye.

Dennis points at me. "Your wife invited me for dinner. Are you gonna make me leave?"

"My wife didn't invite you for anything." Ray's voice is low, and in the flickering light, his jaw clicks so quickly I step towards them as well. There is something in the air, like we're sitting at the edge of a knife, and I can't put words to it, but there's the acidic taste of fear in my mouth. "My wife and I invited you to dinner, and now we are uninviting you."

"That true, Iris? Am I uninvited?" Dennis looks at me again.

I don't hesitate. "You need to go home. Someone can drive you."

"I'll do it." Naomi stands up, tossing her cloth napkin on the table.

"Why not Iris? She's pretty good at getting me home when I'm loaded. You up for it again?"

And Dennis throws me a look so personal I step back.

"What's this?" Ray asks, and Dennis says, his tone joyful, "You didn't tell him? Iris, that's not good."

He is drunk. He is *a* drunk. These are things I remind myself, but I'm livid at how he's pulling me into this, and even worse, that old tug of shame, that sense I've done something wrong stirs in my chest.

"Nothing happened," I say at once, and this only sounds incriminating. Anger is dying, and embarrassment floods me as people look between us, curious and confused. Instead of red-faced and furious, I'm red-faced and sweating.

"What are you talking about?" Ray watches me.

I press my lips together, shaking my head. "Nothing, absolutely nothing. Stephanie can tell you."

"What's Stephanie got to do with this?" He looks to his sister. And, to my absolute disbelief, she keeps her head down, eyes fixed on her plate.

Feeling helpless, tears springing to my eyes, I shake my head again. "It was nothing. Nothing. Dennis was drunk, and he needed someone to pick him up. He called me–"

"Why would he call you?"

The coldness in Ray's voice stops me. "I, I don't know."

"Are you sure, Iris? Are you sure you don't know?" Ray's expression is guarded and unfriendly.

"Yes, I'm sure."

"Ray." It's a murmur from The Lovely Naomi. She's in the mix now, standing near Dennis' truck.

It's too much, the accusatory face of my husband, his brother leering at me, and Ray's family, my new friends, or so I thought, refusing to stand up for me. I'm not proud of it, but I round on her and exclaim, "Don't you 'Ray' him!"

Her head snaps back, eyes wide.

"He is my husband. I am the only one who will 'Ray' him, thank you very much." As I speak, I point my finger at the ground, punctuating each statement.

Why am I shouting at Naomi? I don't know what 'Ray' meant, but it's possible it was said in my defense.

"That's enough from you."

Myrtle pushes back from the table and stands. I look between her and Dennis, her and Ray, waiting.

"I'll tolerate it a bit, but you're not going to snap at my employees."

I look at Myrtle. Her gaze is level on my face.

And it becomes clear. She's not shouting at either of her sons. She's shouting at me.

And she's not done.

59.

I open my mouth to protest, but Myrtle holds up a hand. "You owe her an apology." She gestures to Naomi.

Naomi, to her credit, shakes her head at me.

"Hey! Do you hear me?" Myrtle's sharpness makes me jump.

"Mother," Ray says, and he takes a step towards her.

"No, Ray. I am done with this. She has caused more than enough trouble. I've held my tongue. But I'm not holding it any longer." And here she points a chubby finger at me. "Where do you get off, thinking you can come onto my farm and throw all these wrenches in the works?"

"What are you talking about?" My voice is too loud, but I don't care. It's Myrtle, the crackle of the candles, and the cool spring evening on my skin, that's what I'm aware of.

Myrtle throws her head back and snorts. "'What are you talking about?' she says," and the voice she uses to mimic me is breathy and childish and makes me squeeze my hands into fists. "I'm talking about all of it. All of it. You've married Ray and latched yourself onto his inheritance. You've led Dennis on, now Shawna's moved out, and, I believe, you're the cause. Stephanie told me she's thinking about moving back to Atlanta after apparently some good talks with you." Myrtle throws some air quotes up at that phrase. "Brandon is the only one you haven't hurt as far as I'm aware. But maybe she has?" She swings around and glares at her youngest, and he puts both hands in the air, palms up. Turning back to me, Myrtle steps closer, breathing hard. "We were a perfectly happy family until you showed up. You've wrecked everything."

"Myrtle," Ricky murmurs, and he half stands.

"Mother!" Ray says at the same time, but I talk over them.

"Were you? A perfectly happy family?"

Myrtle raises an eyebrow, daring me. "You heard me."

The moment feels long, but it's not. There's a matter of seconds for me to decide how far I want to wade, how deep I'm willing to plunge.

It's a matter of seconds, maybe less.

And I don't so much step forward as hurl myself in.

"You're right, Myrtle. You always are. You and your happy family. You are such a happy family that your oldest son has a drinking problem and everyone looks the other way. Is that right?"

Myrtle draws back, only a fraction, but I've chinked her armor. There's a rush, and I keep diving.

"And your daughter loves being here so much she only comes home at Christmas. That's odd, isn't it, considering you're so close? Yeah, that's weird. And that same daughter has never said a word about the Saudi man she's lived with the last decade, has she?" My tone is light, conversational; it's a thrill. I'm not the one struggling to stay in it. I'm the one on top.

For once.

Myrtle's face goes slack. Take that, Battleship Myrtle. "What?" She glances at Stephanie, but not for long.

I plow forward. "And good thing I haven't wrecked your precious baby boy. Nope, not a bit. Brandon is untouched by me. I mean, he's going to get the hell out of here as soon as he finishes his degree in Engineering. But you knew that already, right Myrtle? Y'all are close, so you're well aware of that decision he's made."

"What?" Ray and Dennis say simultaneously, and, for a moment, they're a united front. Brandon only has eyes for me, his expression so hurt it almost stops me.

But not quite.

"Gosh, Myrtle, it's so weird, such a happy family. So except for your son who's an alcoholic and your daughter who doesn't trust you to meet the love of her life or your other son who's been lying to you about working for the family business, you've pretty much got it all nailed down. Of course, the one thing you might not know, the thing you might not be aware of is that your beloved employee right over there is sleeping with your married son."

Heads whip around to Naomi. "How did you know that?" Ray demands.

Naomi bursts into tears.

And those tears serve two purposes. They distract me from my meltdown, and they confirm what I've most feared since I moved here.

Naomi is having an affair with my husband.

60.

Waking up, the room is too bright, sunlight streaming through gauzy curtains. I peek through one eye, then the other, my location unclear.

My white wrought iron bed. My old dresser. My bedroom. My parents' house. This is where I live or, at least, this is where the boys and I are staying.

And that brings everything back. Myrtle's hateful accusations. My detonation, ending in accusing Naomi of infidelity with my husband and Naomi sobbing. And, even after all that, I wasn't done.

Seeing that gorgeous young woman bawling, realizing my worst fears about Ray, I turned to Myrtle with fury.

"You are to blame for all of this," I growled. She squared back up but didn't seem as confident now. "You." And I jabbed a finger in her direction, lest there be doubt. "Your children are afraid of you so they lie to you. They lie about their work, their health, and their relationships." This last one made me swallow hard, but I dropped my foot on the pedal, all the way to the floor. "You are a judgmental, overbearing, unkind woman. You might have kept it together after your divorce, but you have never let them go. Now you've got your hooks in them, and you won't let them be who they want to be. You won't let them grow up. They shouldn't be leaving. They should be *fleeing* from you. You are what's wrecking this farm."

Dramatic? Definitely. Over the top? For sure. Words spoken by a woman whose heart had just been broken to pieces? Absolutely.

Leaving the others to comfort Naomi, I went inside, found an old canvas satchel, and started chucking things into it. In went a couple of pajama sets for the boys, Ernie's Sleep Elephant, and Atticus' favorite comic book. I might have grabbed a few unnecessary items only because they were close, like my house shoes and a t-shirt that Ernie outgrew last year, giving him the look of a miniaturized Hulk.

"What are you doing?"

It surprised me that it was Ray who came to check on me. Poor Naomi surely needed condolences more than I did.

Because I wasn't a woman bereaved or bereft. I was a woman on fire. I was a woman who would burn this whole house to the ground if someone didn't remove her from the premises within the next five minutes.

So when Ray asked what I was doing, I knew I needed to stick to monosyllables, lest my rage might result in choices with irreparable consequences.

"Packing."

"For what?" He leaned in the doorway of our bedroom, hands shoved in his pockets. Always cool, always calm, that was Ray.

I flung items out of my dresser looking for a sweater I was nearly certain was in the laundry but couldn't stop wanting.

As I flung, I muttered, "Don't be stupid."

"Am I being stupid? Because I don't know what you're doing anymore. You just insulted my entire family, including me, in front of your family and some employees. You just made up a bunch of lies about us, too, plus spilled some painful secrets. Naomi's wrecked. How could you do that, Iris?"

There was nothing, nothing at all, moving me besides the hurt and humiliation I felt at Ray's betrayal. The fact he could say Naomi's name in front of me was crazy-making. I gave him a look, all eyeballs and open mouth, and he actually stepped back.

Still, he tried again. "Iris, please. I do not understand what's going on right now."

Words piled in my throat, but they had no outlet. Bag packed, I pushed past Ray into the living room.

"Where's my purse?"

"Why do you need it?" Ray followed me as I stormed through the house, head down, eyes peeled for my handbag.

"I think it was over here." How could I not find it? Our house is smaller than Frodo's hobbit hole, and yet my enormous satchel of a handbag was missing. "Did one of the boys move it...?"

"Iris!" It was the first time Ray had ever raised his voice at me. He caught my elbow and stopped me short, the two of us glaring at each other.

There were those dark brown eyes I loved, so clear and honest, and yet it turned out, the eyes of a liar. The thought snatched my breath and held it. Tears in my eyes, tears of fury and injustice, I shook my head. "How could you?" I hated how my voice caught, how it broke.

"Iris, I didn't know what to do. I don't know how to be married. This is, this is all a lot for me."

The most painful guffaw erupted from my mouth, one that made my chest hurt. "Too much? Is marriage too much?"

He still had my arm, eyes piercing into mine. But his only answer was to lift one of his thin, strong shoulders and shrug.

That was enough. That was what I needed to know.

I pulled from his grasp, and he let go, easily. Effortlessly. "We're going to my parents. I'll be in touch."

Now here I am, only a few nights later, after the most disastrous Sunday supper, I expect, in Fox family history. Lying in my twin bed in my old bedroom in my parents' house, Ernie and Atticus sleeping on the blow-up mattress on the floor.

61.

"Can we watch TV?" Ernie's already racing to the television, yanking a shirt over his head. A few days into staying here, and we've started a routine without even trying.

"Yep."

"And doughnuts?" Ernie whips his head around.

I feign a hard stare, eyebrow crooked at him. "Don't push it, bub."

Both boys dissolve into laughter, and Ernie takes the rejection with good humor. And as well he should what with his efforts to take advantage of his mother.

"I didn't know what to make for the boys for lunch." My mom's wringing her hands at me as soon as I walk in the kitchen.

"It's OK. I'll figure it out." Pushing my hair out of my face and fixing it into a loose bun, I dig into lunch.

Practical life. It's the last thing I want right now, but the thing I most need. We've managed lunches the last few days, and I've done a load of laundry once. It's normal-ish.

I forgot their backpacks, and Atticus panicked about that Monday morning. I could only shrug, feeling helpless, and promise I'd get the bags back as soon as possible.

Mom and Dad have a random assortment of items I've sent to their house through the years. They were able to provide a lunchbox and a small water bottle for each boy, and we've limped along like this, living in this suspended reality. Monday morning, on the drive to school, I offered a weak story of getting a few days break from driving to and from the farm. "School's almost out," I pointed out, "And this gives us a rest before we get a real rest this summer."

And they both seemed to take it in stride.

My parents, too, didn't balk when I suggested I needed some brain space, some time to talk to Ray and sort through the disaster of Sunday's dinner.

And even Ray didn't push back when we spoke Monday afternoon. I shouldn't have been surprised that he called me. That was Ray's style, voice to voice, not typing a message.

"So what are we doing here, Iris?" he asked, no preamble or small talk.

"I don't know." My voice was husky. I hadn't spoken much that day, choosing, while the boys were at school, to hole up in my childhood bedroom and gaze out the window, mind churning. The fact it was a stormy day, and I could watch the rain only added to my inertia.

He sighed, a long, slow breath down the line. "Will I see you and the boys tonight?"

I shook my head at the window, at my own reflection. "I don't think so." And a lump caught in my throat.

He was silent. We both were. At last, I tried. "I need some time. I need to think."

"Any idea how much?"

Even though he sounded exhausted, Ray managed a light tone, poking. It made me laugh.

It also gave me the energy to suggest, "Not too long. A few days. Just some space from the farm. Not driving so much with school. From all the things."

He didn't ask, and I didn't say whether he was included in "all the things." I think we both knew the answer.

62.

As I sit by the front door, tying my shoelaces, I beat a circular pattern in my head, the same two words circling each other. *Stay? Go?*

The boys thunder downstairs, substitute backpacks on, but Atticus draws back as I hand him a lunch.

"I want my lunchbox."

The one I'm holding has three brightly colored cartoon sharks grinning at me. I look at it like I'm seeing it for the first time. "What's wrong with this one? It's fine."

He shakes his head, backing up from me. "I'm not carrying that. It's for babies."

I sigh. "It's only temporary, Atticus. This isn't a big deal."

"I want that one." Atticus jerks his chin at the second lunchbox in my hand, this one with smiling dogs in emergency worker uniforms.

It's not worth a fight. "Fine." I switch the bags in my hands and hold them out.

"I don't know." Ernie squints at the bag. "I like the dogs one better. Change them back."

Oh, for THE LOVE.

"No!" And Atticus howls in a way he's only sounded a few times in his life. "I'm not carrying that. It's for babies. I want my lunchbox. With the dinosaurs."

"That lunchbox isn't here! It's at the farm!" my voice rises.

"I don't care! You said you'd get it! Go get it!" Atticus screams back. His dark eyes stand out, his cheeks red.

I gape at him. "I will not go get it. It's a lunchbox, Atticus. You can deal with it. And frankly, I'm disappointed in you. This is not the way you behave."

"Well, I'm disappointed in you!" he bellows back, and I freeze. "I'm disappointed in you! You took us there, and then you took us away again. How could you do that? You ruined it! You ruin everything!"

"I didn't ruin anything!" I exclaim. "Ray ruined it, not me."

"No, he didn't. He was great. He loved us, and he did stuff with us. He acted like he was our–our–" He chokes on the word. "And you packed us up and left, just like every other place we've ever lived..."

I'm absolutely baffled. "We left those other houses because we had to. Because they raised the rent, or they wanted to move into the house, or they wanted to sell it. That wasn't my fault."

"Why can't you be normal? Why can't you be like other moms?" And Atticus breaks into a torrent of noisy sobs.

I stagger back, hand to my chest.

It's the same feeling I had when Ray called me dramatic.

How can he say that? How can he throw that at me?

Be normal?

Like the other moms?

It's like he's stuck his head inside my chest, taken a peek at my heart, and thought, "Oh, I know exactly how to smash this."

Be normal. Be like other moms.

"How could you say..." I start, and another voice interrupts.

"That's enough."

None of us are used to men. Even after a few months with Ray, I see it startles all three of us when my dad interjects.

"That's enough, Iris. Atticus, I can see you're upset. But that's enough right now. You have to go to school."

I gape at my dad and then throw a look at my red-eyed, snotty-faced son. "Look at him. He can't go to school."

"He'll calm down." Dad's voice is calm and measured.

It takes me right back to middle school, me shrieking I couldn't go to school after what that witch Misty Hale said about me and my father, looking me in the eye and saying, "Iris. You are going to school."

In those cases, my mother intervened. She would wrap a protective arm around me, hold me close, and say, "You go on. I'll take care of it."

Over time, Dad realized what this meant. Mom and I would stay home together, watching morning network television, getting some kind of takeout for lunch, and me doing my homework in the afternoon to prove nothing was missed by the time out of school.

Looking at my dad's face, now more lined, jaws a little saggier, but eyes no less determined than when I was sixteen, I don't think this standoff is going to end like all those other times.

"Atticus is going to school. He's seven years old. They won't demand that much of him. He'll be fine."

I cross my arms. "Exactly the reason you can make the argument the other way. There's not much to demand of a seven-year-old, so why put him through this when he's so upset?"

And then Dad gives me one of the strangest looks I've ever seen from him, shaking his head, eyebrows knit together, as though he has no idea who I am. "Because he has to learn that sometimes, often, in fact, you must push through what's hard and keep going. Not forever. But for now."

My mouth's open, ready to protest, but Dad's already called out, "Cynthia!"

And it's inexplicable to me how this is happening, how my dad appears to be winning this conversation, but he is, and we both know it.

Mom appears as I notice my handbag by the front door. It's where I dropped it yesterday, and I'm embarrassed at how it gapes open, a scarf and notebook spilling onto the floor. Possibly I am messier than I've wanted to admit to Ray.

"Fine." I grab my purse and sling it up my shoulder. "Get in the car, boys. We're going."

"No, no, no," Dad interjects.

And I wheel on him, keys out and pointed right at his chest. "What do you want from me?" I bellow. "Isn't this enough?"

"No. Your mother is taking them."

"That's ridiculous. We'd have to move their boosters, and it's a hassle."

"She can take your car. Cynthia," he nods at Mom, "the keys."

"Are you kidding me?"

Mom takes the keys, not meeting my eyes. They've planned this. She probably pushed back, but Dad insisted. Now she's his minion carrying out whatever dastardly deeds he assigns.

"Are you really doing this?" I ask her.

"It'll give you a break, sweetie." She keeps her face down. It's almost comical how miserable it makes her to work against my wishes, except I'm so angry I can't laugh.

Dad meets my gaze, his hands in his pockets, rocking back and forth on the balls of his feet. A man without a care in the world. I see red.

"Why are you doing this?"

He stops rocking. And he replies in a tight voice, "Because you and I need to have a little talk."

I'm holding my breath at those words.

"Ooo!"

It's Ernie, looking between Dad and me, his eyes bright with delight. "Mommy's in trouble! Mommy's in trou-ble!" He's gleeful as my mom hustles both boys out the door.

63.

You don't run a school for more than forty years without building a passive expression and an ability to wait in silence unrivaled by any other profession. He's an expert at this, my father.

We're in the former dining room, now his new office. Dad sits at his desk, his chair swiveled towards me. I sit in the short green armchair with the ruffled skirt and big buttons. My mother loves this chair.

"That's your mother's chair," he starts.

"I know that." My stare is hard.

"When we made this room a library, of sorts, your mother put her chair in that corner where she could read in here when I needed to work late."

My jaw twitches. "Fascinating."

And Dad, the absolute nerve of him, looks amused. "Do you know why she did that, Iris?"

It's infuriating, being quizzed like a mischievous high schooler caught in the act of leading a topless walkout.

However, at the same time that I want to tell my dad to shove it and storm out, I don't currently have any place to storm to. What, am I going up to my old bedroom in a pique of anger? That hardly sets the tone I'm looking for.

I have no place to go. Now or later. And the thought holds me in place.

Dad puts up his hands, palms towards me, a symbol of peace. "Iris?"

It's possible I've lost track of the conversation. With as much dignity as I can muster, I say, "Can you repeat the question?"

He's amused, but I don't care. "I asked, Do you know why your mother moved her favorite chair from the living room into here?"

I could be staring out my bedroom window in the throes of misery. But here I am, working through some kind of riddle with my dad. I lift my shoulders. "I don't."

"I'm really asking you this question. Your mother and I have been married for–how old are you?"

"Thirty-six."

"Goodness, are you really?" Dad gives a low whistle and shakes his head. "Time flies. Anyway, we've been married for over forty years now. That's four decades of being around the same woman every day and every night. And yet, when your mom and I redid this room into an office, what did she do? She put a chair in here for herself. So for the purposes of moving this conversation along, I'll answer my own question. Your mother put that chair in here, so she could sit with me while I work in the evening. Because she wanted to be near me. And I, in turn, put my desk against this wall, so she might have the window view for herself. Do you see that?"

He gestures to the chair and the window next to it, and I follow his gaze. But there's no room for me to speak; he's still talking. "I originally wanted that spot for my desk, so I could look outside while I work.

But when I realized your mother wanted to have a place in here, too, to keep me company, I insisted she take that spot there. It is without a doubt the best view in the room, and it was important to me that she has it. Do you know why?"

I sigh. "Because you're a good guy."

Dad barks a laugh so loud and surprising I jump. "No! Good grief, what made you think that? I'm as selfish as the next man, God forgive me. No." He shakes his head, still chuckling. "I gave your mother that spot, the best spot in the room, because I love her. And I wanted to show her that by doing something kind for her. It's a small gesture, yes, but I hope if I make enough of these small gestures towards her, that when I say, 'I love you,' she'll believe me."

Now it's my turn to make a noise, a weird, choked sound. He's caught me off guard and tears pool in my eyes.

Why am I crying? Because I'm with my dad and not in a room by myself, I take great, shaky breaths trying to keep from sobbing openly.

Dad nods. "I know. It's a lot. But it's true. That's what love is, Iris. It's all these tiny, thoughtful gestures made over days and weeks and months, and eventually years. That's how we show our tenderness, our affection, our passion for someone else."

I take a deep breath, hoping to stem the tide. Where he's going isn't clear, but I sense it's not a place I want to follow.

"Now, I only do these things because your mother is a good person, deeply deserving of love. If she were selfish, unkind, or hateful most of the time, I probably wouldn't feel this way. But I know, despite her small flaws and faults, she is a genuinely good person. Which makes me want to be a genuinely good person and give her everything I can to show how much I appreciate and respect her. People, all of us, want to offer love with flowery words and big gestures." My dad twists his mouth, like he's sucked a lemon. "It's misguided, and it never leads to lasting happiness. Which you, my dear, need to know by a different name."

I hiccup and wipe my wet face. "What?"

"Contentment." And here Dad takes both my hands in his, ignoring the fact they're damp. "That is what I worry about most for you. I don't think you know what contentment is."

I don't have an answer. Before, I was all prickles and walls. Now, my prickles are shorn, my walls demolished.

So instead of bristling or shouting, I shrug. "I don't know. What do you mean?"

"What I mean is you need to be looking more for contentment in love. Not excitement or thrills."

He releases my hands and sits back. "Please. Let me finish. I've been teaching high schoolers long enough to know, telling them exactly what they need to do rarely leads to them doing it. And I know, no one else can live our life for us. And yet, as your father, if I don't say this to you at least once, I believe I'll have done you a disservice. Your mother is wonderful at seeing the best qualities in you, Iris. It's one of my favorite things about her. She genuinely thinks you hung the moon. You know, getting pregnant wasn't easy, and when it happened, she felt God had answered every prayer she'd asked. 'For this child I prayed—'"

"'And the Lord has granted me my petition that I made to him.'" I recite with him. Scripture memorization has never been my strong suit, but I know this verse by heart. My mother has said it to me a million and one times throughout my life, often with her hand on my cheek or the top of my head.

Dad smiles. "Yes. You know. We were both so glad. I hope you know that. Your mother's better at expressing it, but please don't doubt I feel it as deeply as she does. Still, I've tried to show you more with small gestures than words and some of those gestures amount to letting your mother take the lead on how to discipline you and raise you. And she did, I believe, a magnificent job." His eyes are damp, and for a moment, it's only the two of us, looking into each other's eyes, in the quiet house, the spring sun streaming through the windows. "And still, Iris, I have to say this to you, you haven't seemed to be a content person."

I open my mouth, but words don't come out. It's one long sigh. And instead of interrupting, I stay silent and wait.

"We all have character faults. And, to my mind, you don't have many. Absent-minded, yes. Messy, for sure." And here he laughs. "But your lack of contentment is the only one that worries me. Because it's such an important thing. To love well and be content. I don't know that a life well lived is much more than that, in the end. And I see how well you love. I see how you love your boys. And how you love your mother and me. Your friends. You are kind, you are fierce, you are devoted. But you've not been fortunate in romantic love. And now you're married to Ray, and while I don't know that I supported this marriage, I do now."

It's a blow. "How can you say that, knowing what you know?"

"That's the thing. I don't know anything." I crook my head to the side. Dad tries again. "I mean, I don't know what's happened between Ray and this young woman—that's what you're referring to, correct? That there's been some kind of indiscretion between them?"

"Indiscretion? That's a quaint and old-fashioned way to say it."

Dad shrugs. "Call me quaint and old-fashioned then. Do you know what happened?"

"Yes, I know what happened. I said as much at dinner, and Ray all but agreed. Naomi started crying."

"And none of that is conclusive. I was there and it's still not clear to me what was suggested and to whom it was suggested." Dad raises an eyebrow at me. "Do you see what I mean?"

"Nope." I cross my arms over my chest.

He sighs. "Well, I won't say more than that on this subject. But I am going to tell you, go talk to your husband. And get clear, absolutely clear, on what happened."

"Why should I go to him? He's the one who's made this mess, who broke my trust, broke our vows." My voice trembles, but I don't back down, chin out.

"This isn't a film. Or a novel. Something has gone sideways in your marriage. That much was clear to anyone at your house the other night." I wince. Shame washes over me, remembering some of what was said and all the people who witnessed it. "You have to talk to him."

"Why shouldn't he come to me?"

"Because you're not eleven years old. Grow up, my dear daughter, before you lose what is possibly your best chance at a contented marriage."

We're both silent. Blood pulses in my ears, my heart races in my chest. There's a struggle in me to argue and disagree, to stick to what I believe and refuse to hear anyone else.

Except.

Except.

What if he's right?

About my childishness, my discontentment, my marriage? About me?

What if he's right?

I swallow. "Ray's working today."

"I imagine he would stop if you asked him to." Dad's tone is wry. "I saw his face, Iris. Whatever conclusions you may have drawn, that's the face of a man in love. With you. Not anyone else."

"Mom has my car."

"I've got the keys."

"Agh!" I shriek, and Dad shouts, "Good Lord, Cynthia! What are you doing, sneaking in like that?"

Mom hovers in the office doorway, keys outstretched. "I didn't sneak. You just didn't hear me."

And then she beams at both of us, my affectionate mother. "It was such a nice moment, I couldn't bring myself to interrupt. The boys are fine," she adds. "And actually, you take my car. I'll pick them up from school and give you more time at the farm." She slips her handbag off her shoulder and fishes out her keys.

I'm on my feet shifting from side to side. "Maybe I should just call."

"Sweetheart," Mom's eyes are on me, so loving and kind, "get your butt in the car and go talk to your husband. Right now."

64.

It's strange, going to the farm instead of away from it. I've become so accustomed to this drive, but backwards. I loaded up at the farm and took the boys to school. Then I drove straight back home.

Now, I'm driving to the farm, and I see it with fresh eyes. The trees that line the four-lane highway. The rolling green and the hovering mist of the Smoky Mountains surrounding me. Seeing those hills brings flashbacks of our honeymoon, however brief, to Gatlinburg, and my stomach aches.

Those days felt so hopeful. It was dewy, exciting. Now we're in this place–what is this place? Have I left Ray? Did he leave me? Have I moved out? It's unclear.

And I hear my father's voice, "That's what love is, Iris. It's all these tiny, thoughtful gestures made over days and weeks and months, and eventually years. That's how we show our tenderness, our affection, our passion for someone else."

Have I given Ray that marriage? Tiny, thoughtful gestures made over days and weeks and months?

What about Ray and Naomi? The question rears up in my mind, and I forcibly push it aside, like seizing the steering wheel from my worst side's hands. That's not the question right now. The question is, Have I given this marriage what it deserved?

Have I committed? Have I dug in?

Driving the boys has worn me down more than I expected. I know there are so many people who spend hours a day in their car, but driving them back and forth, that's made me done in. *But there's the local school*, my better side reminds me. The one Ray keeps encouraging me to look into. The one I balked against.

I did help at the farm. I did. Of course, it was harder than I anticipated. And Naomi's presence made me uncomfortable.

Not to mention Myrtle.

Always Myrtle at the back of this or the center, depending on how you see it.

My hands grip the steering wheel, a new plan forming in my brain. Myrtle. On the farm. At my house bringing my unprompted and unwanted items to decorate my house.

I know what my dad said. And I know what my mom said. They were both adamant: Go see your husband.

I turn into the main entrance. And as I pull into the driveway, I park in front of the house, take a moment to comb my fingers through my hair, run lip gloss over my mouth. And then set out, in search of my target.

She's in her greenhouse. Of course, she is.

Working silently with a pair of gardening shears snipping dead heads, she's focused and doesn't hear me until I say, "Myrtle."

Myrtle looks up. An expression crosses her face, fleeting, but something I've not seen before. What is it?

Fear. That's my instinct, and I decide to trust it.

However, when she speaks, you'd never know she had a moment's pause.

"Iris," she says, her tone neutral. "Did you have something else to yell at me? Some other bombshell to drop?"

I flinch, but I don't retreat. "That's not fair." Somehow I keep my voice calm. "You attacked first."

It sounds a bit dramatic, sure. But I stand by it. Myrtle fired first.

She sets her shears down, rests her hands on the table, and looks up at me. "I am a sixty-six-year-old woman, a single mom. I'm retired, for Pete's sake! And I threatened you? Is that what you're saying?"

I open my mouth to reply, shoot back fast. But Myrtle raises her voice and overrides me.

"In the last twenty years, I've kept everyone fed and clothed and kept this farm going, and I've done it all alone." Her voice breaks, and that catches my attention. I watch Myrtle, always imperturbable, a bastion of composure and cool as they come, now bow her head, voice trembling. And it stops me. Right there. This isn't a monster in front of me. It's, as she said, a sixty-six-year-old, retired, single mother.

And she suddenly looks so vulnerable. And tired.

So instead of snapping back, I venture to say, "Please, finish what you were saying."

Myrtle raises her eyes and meets mine for a moment. And then she picks her shears back up, gets back to work. When she speaks, her tone is conversational.

"Did you know when the kids were little I worked at an attorney's office? Brandon was tiny, not even a year old. Their dad had run off. And I knew the farm couldn't support us. Hell, we couldn't pump enough money into it to keep going. So I got a job real quick."

As she works, she talks. *Snip, snip, snip* go the metal shears, and it's strangely calming, this warm, sunlit space, smelling of damp earth and pollen. No wonder Myrtle hides here.

Hide? Did I just think that? Is she hiding?

"It was the best paid work I could find and still get me home in time for supper. It gave me the extra money I needed to pay Ricky and to keep this place going until we could start turning a profit again. There were times it looked like we'd have to sell, but this was my father's house, my house, and I wasn't about to do that."

She swallows hard and again meets my gaze. Briefly. "I've given everything I have to this farm and this family. When their dad left, good riddance. I did this alone. And I didn't hitch myself to the first fellow who came along, hoping he'd look after us." Myrtle raises an eyebrow at me, challenging me. When I stay quiet, she shakes her head and throws her hands in the air. "I do all that, all that, and never an argument between any of us. Not until you came along. Now you're here, it's all gone to hell, and I'm the aggressor? Now that is funny."

I take a breath waiting, her words settling in the humid greenhouse around us. And I don't answer right away. Instead, I rest against a table behind me, careful not to disturb her foliage.

Fighting isn't helping. I'm not a fighter. I love deep words, heart-to-heart conversations. And here it is, Myrtle's offering it to me. But I can't come in full-Iris either and scare her off. So I choose my words carefully.

"Aggressor is harsh. I wouldn't call it that. But just because you and your children don't argue doesn't mean you're not responsible. You're as culpable as them. Honestly, more, I think. You have a strong personality, and if it's not your way, it's the highway."

Her jaw is set, and she's looking past me into the middle distance. I can practically see my words hit her armor and bounce off, and it's maddening.

But also sad. That's clear now. Look at Myrtle. She is a sixty-six-year-old woman. She is a single mom. And hearing these pieces of her story leak out from tight lips makes my heart hurt for her. What a life, head down, working hard to keep her family and this place together and on her own.

Ray's never said anything like this to me before. Does he know? And if he does, is that what keeps him quiet, obedient to the point of losing his own life to the life of the Fox family?

I exhale a deep, gusty sigh. The fight has slipped away, a balloon fizzing away through the air into the distance.

"It all sounds so hard, Myrtle." I shake my head, feeling the load of her words weighing me down, too. "I don't know how you did it. I've been a single mom since Ernie was a baby, but I only had two boys. And my parents were around to help. I only have one job, and there have been days I've thought, I can't do this. I can't take another step."

I raise my eyes and see Myrtle watching me, hands still. And she's nodding.

"That must have been tough," she says. "Having two boys in diapers and no one to help. Not that my ex raised a hand to change a diaper."

"Or mine," I say, and we exchange a look, the look of two women who know what it's like to be responsible for little ones, changing the diaper of the tiniest, while the older tries to tear the curtain rods down and a selfish man clutters up the background, doing nothing to help.

Myrtle laughs. "Useless," she says, and I nod.

I take a deep breath appreciating the earthy scent that fills my nose. Nothing like dirt and the ground to bring us out of our heads and back into our bodies.

Nothing like the earth to remind us of what's true and what's real. And the words that are true and real come to me right then. So I say them.

65.

"Myrtle, I'm sorry." My voice is steady, and I meet her gaze. What I'm apologizing for isn't clear to me. For my behavior? For the behavior of her "useless" ex? For the many lies and hurts her children have handed her most of their lives, both to protect her and to protect themselves?

She got dealt a tough hand. Yes, it included a little piece of heaven on earth, acres of gorgeous land, and one big beautiful house. And four healthy, capable children. It also included the pressure of financing said piece of heaven and raising those children on her own. What an impossible situation, a blessing, and a curse in the same hands.

Not unlike myself. Or so many other people I knew.

"I don't know how to be gentle, like you. Or playful."

I'm so lost in my own thoughts, my private mourning for Myrtle that her words startle me.

"What's that?"

She takes a breath and repeats herself.

I shake my head at her. "What do you mean?"

"Good grief, Iris. Don't be dumb!" She hears herself, and a smile breaks out across her face. "Well, that's me in one sentence. You're so good with your boys. I see you with them, the way you're soft, the way you listen. I–I've never had that."

The words wash over me. Myrtle complimented me. Full-fledged praise. "Some things come more naturally," I start, but she holds up a hand.

"That's not it. You work on it, being gentle. I never have. If something sets me off, I let it fly. If–if there's any truth to what you're saying, about my kids being afraid of me," and here she shoots me a side-eye indicating she's not yet willing to capitulate that much, "My temper's the root of it."

And suddenly the words are there and pouring from me. "But that's not it, Myrtle, or that's not only it. They're not afraid of you because you have a temper. They love you and respect you. They want to make you proud, and they don't want to let you down. That's the thing, isn't it? It comes from a good place. It comes from their love, the thing that makes them run away," I say, thinking of Stephanie. "Or give in," I say, thinking of Ray. "Or drown it," I finish, thinking of Dennis.

Myrtle chuckles. "So you're saying it's because they love me we have a terrible relationship?"

But I'm not laughing. Leaning against the edge of a table, eyes fixed hard on a spot on the floor, I'm concentrating. Because something is coming to me, but it's hazy. What is it?

"No, not that. It's, it's..." My brain reaches for the words, and then there they are. "They don't totally trust you. That's why you have a terrible relationship."

I lift my eyes until Myrtle and I are looking right at each other. She's squirming, but, full credit to her, she doesn't look away.

"They don't trust me?" she says.

I lift one shoulder. Unlike my father, who's been dispensing advice since the dawn of time, I'm not comfortable diagnosing the dysfunction of this woman. And still, it feels accurate.

"Maybe? It's a lot of people keeping secrets in one family. There's a reason they don't want to tell you what's going on."

Myrtle nods, her lips working back and forth, thinking hard. "Now that you've spilled all their secrets for them, they don't need to, do they? Talk about breaking trust."

I wince. It's a piece I haven't let myself consider. But it's true. I blew every trust given to me in these last few months. Stephanie, Brandon, Dennis...they have no reason to trust me again.

Still, that's not the point right now. I understand why Myrtle says what she says. Easier to spotlight my failings than consider her own. Remembering that, remembering Myrtle and the tough shell she wears, she has to be struggling in the face of so much vulnerable conversation. So I don't retaliate.

In fact, I realize, there isn't much more for me to say. "I owe everyone an apology. And I'll be sure to give them. But, first, to you, Myrtle, I am really sorry for all the hateful things I said the other night. It was my hurt and insecurity talking. You didn't deserve any of that."

"Ehhh." Myrtle's eyes roll side to side. "I deserved it a little. I know I'm not an easy person to get along with. And I've had people recommending I back off, maybe open up a little."

Who, my brain immediately demands, losing track.

Ray?

Stephanie?

Ricky, that same voice answers its own question. I bite back a smile and stay quiet.

"I'm a–a protective person, especially when it comes to these kids, whatever they may think of me. I could see Ray, I could see how taken he was with you. You made me more nervous than the other one, the first one."

"Heidi?"

"Yeah, her." She's back to work, snipping those flower heads. "I didn't like her. But she didn't scare me either. I knew Ray liked her, maybe loved her. But he'd never have left the farm for her. You," she shook her head, "it was the first time I could see Ray going."

"Why would I want Ray to leave? I love it here."

She cocks an eyebrow at me. "Do you?"

Now it's my turn to sigh. "I do when you people aren't making it impossible."

And Myrtle laughs, a deep belly laugh. "I haven't made your move here easy, Iris. I expect I owe you an apology as well."

We're both quiet. I wait.

Nothing happens.

OK then. That was the apology.

Take what you can get, Iris, and I give myself a mental nod.

"You don't need to worry about my taking Ray away from here," I say.

Myrtle gives me an appraising look, cagey. "No, that's not my concern anymore. After that display you put on the other night, I'm not sure you'd want to take him with you."

66.

It's my turn to squirm. "This has been a lot harder than I expected," I say.

"You know, I'm yet to hear a married person say, 'Gosh, this marriage deal is a real walk in the park.'" She's gone back to her plants.

Wow, Myrtle the comedian. I don't think I love her in this role. And being compared to everyone else feels like a real knife to my heart.

But she's right, and I have to take my lumps.

"I see that now."

We're both quiet. When I look up again, Myrtle's expression is as close to gentle as I've ever seen. "People have gone a lot more off track than this. Don't be too hard on yourself."

"After three months?" I shoot back.

She laughs. "Duration doesn't indicate dedication. My ex hung stuck around for fifteen years, but he was completely useless that whole time."

"I don't love that comparison."

Myrtle waves a hand. "I only mean to say, if that dummy can hang in there for so long, you'll be fine."

Watching her, at the lack of emotion that crosses her face as she mentions her ex, it's clear: Myrtle isn't pining for lost love. This is the most honest conversation Myrtle and I have had. Is it worth a mention?

"Speaking of exes, if anyone understands being scared of remarriage, it's me," I start. Myrtle watches me, impassive. "But I will say if there's a way to shake off the experience of a bad man, it's finding a good one."

Now both eyebrows pop up. "Is that right, missy?"

There's a storm brewing in those dark brown eyes, but I make a point to stay firm. *Say what needs to be said, Iris.*

"And I would say, if I've ever seen a good man–" *and one willing to put up with some crazy, considering this loony family*, I think, but don't add– "it's Ricky."

"Is that so?" Myrtle's tone is cooler than ever. But her eyes dart side to side, and I know I've planted or loosened an idea that's been in her brain before.

I hold up both hands, palms out, a gesture I've used constantly with this wild, antagonistic bunch. "Just a thought, Myrtle. A thought from a friend."

I'm moving on already. Peace has been made here or, at least, the idea of peace has been made. I need to find my husband and salvage the relationship I've blown to bits.

"Myrtle, I need to go." I start to back out. "I've got more business here."

"Are you talking about Ray?" Welp, there's Myrtle bludgeoning any softness I might bring to the situation. "He's gone."

My heart leaps to my throat. "He's what?"

"SAS, remember?" When I remain impassive, Myrtle rolls her eyes again. "Lordy, we have a lot of work to do with you. The Southeastern Agriculture Symposium. It starts today."

The conference! Yes, that started today.

"I completely forgot." And then, in a smaller voice, I can't help but ask, "So he still went?"

Because, honestly, it's hurtful that after everything that's happened, Ray still woke up, got packed, and headed out on a trip this morning.

"Yes, he went. He's a speaker, they're paying him a fee. He can't call and say, 'Sorry, folks, stormy weather at home, gonna have to pass on those lectures I agreed to six months ago.'" Myrtle makes an exasperated sound at me, a cross between a sigh and *tsk tsk*.

"He's home Sunday," Myrtle says, showing an unexpected moment of intuition. "He'll be home Sunday."

And it's only Thursday.

67.

I realize I left the farm four nights ago. And I've only spoken to Ray once in that time. To tell him I needed space. And we shouldn't talk.

But right now, the idea of not talking to Ray for four more days? Of not seeing him?

Not possible. I can't do it.

How do I jump from one to the other in the span of one conversation with his mother?

I can't say.

But it's true, and as I reach my car, my mind's a jumble, formulating a plan. I have to go now. There isn't any time.

"Hey, Iris."

I stop, startled and swing around.

Naomi approaches me, and even though she's clearly been at work, dirt patches all over her jeans, her hair pulled back in a tight ponytail, face flushed and sweaty, she's still as lovely as ever.

Dang her.

"I really can't talk," I start, but that only makes her pick up her pace until she's much too close.

"I'm so sorry about everything," she starts.

My stomach knots. Here it is, the big confession, the explanation, the apology for whatever has happened between my husband and her. I swallow hard, biting back the sharp words that rise to my tongue. My fight is with Ray not her. He's the one who made the vows, not Naomi.

That still doesn't mean I want to hang out with her right now.

"Look, Naomi, I'd rather talk to Ray–"

"It wasn't Ray. You need to know that." She steps closer, her eyes wide and desperate. "I heard what you said at your party, and that's not what happened."

My heart picks up, suddenly racing, like I've downed a few espresso and set off on a run. "What do you mean?"

"You said," she swallows. "You said something to Myrtle about me sleeping with her married son. I think that was it?"

She's flushed, but she holds her ground. "It's not what you think."

My knees want to buckle, but I work to stay upright and strong. "I do not want to do this with you," I protest. "Not you. I'll talk to Ray, but this isn't OK."

"It isn't Ray," she insists.

It makes my blood boil. Is Naomi casting herself as the hero, sacrificing herself on the blame altar for my husband? Absolutely not. If I'm screaming at anyone, it's him. "How dare you? Do you think you have any right to talk with me about you and–"

"It's Dennis." Naomi keeps going, blabbing the words right over me. "Dennis. Not Ray."

And that silences me.

Dennis? It's Dennis. What does that mean?

Except seeing her face and hearing these words, I have an inkling.

I hold up a hand, working to keep up. "Wait. I said–and then Ray said– and you cried."

Scenes from that horrible night slip past my eyes like a slot machine lining up for the winning pull.

Myrtle has two married sons.

One of them is unhappily married and struggling to stay within the confines of that commitment. One of them is Ray.

I accused Naomi of sleeping with one of Myrtle's sons. And she cried because she had.

I meet Naomi's gaze, bringing a hand to my forehead, taking it all in. "Dennis."

And she nods, tears pooling in her eyes. "I'm so sorry you thought it was Ray," she whispers. "I begged him not to tell anyone. He promised he wouldn't. But I shouldn't have done that."

What can I do? She's giving herself more than enough grief for the two of us.

"I can only imagine what you must think of me," Naomi mutters, staring at the ground.

I'm not thinking about her at all. I'm thinking about my husband. But at those words, I pull myself back into the moment..

And I take her hand. "It's OK. We all do stupid things sometimes." It burns my lips, saying those words. Stupid things like accusing faithful husbands of infidelity?

I've got to see Ray.

I squeeze her fingers and say, "Naomi, this is going to be OK. I'm so sorry I thought you had, had done anything." I finish lamely. "But I have to go now."

She nods, sniffing and working to pull herself together. She's like a snotty, red-faced lovely messenger angel sent to deliver me of my stupidity. "Thanks for listening."

"Of course. Anytime." But I'm already backing away, desperate to get to my car.

I have to find my husband.

There's no way I'm waiting until Sunday to talk to Ray.

68.

There are brash, impulsive people in the world who can make a hair-trigger decision and move forward at full steam on this idea. These people are sometimes called thoughtless. Flaky. Reckless.

I am absolutely one of those people.

About ten minutes away from the hotel where the Southeastern Agriculture Symposium is being held and I haven't for a second questioned my decisions.

It was easy to put together. It was a quick zip back to my parents to collect any clean clothes I had there and throw them in a bag. And also to update my parents.

"You're driving to Lexington? Today?" My mother was already up, reading glasses in one hand, headed to the refrigerator.

She moved through her surprise at lightspeed, sending me with a packed lunch and the assurance she'd take care of the boys.

Dad wasn't as encouraging.

"Surprising Ray at this event is a terrible idea," were his exact words. I ignored him. He doesn't know everything.

And, to give me some credit, surprising him wasn't my exact intention. I have, in fact, called Ray. Several times.

And he hasn't answered once, which worries me to no end. Is that where we're at? He won't take my call?

I work on taking slow, measured breaths. It's possible Ray's done.

But that's not on me. All I can do is try, and that's what I'm doing now.

Dad did say, "Good luck. You know what they say."

"'Fortune favors the bold.'"

"You got it."

I took it and was headed to Lexington two minutes later.

Now, as I pull into the hotel parking lot, my stomach is in knots.

Contrary to my father's assumption I prefer working from the angle of surprise, I wish Ray would respond to my calls. Or my one text.

It was simple: **I know you're busy, but could we talk?**

An abrupt answer, even a refusal would feel better than this absolute silence. But what can I do? If he's not answering, he's not answering.

There's a *ping!* And I admit my first thought is: *divine timing!*

I dive for my phone only to let my breath out in one disappointed sigh. It's my mother. **I've got your boys.**

I wonder if she ever considers that her messages, if seen in a different context, sound threatening as opposed to reassuring.

Don't take it out on your mother rises up in my brain. After all, she agreed to watch my wild children for the night. And I'm still being nourished by the string cheese and bountiful bag of peanut butter crackers she provided.

I text back: **Thanks! I'll check in soon! I'm at the hotel.**

She sends back the prayer hands emoji.

It's time to get out of the car.

It's a pretty hotel, fancy-feeling without being actual fancy. People are sitting on benches, chatting, and in line at the Starbucks, all wearing lanyards with name tags.

I stand still, scanning the group, finding my bearings.

"Are you here for the conference?" A woman at a table to my right asks.

I exhale. "Maybe."

She smiles and pushes a brochure to me. "If you don't have a ticket, there's still time to get one. Talk to that lady over there." She gestures, but I'm not paying attention.

The brochure folds open and offers a map of events for the next few days. There's a clear rundown of the events taking place right now. In the top spot is *Meet the Speakers!*

And there, listed alphabetically, only a few spaces down, is my husband Ray Fox.

69.

It's a large conference room, and it's packed.

I remember Ray describing it as "the agricultural Oscars of the South."

He agreed to come months ago before we ever married. Apparently, the Southeastern Agriculture Symposium has more sense than I do. They've known they wanted my husband for more than six months. I've only known it, deeply known it, for about three hours.

There are dozens of rows of folding chairs ahead of me, and everyone, from Ma and Pa Farmer in their sixties with gray hair and permanently sunburned faces, to Hippies are welcome, tall, stringy, with long oily hair (men and women) and clothes that might have been pulled off an abandoned scarecrow, is in attendance.

I take an empty seat in the back row. No one seems to have noticed I slipped in without a lanyard.

At the front of the room is a long table, draped in white tablecloths. About a dozen people in total, there's a microphone clamped to the table at every third speaker or so.

And there, front and center, is Ray.

Of course, he is. If you have a speaker who looks that good, all bronzed and square jawed, with wild hair and an impossible to resist smile, wouldn't you put him at the front?

And, honestly, by comparison, some of these agricultural folk haven't taken great care of themselves. I probably wouldn't highlight that big ol' boy, with his belly pushing the confines of his overalls and his red splotchy skin indicating he liked his bourbon too much. Nor would I have chosen the whippersnapper with his blonde dreadlocked hair and his Grateful Dead t-shirt who's shown up barefoot and now displays two enormous pale white feet crusty with some kind of fungus.

No, these are not top of the class for the conference's speakers. But there's my Ray, next to a clear-skinned, bright-eyed, middle-aged Black woman wearing an African turban in the most stunning color palette of grays, blues, and greens. She's smiling, nodding at what he says, and when he finishes, he looks at her, and she picks it up.

"Yes, and to add to Mr. Fox's thoughts, I'd also recommend attending..."

They're answering a question. Dragging my eyes from Ray, I notice a single microphone set up dead center to the stage. There's a conference worker monitoring it, nodding at each thing the current speaker offers.

Ray's right up there. Fingers fumbling, I have my phone out of my pocket and in my hand.

Can we talk? Please.

Ray touches his leg, looks down at his side, and when he looks back up, he's frowning.

He's ignored it. I've watched him ignore my message. My plea.

"It's a shame that for the conference Mr. Fox won't be able to go further into this for you. It's a fascinating subject." Now the speaker looks back to Ray.

"Ah, Dr. Habimana, you are too kind," he says, and they exchange smiles. "You'll be far better prepared to handle this. And, like I said, I am sorry to miss meeting with more people. A family situation requires my attention, and I'll be heading out as soon as we finish here." He nods to the crowd, and I find myself craning for him to notice me, to catch my eye.

"And on that note, we should wrap up. Ray, we hope you get that squared away, and everyone is OK. And a big thanks to Dennis Fox for agreeing to step in." A blonde woman, with thick hips and a bright face, has a microphone, and she's taken center stage. She gestures to Dennis, who inclines his head at the crowd. If he had a cowboy hat, he'd tip it at us. I swear, the woman next to me actually sighs.

Dennis is taking Ray's presentations? Ray's leaving?

The blonde lady barrels on. "And that's about it for today's panel. We need to let our speakers get settled and prepared for the next couple of days. But let's give them one more hand!"

She tucks the mic under her arm and leads the smattering of applause that breaks out.

What is happening? There's shuffling. I watch the presenters turn towards each other. Ray and Dr. Habimana exchange words, and she laughs. And then he turns away from the table.

"Wait, I have a question." I look side to side and scramble to my feet. "I have a question. I have a question!"

Clutching my bag to my chest, I throw the other hand in the air. I couldn't say that I'm aware of what I'm doing, but I am moving, running up the makeshift aisle to the microphone stand.

"What's that?" The blonde lady peers into the audience.

"I have a question!" I bellow, and several speakers look up now.

"You'll have all weekend," the blonde woman starts, but I'm at the microphone now and I blurt, "It's for Ray Fox. And only Ray Fox. He's the only person who can answer it."

It's too loud, and instinctively I step back. But it's enough. My husband notices me. He turns back to the room, eyes wide.

My heart hammers in my chest, my mouth's gone dry. But what else could I do? I didn't drive all this way so he could get lost in a sea of people, hop in his car, and head home again. What kind of pathetic story would that be?

It's now or never. I take a breath and work to steady my voice. "I have a question for Ray Fox. Please."

The blonde lady glances at Ray, who nods, and she shrugs. "Alright, then go ahead." And she returns to her nearby folding chair where she proceeds to slip off her low-heel shoe and massage her ankle.

I can't be distracted by that now. I look at Ray and say, "I have a question."

70.

It's the blonde woman who answers.

"Yes, dear, we know that," she says, and a few people chuckle.

I try to smile, but my brain feels frozen. What am I doing? What am I supposed to ask?

Would you come back to me?

Do you still want to be married to me?

Can we fix this?

No, nope, and no, thank you. I take a breath. The room is waiting. I need to speak. "My question is, is about...working with your family. As a farmer."

I can see him tense. They're tiny details: the way the back of his jaw tightens, the way he shifts his shoulders. But after eight months of dating and three months of marriage, I know the signs.

Please, please, LORD, help me fix this.

"Do you have a specific question?" he asks.

"Yes. Is it hard working with family members?"

Ray looks to the left, then shakes his head. When he looks back to me, his expression is wry. "It ain't easy," he says, and this time people are definitely laughing.

"Then how do you do it?" I'm desperate for this answer. "Why not do something else?"

"It's a brutal industry to jump into without some support. Whether that's your relatives or creating some kind of partnership with friends, it's almost impossible to do this work alone." He sighs. "And I love it. I'm not saying it's the only kind of work I could enjoy, but it's the work I want to do."

Watching his face, surrounded by his peers, many of them nodding, it's like seeing the farm through Ray's eyes for the first time. The expression he has, the way his posture, his animation, his spirit changes when he talks about the farm, there's only one other time I've seen that look on his face.

I wouldn't want to take that away from him. And surely, I can figure out this piece with his family. Surely we can work this out together.

But Ray's speaking again, and it jolts me back into the moment. "Is that something you, I mean, people outside of the farming industry can understand, do you think?"

I nod, a lump rising in my throat. "I think I—people outside of the farming industry could understand for sure. In time. And especially if y—the farmer in question was able to draw...good boundaries. Around his relatives. And their...input."

Ray's eyes are dark and bright at the same time. "I expect a farmer would work hard to do that, if he were given the chance."

I smile. It's the first time my mouth's made this shape in days, and it feels good.

"But it's also important that the people outside of the farming industry make good boundaries, too."

What's this now?

I focus on him. "What do you mean?"

"Well, I think it can be as easy for...people outside of the farming industry to get drawn into the lives of those relatives, too. Parts those people don't need to be in."

I tilt my head at him. What in the world?

And then, there's a cough. It's slight, but the room is so silent it makes me jump.

Dennis. He leans over, looking at me, and he puts his hand in the air, for a moment as if to say: me.

I swivel back to Ray, who gives a tiny inclination of his head.

This is about his brother. His brother and me.

I've had my answer when it comes to Ray's faithfulness. But he hasn't had his.

"I think the people outside of the farming industry would want to make it clear they have always been respectful of those boundaries around relatives. And maybe they've been sucked into...challenging situations they didn't expect. But never, not once, have the people outside the farming industry wanted anything other than to work with their own farmer. Nor have they done that." I subside. Those sentences deteriorated the longer I went on. The folks around are murmuring to each other. But when I look at Ray, he's only got eyes for me.

"Really?" he asks.

"Really," I say with so much force I cause the microphone to squeak. I tilt back but say again, "Really. Only their farmer. That's it."

"We don't have to rub it in," Dennis speaks up into his own mic. "We get it. The people outside of the...whatever, they only like the one farmer. Can we move on?"

I meet his eyes, and he winks. But it's different. Warm and friendly, like a brother. When I look back to Ray, a smile is starting to break across his face. Heat rises in my cheeks, and I blurt, "There's one last thing."

Ray's eyes are fixed on mine. He nods. "Go on."

"What about having a family of your own. And being a farmer, too. Do you, uh, think that's possible? For you? For the farmer, that is?"

The room is quiet. No one seems anxious to leave.

At last, Ray nods his head. "I do. I think there are drawbacks. But I think it's possible."

"What kind of drawbacks?" I hate how small my voice sounds.

Ray takes a minute, and when he answers, he speaks slowly. "Farming is a full-time occupation," he starts. A few folks around me mutter, "Amen," and "Yeah, it is." I resist the urge to "shh" them.

"During the farming season, there's no time off. And if you've got animals, shoot, there's no vacation, no trips to get away." There's more grumbling, all seemingly in agreement with Ray. "Ground needs to be worked, prepped, tilled, seeds need to be started, everything needs to be watered, and it all happens on a tight schedule. There's no fooling around, not if you want to do this as a profession."

My breathing is quick, my palms sweaty. Staying put, listening to the full answer, takes all my energy.

"It's time-consuming, and it's hard work. Not only physically but mentally, too." This gets more murmurs, more sounds of agreement. "It's exhausting, all of it. You hit May, when you're harvesting spring crops, getting summer crops in the ground, and going to farmers' markets, and, Lordy, it's like to kill you some years. Repeat that again in July and August for the fall this time, but now it's hotter than blue blazes. It is constant, never-ending, and sometimes all-consuming. Or, at least, it feels that way. "

He takes a breath. The audience isn't moving.

"It's also living with the seasons, harvesting your food with your own hands, and eating what you grew. It's providing for people, people you love most in the world if you're lucky. It's exhausting, but it's satisfying. And, as far as I've seen, that makes it almost exactly like having a family. Farming will damn near kill you. Bankrupt you. And it is work that will leave you happier than anything else on God's green earth, same as being married and raising kids. In fact, I don't know if there's a more apt metaphor."

There's a lump in my throat, and tears pool in my eyes. Ray's watching me.

"So you're all in?" I ask. "Farming...and family?"

"I expect some days my beliefs might need reinforcement. But isn't that just about anybody in this situation?" He taps his fist on the table, gives his head a single shake. And then he leans into the mic and says, "So to answer your question, yes, ma'am, I am one hundred percent all in."

71.

Where is my husband?

When the moderator closed the session, people flooded the doors or plodded towards them at least. And I, in the middle of the room, ended up in the center of the crush. I wanted to rush the table, as some folks did, but some scholarly looking folks blocked my way, a family with about six rather Amish looking teenagers surged towards me, and now here I am, in a lobby filled with bodies, and I'm turning in a circle.

Panic rises inside me. Where's Ray? I want–I need–I have to say–

"Excuse me, young lady, you seem to be lost."

And he's here, hand on my elbow, eyes so tender and loving. In the middle of that crowded room, amidst the hubbub and noise, I throw my arms around his neck and vow to hold on.

It's only been a few days, but it's been so much longer, too. So long since we've held onto each other with nothing between us, nothing to separate us. Feeling his strong, wiry body against mine, the safety of our arms encircling each other, I give in and sob. Loud, noisy sobs.

A woman in large square glasses startles and asks, "Is she alright?"

Ray, his hand stroking the back of my head, rocking us side to side, nods. "She's fine. This one's a crier."

I laugh, but my weeping is stronger. Joy might come in the morning, but it can also come in the late afternoon, and it can come with a bucket of tears.

"C'mon, honey, let's get out of this mess before you start scaring the children," he murmurs in my ear.

He steers us all the way out the door and to a bench in front of the hotel. Out here, it's quiet, and we're staring at a Waffle House across from us. How romantic. That thought makes me laugh harder. I hiccup, and now I'm roaring.

Ray watches me while he feels around in his shirt pocket. "You really are a barrel of emotions, Iris."

I shrug. Ray produces a handkerchief and hands it to me. A handkerchief!

"How did I not know you carry a handkerchief?"

"Well, that's a funny story. I don't, or, at least, I didn't. But once I got a sense of," and here he glances at me and nods his chin, "how...tender you are, I thought it might be a good idea to procure a few."

Tears rise again, but I'm working so hard to keep myself in check. "That's, that's really kind," I manage.

Ray rests his elbows on his knees, leaning forward. "I know it might not look like it, but I am a kind man. At least, I think so."

"I know. I know." I feel so stupid having imagined him to be any less the person than he is. How could I have been so lost? And still... "Why didn't you call? I haven't heard from you since Monday. Not a peep."

He looks confused. "Honey, you told me you needed space. You needed time away. I was trying to give it to you."

"And you took me seriously?"

"Yes, I tend to take people at their word. Did you not mean it?"

Nuts. Somehow, said like that, it makes sense he didn't call. "I probably said some of that for dramatic effect," I say.

Ray chuckles. "Yeah. You do that sometimes, don't you?" And he squints at me, smiling.

"A little."

He sighs. "That's new for me. I have to get used to that."

"I did call you. And text you. A lot today."

"Yeah, that's on me. I had finally realized I was being a horse's ass not coming after you."

"Yeah?"

"Yeah. And to be honest, I didn't realize it. Dennis said it to me."

"Really?" Gosh, I love a behind-the-scenes peek. I dab at my runny nose and ask, "What did he say?"

"He said, 'Ray, you're being a horse's ass not fighting for Iris. You need to go get her.'"

"Wow." We're both quiet, marveling over the words and the speaker.

"Yeah. And he was right. Look, Iris," and he straightens and turns toward me. "My pride was hurt. I didn't know what was happening between you and him—"

"Nothing! Absolutely nothing!"

Ray nods and holds up a hand. "I know that now. Just let me finish, OK? And try not to storm away when I do."

"I don't do that." My temper flares.

"Honey," and he doesn't say it as a term of endearment, but more as the Southern way of "I'm about to shoot you straight and you're not going to like it" honey. "You have walked out of every argument you and I have ever had."

"That's not true." My chin juts out, my arms crossing over my chest. How were we making up two minutes ago, and now I feel irritation sweeping over me?

"Iris, if you don't like it, you leave it."

I open my mouth, retaliation at the ready. And then my dad pops into my brain.

Again, the last person I would like to be thinking about during a reconciliation with my estranged husband.

Yet his reminder. To be kind, and make those tiny thoughtful gestures.

Right now, the thoughtful gesture might be to listen. And, if I'm being completely honest, it might not even be that thoughtful. It might be good common sense.

So I look to Ray. He's watching me, eyes searching my face, no doubt expecting my rebuttal. I breathe and say, "Go on. What were you saying?"

And just like that, the dynamic changes. Instead of bracing himself for shouting or an abrupt exit, Ray's able to relax. His shoulders soften, his jaw loosens, and his eyes are warmer than before.

"I don't want to sit here and criticize. I want to say, I messed up. And I'm sorry."

As soon as those words are out of his mouth, I'm remorseful.

"No, it's me. I'm sorry, so, so sorry. I wish I had told you, clearly, how hard it was for me, dealing with your family on top of the marriage and the move."

Ray nods, and he doesn't seem a bit offended. "Yeah. I wish I had listened better when you tried."

I turn towards him, and Ray relaxes into the bench, arms thrown along the back.

I keep going. "And I really wish I would have asked you about Naomi. Or just told you what I was seeing and why it upset me."

He runs a hand over his face. "Man, that was an impossible situation." He looks at me. "I hope you know, I never wanted to keep you in the dark like that." I nod and manage, somehow, to wait quietly, desperate to understand. "I was stuck. I had Naomi on one side of me, humiliated and honestly heartbroken. For all his faults, she genuinely cares about my brother. And then I had my brother on the other side silently strong-arming me into staying quiet. And I just, I didn't have the mental capacity to deal with...whatever your thoughts might be on the situation."

That feels like a critique, and I twinge. But I stay in the conversation.

"What do you mean?"

He turns towards me, too, and his arm is around my shoulders. "You're so interested in people. What they're feeling, what they're thinking. Interests I, frankly, don't have. And I thought, if I told you about that whole mess, besides breaking their confidences I'd get pulled into some kind of deep, philosophical conversation on what they did, and why they did it, and what that means." Ray exhales. "I feel awful saying this. And hearing it out loud, I see what a chicken that makes me. But I was maxed out between the farm and you and the boys. I didn't have the energy to dig into Dennis' mess as well. So I kept this secret. From you. And for that, I'm truly sorry. I see now how that would have caused a mess, you seeing Naomi and her always bawling, me there with her. I was an idiot. Can you forgive me?"

His eyes are darker than ever, remorseful and sincere. And I, much as I don't want to, have my own confession to make.

"Yes. I can. If you forgive me, too. The things I kept from you about Dennis and picking him up that day. We'd been arguing so much, and even though I knew it was completely innocent, I thought if I told you, we'd fight more."

Ray sighs. "I can see that."

"And then Stephanie opened up to me, and I was so happy. I thought we might be friends. But then Brandon on top of that, it was so much." I hold my hands up as though helpless. Except I wasn't helpless and I see that now. I put them back in my lap and work to say the honest words. "I didn't want to keep arguing. And I was afraid telling you about all these issues in your family would lead to more of that. So I kept it to myself."

We're both quiet. It's hard to believe how much pain and hurt we've each endured because the other feared the consequences of being honest. "I mean, what if these are signs? What if we're not compatible? All this hiding and secrets. That's not good." I'm despondent, struggling to find a way through the mire back to each other.

"Oh, honey, that's not it at all. I think we kept these secrets because we love each other. You didn't want to fight because you love me and you wanted to give us a peaceful home. And I didn't want to waste one second of the precious time and energy I have for you and the boys worrying about other people's problems." Suddenly Ray's sitting up, drawing me into his arms. "Don't you think?"

My goodness. If this doesn't remind me of a conversation I had only that morning with his mother.

"Why are you smiling?" He's bemused.

I shake my head. "People are stupid when it comes to love."

"Yeah, but only sometimes. This one's easy, right? Be honest. There. Lesson learned. You and I are going to get through it fine if we'll just be honest. And if you just stay put." His lips twitch.

"That's not fair! I could have left so many times." My cheeks flush.

"That's true. You gave it a whole three months before you called it quits." He's actually laughing now while I'm struggling to pull away. "Don't you try to get away! Don't you even think about it!" He crows and pulls me in so tight I can barely breathe.

It is exactly where I want to be. My arms go around his neck and hold me there, right there, safe with each other, our own bubble, just us.

He leans in, lips to my ear, and I shiver. "I have one more question." His voice is low.

"What's that?" I'm almost breathless from his nearness, the feeling of his lips on my neck where he puts one small, soft kiss exactly like that kiss from the Christmas Festival. When he first said he loved me. When I first realized I loved him.

"Did you," and he puts another kiss on my neck, "by chance," and another one below that, "think to get," one kiss at my collarbone, "a room?"

I straighten up. "You want me to get my own room?"

Ray looks up, and his eyes are dancing. "No, but I'm sharing mine with Dennis. And I thought you and I might need our own space."

I laugh so hard my belly hurts, but Ray's got his arms around me, and he's focused. "Mrs. Fox, I think it's time we get inside." And as we march into the hotel, arms wrapped around each other's waists, he murmurs, "I told you we'd have more than one honeymoon, didn't I?"

72.

It takes almost two months to implement Ray's request. By the time we're ready, the farmers' market season is back in full swing.

Lincoln Country Farmers' Market is going, and now they offer a new vendor: Fox Family Farm. The booth was at Myrtle's insistence. Dennis and Ray protested at first, but she was adamant.

"I run the market. It's an embarrassment my farm isn't there," she said, and her tone and jaw were so mulish they didn't fight her. Dennis agreed to run that market with Brandon for backup.

Dennis no longer needed his Saturdays free to work on his marriage. He and Shawna had quietly filed for divorce, and it was only a matter of weeks before that was complete.

He offered to do the Saturday markets in Harrisville in Ray's stead. Ray, however, made the point that all of his family would be at the market, as I would still be maintaining my booth and the boys would be with me. And to me, he muttered, "If that guy thinks for a second, he's spending every Saturday with you..."

It made me roll my eyes and shake my head. After the experience in Lexington, Ray and I rarely touched on the topic of Dennis and his feelings for me. Whatever they were, pure or otherwise, they would fade. Dennis couldn't stay in love with someone so clearly in love with someone else.

Someone so clearly in love with his brother, to be specific.

"It's best if Dennis is at the Lincoln County market," I agreed. "The women of Harrisville are not ready for an unmarried Dennis to be unleashed upon them."

It was clear Myrtle liked having a booth at the market. Now, she could boast about having the best meat and vegetable offerings available in their little neck of the woods.

Because of the Saturday market and because of the number of Foxes participating in those markets, our event is on a Tuesday. Also, the court isn't open on Saturday. And that's a critical element.

"This is itchy." Ernie squirms in his long-sleeved button-up shirt. I know it's not itchy, it's one hundred percent cotton. He's grumbly because he doesn't like dressing up. To be fair, not many six-year-olds do. But it looks so cute with his little khaki shorts, especially with the–

"Suspenders? Really?" Angie pops up behind me, eyebrow quirked.

I hug her and at the same time say, "Oh, you can't complain about this. Look at them."

We both look at the boys. Little khaki shorts, long-sleeved button-ups, suspenders and–

"It's the bowties I'm protesting." This from Stephanie, who's now on the other side of me. "What kind of dictator puts a kid in a bowtie?"

"One with an amazing sense of style," I reply and hug her, too. This is a more tentative hug, first as Stephanie isn't much of a hugger, and second, I'm still not confident I've been forgiven.

I definitely required forgiveness. Busting her secret relationship in front of her entire family, and some folks she didn't know, had to be one of my worst moments.

I went to see her as soon as the boys and I were back at the farm. If anything, this awful experience taught me to seize the moment. No more waiting and hoping everything would sort itself out.

She was in her childhood bedroom, packing.

I saw her suitcase on the bed, the piles of tote bags at her feet, and panic shot through me. "Oh, no, oh, Stephanie, I'm so so sorry," I blurted, marching into the room.

She looked up. "You're sorry for telling my entire family I've been living in sin the last decade? With a non-Christian no less?"

I winced. "Yes, that's exactly it," I whispered. "Are you, is Myrtle, did you get kicked out?"

Stephanie paused, hand hovering over her suitcase. "No, I, uh, actually, no." She struggled for words, and all the while my heart was in my throat wondering what punishment got laid down. "I'm going back to Atlanta."

"Do you need help? Do you need money?" I was nearly in tears.

"Do you have some?" she asked, brow wrinkled, and I shook my head. Something broke in her, and she barked out a laugh. "Oh, my gosh, Iris, Mom is right. You're too serious." She dropped her shirt into the case and plopped down on the bed. "I don't need your money. And I don't know that I need your apology. I, uh, called Em."

"What?"

"And he misses me. As much as I miss him. And I apologized. A lot. And told him I wanted him to come home with me. To meet everyone." She spit the words out fast. When she looked up, she was flushed deep red. "I think you may have been right."

It was more than I could take in. I sat down on the bed, too, and stared at her. "You made up?"

"Yes."

"And you're going back to Atlanta. To live with him?"

She paused. "Yes to the first. No to the second. Em said," she cleared her throat. "He said, he knows what he wants. And it's not to just live together for the rest of our lives."

She met my gaze and her eyes were bright. "He wants us to work on our differences. And then take...the next steps."

I didn't realize I was holding my breath until I released it with a *whoosh*. "So what does that look like?"

"My coworker, Amy, is subletting her apartment for the next six months. So I'm taking on her lease. Em's living in his place and he's coming to church with me. And we're going to figure this out." She thrust out her chin, her expression every bit as determined as I'd ever seen her mother look.

I shook my head, amazed. "And what did Myrtle say?"

"That this is my life. And it's time I act like it." Steph stared out of her window. "I don't know, Iris. I don't know if we've all been misreading her or if she's trying to change, fast, after everything you said to her. But whatever it is, she's different than before."

We were both quiet until Steph nudged me with her elbow. "Maybe you're not the worst thing to ever happen to this family. Besides my dad. I guess he's the worst-worst thing. But maybe you're only, like, medium-worst."

It made me laugh, but it still stung. She must have seen something because impulsively she put an arm around me. "I'm kidding. I think you've been a great thing to happen to our family. Things are changing for the better. That's on you."

That was a balm to the wound. "Yeah?"

Steph nodded. "For sure." She withdrew her arm and said, "So enough of the mushy stuff..." and got to packing.

Seeing her now, nearly two months since that time, she's such a different Steph. Shiny hair, bright eyes, wearing some cool ripped jeans with a cropped blue blazer and a tight white t-shirt, she's vibrant in a way I couldn't have imagined when I first met her in January.

She's also holding hands with someone, and I look up to see a shockingly handsome man. His skin's a rich coppery brown, his eyes are nearly black, and he's got the faintest hint of a beard and bright white teeth against full lips. It takes me a second to wrap my head around it as Steph says, "Iris, I'd like you to meet my boyfriend, Emad. Em, this is the gal I told you about." I want to laugh. She sounds like Ray, throwing around words like "gal." It makes me happy.

He puts out his hand, and we shake. "The infamous sister-in-law?" His voice is soft and deep, and I'm pretty sure he's done some kind of hypnotic thing with his eyes....

"Iris. Iris!"

I blink, dazed. Steph's snapping her fingers in front of my face. "That's me," I say to Emad. "The infamous one."

He smiles, and I have to work not to stare again. "Well, I appreciate your assistance. Steph told me you were instrumental in her coming to her senses."

"I'm helpful like that," I say with a self-deprecating shrug. An arm slips around me, and I startle to find Ray standing next to me. There he is. My own handsome man. My husband. My person.

"We're about to get started, if y'all want to take a seat," he says to Steph and Emad. He claps Emad on the arm and adds, "Real glad you're here, Em. Can't wait to show you around the farm."

Emad smiles and says more words, but I don't hear them, suddenly nervous, my stomach tight and fluttery at the same time.

They're all here. Everyone we love. My parents, Angie, José, and their kids. And all of Ray's family, including Ricky and Naomi. They're the only ones in the seats in the courtroom.

Normally, we'd have met in the judge's chambers. However, Ray explained the circumstances, and the judge agreed he was happy to use the court itself for a private service.

"You ready?" Ray looks at me, eyes bright, his hand clasped in mine. I look down at our fingers, linked together, his wedding ring glinting up at me. This is it. This is when the three of us become the four of us.

So hand in hand we walk to the front of the courtroom. He marshals the boys in front of us, Ernie squirming, but Atticus leaning into Ray. It's clear from the slope of his shoulders and the softness of his neck, he's relaxed. My tense little guy, the one who's been on the watch for as long as I can remember, is calm and settled under the gentle grasp of his stepdad.

Dad, now. Or about to be.

When I called Parker about the idea of adoption, I was nervous. Also, a little combative. "If he has the nerve to say 'no' when he does nothing with these boys," I ranted to Ray for days before making the call.

And Ray would nod and say, "I know. Just make the call."

When I did, Parker answered at once. He let me speak, let me say everything. When I finished, he said, "You think this guy is it? This is 'the one'?"

If anything has ever made me roll my eyes up into my head, it's hearing my ex-husband quiz me on if I had genuinely found my soulmate. Ray was there, listening silently on speakerphone. He shook his head at me, and I stayed calm. "Yep, I do. And the boys love him."

It could have felt hateful, vindictive even to say as much. But it was true. And Parker, who left when the boys were under the age of two and hadn't looked back, didn't claim any further right.

"If you're good with it, I'm good with it," he said, and that was when I burst into tears. Who knew I was so nervous?

Parker, happy with his new wife and new kids, sent the paperwork, we filed with the judge, and now here we are, at the last stage.

The judge walks us through the legal jargon. And then, before he signs the paperwork, he glances at the boys. "And you're both in agreement with this?"

"Yes, sir," Atticus' voice quivers. Ray hears it, too, and he rubs Atty's shoulders. Atticus looks up at him, Ray grins, and Atticus smiles, relaxing again.

"And you?" The judge checks with Ernie.

"Yup," Ernie says and follows it up with, "Are we going to eat soon? I'm starving."

The judge isn't listening. Head bowed, he signs the paperwork.

And that's it.

Ray, Iris, Atticus, and Ernest Fox. The Foxes.

I burst into tears again.

"Lordy, you think she's going to do this all day?" Ray murmurs to Atticus, who shrugs and says, "Probably. You know Mom."

"Yes, I do." Ray beams at me.

Myrtle, done with the ceremony, stands up and claps once for attention. I notice my mom bristles, but she still listens.

"If y'all all hop in your cars and come back to the house, we'll have dinner and drinks. Non-alcoholic, of course." Myrtle throws Dennis a stern look, and he gives a single nod. His sobriety of about eight weeks was a highly celebrated and much-noted situation at the farm. Myrtle, in her effort to be supportive, often sounded as if addressing a truculent toddler instead of a grown man who'd realized he needed help and sought it out.

"Keep it clean for the alkyholic!" Brandon hoots, and Dennis laughs. I have the sense, now that Shawna has moved out, Brandon spends more with his brother. It makes me thankful for both of them. Dennis needs someone who could love him pretty unconditionally. And Brandon needs a break from his mama's house. Win-win.

Brandon and I made our peace as well. Feeling good after my conversation with Steph, I went straight to Brandon's room.

Where it took several knocks and a request through the door for him to let me in. Of anyone I expected to hold a grudge, it wasn't Brandon.

He settled back in at his desk, back to me.

"Lots of homework?" I asked.

He shrugged and tapped the keyboard.

"If you need help studying, I'm pretty good at it," I offered.

He made a noise, a sort of grunt, and didn't turn around.

All words of apology, of asking forgiveness and making amends flew out of my head. My own husband, who had been hurt, furious, and terribly sad, hadn't given me a shoulder as cold as this one.

"Well, I don't want to bother you."

He pointed. "Door's that way."

"Brandon! C'mon, what the heck? I'm sorry, OK? I'm sorry. But this–this seems a little much, don't you think?"

He wheeled around in his office chair. "You spilled the beans to my family about the one thing I told you in complete secrecy, and now I'm supposed to accept that you're 'sorry'?"

"It was a big ask. I shouldn't be keeping your secrets. From your mother. From your brother. Who happens to be my husband, by the way. That was a lot to put on me."

The words surprised me. At the time, I felt weighed down, but I don't think I realized how much until right then, saying them to him. No wonder Ray looked so guilty every time I came across him and Naomi; the weight of keeping secrets from people you love is too heavy.

Brandon studied me for a long moment, his young, handsome face as stern and serious as I'd ever seen it. I held my breath. Of all the folks in Ray's family, I liked Brandon so much. He was easy, he was funny, he'd already shown he could be a big brother-type to my boys. And now my thoughtless and hurtful rant cost us that? Was that how this played out?

Brandon shook his head at me. "I don't know, Iris," he said. "I trusted you."

If he could cut me with anything, it was that. I choked up, regretful, humiliated.

"Brandon, I, I am sorry. If I could take it back...."

"Bahaha!"

The burst of laughter made me jump. Brandon's head was thrown back, and he slapped his knee. "Oh, Lord, Iris, you are too serious."

"What? What is, what are you...?" I gaped at him. "Were you messing with me?"

"Of course, I was! C'mon, Iris, you told my family I changed my major not that I was a serial killer. What's the big deal? I was a chicken for not saying so earlier. Someone needed to knock me out of it."

I let out a long trembling breath and exclaimed, "Brandon Fox, you are toe-jam."

He chortled. "Who, me?"

"You are the jammiest of gross stuff between the dirtiest toes. That's how awful you are."

He punched his fists in the air, feet tip-tapping the ground, hee-hawing. "Oh, that was good. Too easy, but good. Holy moly."

Thinking about it now leads me to pinch the back of his arm as we follow him into the parking lot. Brandon yelps, sees me, and grins. "Still not over it?"

"Nope."

He looks at Ray, smiling ear to ear. "She's still mad at me."

"I'd expect her to hang onto that for a bit," Ray says, his tone dry, and I shoot him a suspicious look. "Rightly so, my dear," he adds. "Rightly so."

The people we love get into their cars, or their church van in the case of Angie and her family of seven, and head to the farm. My home. Our home.

I watch Myrtle climb into her SUV and notice Ricky there. He helps her in, closes the door, then walks to the passenger side. Paused at the open door, he catches my eye.

I raise my eyebrows at him, give them a wiggle. *What's going on here?*

He smiles and, so help me, blushes. He blushes! He shakes his head, but the grin doesn't dissipate, and to no one in particular, I murmur, "Will wonders never cease?"

"Hey, honey?"

I glance at Ray. He's standing across from me, arms across the top of the car. The boys are strapped in, windows rolled down. It's already warm in May.

"You coming?"

I'm caught off guard and blurt, "Where?"

Ray throws his head back and cackles, then calls to the boys, "Did you hear that?"

"Mom!" Atticus hollers. "We want cake."

"And ice cream," Ernie pipes up.

Now I'm blushing. "Yes, I'm coming." I shake my head, climbing into the car. "Of course, I am."

"Good." Ray pats my knee and meets my gaze. "'Cause we belong together. And we're not going anywhere without you, are we, boys?"

"No!" they call back.

Ray touches my chin, brushes his lips over mine so slowly and murmurs. "Where you're going, I'm going. Don't forget that, OK?"

And I press my forehead to his, so filled with joy and love I could pop. I want to swim in this moment forever.

Of course, I can't. And somehow that's OK. We have a long life in front of us, God willing and the creek don't rise. There's so much time, some of it awash in loving moments like this, some peppered with fights and tempers, and there will always be a little sadness. And most of it will be little, ordinary, everyday moments.

I stare out the window as he fires up the car, the idea of this life we're about to make spooling out before me. What I've always wanted, but better. Real.

Real and rich. With this man. I glance at him and mouth, "I love you."

And eyes bright, he mouths back, "You better believe it." Which makes me laugh.

It's sunny and warm, the wind whips through my hair, and I feel such a strange, tingly, new sensation.

Contentment. That's what this is. I am content with exactly what I have in life right now.

Possibly for the first time ever.

And it feels amazing.

Also By

First Comes Love

A career woman. A divorced dad.

And a connection they can't seem to break.

Andie Werking has never worried about finding true love. She's been busy building a successful small business and a few tight friendships. But now, at thirty-eight, her "no kids" decision seems to have left her permanently single.

Until Joe McIntyre walks into her life with a chance for that happily ever after...if Andie's willing to welcome the three kids, amicable divorce, and fifty-fifty custody split he brings with him. On one hand, there's Joe's kind, steady character, and his electrifying kisses. On the other, there's her terror of mothering anything more demanding than her beloved dogs.

And just when Andie needs her friendships most, her best friend disappears as both her number one confidant and irreplaceable store manager...leaving Andie to wonder if she's capable of any long-term relationship.

As Joe brings everyone together for soccer games, group outings, and family trips, Andie clings to the carefree life she once knew. She can't compromise on a "'til death do us part" decision, even for the sweetest man she's ever met...can she?

Grab First Comes Love by Emily B. Riddle today!

About the Author

Most of the time, Emily's busy wrangling a teen, a toddler, and her farmer husband. When they're asleep, she writes. She and her crew live in Knoxville, Tennessee, run a farm, and have too many dogs.

Emily started reading in kindergarten and writing right after that. She writes funny, hopeful love stories about women who love Jesus but cuss a little. This is her second published novel. Her first novel, First Comes Love, is available in indie bookstores and on Amazon.

For updates on her latest books or just to chat, follow her on Instagram at @emilybriddlewrites, and visit her website at www.emilybriddle.com.

Acknowledgements

For all the folks who made this book possible...

Thank you to Michele Mathews, of Beach Girl Publishing, for your excellent attention to detail when proofreading this manuscript.

Thank you to Staci Frenes, of Grammar Boss Editing Services, for your encouraging praise and, more importantly, insightful critique of this manuscript.

Thank you to Jessie Cunniffe, of Book Blurb Magic, for taking the skeleton of a book blurb I brought you and giving it life.

Thank you to Karla Colahan, of The Inspired Foundry, for this stunning cover. Your Tiny Brand is magic and you, my friend, are a magician.

Always huge thanks and appreciation for my writing colleagues, friends, and early readers, Sarah E. Strong and Louise French, who are so generous with their time and their praise and so gentle with their criticism.

And thank goodness for my Writing Mastermind, Brittany Tinsley, Deb Alexander, and Maeve Gerboth. Y'all inspire me with your words. I'm so glad to be doing this writing life and this real life with you.

I'm so excited to share this book with my parents, Patti Broyles and Jim & Suzanne Broyles. You three are the most constant of constants in your support of me as a person. Who knew you'd still have to read all my writing assignments and come to my presentations long after I was done with school? You're so faithful and I'm so thankful.

And the biggest, most heartfelt thank you to my little family. To my husband Jim, and to my kiddos, Dorothy and Ben, you guys make this world brighter, louder, funnier, and lovelier. And you're always the first to like my posts. How in the world did I get so lucky to end up with you three? I'm grateful every single day.

Milton Keynes UK
Ingram Content Group UK Ltd.
UKHW040631301023
431584UK00004B/239

9 781088 097991